Praise f...
of Al...

Most Eagerly Yours

"I thoroughly enjoyed *Most Eagerly Yours*. Allison Chase is a masterful storyteller. Her plots are intriguing, her talent for crafting a mystery unparalleled, and her love stories are touching as well as sensual. I am now a fan! She is a writer who delivers a book that delights me in every way, interlacing sensuality and romance with stunning detail, gripping mystery and intrigue, plus fabulous characters who steal into my heart and keep me turning the pages. If you yearn for a story that engages all your senses and makes you sigh with satisfaction at the end, I highly recommend an Allison Chase book."
—*New York Times* bestselling
author Catherine Anderson

Dark Temptation
Winner of the *Romantic Times* Award
for Best Historical Romantic Gothic

"The windswept, forbidding coastline is the ideal location for Chase's second Blackheath Moor gothic, where fear, deception, and passion dwell together. She sends chills down your spine as she heats up the pages with passionate love scenes and frightening incidents. Chase's name is fast becoming synonymous with delicious, heart-stopping thrillers." —*Romantic Times* (Top Pick)

"An enthralling adventure. Sophie is a spirited, witty heroine and Chad is a tortured hero who truly has some heavy crimes on his conscience. . . . Allison Chase takes the classic gothic romance style of Victoria Holt or Daphne du Maurier and brings it into the twenty-first century with her addition of some spicy love scenes . . . makes an enthralling read." —Romance Junkies

continued . . .

"In *Dark Temptation*, the reader will want to go all the way to the end.... An interesting read for both mystery and romance fans. Get cozy and prepare to have an adventure."   —Romance Reviews Today

Dark Obsession

"This wonderfully moody and atmospheric tale, with its brooding hero, troubled young child, unquiet spirits, and unfriendly housekeeper, has many of the accoutrements of the classic gothic of the sixties. In fact, except for the ramped-up sensuality . . . it is reminiscent of Victoria Holt.... The solid writing, riveting opening, and clever plot twists recommend this worthy debut."
                    —*Library Journal* (Starred Review)

"Allison Chase's *Dark Obsession* dishes up a wonderful story in a charming, romantic tradition, complete with a handsome and tortured hero, real conflict, and a touch of mystery! Anyone who loves . . . a well-written historical romance will relish this tale."
—*New York Times* bestselling author Heather Graham

"Following in the footsteps of Daphne du Maurier, Victoria Holt, and Phyllis Whitney, Chase delivers a classic gothic complete with a haunted house, an intrepid heroine, dark secrets, and grand passion that will enthrall readers."   —*Romantic Times*

"A compelling and exquisitely written love story that raises such dark questions along the way, you've no choice but to keep turning the pages to its stunning conclusion. Allison Chase is a master at touching your heart."   —Jennifer St. Giles, author of *Bride of the Wolf*

"Intriguing! A beguiling tale. Moody and atmospheric."
                    —Eve Silver, author of *Seduced by a Stranger*

Also by Allison Chase

The Blackheath Moor Series

Dark Obsession
Dark Temptation

Most Eagerly Yours

HER MAJESTY'S SECRET SERVANTS

ALLISON CHASE

A SIGNET ECLIPSE BOOK

SIGNET ECLIPSE
Published by New American Library, a division of
Penguin Group (USA) Inc., 375 Hudson Street,
New York, New York 10014, USA
Penguin Group (Canada), 90 Eglinton Avenue East, Suite 700, Toronto,
Ontario M4P 2Y3, Canada (a division of Pearson Penguin Canada Inc.)
Penguin Books Ltd., 80 Strand, London WC2R 0RL, England
Penguin Ireland, 25 St. Stephen's Green, Dublin 2,
Ireland (a division of Penguin Books Ltd.)
Penguin Group (Australia), 250 Camberwell Road, Camberwell, Victoria 3124,
Australia (a division of Pearson Australia Group Pty. Ltd.)
Penguin Books India Pvt. Ltd., 11 Community Centre, Panchsheel Park,
New Delhi - 110 017, India
Penguin Group (NZ), 67 Apollo Drive, Rosedale, North Shore 0632,
New Zealand (a division of Pearson New Zealand Ltd.)
Penguin Books (South Africa) (Pty.) Ltd., 24 Sturdee Avenue,
Rosebank, Johannesburg 2196, South Africa

Penguin Books Ltd., Registered Offices:
80 Strand, London WC2R 0RL, England

First published by Signet Eclipse, an imprint of New American Library,
a division of Penguin Group (USA) Inc.

First Printing, March 2010
10   9   8   7   6   5   4   3   2   1

To Joan Hammond,
a dear friend and a true champion of historical romance.

ACKNOWLEDGMENTS

Many thanks again to Ellen Edwards and Becky Vinter for continuing to encourage me to achieve my best work, and for keeping their faith in me; and to Evan Marshall for his professionalism, and for being that calm voice on the other end of the line.

Special thanks to my good friend Benay Unger, who is always eager to talk books and history, and is willing to drop everything at a moment's notice to help me hunt down a historical fact or dig up some invaluable research materials . . . and doesn't seem to mind when I don't return them for a really long time.

And my thanks and love to Paul, who never fails to be there when I need him.

Prologue

June 1830
From the Diary of Miss Laurel Sutherland

Guests came to Thorn Grove today, and with them came the knowledge that the close little world I have shared with my three sisters these past eleven years will change, change for always.

Only rarely do we receive visitors on the small Surrey estate we have called home since the death of our parents. So young were we when we came to be in our uncle Edward's care that I cannot now discern what I recall of my early life and what my imagination has conjured. I do know I have been happy here, and that I never suspected how readily the larger world might intrude upon our quiet borders and upset our peaceful existence.

Princess Victoria arrived this morning with her mother, her uncle Leopold, and the small host of servants who habitually travel with them. Her beloved King Charles spaniel, Dash, accompanied her, too, bounding from the open coach door like a windy shadow to scamper about our skirt hems and convey his enthusiastic if rather wet salutations.

Our ties to Victoria's family stretch back to before I was born. Under the command of Victoria's father, the Duke

of Kent, Uncle Edward and my father served as officers in
the Seventh Royal Fusiliers in Canada. They attended the
duke again some years later, during his governorship of
Gibraltar. I am told my family used to visit with the Duke
and Duchess of Kent at their seaside cottage in Sidmouth,
but I retain no memories of those occasions.

Today, as soon as the watchful eyes of the adults
seemed sufficiently distracted with tea and conversation,
the princess caught my hands and with urgent whispers
drew my three sisters and I down the terrace steps. Dash
followed, his nose working furiously as he darted into
the edges of the flower beds and back again to tangle
in our feet. With a backward glance at her mother and
uncle, Victoria led us into the rose-edged yard of what
was once the estate's dovecote.

Surrounded by a fragrant stillness broken only by
buzzing bees and the spaniel's playful whimpers, Victoria
turned as somber as I have ever seen her. My sisters and
I sat on the stone bench, but as she remained standing
before us, a chill of foreboding grazed my nape. Silently
I waited as she drew a fortifying breath that squared her
shoulders and imparted definition to the soft curve of
her chin.

She had passed her eleventh birthday but a month
ago, and I pondered what could possibly etch such grav-
ity upon those childish features and cause her to seem
so much older, older even than I, though at seventeen I
am six years her elder.

"I am not who I was last time we met." Her statement
took us aback, but waiting for more, we said nothing. "I
may continue to call you Laurel, Ivy, Holly, and Willow
as I have always done. But you may no longer call me
Victoria. At least not . . ." Here she faltered, her lower
lip trembling. Tears magnified her eyes and reminded
me once more of her tender age. "At least, you must not
within the hearing of others. For you see, I have but two
days ago come to an astonishing realization."

My heart stood still as she spoke her next words: "I will one day be your queen."

My queen. The Queen of England.

I suppose had I ever paused to consider the origins of my little friend, I would have reached this obvious conclusion long ago. But the workings of the monarchy were so far removed from our safe little haven at Thorn Grove.

The truth was that Victoria, with her large solemn eyes, sweet smile, and tiny stature, would someday assume the weight of an empire, because neither the recently deceased George IV nor his brother, the newly ascended King William, had produced a legitimate heir. Victoria's own father, who might have one day succeeded William, had died many years ago, quite soon after my own parents passed away.

Dash, grown weary of chasing insects, came to stand with his forepaws propped on my knee. Absently I petted him behind his drooping ears as my sisters and I stared dumbfounded at Victoria. My throat closed around everything I might have said, for good or ill. Reassurances, warnings, and a deep, sorrowful lament stormed through my mind as I remembered the tales of intrigue and rivalry, along with the excesses and downright corruption of the Hanover family.

Would Victoria be spared all that? King William was elderly. What if he passed away a mere year from now? Or a week? What then for the little girl standing so bravely before us?

The bees echoed loudly in my ears. The air, thick from the recent rains and stiflingly sweet from the close circle of roses, weighed heavily in my lungs. Then Willow, barely older than Victoria, slid from the bench and sank to the grass in a deep curtsy.

"Your Highness," she whispered. Tears beaded the tips of her thick lashes.

The twins, Ivy and Holly, followed, their heads bowed

to the hot summer sun and the alarmed gaze of the princess. Perhaps thinking it a game, Dash pranced around them, nudging them with his moist nose.

Victoria's gaze shifted and locked with mine, and the raw emotion in its dark depths prompted me to jump up and throw my arms around her. Drawing her deeper into the concealing curve of the rose hedges so that the adults on the terrace could no longer see us, I held the princess tight as she sobbed against my bosom.

In an instant Holly, Ivy, and Willow formed a tight ring around us, their arms interlocking and their heads bent over Victoria's. Their tears—our tears—mingled with hers.

"I am frightened," she whispered. "So frightened of the future. I feel so alone."

"You need not be afraid, dearest." Pressing kisses to her hair, I murmured reassurances. The spaniel sat looking up at us, his head cocked in an aspect of sympathy. My heart nearly broke as I considered that, aside from my sisters and me, Dash was the princess's truest friend in all the world.

"One day, many years from now, you shall make a splendid queen," I told her. "And you will always have us. We shall always be your friends, your servants if ever you need us."

For all my attempts to comfort her, I wondered: how long before her mother and the royal court deemed my sisters and I, common-born and lacking in fortune, unfit to keep company with the future Queen of England? Were it not for the military ties among our father, our uncle, and the Duke of Kent, we should never have crossed paths.

Yet we had loved her—adored her—from the moment she first tottered into the front hall of Thorn Grove some nine years before. Perhaps it was our mutual lack of a father that forged the initial bonds among us; who better than the Sutherland sisters to understand the sad, wistful yearnings of a fatherless child?

Some minutes passed before I felt Victoria pulling straighter, taller. She stepped back from our embraces. With a brave sniffle, she raised her chin. "We shall remain friends, shan't we? I do so wish us to."

"Of course we shall." The assertion came from Willow, who, a year older, stood head and shoulders above Victoria. Dearest Willow, young enough to retain her optimism, too young to realize the truth.

I gazed at Holly and Ivy, who at fifteen could not be more different despite their being twins. Holly, with her auburn hair, freckles, and violet-blue eyes, nodded vigorously in agreement with Willow's sentiment. Ivy, her expression as dark as her coloring, managed a shaky smile even as she flashed me a look of despondency.

The certainty that time and circumstance would inevitably remove Victoria from our intimate circle filled me with sadness. But, as my sisters did, I conjured a smile for my little friend, took her hand in mine, and knelt before her to look her in the face.

"You will always have us," I repeated. "Ivy, Holly, Willow, and I will always be your friends. Your secret friends, if need be. You must always remember that. When you are queen, if there is ever anything you need, any way that we may serve you, you have only to call on us."

"My secret friends," the princess repeated, tilting her head to savor the words. She glanced down at Dash, still sitting quietly as if grasping the solemnity of the occasion. Suddenly the fear and apprehension drained from Victoria's features. Squeezing my hand, she gave a resolute nod. "My secret servants . . ."

Chapter 1

London, July 1837

Beneath what was, for London, a dazzling noonday sun, Aidan Phillips, ninth Earl of Barensforth, suddenly found himself short one illegitimate, slightly inebriated prince, and he was damned unhappy about it.

Maneuvering his gelding through Knightsbridge Street's close-packed crowds, he avoided colliding with the other riders, carriages, and carts, and the constant zigzag of hurrying pedestrians. The sidewalks bore an even heftier burden, jammed tight as if with several days' worth of shoppers all at once.

Despite the inconvenience, a festive air hung over the multitude, as cheerful as the red, white, and blue striped bunting draped along the building fronts. Costermongers squeezed through, hawking the delicacies brimming from their handbarrows, their shouts of "Pasties," "Gingerbread cakes," "Oranges," "Pickles" . . . rising above the general din. Young children sat breathlessly atop their father's shoulders. Older boys climbed halfway up lampposts and clung there.

"Sir! Excuse me, sir!" A uniformed policeman came briskly alongside Aidan's horse and placed a hand on the bridle. "You'll have to move off onto a side street, sir. We're closing off Knightsbridge now. The queen will be coming through shortly."

Aidan replied with a quick salute. The officer moved away to repeat the order to others clogging the way.

Squinting against the glare, Aidan peered into the westward distance. The royal procession would soon pass by on its way to the recently renovated Buckingham Palace, conveying England's brand-new queen to her brand-new home. Aidan saw no sign yet of the cavalcade, and for that bit of good luck he breathed a sigh of thanks.

An oath of frustration followed. He was supposed to have kept a sharp eye on the queen's cousin George Fitzclarence, eldest son of the late King William and as unhappy a royal as Aidan had ever encountered. Not that old Fitz was royal in the strictest sense, mind you, for he'd had the ill fortune of being born on the wrong side of the imperial sheets.

Hence the problem, and Aidan's present dilemma. Fitz wanted to be king. Badly. And he could not be convinced of the futility of that wish. Not even being Earl of Munster, a title conferred upon him by his father, proved sufficient balm to ease his blistering disappointment.

To make matters worse, despite his recent appointment as aide-de-camp to the queen, George Fitzclarence had not been invited to join today's procession. As Fitz had vociferously complained just last night, his new post amounted to little more than a patronizing pat on the head.

Since the old king's death two months ago, Fitz had engaged in a downward spiral of drunkenness and dangerous ideas, ones he spewed eagerly to whoever lent a sympathetic ear. Several nights before at a soiree at the home of the French-born Comtesse de Regny, Fitz had openly advocated the radical strategy of doing away with the monarchy altogether.

Blasted hell.

Aidan had been sorely tempted to toss Fitz over the comtesse's balcony railing rather than allow him to continue his treasonous tirade. As it was, Aidan had stuffed a pickled whelk into the inebriate's mouth to shut him up and soon after bustled him from the party.

Regardless, word had gotten back to the Home Office, which now expected Aidan to continue playing nursemaid to the Earl of Munster until further notice.

Aidan's eyes burned from lack of sleep. They had spent the previous night gambling at Crockfords, then gone across the way to Whites, where Fitz had sipped enough sherry to sink him into a contented and, Aidan hoped, Victoria-free doze. Unfortunately, quite without warning, about an hour ago the old boy had pushed out of his wing chair, declared a change of scenery just the thing, and called for his horse.

Aidan flinched as a short blast on a whistle heralded the return of the police constable. A scowl replaced deference as he shouted, "Thought I warned you to get a move on."

Skirting a family of six that was attempting to wedge itself into a space big enough for three, Aidan offered the official a compliant nod and turned his horse south. William Street led into Lowndes Square and eventually over to Sloane, where the Earl of Munster might have slipped into any number of drinking establishments.

The blue-coated policemen now arranged themselves as human barriers at intervals along Knightsbridge to hold back the crowd. The distant blare of trumpets announced the queen's imminent approach. Shading his eyes with his hand, Aidan made out the distant dust clouds of the riders preceding the royal coach.

A cry of sheer panic ripped through the clamor, startling his gelding. A few soothing words calmed the horse, but the desperate shouts continued. Aidan scanned the crowd.

Several doors down from the corner of William

Street, two policemen were attempting to herd a mob of spectators—too many for so small an area—farther back off the street. With the shop fronts directly behind them, they had nowhere to go. An out-of-control hysteria threatened to take hold.

The feminine cries took on a shriller urgency. In the middle of the surging multitude, Aidan caught flashes of lustrous gold hair that had half fallen from its pins; a gust of wind lifted the disheveled strands away from her beautiful but alarm-pinched features. The woman held a child high in her arms.

Tears of terror streaked the little girl's face as her rescuer continued shouting for someone to take the child. A pair of arms clad in tweed reached over heads and grabbed her, then passed her through the crowd. Finally she reached a shawl-wrapped figure that must have been her mother, for the woman clasped the child close and shed tears of relief.

But the golden-haired beauty had been shoved farther into the press of bodies until she stood trapped against the window of a shop whose sign read WINSTON'S HABERDASHERY. Her chin high, her arms stretched above her head, she attempted in vain to squeeze her way out. From all sides, the mob pinned her in place.

At the edge of the street, a redhead struggled without success to push her way through the crowd. She jumped to see over heads, shouting something Aidan could not make out. Seeming to believe she wished only to usurp their vantage points, the spectators shoved her impatiently away.

In defiance of the officer waving him off, Aidan guided his gelding to the side of the road. He intended to swing down from the saddle and shoulder his way through, but at the last second he changed his mind.

"Coming through," he shouted in his most authoritative voice. "Make way!"

Despite his impatience he eased his powerful gray

forward one cautious step at a time. Behind him, the policemen blew their whistles and ordered him to cease and desist, while those lurching out of his way spat blasphemies gritty enough to peel the paint from the storefronts.

Though the woman's cries continued to draw him on, he lost sight of his quarry as she slid down the building front and disappeared behind the press of bodies. Around her the people pushed and shoved. The police whistles shrieked furiously—and uselessly. Aidan urged Ferdinand onward.

Her throat raw from pleading, Laurel gasped for air. No one listened. No one heard her. She felt as though she were drowning—drowning in people. With dizzying closeness, arms and legs, silks, cottons, and dark serge reeled in her vision. Behind her, the window made ominous creaking sounds.

A shove took her off her feet. Someone trod on her hems. She heard tearing and felt herself going down, down to where no one would see her. Where she would be kicked, trampled. Panic rose in a stranglehold. . . .

Suddenly, astoundingly, the crowd parted, and cool air rushed into the spaces where bodies had been. A giant figure, towering and gray, appeared between skirts and trouser legs. In her confusion she could not make out what it could be; then, to her amazement, the figure formed itself into the hooves, fetlocks, flanks, and, finally, powerful neck and head of a horse. A hand—broad, long-fingered, sinewy—reached toward her.

Fingers of steady, heartening strength closed around her wrist and drew her effortlessly to her feet. Briefly she glimpsed a polished Hessian boot, riding breeches stretched tight over a muscled thigh, and the hair-sprinkled width of that powerful hand—powerful enough to save her life. Then she stepped into the offered stirrup and was swung up onto the horse's back.

Her arms went around a tight, trim waist; her cheek pressed against a shoulder as unyielding as steel. She shut her eyes and hung on tight, or as tight as her trembling limbs permitted.

Though she would likely die of embarrassment when she considered it later, she could not prevent herself from uttering a cry of mixed terror, relief, and sheer, unbridled gratitude, an outburst absorbed into the collar of a coat that fit the gentleman sitting in front of her like an elegant second skin. If he noticed, which he assuredly must have, he gave no indication, not the slightest wince, though Laurel voiced her emotions exceedingly close to his ear.

Without lifting her face, she braved a peek at her surroundings. From high atop the horse, the crowd appeared surprisingly innocuous, an undulating vista of dark hats and bright bonnets.

A trumpet sounded and a cheer went up. Twisting, she spotted the queen's open coach proceeding up the road toward them. The diminutive figure inside, draped in velvet and crowned with a coronet of flashing gold, waved a white-gloved hand at her subjects.

Pride, delight, and bitter disappointment rose in Laurel. Oh, she had hoped to stand out in front, give a call that might attract Victoria's attention and prompt some personal response that only Laurel and her sisters, and the queen herself, would understand.

My secret friends . . . my secret servants . . .

Earlier, Laurel and her sisters had crossed to the north side of Knightsbridge Street with the intention of walking to the open verge outside Hyde Park, where they might watch from the comfort of a thinner and less turbulent crowd. Partway there, Laurel had realized that none of them had remembered to bring the flowers they intended to toss to the queen's passing coach.

When she had gone back for them, she had seen little Lucy Brock yanked by the surging crowd away from her mother. The last thing Laurel had witnessed before being swallowed into the horde was Lucy being swung back into Mrs. Brock's arms.

Her rescuer wove a cautious but steadfast path along the storefronts until they managed to squeeze around the corner onto William Street. Uncle Edward's town house stood a few buildings away. Here, the din of the celebrations faded to a distant roar.

"Good heavens, sir, thank you. Thank you ever so much." Only now did Laurel realize how snugly she was leaning against his back, a rippling wall of muscle and safety. With a start, she allowed a few proper inches between them.

His hair, just brushing his collar, was a rich, shadowed mahogany infused with brighter glints where the sunlight kissed it. The breeze sifted through the strands, releasing a vague hint of something masculine and mysteriously musky. The scent crawled inside her, raising an ache of awareness and a whisper of warning.

She removed her arms from around him and cleared her throat. "I dare not consider the outcome, sir, if not for your timely and most thoughtful assistance."

A silent chuckle ran through him, communicated across the broad sweep of his back. "Quite happy to have been of service, madam. I thought it exceedingly brave of you, saving that little girl."

"Lucy is a neighbor. Someone had to do something."

"Still and all." He tossed a glance back at her, revealing the strong line of his profile, and the softer curve of his generous lips. "Were you hurt?"

"I . . . no, I do not believe I am. But my sisters . . . I must find them." She twisted around, hoping in vain for a glimpse of them.

"Is one perhaps a rather attractive redhead? She seemed frantic on your behalf but otherwise unscathed."

"That would be Holly. Were the others with her? I have three sisters, you see."

"Three?" Again, an amused current rippled through him. "I am afraid I saw no one else who appeared to be associated with her."

"Oh, dear."

"Fret not. I harbor no doubts that they are safe."

He could not, of course, know any such thing, yet his reassurance set Laurel at ease.

He drew to the side of the street and dismounted by effortlessly tossing a leg over the horse's gray withers. Reaching up, he spanned her waist with his hands in a manner that caused her breath to hitch. As he set her gently on the ground, she saw him—*truly* saw him—for the first time.

Her insides stirred. However rude, however giddy and girlish, she could not help gaping up at him, arrested by crisp blue eyes, full lips, and sturdy, well-hewn features that suggested both a keen intellect and a sensuality she found thoroughly disconcerting.

Then she noticed that he, too, was staring as though taken aback by her appearance. . . .

Oh. Embarrassment rushing through her in hot torrents, she raised a hand to her hair to discover her bonnet gone, crushed no doubt beneath the tramping feet. Meanwhile her hairpins had scattered, reducing the fashionable chignon Ivy had helped her arrange that morning to a tangle around her shoulders.

His gaze lingered on her face for another moment, then dipped lower. Remembering the tearing she had heard, she glanced down at a rip between her skirt and bodice that indecently exposed her petticoat.

Her new marigold muslin, ruined. She slid a hand to cover the offending garment. Good grief, *why* could she not have met this man earlier this morning, or yesterday, or tomorrow?

"Is there anything more I may do for you, madam?" He sounded the perfect gentleman, which miraculously restored a measure of her dignity.

"Thank you, sir, but no." The words were feeble, breathless. "I am a bit shaken, to be sure, and . . . well . . . rather disheveled, I will admit. . . ."

"If we continue on to Sloane, I should be able to flag you a hackney."

"That will not be necessary, for you have brought me nearly home. My uncle's town house is just there." She pointed down the street.

At that moment trumpets blared. At the corner, visible above the heads of the onlookers, the plumed helmets of the queen's rear guard disappeared from view as they passed beyond William Street.

Laurel's heart sank. She had missed her friend's glorious moment, lost the chance to toss flowers, wish the new queen Godspeed, and perhaps be rewarded with a private glance of recognition.

She and her sisters had not visited with Victoria in more than three years. At first they had traded frequent letters, but even those had grown rare as the old king's health failed and it became apparent that Victoria would shortly assume the burdens of the Crown.

The Sutherland sisters had *so* wanted Victoria to know they still thought of her, still wished the very best for her, still loved her.

In the wake of the procession, police whistles sounded and a commotion broke out at the corner of Knightsbridge and William streets. Several high blue hats bobbed above the crowd.

"The police appear to be fighting their way through," Laurel observed.

"Ah, yes. Odds are they're coming for me." The man before her grinned, a gesture she found utterly devastating in its capacity to trip the beat of her pulse. "They seemed rather disgruntled when I rode my horse onto the sidewalk."

"But you only did so to rescue me."

"Indeed, and well worth my pains. However, from

their point of view I no doubt appeared a drunken lout attempting to plow my horse through the hapless crowd. I hope you understand that I have little desire to spend the next several hours down at the Chelsea Station clarifying who I am and why I acted as I did."

"Oh, I can fully appreciate your disinclination to do that, sir."

"Then if you will be so good as to excuse me." He raised her hand to his lips, imparting a tingling sensation that began at her fingertips and swept like wildfire all through her.

"Aidan? By God, that you, old b-boy?"

Laurel's rescuer—Aidan?—straightened and turned in the direction of the hail. His dark eyebrows converged.

Mounted on a sleek chestnut, a man of sallow complexion and thinning russet hair approached from the quieter south end of William Street. Despite the expensive cut of his riding attire, his uneven slouch, slack mouth, and slightly unfocused gaze lent him a slovenly aspect.

"I s-say," the rider slurred, confirming Laurel's suspicions that, despite the earliness of the hour, he was fairly into his cups, "what d-damned devilry are you up to now? Might have known you'd p-pluck yourself a tasty little treat from the crush."

Laurel gasped, once more steeped in shame over the state of her appearance. Beside her, Aidan's skin darkened, but before he replied, a shout from the opposite corner heralded the approach of two constables.

"You there!"

"Time for me to take my leave."

Laurel was surprised to realize that her hand still rested in his. He broke into a grin that filled her with delight. "By God, what you did for that little girl took courage."

Before she knew what he was about, he tipped her

chin and brought his mouth down to hers for a fleeting yet thorough kiss. Her pulse rocketed like a celebration day firework.

Then, with no particular effort that Laurel could perceive, he was atop his horse and making rapid progress down the street. His friend fell in beside him and the two sped away at a canter. With no choice but to abandon their pursuit, the shouting constables came to frustrated halts. They glanced at Laurel, dismissed her with disparaging shrugs, and about-faced.

The crowd up at the corner dispersed, and Holly's worried face appeared. As the girl hurried closer, Laurel pressed her fingertips to her quivering lips and tried to master her breathing. Her shocked sensibilities were another matter. If the impulsive kiss had revealed her rescuer as rather less than chivalrous, neither could she quite claim being a lady.

Because the truth was, as improper and insulting as that kiss had been—or *should* have been—she had wholeheartedly, unreservedly, and in defiance of everything she had been raised to believe, enjoyed it.

Chapter 2

London, March 1838

Aidan's first hint that his pleasant night had reached its inevitable conclusion came with an irritating burst of brightness against his eyelids. The second was the slap of his own dress shirt against his face. Though he had not yet opened his eyes, he immediately recognized the garment as his own by the scent of his companion's flowery perfume clinging to the linen.

Miss Delilah, the lovely creature whose acquaintance he'd had the pleasure of making after winning several hundred at hazard last night, and who had done him the honor not only of joining him for a late supper but also of serving up a rousing bit of dessert afterward in this very room, deposited a kiss on his brow and disentangled herself from the sheets.

The satin coverlet slithered from the bed as she drew it around her splendidly supple body. An image crept into his mind of the contortionlike poses the young lady had achieved with her long arms and shapely legs. A professional, she had made the distasteful task of sullying his own reputation rather more palatable, and he would be sure to leave her an ample reward.

While he couldn't claim to detest his occasional visits

to London's finer brothels, the pleasure he took in such episodes typically proved fleeting. Like gambling and drinking, whoring had become part of the persona he showed the world.

Last night he had also needed an alibi. No one who knew him would ever suspect that before retiring to seek his pleasure here, at Mrs. Wellington's Gentlemen's Sanctum, he had sent his carriage—with Delilah inside it—circling the London Docks while he had picked a lock and stolen inside a certain warehouse, seeking evidence against a certain notable solicitor.

Delilah herself had asked no questions. But then, she had known that he would pay as dearly for her silence as for her other professional services.

Her padding footsteps faded from the room, followed by a pronounced throat clearing. "Wake up, Barensforth. We've business to discuss."

With a groan, Aidan buried his face into the pillow. His head ached like the dickens, and he feared opening his eyes would send the room spinning. "Later."

"Now." The mattress jerked beneath the force of what could only have been the bottom of the intruder's boot. A second article of clothing that felt suspiciously like his waistcoat landed on his shoulder. "We have a situation."

He gingerly opened an eye to a partial view of the stocking-draped washstand on the opposite wall. "I say, Wescott, will you kindly cease bombarding me with my own wardrobe? That's no way to treat a peer of the realm, not to mention the man who single-handedly saved your financially inept arse and restored your family's security and your damned bloody dignity."

"Yes, well." Lewis Wescott released a long-suffering sigh. "You, of course, have my undying gratitude, my dear Lord Barensforth. Be that as it may, it has taken me two full days to track you down. Has it never occurred to you to check in before vanishing on one of your binges?"

"A binge? Is that what you'd call it?"

Wescott huffed. "What *have* you been up to?"

Aidan peered up at the man and curled his lips into a satisfied smile. "The *Anne Dorian*, which supposedly sank in the Atlantic last month, taking down with it a fortune in cotton, sugar, and the life savings of several prominent Londoners, didn't."

"Didn't *what*?"

"Sink. I've spent the past fortnight poring over recent commodities figures, staring at ship manifests until my eyes crossed, and questioning every drunken sailor I could find who had lately been to the Americas. There was no storm. From what I've been able to piece together, the *Anne Dorian* was refitted before leaving the West Indies and returned home as the *Wild Rose*, falsely registered as a Jamaican vessel. She has unfortunately sailed away again, but you'll find her illicit cargo tucked away in a warehouse on the West India Quay. Ah, and here's the best part. I've uncovered a silent partner who stood to profit enormously from the scheme. One Oscar Littleton."

Wescott started as if poked from behind. "The foreign secretary's private solicitor?"

"The very same."

"Well-done, Barensforth! Well-done, indeed."

"Yes, yes." Aidan cut the man short with a wave, hauled himself semiupright against the pillows, and scrubbed the bleariness from his eyes. "As long as I'm awake, why don't you tell me what has you as flushed as a maiden on her wedding night?"

Aidan's barrel-chested, paunch-bellied contact from the Home Office plunged into a rapid elucidation of the latest matter threatening the financial well-being of the kingdom.

"There hasn't been much in the way of new building in Bath in more than a decade, and now suddenly the quality is flocking there to invest in something called the Summit Pavilion," Wescott explained. "Some kind of spa. We might not have noticed except that there have been multiple delays in breaking ground. . . ."

As Wescott continued spouting the details, Aidan sighed. The *Anne Dorian* affair had taken a good deal of energy on his part, not to mention the risk to life and limb, and here Wescott expected him to jump on command—again.

There were moments when he regretted having ever made Lewis Wescott's acquaintance.

Five years ago a lucrative investment opportunity had swept through London's aristocratic and upper-middle-class drawing rooms. Scores of men, including Lewis Wescott, had scampered to stake their claim in a West African diamond mine whose yield promised to make them overnight millionaires.

Not long prior, Aidan had discovered he had a proficiency at the gaming tables that allowed him to rebuild the fortune his father had lost before his death. Aidan's talent with numbers extended to financial speculation as well, and the idea of wealth gleaned from glittering pebbles had appealed to him.

Upon closer inspection, however, the figures presented to potential investors simply didn't wash. Workforce, expenses, payload . . . the inconsistencies were subtle, easily missed, but within minutes of perusing the so-called records, his uncanny mind had detected a pattern that shouted fraud.

Very quietly, he had brought his suspicions to the Home Office, which in turn had contacted the Foreign Office, which had sent its people to investigate. In many instances entire life savings had been spared. And while Aidan had kept his assistance mostly anonymous, he had come away with a lasting if often contentious partnership with the man blustering before him now.

Wescott paused for breath, then with obvious frustration burst out, "For the love of God, Barensforth, have you heard a blasted word I've said?"

"Of course." Aidan ran his fingers through his hair and frowned. "Ah . . . a new spa, some sort of pavilion, and something rather melodramatic about looming financial ruin, I believe?"

"Oh, for heaven's sake." With a disgusted shake of his head, Wescott went to the door and flung it wide. "The Earl of Barensforth requires coffee," he bellowed into the brothel's second-floor corridor, "and damned plenty of it."

"Thank you, Wescott. Most considerate of you."

After slamming the door closed, the man sneered at Aidan down the length of his bulbous nose. "Barensforth, do get up and make yourself decent. By God, look at you." He gave the coverlet a disgusted flick. "Do you never tire of carousing?"

"Only doing my bit for my country. As ordered, I might remind you."

"You play your part rather too diligently, I should think."

"My dear Wescott, you should have taken that into consideration a good deal sooner." He stretched an arm behind his head. "Now tell me the rest. What makes this pavilion project so urgent that you needed to come barging in on me at this ungodly hour?"

Wescott met his gaze evenly. "A dead MP, a French traitor's son, and the Earl of Munster."

Aidan sat up straighter, letting the bed linens slide from his chest to pool in his lap. "One matter at a time. Who died?"

"Roger Babcock, Whig member of the Commons."

"Cause of death?"

"Drowning, it would seem, but we don't know if it was deliberate or accidental. An attendant found him facedown in the Cross Bath three mornings ago, an hour before the facility opened to the public. The Bath authorities, damned half-wits that they are, seem content to call it a mishap and close the case."

"Any injuries or wounds on the body?"

"A knot on the back of the head, but the coroner found that consistent with Babcock having fallen and hitting his head on the ledge of the pool, thus knocking him out and facilitating his drowning."

Aidan frowned in thought. "Does anyone remember seeing him at the bath the night before?"

"He signed in shortly after six in the evening. Beyond that, however, no one seems to know anything, not even if he came alone or accompanied."

"Hmm. Someone knows something. . . . They simply aren't telling. What was he wearing when he was found?"

"Only his linens, as if he fell in before fully disrobing."

"That makes no sense. He would have disrobed in one of the dressing rooms and donned a gown before going out to the pool." Aidan rubbed his palm against the morning stubble on his chin. "Any chance it was suicide?"

Wescott shrugged. "Can't think why. The man had no substantial debts, his wife was faithful, and he was in fair health except for recurring gout and a bit of a cough."

"Enemies?"

"None that we know of."

Aidan considered a moment. "What's his connection, if any, to this pavilion?"

"He was one of the chief investors, as a matter of fact."

"And Fitz? How does he play into it?"

Wescott perched his bulky figure at the foot of the bed. "That's for you to discover. We consider it highly suspicious that Lord Munster should betake himself to Bath at this of all times."

Aidan pushed a breath between his clenched teeth. "You've been suspecting him of foul play for years, and time and again he proves you wrong. George Fitzclarence is no more a threat to decent people than I am. He's a blowhard, nothing more."

He would know. For three years he had stuck close to George Fitzclarence under the guise of being his friend. When the Home Office wasn't suspecting Fitz of treason, they made convenient use of him. Through his friendship, Aidan had gained access to the back parlors and smoky cardrooms where illicit plans were made and sizable sums exchanged. Not once had anyone suspected the Earl of Munster's inebriated, irreverent friend of foiling numerous financial scams.

Along the way, Aidan had developed a genuine fondness for King William's eldest by-blow; his antics and overindulgences and the slight stutter that increased when he drank had become endearing if exasperating traits to Aidan.

"The Earl of Munster is what he is." Wescott's upper lip curled. "A royal malcontent with an irrational grudge that will never fade. Never. You would do best to remember that." He tugged at his cravat, tied too snugly against the slack skin of his neck. "And of late he's become altogether too chummy with Claude Rousseau."

"The traitor's son," Aidan murmured. At the close of the wars with Napoleon, Rousseau's father, André, had been hanged as a traitor to the French crown. Though an aristocrat himself, he had secretly aided in the Terror, helping to send scores of his peers to the guillotine. Later he had spied for Napoleon's troops. The discovery of his betrayal had rocked French society.

"To my knowledge Fitz and Rousseau are barely acquainted," Aidan said. "Besides, despite his father's sins, Claude Rousseau is a scholar and a scientist, not a politician. Certainly not a rabble-rouser. Since arriving in England nearly two decades ago, he hasn't attached himself to the slightest hint of scandal."

"Perhaps not, but he *has* attached himself to the Summit Pavilion in a way that makes me highly uncomfortable." Wescott pulled a handkerchief from his inner coat pocket and mopped his forehead. "He's supposedly creating a revitalizing elixir by enhancing Bath's mineral waters with alchemical elements. Word is he has set up a secret laboratory to protect his patent, and those who have tried his formula swear by its invigorating properties."

"What a load of bosh." Aidan's hand fisted around the bed linens. "Why don't the Bath authorities simply arrest him?"

"For what? People have long believed in the benefits of Bath's waters. Rousseau is merely claiming to boost those effects with a blend of herbal remedies already in use in the Americas. I believe coneflower is one of them."

"And what's he charging people for samples of this so-called elixir?"

"Not a thing. Oh, he seems to have a few voluntary investors, but beyond that, the samples have been free. That is why the authorities are leaving him alone."

"Foolishness."

Wescott tipped a nod. "Perhaps, but this is how medical advances are made. One cannot pooh-pooh them all."

"I can." Aidan threw off the covers, ignoring Wescott's obvious discomfort as he collected his clothing from around the room. "I'll leave for Bath first thing tomorrow."

For all Aidan's outward show of calm, the rage he had not completely conquered during the half dozen years since his father's death writhed in his gullet. The virulence of his mother's last illness had prompted Charles Phillips to seek unconventional treatments, to invest his trust and vast sums of money in promises of a miracle cure.

He'd been a desperate man, so desperate that when his wife lay dead, he retired alone to his study, put a pis-

tol in his mouth, and pulled the trigger. Aidan had been
standing on the other side of the door at the time, his
hand raised to knock when the gun exploded. . . .

Following a tap, Delilah shouldered her way through
the doorway. The tray in her hands exuded the rich aro-
mas of coffee and warm scones. Aidan's stomach grumbled. After setting down her burden, she poured a cup
and handed it to him, at the same time leaning close to
brush her lips across his.

She cast Wescott a sidelong glance. "Shall we crawl
back into bed after your mate leaves, milord?"

Aidan stroked her cheek. "I'm afraid not, love, for I
must be off." Retrieving his frock coat from the brass
footboard, he reached into the pocket, drew out a handful of coins, and pressed them into her palm. "Should
anyone ask if I was here last night, be a good girl, do, and
reply with a resounding yes."

Laurel stared out onto rainy William Street and sighed.
The clouds had spread an early dusk over the city, and
the sodden weather had sent people scurrying indoors.
The air of abandonment hanging over the streets had an
equally dampening effect on Laurel's spirits.

As often happened in such gloomy moments, her
mind conjured a forbidden fantasy. . . .

He would appear out of the mist, ride his powerful
gray to her doorstep, scoop her onto the saddle, kiss
her—oh, she could taste those lips even now—and
profess how desperately he had searched for her these
many months.

His name was Aidan. . . .

Ah, yes, but he had not bothered to inquire after her
name, had he? No, he'd saved her life, claimed his reward in a quick kiss, and, she felt certain, forgotten her
as swiftly as he and his friend had rounded the corner
and disappeared from sight.

The rain-speckled windowpanes reflected the bookshop behind her. Seated on a high stool behind the counter, her sister Ivy pored over columns of figures scrawled in the shop's account ledger. The Knightsbridge Readers' Emporium had not sold a book, or seen so much as a single customer, in two entire days.

It was partly due to this wretched weather. But then, the Emporium rarely saw more than a customer or two per day, and an entire week had been known to pass without the sisters once hearing the jangle of the bell above the street door.

Laurel supposed it didn't much matter. The annuities left to them by their parents and dear Uncle Edward saw to their needs and a few luxuries besides. They were able to restock their inventory regularly as well as continue the lease on their guardian's tiny London town house, which they had converted to a shop on the ground floor with living space above.

Poor Uncle Edward had succumbed to pneumonia during last autumn's incessant rains; indeed, Laurel and her sisters still wore black bombazine in his memory. He had been like a father to them. Thorn Grove, however, had passed to a distant relative, a second or third cousin whom the girls had never met prior to the funeral and who had showed little interest in furthering their acquaintance afterward.

The Sutherland sisters were on their own.

Seeing no signs of impending business, Laurel sighed again and turned away from the window. Willow spared her a quick smile as she moved about the room swiping a feather duster across the tops of books lining the oak shelves. Behind the counter, Ivy frowned down at the account book and scrunched up her nose. Absently she tucked a strand of dark hair behind her ear and scratched her quill across the page.

"Ivy, why are you laboring so?" Laurel could hardly suppress her impatience. "We haven't sold a book in days."

"I am perfectly aware of that, Laurel," Ivy replied with her typical businesslike aplomb. She did not lift her gaze from the page. "But I have found a discrepancy. I fear Holly has muddled the figures again."

Ivy never hesitated to blame her twin whenever the numbers failed to tally. Thank goodness Holly's decision to brave the drizzle in favor of a trip to the bakeshop prevented her from hearing the charge, which surely would have set off another of the twins' infamous arguments.

Laurel circled the counter. "Let me have a look."

Ivy whisked the ledger out of reach. "If ever I am in a quandary as to an historical fact or a literary quote, I shall certainly consult you, Laurel. But we all know that when it comes to ciphering, well . . ." A lift of her brows completed the sentiment.

Laurel raised her hands and backed away. Ivy was right; neither she nor Holly had ever shown much aptitude for numbers.

"Why don't you go on up and prepare tea, Laurel?" Dear Willow, always the diplomat. She attempted to diffuse the tension with a flick of her duster. "We'll be up as soon as Holly returns. No use staying open any longer on an evening like this."

An impulse sent Laurel across the room to wrap her arms around the baby of the family. The months since Uncle Edward's death had not been easy on any of them, least of all Willow, who at nineteen should have been looking forward to her first, perhaps even second season here in London.

Ah, but there had been no seasons for any of them, no advantageous social connections or prospects of any sort. There had only ever been the four of them and Uncle Edward. Kind, if somewhat distant, their mother's elder brother had always seen to their basic needs, but the extras, such as parties and seasons and introductions to eligible young bachelors, had been overlooked.

They had never discussed the reasons for this lack,

not even among themselves. They had simply accepted their quiet life at Thorn Grove for what it had been: safe, tranquil, and thoroughly predictable. A retired army officer, Uncle Edward had shunned most social occasions, preferring his books and long walks with his hounds on Thorn Grove's woodland paths.

Life might have been considerably worse. Laurel *knew* that, yet as the eldest she wished she could give her sisters all they deserved. To see both twins married and raising a baby or two . . . and for Willow, the prettiest of them all, a white silk gown, dove's feathers in her hair, presentation at court, and a glorious season ending with a brilliant proposal of marriage . . .

As for herself . . . yes, she had wants, needs, that could not be met within the confines of their limited sphere. Adventure, travel—to see firsthand the sights she had only ever visited in books, to savor even a small taste of excitement, spontaneity.

Oh, such a capricious host of wishes, but what did it matter? Wishes, like daydreams, never came true.

Willow studied her intently. "What's troubling you, Laurel?"

"Nothing. Can I not hug my dearest little sister?" She released Willow and turned away, blinking to clear her eyes. It wouldn't do for the others to see signs of weakness in her, such futile wistfulness. Though they might not wish to admit it—especially the twins—her sisters looked to her for guidance and security, especially now that they were alone in the world.

She paused again to glance out at the gleaming street and the slick stones of the buildings across the way. Wishing Holly had not gone out so close to dusk and hoping she would be home soon, Laurel started up the back stairs.

A sharp clatter of the bell and a burst of wind and rain stopped her short. Instead of Holly stepping inside and shaking the wetness from her cloak, a tall young man stood on the threshold, holding the door open against his back. Laurel's first thought was one of gratification. Apparently someone in this city enjoyed his books more than he feared inclement weather.

Raindrops streamed off his cloak to splatter the floor; a chilly gust fanned the pages of Ivy's account book. The man said nothing. His bland expression betrayed no emotion. Taking in his superior height and attentive if uncommunicative stance, Laurel decided he must be a footman, though his dark, nondescript clothing revealed nothing about the personage he served.

Through the open doorway, carriage lanterns illuminated misty gold circles of rain. Black and sleek and of fine quality, the vehicle displayed no identifying crest or insignia. Laurel heard the carriage door opening, the lowering of the step, someone being handed down to the street. A figure moved into view, cloaked and bowed to the rain despite a second servant standing just behind with an umbrella.

Something about the size of that figure, and the prim, dancelike step that brought her over the threshold, sent a tingle of recognition up Laurel's arms.

Just as two plump hands reached up to draw the hood back, a King Charles spaniel, grown squat and gray-muzzled with age, clambered through the doorway. His wet paws slid on the hardwood floor, and he gave a rapid shake that showered Laurel's skirts with water. He raised moist, velvety eyes to her while a whine of recognition squealed in his throat.

"Please forgive this intrusion." Though it had been several years since she had heard that high, clear voice, Laurel well remembered it. Victoria pushed her hood to her shoulders. "I did not know where else to turn."

Chapter 3

"With my coronation still three months away, I find myself facing my first potential crisis. My dear friends, I need your help."

Upstairs in the Sutherlands' cramped parlor, the rain beat steadily against the windows, while a coal fire hissed in the hearth. Between sips of tea and bites of the hot venison pasties Holly had brought home from the bakeshop, Victoria explained her dilemma.

"It's my cousin George," she said bluntly. "He detests and resents me for occupying the throne he has long believed should rightfully belong to him."

The years had done little to take the childlike frankness from Victoria's features, and though she had grown taller, Willow still towered a good head above her. Victoria's figure had acquired the curves of womanhood, yet had retained something of the doll-like proportions that had always prompted Laurel and her sisters to be so protective of her.

Downstairs, their erstwhile friend had greeted them all warmly with embraces and kisses on their cheeks. But Laurel had sensed restraint, and she felt it now in the awkwardness that hovered over the parlor.

With a pang she acknowledged that their childhood camaraderie could never be entirely recaptured. Perhaps that was as it should be. The Sutherland sisters were no longer Princess Victoria's playmates; they were now merely Her Majesty's subjects.

"George has openly defied me," the queen said. "The man is a shameless reprobate with no respect for authority. I believe he is up to no good, and I tell you truly, I fear what he might do."

Those words heightened Laurel's sense of unreality. Surely the Queen of England could not be sitting in this shabby parlor, on the worn seat cushion of the faded settee, sipping tea from secondhand china and discussing the particulars of possible treason.

"But with or without Your Majesty," Laurel said, "the throne could not have passed to George Fitzclarence. Not when he is, well . . ."

"A bastard, yes." Victoria completed the sentiment with a lift of her eyebrow. "It is no secret that within the Hanover family, legitimate heirs have been as rare as daisies in winter."

She paused, studying each of the sisters as she sipped her tea. Dash, having grown tired of begging scraps from his mistress's plate, curled up by the fire with his chin on his paws.

A sad smile tugging her mouth, Victoria set her cup aside. "Years ago when I learned what my future held, I told you that you must no longer call me by my given name within the hearing of others. You always remembered to adhere to that rule. But we are quite alone now. There is no one to overhear, not even my footmen."

Laurel saw her own thoughts mirrored in her sisters' faces. Yes, they had all once been on the most familiar of terms. But that was before extraordinary circumstances created a chasm between them. The thought of treating their queen as an equal . . .

"The reason I came tonight has little enough to do with propriety," Victoria said. "Even a queen must live by certain rules, and in being here I am breaking several.

Two ladies-in-waiting in my coach are willing to lie for me no matter the reasons. My footmen as well. The rest of the palace believes me in bed with a headache."

Her features became taut with urgency. "As I said, I had nowhere else to turn. No one must ever know I sought your help. But seek it I do, because of your promise years ago that you would always remain my friends. My *secret* friends."

"We always will," Laurel said with conviction. "You may depend upon it . . . Victoria."

The others echoed their wholehearted agreement.

"Good. Then within this room, I am merely your childhood friend who seeks your assistance."

Her somber tone wrapped a sense of foreboding around Laurel. "Has your cousin threatened you?"

"Not openly," Victoria replied, "but in a manner of speaking, yes. Or perhaps he believes that reports of his impertinent remarks and outrageous behavior fail to make their way to my court. Drinking, carousing, consorting with individuals of questionable repute—it's all quite disgraceful. Not to mention insufferably embarrassing to me personally. I believe he takes great pleasure in humiliating me in the eyes of my subjects with the hope of rendering me an ineffectual ruler."

"Surely his antics are beneath your notice." Willow stood to pass around a platter of tea cakes. "Perhaps if you ignore him, he'll grow weary of baiting you."

"I wish I could believe that." Victoria plucked a biscuit from the tray and dunked it into her tea before taking a bite. "Two weeks ago I summoned him to court, and do you know how he responded?"

Laurel and each of her sisters shook their heads.

"By ignoring me." Victoria swallowed, flattened a palm to her bosom, and screwed up her features in a show of anger that made Laurel flinch beneath the royal displeasure. "*Me*, his queen! Such brazen disobedience is beyond insolent. It is more than I can bear and more than I dare tolerate. Understand, there are many subtleties at work here. Factions exist in this country that wish to do away with the monarchy altogether, and I fear that, ultimately, George hopes to incite them to action."

"The Radical Reformers," Laurel said. Throughout the reigns of Victoria's uncles and grandfather, distrust of the royal family had mounted in direct correlation to the scandals surrounding them. Unpopular foreign marriages, extravagant spending, adultery, madness . . . all had fueled a growing resentment among certain segments of the population, especially those that wished to institute democratic reforms similar to those in America.

Victoria nodded. "Precisely. And since I am young and female, such rabble considers my reign a perfect opportunity to press their views on the public."

"If indeed your cousin is entangled in some sort of treason," Laurel said, "should you not inform your prime minister?"

"Yes," Ivy put in, "surely Mr. Melbourne can set things to rights."

"Goodness, no!" Victoria flashed a startled look. "I need this dealt with quietly. Discreetly. The notion of a member of my own family scheming against me would only fuel sentiments that the Hanovers are a corrupt lot who have been plotting against each other for generations. It's just the sort of hullabaloo that could turn public opinion against me."

Laurel stared down into her own tea, now grown cold, then once more met Victoria's gaze. "How can we help?"

"George is presently in Bath. Laurel, I am hoping that you will agree to go there and do a little . . . well . . . spying. I want you to find out what he is up to and with whom. And if you can, dissuade him from whatever tomfoolery he's involved in and guide him back to me."

Before Laurel's astonishment had fully registered, Ivy sprang to her feet, startling Dash out of his slumber.

"What about the rest of us? Surely you can't mean for us to sit home while our sister—"

"Yes, we should go along." Holly's violet eyes snapped with excitement as she clapped her hands together. "It all sounds so diabolical and dangerous."

"Ivy, Holly, please. This is no game." Laurel knew she had to quell her sisters' enthusiasm immediately or they would follow her all the way to Bath. "Obviously Victoria cannot send all of us, for how would it look for four unknown sisters to suddenly appear on the social scene?"

"Laurel is correct," Victoria said. "One of you can be easily explained. A young widow from the country, recently out of mourning. A squire's wife, perhaps, who would not be readily known among the *ton*. Sending more of you would only complicate matters, and should one of you confuse your stories, my cousin might grow suspicious."

Once more she turned to Laurel. "Of the four of you, I believe you, Laurel, possess the right steadiness and experience to be successful. Will you do it? Will you help me?"

Had Laurel just this evening wished for adventure and excitement? What did she know about maneuvering in society, or about politics and treason? Good heavens, was she to transform from surrogate mother to surrogate spy in the span of a mere breath?

Could she?

The tapping of Victoria's pointed-toed boot confirmed a suspicion. "You haven't yet told us everything," Laurel ventured. Her voice gentled as she added, "It might help if I knew the entire truth of the matter."

Victoria hesitated, looking suddenly younger, apprehensive. She stilled her foot. "The reason I ordered George to court is because I'd made a troubling discovery among my late uncle's possessions. It appears that before the wars Uncle William maintained an ongoing correspondence between a Frenchman named André Rousseau and . . . my own dear father."

"*No.*" The word was a rusty squeak from Willow. Holly's and Ivy's mouths gaped in horrified silence. The blood drained from Laurel's cheeks. They had all heard of this man—who *hadn't* heard of the French aristocrat who betrayed his family, friends, and peers during France's Reign of Terror and throughout the wars with Napoleon?

Victoria continued. "It appears that some of the letters have gone missing and I believe George took them, for no one else had access to the locked files in his father's private study." A shudder ran through her slight shoulders. "Depending on what those missives contain, he could potentially do great damage to me and to England's future. And with my father's good name at stake, you'll understand why I cannot—simply *will* not—alert my ministers or anyone else as to the nature of my concerns."

No indeed. A vise closed around Laurel's throat. Treason, not merely from a discontented royal by-blow, but entrenched in the legitimate line as well? A line that led directly to Victoria herself?

"Victoria, I am not possibly qualified. . . ."

The young queen's lost, desperate look silenced Laurel's objections. Eight years ago, she had made a *vow* to her friend, her queen, and, by association, her country. She had pledged her loyalty with the whole of her heart and she must honor that vow now, when her dear friend needed her most.

Standing, she steadied her nerves and smiled down into Victoria's solemn dark eyes. "I shall do whatever you wish of me. Most eagerly."

Ivy tried unsuccessfully to muffle a groan of exasperation. Willow and Holly looked on as if thunderstruck.

Victoria sighed with evident relief. "Good. You will not be entirely on your own. I will arrange for a former lady-in-waiting to my aunt Princess Sophia to be your escort into Bath society. I know the Countess of Fairmont tolerably well and I trust her integrity, but she will know nothing, Laurel, beyond the fiction of your widow's identity. She will not even know the request comes from me, for I intend to send it through Lehzen."

Laurel nodded her understanding. She remembered Louise Lehzen, Victoria's German governess, from years ago. Steady and stoic, often to the point of seeming humorless and stern, the woman had nonetheless remained fiercely devoted to her royal charge. If anyone could be trusted with Victoria's secrets, it was Lehzen.

Victoria went on, "Through Lady Fairmont, you will gain an introduction to my cousin and then—how shall I say it?—you will work your charms on him until he warms toward you and you can persuade him to confide in you."

Laurel's stomach gave a twist. "You wish me to seduce your cousin?"

"Good heavens, no!" Victoria's hand flew to her bosom. "I would never ask you to compromise your virtue, not even in a matter of such vital urgency. I only suggest that you give the *appearance* of flirting with George, just enough to lower his guard."

As though they were in the schoolroom, Ivy's hand came up. "Are we not forgetting one complication— Mary Wyndham Fox?"

"George Fitzclarence's wife." Laurel didn't dare glance at her sisters.

"Oh, his wife has never stopped George," Victoria said with an indifferent wave. "He and Mary are estranged. He stops home every now and again to get her with child, but he hasn't even seen his newest son yet. However, Laurel, if your conscience prevents it, I shall press you no further."

Ivy pulled up taller in her chair, seeming about to speak.

Laurel didn't give her the chance. "No, I shall do it. . . ."

But if she knew little about society or the world, she knew even less about the art of flirtation. The only man, a neighboring landowner, who had ever shown an interest in her had immediately withdrawn his regard the moment he learned the size of her inheritance.

But, oh, dear. She, Laurel Sutherland, practical, ordinary, inexperienced spinster, was to go to Bath and seduce—she didn't care how Victoria termed it; the meaning was the same—a *married*, debauched scoundrel.

With a resigned sigh she clasped her hands at her waist. "When would you like me to leave?"

"In a week. That will give us time to assemble a proper wardrobe for you. I will also arrange for your accommodations and provide you with ample spending money. Oh, and here, just in case." Lifting her brocade reticule, Victoria pulled an item from inside and held it out to Laurel.

Laurel's eyes widened as she reached out and closed her hand around the butt of a small silver percussion pistol.

"You should not need that," Victoria told her, "but I would have you prepared for all contingencies. I leave you with one warning."

Only one? Laurel pulled her gaze from the gleaming weapon and mustered a brave expression. "Yes?"

"Beware of George's friends, and do not be fooled by genteel appearances. Many are individuals of the very worst sort, hardly fit to be called gentlemen. One is a rogue of particularly low morals and few scruples. I speak, of course, of the Earl of Barensforth."

The cards shot facedown across the felt-topped table, spinning to rest in front of each player. A fourth round of vingt-et-un had begun, and although the dealer used two decks shuffled together, Aidan had no trouble keeping a mental tally of the cards already played as well as those likely to surface in the next few minutes.

He had arrived in Bath that afternoon. Despite the suddenness of his plans, he had managed to lease a town house in the Royal Crescent, at the northwest corner of town. Fitz was staying a short walk away in the King's Circus town house he had inherited from his father.

Word of Aidan's presence in the city had quickly spread, and invitations to numerous affairs had piled up on the silver post salver.

Tonight's Assembly Rooms ball constituted the first of those affairs, and as he contemplated the faces circling the various tables in the cardroom, a troubling current ran under his skin. It was nothing he could put a name to, simply a sense that, within the banal normalcy of this typically masculine scene, something was . . . off . . . and therefore not normal at all.

Turning his focus to the game, he raised a corner of the card dealt him. Ace of diamonds. He added its count value—negative one—to the running tabulation in his mind and calculated the odds of what his next card would likely be. High? Low?

A low card was practically guaranteed, he decided. He pushed a five-hundred-pound chip, double the minimum wager for the table, in front of his card. To his left, Arthur Steele, who had recently inherited the title of Viscount Devonlea, patted his perfectly slicked-back hair and doubled his wager as well.

Lord Julian Stoddard, sent down from Oxford a month ago but apparently suffering little shame over the matter, did likewise. Besides healthy good looks and a savoir faire that ladies found universally appealing, the young Stoddard possessed a sharp eye and a deceptively quick wit, leading Aidan to agree with Julian's smug assertion that this second son of a marquess would one day gamble his way to considerable wealth.

"From what I heard," Stoddard said as he pushed his wager to the center of the table, "Babcock floated in the thermal waters for so long that he"—he paused, his gaze lighting on each of the others in turn before he gave a theatrical shudder—"he actually *stewed*. As cooked as a shank of boiled mutton."

"Oh, I say, Stoddard."

"Good God."

"Really, Stoddard, must you?"

"I'm only passing on what I was told," the young man said with a defensive shrug. Pushing his chair back a few inches, he stretched out his left leg and released a soft groan.

Aidan noticed the silver-handled walking stick leaning against the edge of the table. "I say, Stoddard, rather young for one of those, aren't you?"

"Sprained ankle. Had a bit of a riding mishap last week."

"Give it a good soak." Devonlea flashed a nasty leer. "Just not at the Cross Bath."

"What I can't help wondering is how Babcock could have remained all alone in the bathhouse after everyone else left." Aidan raised a glass of port to his lips and waited for an answer.

"If you ask me, he'd been drinking and dozed off, perhaps in the corner of one of the dressing rooms." Captain Geoffrey Taft considered his cards and tossed in the table's minimum wager of 250 pounds. "Then upon waking, he stumbled into the bath and drowned."

A retired naval officer who presented the very picture of stodgy English tradition with his serviceable suits and stoic, unflappable demeanor, Captain Taft had nonetheless scandalized the *ton* two years earlier. His wife had died, and months short of the proper mourning period the man had taken up quite openly with a much younger woman no one had ever heard of.

Her name was Margaret Whitfield—*Mrs.* Whitfield,

though Aidan doubted she had ever been married. Like Fitz's mother, Dorothea Jordan, the petite and pretty Mrs. Whitfield had once made her living as an actress, but *un*like Dorothea Jordan, the stages this woman had graced were accessed through back doors in seedy alleyways. Apparently, Geoffrey Taft had wandered into a playhouse one night and come out smitten.

No one in society would know that, of course. Aidan knew only because he'd done a little checking up on Mrs. Whitfield. Taft had been a friend of his father's and, quite simply, Aidan liked the man and hadn't wished to see him cuckolded. So far, much to Aidan's surprise, he had not been.

"So Babcock was an inebriate," he commented to no one in particular.

"No more than any of the rest of us," Devonlea said with a laugh. He gestured at Aidan's hand. "Are you sticking?"

Aidan glanced at his ace and four of clubs and increased his stake by another five hundred. Deciding to play the ace as a one rather than an eleven, he bought three more cards and raised his wager accordingly.

As each of the other players bought cards, twisted, or stuck, he analyzed their facial expressions. Taft appeared tense, whereas Devonlea and Stoddard leaned casually back in their chairs. Henri de Vere, the dealer for this round, dealt his own final cards.

Aidan considered de Vere something of an enigma. Like Claude Rousseau's father, de Vere had served as a spy during the wars, but he had chosen to aid the British and European forces rather than Napoleon's. It was even rumored that de Vere provided Wellington with information that facilitated Napoleon's defeat at Waterloo, though de Vere had never confirmed or denied the claim. Still, his service record made him a hero in both the British and French courts, and instead of channeling this favor to his advantage, he chose to live quietly in relative obscurity.

The Frenchman turned his cards over one by one with a dramatic flair to reveal four cards totaling twenty-one. The other men around the table sighed in defeat.

"Well, Barensforth?" Lord Devonlea gestured at Aidan's cards, still facedown on the table. Unlike either de Vere or Taft, Devonlea, a man whose expenses generally exceeded his income, left little to wonder about. Only a year or two older than Aidan, he was nevertheless a gentleman of the old school, with deeply entrenched Tory philosophies and a strict belief in the separation of the classes.

In other words, Arthur Steele, Viscount Devonlea, was as colossal a snob as could be imagined, but otherwise harmless and thoroughly predicable.

He also happened to be George Fitzclarence's brother-in-law.

Remaining mysteriously silent, Aidan again reached for his port. In the past hour he had contrived to part with a considerable sum, a circumstance he loathed, not merely because losing grated against his competitive instincts, but also because the effort to lose taxed his brain to an even greater extent than winning did.

Yet ceaseless victories would raise suspicions and eventually lead some clever opponent to realize it wasn't mere luck that filled Aidan's pockets at the gaming tables. No, it was important to temper his successes with occasional failures . . . but damned if his pride didn't sometimes ride roughshod over his good sense.

To the accompaniment of muttered oaths and exclamations of reluctant praise, he revealed his hand.

De Vere's lip curled, yet with good-natured censure he observed in his lightly accented English, "A five-card trick beats my hand. Damn you again, Barensforth."

"And to think, it seemed Lady Luck had abandoned you tonight." With a snap, Devonlea summoned a waiter to replenish his brandy.

"Dev, old boy," Aidan said, "our dear Lady Luck may

run off for the occasional fling now and again, but rest assured she never stays away for long. Seems the old girl cannot resist me."

Aidan drained his port and splashed another measure into his glass from the bottle at his elbow. In keeping with his reputed ability to drink all night without falling into his cups, he pushed smoothly to his feet. This was only his second glass since his arrival in the cardroom, but a few clever sleights of hand had made it appear to be his fifth or sixth. "Gentlemen, it has been a pleasure."

He sauntered over to another table, where he hovered for the next twenty minutes conveying subtle signals to aid Fitz in his game of loo—a twitch of his brow, the quirk of his mouth, a deep or shallow sip of his port. If his own profits tended to run audaciously high, the opposite could be said of George Fitzclarence, evidenced by the dwindling stack of chips at his elbow. Aidan sought merely to give Fitz a fighting chance.

Aidan lingered long enough to ensure that ample spending money found its way into the man's pockets. It wouldn't do for Fitz to run out of cash and suddenly decide to cut short his visit to Bath. Aidan needed him here, performing whatever ill deeds the Home Office wanted investigated.

Stepping out into the centrally located octagon room brought to Aidan a shock of noisy bustle that contrasted sharply with the hush of the cardroom. Returning greetings, shaking and kissing hands as he went, he proceeded through to the ballroom.

A reel was presently under way, a colorful flurry of youthful energy. Tiers of seats lined the walls, from where the elders and infirm and those not lucky enough to have found partners looked on. Overhead, five massive cut-glass chandeliers blazed at full brilliance, and lively hearth fires warded off the March chill.

As Aidan made his way through the long room, scanning faces and taking mental notes, a number of bright-faced young ladies in colorful silks waved their dance cards under his nose. He stopped to offer a compliment here, chuck a curl there, and chat a moment with their fathers. In every case he left behind a trail of blushing disappointment.

"My lord, a word if you please."

Ah. Smile in place, he came to an abrupt if somewhat reluctant halt. Lady Amanda Beecham's tone matched the frosty diamonds glittering around her slender neck. A sliver of white blond eyebrow arched in disdain as she regarded him.

They stood not far from the orchestra. The lady slipped her hand into the crook of his arm and drew him behind the carved Oriental screen that concealed the musicians from their audience. In the relative privacy, she slid her hand from his elbow and let it fly open-palmed against his cheek.

The violinist missed a note. Although the blow left a rather commendable sting, Aidan merely tilted his head and frowned in puzzlement.

"That, my lord, is for ignoring my notes."

In point of fact he hadn't ignored them at all. He had dutifully read each carefully penned, scalding condemnation of his character and then tossed it into the hearth.

He also might have mentioned that by Amanda's own decree, their affair had never been meant to last more than the fortnight her husband had been away from home, and that had been more than a month ago. Aidan had believed their liaison long over.

His work for the Home Office didn't allow for more than brief affairs. When he took up with a woman, he always made certain it was someone who shared his aversion to permanent attachments. That typically meant married women of less-than-spotless virtue. He was neither Lady Amanda's first paramour nor her last, and he suspected tonight's outburst had more to do with her frustration in a loveless marriage than with his own conduct.

Ah well, this was not the first time one of his affairs had ended with the imprint of a feminine hand across his cheek, and he could think of several that had begun that way as well.

Amanda leaned in close and hissed, "I am not some old cloak to be worn when one feels a chill and cast off when the sun returns. How *dare* you?"

The question, it seemed, was rhetorical. She swept away without having secured an answer. Aidan adjusted his cravat, shot his cuffs, and exchanged an apologetic look with the musicians.

He shrugged off the interlude and returned his focus to the assembly. For the most part these well-heeled individuals were here on holiday, seeking cures for their minor ailments and hoping to acquire a feeling of youthful vitality. As for the young people . . : they were here because their parents were, and they seemed intent on making the best of the situation.

Yet a man from among their rank had recently died in one of the very facilities where many of those present tonight intended to soak their aching limbs. Though there had been no conclusive evidence of villainy, the circumstances of Babcock's death remained suspicious. Aidan would have expected a dampening of merriment, a more somber demeanor, out of respect. Looking about, he saw quite the opposite.

Had Babcock been without friends here in Bath?

He once more considered Captain Taft's theory that an inebriated Babcock had stumbled into the water. Aidan didn't believe it. Babcock had a reputation for honor and responsible behavior in the Commons, and nothing the Home Office had dug up on the man suggested a tendency toward overimbibing.

Then again, some men were skilled at hiding their

vices until, of course, those vices suddenly got the better of them. Had that been the case with Babcock?

Aidan had done enough mingling; it was time to ask more questions, and near the central fireplace he spotted the perfect opportunity.

"Lord Harcourt, what an agreeable surprise to find you here," Aidan declared, drawing the aging marquess to his side. He adjusted his pace to accommodate the man's mild infirmities.

"Barensforth, my boy. What brings a young buck like you to hobnob with the gout-afflicted?" Harcourt was limping slightly, favoring his right leg over the left, while at the same time appearing determined to keep abreast.

"News of a financial opportunity," Aidan replied lightly. He nodded at a passing acquaintance. "Perhaps you've heard?"

"Indeed. The Summit Pavilion."

"Tell me, what is this I hear about an elixir?"

Harcourt's wiry eyebrows went up. "So news is spreading, is it?" He looked about and lowered his voice. "The research is still in its early stages, but should the elixir prove successful, it will be offered exclusively at the pavilion."

"Do tell. Have you tried it?"

"Oh, indeed. I am on the list."

"What list?"

"Rousseau passes out nominal samples from time to time, but to receive a full dosage, one must have a place on his exclusive list. Those of us who are on the list swear by the stuff. I tell you, I have never felt better."

"Fascinating. How does one get on this list?"

"Ah . . . I am afraid for now the list is closed until Rousseau is ready to offer his elixir to all. I tell you, Barensforth, this elixir shall prove a revolutionary development to the field of medicine."

"And a highly profitable endeavor," Aidan added,

contriving to sound impressed while wishing instead to warn the other man of the potential hazards, both to his health and his purse. Instead he said, "I hear Roger Babcock was a huge proponent of the project. An appalling shame, his death."

Harcourt's gait faltered; his nostrils flared. "I shall waste no energy mourning a rapscallion like Babcock. I am sorry for his family. Beyond that, I am little moved by his passing. If you will excuse me, sir."

The liver spots on his temples showing starkly russet against the pallor of his skin, Harcourt limped off. A commotion on the dance floor ensued as he squeezed his unwieldy form through the lines of dancers presently engaged in a quadrille.

As much as Aidan would have liked to follow, he remained where he was, observing through narrowed eyes as Harcourt rejoined his equally stout wife. Aidan had learned something the Home Office had not previously known: Babcock had not been without adversaries, and even the feeble Marquess of Harcourt was not above suspicion.

Chapter 4

"Then I am to understand, Mrs. Sanderson, that your mother was a lady-in-waiting at Kensington Palace at the same time as Lady Fairmont?"

Viscountess Devonlea, formerly Beatrice Fitzclarence, sat facing Laurel inside the velvet-trimmed, luxuriously appointed barouche. Laurel could hardly believe her luck yesterday morning at the Pump Room when Lady Fairmont had introduced her to none other than George Fitzclarence's sister.

The two women apparently cosponsored several charities and were both members of the Ladies' Botanical Society in Bath. When Lady Devonlea had mentioned how tiresome it was that her husband would be arriving at the Assembly Rooms early tonight to play cards, Lady Fairmont had offered her a ride, a fortuitous circumstance that almost convinced Laurel that her mission here would be easy.

Almost.

Now, as they traveled north into the stately environs of Bath's Upper Town, she hesitated before answering the viscountess to be certain she had her "facts" straight.

Her fictional mother, the wife of a baronet, had once attended the Duchess of Kent, but—oh, dear—was that supposed to have been before or *after* the Countess of

Fairmont served as a companion to Princess Sophia, who
had also occupied apartments in Kensington Palace?

So much to remember, so many lies to tell. A slight
ache blossomed behind Laurel's eyes. At the same time,
the silk gown Victoria had supplied, along with the
satin slippers and stunning jeweled reticule, brought an
odd sense of reassurance. These borrowed trappings of
wealth and privilege provided a confident second skin,
like a protective covering, that rendered Laurel Sutherland safe from all the falsehoods the widowed Mrs.
Sanderson must say and act upon.

Even her hesitation worked to her advantage, as the
Countess of Fairmont, sitting beside her, offered Lady
Devonlea what she fully believed to be the correct answer. "Mrs. Sanderson's mother and I never actually had
the pleasure of meeting, for I left the palace the year
before she arrived."

Though in her middle years, Laurel's social patron-
ess was nonetheless a stunning woman, with glossy dark
hair only slightly threaded with silver. Faint lines fanned
from the countess's slanting gray eyes as she covered
Laurel's hand with her own and gave a squeeze. "Apparently your mother was a great favorite of the household.
I do wish I *had* known her."

As the coach turned the corner onto Bennett Street,
the vehicle fell in behind a host of costly carriages rumbling along the cobbled street. Laurel peeked out at the
elegantly attired guests making their way toward the
Palladian facade of the Assembly Rooms and listened
to their animated banter.

Her fingers clenched and unclenched around her reticule as she anticipated the next several hours. She had
little inkling of what to expect, for she had never before attended a ball, much less in borrowed clothes and
under an assumed name—Mrs. Edgar Sanderson, lately
from the village of . . . oh yes, of Fernhurst, in the county
of Hampshire.

Recruiting her sisters' help, she had practiced dance steps all the previous week. Should she happen to step on a gentleman's foot, he would, with any luck, attribute her lack of skill to her having spent the past two years in seclusion, mourning the death of her "husband."

The carriage pulled into an empty space at the curbside. When the footman opened the door, Lady Fairmont slid over to allow the tall, red-haired fellow to hand her down. Lady Devonlea went next, and Laurel followed suit, resisting her natural inclination to step down on her own initiative. Ladies, after all, never descended from carriages unassisted.

The doors to the building's columned portico opened onto a bombardment of colors and textures, faces and voices. Soaring ceilings, carved pillars, and a dizzying array of candelabra made Laurel giddy with nervous excitement.

Breathe. Relax. Believe in the role you are playing.

"Ah, Lady Fairmont. Lady Devonlea. How splendid of you both to grace our assembly tonight."

An elderly gentleman with graying muttonchops and a shaggy mustache bowed smartly over the ladies' hands. With a tap of his heels he straightened. Through silver-rimmed spectacles, his gaze lit on Laurel. "I see you have brought a charming new friend."

Lady Fairmont drew Laurel closer. "Mrs. Sanderson, I should like you to meet Major Calvin Melrose, a dear old friend of my husband's and master of ceremonies here at the Upper Rooms. Major, Mrs. Edgar Sanderson."

"Enchanted, madam, enchanted." His practiced eye appraised her tawny silks, pausing only briefly on the jet brooch pinned to her bodice to signify a lingering sentiment of mourning. Apparently satisfied, he raised her hand and kissed it. "Now let us see, to whom shall I introduce you first? You do mean to dance tonight, Mrs. Sanderson, do you not?"

"She most certainly does," Lady Devonlea supplied

before Laurel had the chance to answer. "Mrs. Sanderson is most accomplished in the art of dancing."

Laurel swung a startled look in the woman's direction, then sent another through the expansive archway into the ballroom where countless couples moved in flawless rhythm.

"That might have been a bit of an exaggeration," Laurel whispered to the viscountess as Major Melrose escorted them into the brilliantly lit ballroom.

"You shall thank me later," the viscountess whispered back. "To have indicated otherwise would have consigned you to a host of ungainly partners."

Laurel sighed. If she hadn't already learned her lesson about the foolishness of making wishes, she would certainly have wished this night long over.

"Aidan Phillips, you scoundrel. I might have known I'd find you here. Why do you skulk here alone like a Spitalfields footpad? And what the devil have you done with my brother?"

Aidan had escaped into the relative quiet of the tea-room to avoid a certain young lady's mother who believed he would make a perfect match for her charmingly bucktoothed but regrettably pin-brained seventeen-year-old daughter. But here, at last, was a welcome feminine voice.

"Bea, my darling." Turning, he closed the space between them and raised her satin-clad hand to his lips. "You grow more beautiful each time I see you."

"And you, dear sir, deliver flattery with more false sincerity than any other man alive."

"I practice before a mirror, you know."

He twirled her in a graceful pirouette. Auburn-haired and generously curvaceous, Beatrice Fitzclarence remained at thirty-two a striking woman, having inherited none of her father's physical shortcomings and virtually all the charms that had made her mother, Dorothea Jordan, a favorite on the London stage. Tonight her peacock silk gown emphasized her finest assets with devil's-bargain perfection. Her hair glittered and her skin glowed. Her lips tilted at their haughtiest.

By God, she never failed to make him smile. "Have you only just arrived?" he asked her.

"Yes. Arthur came earlier, but I drove over with the Countess of Fairmont and a new acquaintance." Using her folded fan, she jabbed at the center of his chest. "You are avoiding my question."

"Fitz is in the cardroom."

The corners of her lightly rouged mouth turned down. "Oh, you can't have left him alone."

"Never fear, he's won enough tonight to offset any funds he might relinquish in my absence."

"Are you quite sure? He very nearly reduced himself to beggary last month."

"Beatrice, upon my honor, Fitz shall leave tonight's festivities with heavier pockets than when he arrived."

She gave a satisfied *humph* and slipped her hand into the crook of his arm. "Dance with me. Or are you promised for this set?"

"No," he said as they made their way through the crowded octagon room and into the ballroom, "I've been maddeningly evasive all evening."

"And you call yourself a gentleman."

"I call myself no such thing. Shall we?"

She placed her hand in his and together they stepped to the center of the dance floor. With an arch look she said, "What an irredeemable bachelor you are. And yet some young hopeful must eventually ensnare you. You must produce an heir."

He set his palm at her waist and guided her in the whirling steps of the waltz. "I had rather contract the pox than submit to the simpering opportunism of the marriage mart. Besides, I'm afraid you broke my heart when you married Devonlea."

She let go a bubble of laughter. "Aidan, dear boy, there is nothing the least bit breakable about you. Not your ego, your pride, certainly not your heart. That is what I like most about you. You are never likely to go to pieces in anyone's hands. Unlike my brother. Tell me, how has he responded to all the fuss over Victoria's impending coronation?"

"Tolerably well. This new pavilion has proved an obliging distraction."

"Yes, how very tedious. The Summit Pavilion is all Arthur speaks of these days."

"Is he investing heavily?"

Looking bored, she shrugged a half-bare shoulder as he moved with her in time to the music. "He believes Bath will suddenly become all the rage again. I have my doubts, but as long as he doesn't bankrupt us, I am content."

"And this so-called elixir? Does he credit Claude Rousseau's promise of eternal youth?"

"A foolish notion, perhaps, but I confess I don't see the harm in it." She gave a momentary lift of her brows. "Convincing people they will feel rejuvenated often produces the desired effect. And who knows? Perhaps Rousseau is on to something."

"Perhaps." But he doubted it, and Beatrice's attitude surprised him. He would have predicted much stronger objections on her part, along with a hearty contempt for anyone gullible enough to believe in magical potions.

"Have you sampled it?" he asked, as though the matter were of little consequence to him.

"Not yet. Having only recently arrived in Bath myself, I am not on the list."

"The list again." Aidan craned his neck to see over heads. "Is Rousseau here tonight?"

"Goodness, no, darling. He never comes to events such as these. You'll find him at the theater, concerts, the occasional private soiree. He's far too scholarly for dancing," she added with a roll of her eyes. Lifting her hand from his shoulder, she bobbed her closed fan in greeting to someone off to their right. A smile blossoming, she said, "There is that new friend I mentioned. The one with whom I shared my coach on the way here."

"Oh?" He tried to sound interested, but he hadn't come to learn about Beatrice's latest social acquisition.

"There, dancing with Raymond Ashley." She used her fan to point. "The delicious-looking young lady in the amber gown."

Aidan rotated with her again and spotted their mutual acquaintance, a thick-limbed, bull-faced man several years his junior. Ashley turned with his partner, and the woman in the amber gown came into view.

The air rushed out of him. Delicious? By heaven, yes, luscious enough to eat. She was golden-haired without quite being blond; her porcelain skin glowed with a country-fresh ripeness, her green eyes with a springtime crispness.

He found himself staring, first out of pure admiration, and then with a vague sense of . . . familiarity.

But surely he would remember encountering a face as beautiful as that. His gaze was drawn to her mouth, to lips as lush as ripe raspberries. Awareness, he'd even call it recognition, danced across his own lips, as if his mouth had once sampled the touch and taste of hers—

"Caught your eye, has she?" Beatrice's rippling laughter mocked him. "I thought she might, but I fear you would only be wasting your time. She is very recently out of mourning, which makes her highly available on that marriage mart you seem so intent on avoiding. More to the point, I'd say she is rather too inexperienced to be your type."

"Who is she?"

Beatrice laughed again. "Mrs. Edgar Sanderson."

"That means nothing to me. Where did you say you found her?"

"I didn't, but it was at the Pump Room yesterday. You really should stop staring. You'll crimp your neck."

But he could not draw his gaze away from her. While her height exceeded that of most of the women in the room, she moved with an effortlessness that somehow reduced poor Ashley to an ungainly jumble of heavy limbs and oafish feet utterly out of step with the music.

Recognition continued to prickle across his shoulders, down his back. Something about the silhouette of her figure and the curve of her slender neck as she glanced up at her partner brought a blaze of certainty that he had once held her in similar fashion, her lovely features tilted just so beneath his own.

A memory, or merely wishful thinking?

"What is her given name?"

"Hmm." Beatrice pursed her lips. "No, I believe I shall leave that for you to discover, if you can."

"Challenge accepted. I'll have her name by the next set."

"I am afraid not. Her dance card is full. Major Melrose saw to that."

"Damn the man, but that has never stopped me before."

"I wish you luck." The waltz ending, Beatrice kissed his cheek and went in search of her brother.

Aidan continued observing the mysterious Mrs. Sanderson as she progressed through the next several names on her dance card. He knew each of her partners, had seen each successfully maneuver on many a dance floor. What about this particular woman rendered these men half-lame in comparison?

And yet they kept coming, practically lining up for their chance to trip over their own feet. At the commencement of another quadrille, Mrs. Sanderson joined hands with the balding, pock-faced Marquess of Wentworth, who proved to have no better luck than his predecessors. Their feet all but tangling on several occasions, poor Wentworth looked downright harried as he attempted to match Mrs. Sanderson's pace.

The sight made Aidan grin; he had never much liked Wentworth. Shaking his head, he looked away, only to glance back to discover a vivid green gaze pinned on him.

The music continued, but for several beats Mrs. Sanderson did not. Wentworth stumbled. Then she was moving again, dancing her way down the line beside Wentworth.

Aidan's senses buzzed. A flurry of sounds and sights invaded his thoughts: jammed sidewalks, bright bunting adorning the shop fronts, the queen's carriage making its way across the city amid the cheering of a joyful crowd.

In the midst of that crowd, a woman struggled against a haberdashery window, in danger of being trampled. He remembered that she had knowingly put herself in peril, risking her life to save a neighbor's child.

Familiar? Yes . . . yes, he remembered her. More important, this delicious young widow of Beatrice's appeared to remember him.

Rather well, he'd say.

Chapter 5

"Mrs. Sanderson, are you quite all right? Have you grown faint? Perhaps you require a breath of air."

For a full ten seconds Laurel failed to respond to her dance partner, whose name she could not remember. Nor did she realize, during those heart-thumping moments, that the Mrs. Sanderson he addressed was in fact her.

He was here. The man who had saved her on Knightsbridge Street, whose handsome face had haunted her dreams and waking fantasies these many months since.

How often had she stood at the Emporium window, staring into the night fog and attempting to conjure his muscular physique atop his powerful gray? How many nights had she lain awake, wondering who he was, where he might be, and whether she would ever see him again?

And now he was here, as imposing and breathtaking as she remembered. No, far more so, for only now did she realize how pale a reproduction her imagination had fashioned.

"What the devil makes Barensforth stare with such impertinence?" drawled the man beside her.

Her heart reached into her throat. Barensforth? The *Earl* of Barensforth?

An individual of the very worst sort, hardly fit to be called a gentleman.

But no, surely Victoria had been mistaken. Certainly a man who risked incurring the wrath of the police to rescue a total stranger must be the very *best* sort of individual, the most honorable of gentlemen. . . .

Who had left her, with the briefest touch of his lips, simmering, vibrating, besieged by a host of emotions a spinster had no right to feel. Sensual, enthralling . . . and utterly *dis*honorable.

"Mrs. Sanderson?"

"Yes? Oh. I am quite well, thank you. Or no, I believe I *am* a trifle warm."

"You do appear flushed," the gentleman agreed. "I believe refreshments are being served in the tearoom. Would you care for some?"

"That would be splendid, thank you, Lord . . . er . . ."

"Wentworth." He placed perplexed emphasis on his name. It was not the first time he had had to remind her. He sucked the pitted skin of his cheeks against his teeth and offered the crook of his arm.

She found the octagon room only marginally less oppressive than the ballroom. Her cheeks felt clammy, her brow both hot and cold. In the blazing glare of scores of candles, faces and fashions blurred into a riot of confusion made all the more intolerable by the combative scents of perfumes and hair tonics. Her airways tightened around a threatening cough she did her best to suppress.

She was not accustomed to such a crush. The closest thing to a ball at Thorn Grove had been the yearly Christmas revelries for the villagers and estate servants. Instead of dancing, she and her sisters had distributed small gifts and served punch and Christmas pudding.

Ah, but it was not the heat or noise or confusion, or

even the assault of masculine shoes against her toes, that put her out of sorts. It was *he*, Lord Barensforth, and what his being here would mean to her mission.

What his being here would mean to *her*.

"I need some air," she said to Lord Wentworth. "I . . . do not feel at all well." Snapping her fan open, she fluttered it in front of her face.

Wentworth's mouth held a trace of annoyance. He conveyed her to the tearoom and handed her into the first available chair, which happened to be at a table occupied by a half dozen young people of about Willow's age. "Wait here. I shall attempt to procure you something cool to drink."

She nodded and continued to fan her face. After initial greetings the others at the table returned to their own lively conversation. Laurel scanned the crowd for Lord Wentworth. Surely he should have returned by now.

Rising and wandering back into the octagon room, she pondered the various doorways and tried to remember Lady Fairmont's explanations of where each one led. Entering the gentlemen's cardroom would raise a scandal sure to keep people twittering late into the night. She avoided that door and chose another.

As soon as the frigid air hit her skin, she realized her mistake, yet the stone terrace overlooking the backs of nearby buildings offered a haven she could not resist. The terrace stood empty, and as the din of the ball faded to a muted hum behind her, she welcomed the chilly air against her cheeks. She tugged off her cream satin gloves and leaned her hands on the balustrade.

Behind her, the door opened. "Good evening. It is Mrs. Sanderson, is it not?"

Laurel whirled and pulled up short at the sight of *him*.

He stood framed in the doorway, the light behind him gilding his silhouette and draping his face in shadow.

Nevertheless, she recognized the Earl of Barensforth immediately. No other man stood as he did, tall and solid and steadfast, with broad shoulders and a bearing she could term only . . . noble. However fanciful a description, she could not help thinking it.

Her heart clamored, then stood still, then clamored again as he stepped toward her like the hero of a beloved fairy tale walking off the timeworn pages.

"Yes, it *is* Mrs. Sanderson." On his lips, her false name took on a world of meaning, of innuendo. Tingles showered her spine. He raised a hand, the light from inside glinting off an object grasped in his long fingers. "I thought perhaps you could use this."

When Laurel merely gaped up at him like a fox at the hounds, he reached for her hand and pressed a champagne glass into her palm.

"I thought only tea and punch were served here."

"Madam, spirits are always available in the cardroom. Drink. It will revive you."

She obeyed with a small sip. He was right. The bubbles tickled her throat, instantly making her feel more alert and not nearly as overheated.

No, the flush warming her skin now had nothing to do with the sweltering crush inside, and everything to do with how Lord Barensforth's eyes held her, traveling a leisurely course across her face and her bared décolletage.

"Thank you." She inhaled, her breath audibly trembling. Why did he make her feel so capricious, so unlike herself? Until this instant, she had even failed to notice a highly pertinent detail. "How do you know my name?"

"We have a mutual friend." He smiled with a quirk of his lips she remembered from Knightsbridge; now, as then, her pulse leaped at the sight of it. "Beatrice Fitzclarence. She pointed you out to me."

"Did she?" Good heavens. How ironically inconvenient for Lady Devonlea to bring her to the attention of the one person Victoria most wished her to avoid. "If you'll excuse me, sir, I must return to the tearoom. Lord Wentworth will—"

"I shouldn't worry about him. His own fault for abandoning you as he did. Any fool could see you were feeling unwell."

"Lord Wentworth didn't abandon me," she clarified. "He went to find me something to drink."

"It looks as though I have beat him to it. His loss." His voice dipped. "And my gain."

Was it? His attentions left her flustered. It had been for George Fitzclarence's benefit that Victoria had meticulously selected her wardrobe to emphasize her very best features—her blond hair, her slim figure, and, yes, her supposed wealth. Her amber gown was of the finest-quality silk; her slippers, reticule, and fan had been purchased at Bond Street's most exclusive shops.

For all the bait they had set, had she hooked the wrong fish?

Unless . . . had the Earl of Barensforth followed her outside because he recognized her from that long-ago summer's day?

Apprehension sent a forced rush of blood to hum in her ears, throb in her temples. She pictured herself as she had appeared to him then: bonnet gone, coif devastated, dress torn, face streaked with dirt. She herself had hardly recognized the image staring back from the glass above her dresser. Surely, then, he did not recognize her now.

Even so, she guarded her face with another sip of champagne, then started to go inside. "Thank you, but I must rejoin—"

He shifted, blocking her path. "Beatrice tells me your dance card is full. A pity. You really ought to dance with me."

She stopped short, nearly colliding with his chest. "Oh, and why is that?"

"I'd spare your feet a good deal of mistreatment."

The candid observation made her laugh in spite of herself. "You noticed that? How horribly embarrassing. I'm afraid the fault was entirely my own. I confess to being a hopeless clod on the dance floor."

"Oh, no, Mrs. Sanderson, I think not. I watched you dance. You were perfection."

He had watched her? The knowledge made her insides flutter.

"Everyone watched you. Or hadn't you noticed?"

She hardly knew what to say, so she said nothing and shook her head.

His hand—the same powerful hand that had once reached through a crowd for her—beckoned now. His proximity made her feel as though she were back in the ballroom crush, heated, pressed in upon, breathless. The darkness carved his features with a brutal beauty. His ebony tailcoat, ivory knee breeches, and glowing white shirtfront seemed sculpted from the smoothest stone.

"With your permission, may I prove a point?"

"I . . . that depends entirely on the point you intend on making."

His smile became devastating in its exuberance. "Can you hear the music from here?"

"Of course I can hear the music. I am not deaf, sir."

He relieved her of both the champagne glass and the gloves she still held in her other hand, and set them on the balustrade. When he returned, he positioned himself toe-to-toe with her, his wide shoulders and broad chest blocking out everything beyond, including the safety to be found through the doorway.

His left hand claimed her waist, settling open-palmed just above her hip. His other hand closed around hers. Heated awareness pulsed through her as she realized that he, too, was gloveless, that his palm lay brazenly naked against her own.

"Madam, prepare yourself as we endeavor to discover the full extent of your talents."

Before she could think of a response to that bit of cheek, she found herself swept in smooth, flowing circles, the crisp breeze filling her skirts, stirring her hair, and uplifting her soul.

He partnered her flawlessly, even over the bumpy flagstones, never once stepping on her foot . . . never once looking away from her eyes. His own eyes, shadowed and fathomless, smoldered with unspoken suggestions, untold implications. She felt keenly aware of everything about him: his superior height, his muscular build, the searing brand of his palm at her waist. . . .

The notion struck her—stunned her—that they were doing something more than dancing, something much more intimate, more sensual.

More forbidden.

As abruptly as they had begun, they came to a halt. Or rather he did, catching her in his arms when she stumbled from lost momentum. His hands slid to her shoulders and he held her at arm's length.

"I do see what the problem is. You, Mrs. Sanderson, do not dance as other women do."

"Yes, I told you. . . ." Her heart sank at the prospect of having proved his earlier conclusion sadly wrong.

Laughing, he shook his head. "You are no clod, Mrs. Sanderson. But most men will have a devil of a time keeping up with you because they fail to understand the obvious. Am I mistaken, or do you prefer to *lead*?"

Laurel's eyebrows shot up. "Is that what I am doing? I never realized. . . ."

His observation made perfect sense. All her life, whenever she had practiced dance steps with her sisters, she had always assumed the lead. She *was* the eldest.

"Mystery solved, I suppose." She laughed ruefully. "I must learn to curb my assertiveness."

"Oh, no, Mrs. Sanderson. I fervently beg you not to do that."

His hands were on her still, the caress of his fingertips on her upper arms generating wicked little waves of heat. A ghost of a smile played about his sensuous mouth.

A sudden notion warmed her nearly as much as his fingertips. "*You* had no trouble dancing with me. None at all."

"We do seem ... well synchronized." His hands drifted away, falling to his sides. Yet the continued force of his scrutiny all but made her squirm.

"What?" she finally asked, bewildered.

His features smoothed. "You seem rather familiar to me, Mrs. Sanderson. Have we met previously?"

She drew a breath. Here it was then, the moment that would determine the success or failure of her mission.

His choice of words struck her. She seemed *rather* familiar, did she? Just as scores of people might seem rather familiar to a man whose sphere encompassed the most fashionable society in England. To him, hers was one more face in a sea of thousands.

She should have been thankful, reassured. But it was neither relief nor gratitude that poured its bitter taste down her throat, but rather disappointment and a quelling sense of foolishness.

All these months of enamored dreams ... and she had meant nothing to him—*nothing*. Merely an incident on a crowded street. Their kiss had made no more lasting impression on him than if he'd kissed a ...

Refusing to finish the demeaning thought, she arched a brow in her best imitation of Viscountess Devonlea. "No, Lord Barensforth, I cannot think where we might have become acquainted."

"And yet you know *my* name."

Her heart gave a thump. "Oh ... I ... Yes, of course. Lord Wentworth pointed you out to me earlier. As he pointed out several others of note," she hastily added.

"Is that so?" When she nodded, his lips turned up in a pensive smile. "Then this is a circumstance we surely must remedy, Mrs. Sanderson, for I believe I should very much enjoy becoming better acquainted with you."

As when they had danced, he seemed to be implying far more than his words suggested. Something sensual and shocking and perhaps a tiny bit dangerous.

The very sort of thing about which Victoria had warned her.

The sort of thing about which she had fantasized ever since that summer's day in Knightsbridge.

Aidan watched the widow's eyes fill with moonlight and a world of uncertainty. He had shocked himself with his less-than-decent innuendo. Christ, what had he been thinking to blurt his desires like a fledgling fresh out of the schoolroom? He liked to believe he possessed more flair than that when it came to the art of seduction.

Typically, he did. But just as this woman sent otherwise-competent dance partners stumbling, she somehow had him tripping over his own intentions. And for the life of him he couldn't fathom why.

For several moments punctuated by her rapid breathing, he could not decide if she might smile or slap him. He found himself bracing for the latter and wishing with all his heart for the former.

Oh, he was not so foolish as to believe in love at first sight, or even, in this circumstance, at second sight, but in the last few minutes he'd found himself tumbling head over heels at her smile, at how one corner of her pretty mouth slanted higher than the other, how her eyes became exotic crescents, and how a single dimple in her right cheek flashed and disappeared, making it a game for him to coax its appearance.

Yet in the end she neither smiled nor struck him, and the lack of either left him unaccountably disappointed. Her gaze veered over his shoulder and her expression changed, became set and determined. She lifted her hems clear of the paving stones.

"I am here tonight in the company of the Countess of Fairmont," she announced as if the words served as armor against him.

"Splendid. I know the lady well."

Her green eyes sparked with alarm, but she replied with composure, "Then please do excuse me, for I see her ladyship inside. One can only suppose she has these many minutes been searching for me."

He allowed her to circle him. Before she stepped through the doorway, she paused, turning to speak over her shoulder. "Thank you for the champagne." Her steely resolve had softened. "And for the dance. Both were most considerate of you."

He was glad she thought so, even if his motivation stemmed more from self-interest than kindness. The same incentive prompted him to ask, "May I be so impertinent as to ask something in return for my consideration?"

She bristled in a way he found delightful. "That depends upon what you would ask of me, sir."

"A trifle, merely. Your name. Mine is Aidan. Will you tell me yours?"

"Oh . . ." The request clearly took her aback. She hovered with one toe pointed toward the doorway as if she might at any moment cut a hasty retreat. One hand absently reached up, fingertips tracing a sheer gold chain that disappeared into her décolleté. His eyes were drawn to the mystery of that chain as he wondered what dangled at the end, lying warm and hidden between her lush breasts.

Realizing the recklessness of such thoughts, he instantly lifted his gaze back to her face. She seemed not to have noticed his lapse. Her lips parted, the tip of her tongue darting out to leave a trace of moisture at the corner of her mouth, another enticement he forced himself to ignore. "Laurel," she whispered, then turned and left him.

Chapter 6

"Laurel." Aidan smiled, liking the sound of the name. He watched her until the crowd inside enveloped the last sweep of her amber skirts.

He liked, too, that he had met Beatrice's challenge. Yet he should have upped the wager by raising the stakes.

He should have kissed the widow, as he had kissed her that day on William Street. After all, hadn't he rendered her a service tonight just as he had done then?

But no, he could see from their brief encounter that, despite having been married, she was too genteel for that sort of dalliance, that she was not a woman who allowed clandestine kisses on darkened terraces. Or on crowded London streets. He could only imagine the fury his impulsive gesture had generated, because he had not lingered long enough to witness her reaction.

No, unless he missed his guess, Laurel Sanderson was a woman who needed gradual and gentle coaxing to . . .

He stopped himself. As Beatrice had obligingly noted, being a widow made Laurel Sanderson all too available, and he did not pursue available women—ever. His work for the Home Office was too important. More to the point, it was often dangerous—too dangerous for him to consider taking a wife.

Besides, he liked his life the way it was. He had purpose, goals. That hadn't always been the case. There had been empty, aimless years following his parents' deaths when he'd stumbled through a haze of alcohol and the occasional opium binge, trying to forget the explosion of a pistol behind a closed door, to blot out the horror he'd discovered after shouldering his way in. . . .

In a way, Lewis Wescott and the Home Office had saved him—saved his very life—by recognizing his talents and insisting he put them to use. Ever since, he had savored the game of ferreting out evidence, piecing together clues, and seeing that bastards like the one who destroyed his father got exactly what they deserved.

Sighing, he raised a gaze to the sky. The constellations took immediate shape. Most people needed time to discern the figures, if they saw them at all. But for him, he supposed due to his uncanny ability with numbers and patterns, they appeared like eager hounds to their master's call: the Big Dipper with the diamondlike Arcturus glittering to the west. Leo to the south. A little to the east, Virgo . . . the maiden.

Mrs. Sanderson could be no maiden, yet in his arms she had seemed as inexperienced as a young virgin. Why was that?

She had been so adamant about their having never met that he had begun to entertain doubts, to believe he had merely mistaken her for the lass he had saved . . . had kissed. His error would have been understandable. He had been exhausted that morning, worn-out from a night spent drinking, gambling, and keeping Fitz in tow.

Tuning out the music and voices from inside, he concentrated on the morning the queen had driven from her childhood home at Kensington Palace to her new home at Buckingham. Frantic shouts for help all but filled his ears. The sight of glittering emerald eyes peering out from a cloud of golden hair filled his vision.

With a wink at Virgo, he shook his head. The similarities were too striking to be a coincidence. Which meant either she didn't remember him—possible, but unlikely—or she had lied.

Back inside the jarring confusion of the octagon room, he spotted Beatrice and Devonlea. Near them stood Lady Fairmont—Melinda to him, for he had known her all his life. She was talking to Fitz. . . .

Mrs. Sanderson stood at his side, seeming to hang on his every word. She gazed up at him as though he were conveying the most fascinating piece of wisdom ever divulged.

The stab to Aidan's gut caught him off guard and momentarily stole his breath.

Jealousy? For a woman he barely knew and had no intention of pursuing?

No. For a woman with the spirit to wade into a dangerously tight crowd and risk her life to save a child because, as she had so ingenuously stated, someone had had to do something. By God, she'd shown remarkable gumption that day.

He started toward them, then came to such an abrupt halt that a gentleman ran into him from behind. Aidan absently apologized while another memory crashed through his thoughts. If Mrs. Sanderson *was* that woman from London, then something was wrong. Very wrong.

She hadn't been wearing black crepe. He couldn't say with any accuracy what she *had* been wearing that day, but . . . yellow. Not amber like tonight but sunny yellow sprigged with a leafy pattern. He specifically remembered because the dress had torn at the waist, revealing an enticing scrap of petticoat.

How could she be recently out of mourning for her husband *now* if she had not been in mourning *then*?

"Aidan! Aidan, dearest!"

Melinda Radcliffe, Countess of Fairmont, stretched her silk-clad arm high and waved her fan above heads. With a speed that belied her years, she wound a circuitous path to him. Upon arriving, she seized his wrists and, with all the license of an honorary aunt, kissed his cheeks.

"Is *this* how I am to learn of your arrival in Bath, by literally running into you in the midst of an assembly crush? For shame, young man."

Until he had gone up to Eton at the age of eight, he had accompanied his mother on her frequent visits to the home of her closest friend, and afterward at least once a year during the summer months. During those final, dark days of Eugenia Phillips's life, Melinda had been at her side, even when—especially when—Aidan's father could no longer bear to be in the room.

"I arrived only this afternoon," he told her. "Upon my honor, I'd have come round tomorrow."

"Well, I've got you now, my boy, and there is no getting away."

Beyond her shoulder, he saw Fitz and Mrs. Sanderson set off together into the ballroom, the "widow's" hand firm in the crook of his arm.

Jealousy lanced him again, this time adding a barbed twist.

With a sharp intake of breath, he steeled himself against the unwelcome sentiment and smiled at Melinda. "I have no intention of going anywhere, or of dancing with anyone else for the duration of the evening."

"Think of the scandal we'll provoke!" Laughing, she poked her fan toward the receding backs of Fitz and Mrs. Sanderson. "Did you notice that charming young lady on the arm of your friend?" She must not have seen the ironic twist to his lips, for she went on, "I am her escort into society while she is in Bath. A favor to the queen, no less, for the service her mother once rendered to the Duchess of Kent as a lady-in-waiting." Melinda's brow puckered.

"Don't tell me you find the task distasteful?" he asked. He fervently hoped not, for here had arisen an

unexpected opportunity to discover more about the
mysterious widow. Playing the domestic spy with his
mother's dearest friend probably didn't constitute the
most honorable of tactics, but in the interest of national
security, or so he told himself, he must seize whatever
advantages came his way.

"Indeed not," she quickly replied. "Laurel Sanderson
is a lovely woman. It is just that Beatrice introduced her
to Lord Munster and . . . oh, I hope you will not be vexed
with me, but . . ."

"Yes?"

She pursed her lips. "I know he is your friend, Aidan,
but even you must admit that George Fitzclarence's attentions are not entirely suitable for respectable young
ladies."

"It is only a dance, Melinda. I am sure no harm will
come of it."

But as they trailed Fitz and Mrs. Sanderson onto the
dance floor, a trace of the young widow's perfume left
him with a sense, stronger than ever, that the situation
was not as it should be.

Laurel carefully schooled her gaze to avoid Lord Barensforth as she hurried past him on the Earl of Munster's
arm.

Oh, but she couldn't help comparing the two men.
Where Aidan Phillips was tall, elegant, and well-defined,
George Fitzclarence sagged and bulged and slouched.
Why, his stomach threatened at any moment to pop his
waistcoat buttons.

Even his large Hanover eyes and rounded chin, which
Laurel had always found charming in Victoria, failed to
provide any benefit at all to his masculine visage and in
fact lent him the aspect of a very large housefly.

And while Lord Barensforth's wit sprang razor sharp
from his tongue, Lord Munster's speech was labored and
halting. Not that that mightn't lend him a certain tender

charm, if only his discourse exhibited more brains than bosh.

It wasn't kind of her, singling out his faults, and she never would have done so if not for the presumptuous way he had planted himself at her side once his sister made the introductions, or how unceremoniously he had placed her hand in the crook of his arm even before she had finished voicing her consent to dance with him.

Odd, but while Lord Barensforth's actions on the terrace had left her unsettled and out of sorts, his forwardness hadn't irked her nearly so much as this man's. And, oh, the whiskey on his breath!

"Another w-waltz, madam. How fortuitous." A smugness in Lord Munster's tone suggested he might have influenced the orchestra's selection, and Laurel suddenly understood the significance of his having quietly addressed an attendant in the octagon room. "Just the opportunity to become b-better acquainted, my d-dear Mrs. Sanderson."

Ouch!

His heel caught the edge of her satin slipper, pinning her smallest toe, yet, apparently oblivious, his lordship continued reeling her about in an awkward, halting pattern that produced a concerning queasiness in the pit of her belly. This time, however, she credited not her tendency to lead but Lord Munster's tipsiness as the root of the problem. He, however, continued unperturbed, or perhaps he believed the occasional lump beneath his foot to be the product of an uneven floor.

Her discomfiture only increased when Lord Barensforth entered the dance floor holding not a young debutante in his arms, but the Countess of Fairmont. She remembered him mentioning that he knew the countess, but Laurel would not have guessed he knew her well enough to be grinning down at her with such fondness, as he was presently doing.

Judging by the reciprocal delight in Lady Fairmont's

eyes, the two of them shared something rather more *en privé* than a casual acquaintance.

Laurel ignored yet another assault on her foot as she pondered the nature of their connection. Together they negotiated the crowded dance floor without ever missing a step. They seemed . . . how had he termed it on the terrace?

Well synchronized.

A scandalous notion lashed Laurel's nerve endings. Could Lord Barensforth and Lady Fairmont be lovers?

Like the blast of a summer wind, envy roared through her, leaving her feeling scorched and not a little bewildered. She was here to do a job, and it should not have mattered one bit what Lord Barensforth or Lady Fairmont did, or with whom they did it.

Shame followed swiftly on the heels of her speculation. The countess had shown Laurel nothing but kindness in taking her under her wing. She did not deserve to be so cruelly judged. Mercifully, the music ended and Laurel wasted no time in curtsying to George Fitzclarence.

"Thank you, Lord Munster. I believe I shall return to your sister now."

"Surely not, Mrs. Sanderson. A charming m-minuet is next. You cannot mean to m-miss it."

"I am afraid I mean to very much. I confess I find myself growing exceedingly weary." An understatement, for her toes ached, her head throbbed . . . and . . . as she watched the Earl of Barensforth prepare to dance again with Lady Fairmont, another, more reprehensible thought occurred to her.

Could Lord Barensforth be after the countess for her fortune?

"Ah, but my dear Mrs. Sanderson, may I p-point out that my sister herself is presently engaged on this very dance floor. J-just there."

He pointed across the way to where a laughing Lady Devonlea waited for the recommencement of the music. At her side stood a robust-looking young gentleman who could not have been more than twenty-five years old.

Humph. Perhaps the pairing of older women with younger men on the dance floor was an accepted break from tradition here in Bath. She should not have found that so refreshingly, vigorously reassuring. But she did.

The musicians played the first notes of the minuet, setting those on the dance floor into graceful motion. A kind of sigh went through the room, a stirring of romantic nostalgia evoked by the archaic dance.

The Earl of Munster stood before her, his hands outstretched. "Dance again, Mrs. Sanderson, d-do. I should s-so enjoy it."

Laurel's reluctance died on her lips. Behind the man's bloodshot eyes, a ghost of desperation pleaded for her acquiescence. A tentative twitch of his lips promised the first genuine smile she had yet seen from him. Suddenly the egotistical rogue Victoria had described seemed . . .

Vulnerable. Uncertain. Heaven help her . . . sweet?

Despite the music and the surrounding voices, a deafening silence echoed through Laurel as she contemplated the man before her. Could such ingenuousness exist in an unruly, unprincipled king's son bent on damaging his cousin's position as monarch? Laurel had arrived in Bath with convictions set in black and white, only to find herself awash in myriad shades of gray when it came to the earls of both Munster and Barensforth.

Compelled by the former's quiet appeal, she returned her hand to his and was startled by the triumphant gratitude that lit up his face.

Which left her not only puzzled but also uneasy about this task Victoria had set her. While the prospect of deceiving a villain did not particularly compromise her scruples, how to proceed if her quarry was less to be reviled and more to be pitied?

*   *   *

Early the next morning, Aidan made his way slowly across the gentlemen's dressing rooms at the Cross Bath, examining each private cubby and scrutinizing every inch of the tiled floor, cupboards, and benches.

He had been standing outside the Bath Street entrance before sunup, waiting for the first attendant to arrive. Initially the man had balked at letting him in, protesting that the facility did not open to the public for another hour and that there were towels to be folded, floors to be swept, refreshments to prepare, etc. Aidan didn't know if it was the silver he'd pressed into the man's hand or his disgruntled explanations that had silenced his objections.

"My physician insisted I come here," Aidan had griped to the man. "Claimed it would cure this bloody stabbing pain in my lower leg."

"That it should, sir, if you'll only be good enough to return at six o'clock."

"No, I must see the place now, before anyone else arrives. I tell you, I am an unqualified stickler for cleanliness and order. I must know the place is properly run and maintained before I dare trust my health to the vagaries of indeterminate conditions. . . ."

Aidan had tossed his hands and ranted about scampering vermin and hidden filth. The attendant, grown red-faced with alarm, had thrown desperate glances up and down the deserted street and hastened to reassure him.

"Please, sir, do come in and look about all you like."

Inside, Aidan searched for signs of a struggle: scuff marks across the floor, scratches on the cupboard doors, threads or bits of torn clothing on the corners of the benches. He followed the narrow corridor from the dressing rooms out to the high-walled courtyard that housed the thermal pool where Roger Babcock's body had been found floating.

Steam curled from the surface of the water. The braziers not yet having been lit, the air held a brisk March snap mixed with a humidity that pressed like a weight on his lungs. In the weak light of a struggling sun, he made a slow circuit of the pool's edge, crouching at intervals to judge the condition of the railings and steps. He examined the coping for loose tiles. Once, he heard a noise and peered over his shoulder to discover the attendant hovering in the arched doorway.

"By God, is this mold I see growing here?" Aidan exclaimed, as if he hadn't noticed the man and were merely expressing his indignation out loud.

He continued his investigation to the accompaniment of rapidly retreating footsteps. Nowhere did he detect any signs of Roger Babcock having been murdered. Yes, the MP had been found floating, but there appeared to be no evidence to support the Home Office's theory of his having been attacked and forced into the water.

So how might he have died? Wescott claimed Babcock hadn't been ill, didn't owe substantial sums of money, and was not the object of anyone's animosity. Yet as Aidan had clearly witnessed last night, that third assertion didn't wash. Not that he could envision the aging, infirm Marquess of Harcourt doing anyone in, but his lordship's show of enmity at the Assembly Rooms did suggest that Babcock had enemies, and perhaps a few skeletons rattling around in his closet.

On his way out, Aidan cornered the attendant in the office. "I understand a man passed away here only a few days ago."

"I swear, sir, the bath was drained and scrubbed. We—"

Aidan cut him off. "Any idea on how he died?"

The man's sandy brows went up in a show of innocence. "The magistrate called it an accident, sir."

"But what would *you* call it?"

Backing up against the desk, the attendant stam-

mered, "I . . . we . . . ah . . . *call* it, sir? I'd call it most un-
fortunate. Will you be bathing, then, sir?"

"I shall have to think about it," Aidan replied. Ignoring the attendant's fallen expression, he headed outside and went briskly on his way. He was to meet Fitz
at the Pump Room later, where he would have his first
glimpse—and perhaps taste—of the so-called magical
elixir.

Chapter 7

Laurel danced, whirling through the room with new-found confidence. Handsome and steady and elegant, her partner never once trod on her toes. In his capable hands, her fears of appearing clumsy and foolish melted away, leaving her with an exhilarating sense of freedom, of being one with the music. One with him.

But as he twirled her gracefully, a wisp of smoke tickled her nose. Her partner's hands fell away, replaced by a pair of wizened ones that grabbed her as flames leaped up all around. She was no longer the grown-up Laurel but a small child grown numb with fear.

Blinding and suffocating, the smoke billowed. The gnarled hands shoved her through a doorway. From somewhere within the crackling flames she heard baby Willow crying, trapped in her crib, shrieking for someone to come.

"Don't be afraid, little one," a woman's voice rasped in her ear. "Close your eyes. You will be safe."

"My sisters—"

"Will be safe as well, I swear it. Come quickly!"

A blast rocked the floor beneath Laurel's feet. She fell hard to her knees, but was lifted up just as quickly. A scream echoed from the hall below, filling her heart with fresh terror. A second blast seared her ears. At the top of *the staircase, a tall figure draped in black appeared and moved toward her. . . .*

A yank on her arm started her running through the smoke. Flames singed her cheeks and hair while the scorching vapors clawed her throat raw. Her eyes stung with tears as she ran through a dark and frightening place, the roar of the flames distant now but no less terrifying.

The smell of dirt and dampness filling her nose, the darkness stretched before her like a never-ending grave. Narrow walls closed tight around her. Fear choked her as she imagined being buried alive under layers of earth. Mama and Papa would never find her here.

Then she and the woman burst into the open air. The morning brightness was stark and startling, the rush of oxygen into her lungs painful in its freshness. She sank to her knees onto the grass, but was scooped up against a hard, male chest.

Uncle Edward. His beard scratched a reassurance against her cheek. Another man Laurel didn't recognize held Willow. The twins were there, too, clinging to Uncle Edward's coattails, their faces stained by tears and blackened with soot. Without explanation the four of them were loaded into a waiting coach.

The vehicle lurched into motion, the horses whipped to a frothing gallop. Beside her, the twins sobbed, calling out for Papa and Mama. Beside them, Laurel cried silently, somehow knowing that she would never see her parents again. . . .

"Laurel! Laurel, wake up."

Her hands groping at the bed linens, Laurel's eyes flew open. A cold wash of panic dappled her brow as her gaze darted about a room thankfully untouched by flames.

It took her a moment to recognize her surroundings, to understand that she had awakened, not in the little bedchamber she shared with Willow atop their Readers'

Emporium in London, but in her comparatively spacious room at the charming Abbey Green lodging house in Bath's Lower Town.

"It's all right, Laurel. You were having a nightmare."

She half expected to see the wrinkled features of the woman in her dream, but the attractive face framed by auburn curls and a plumed hat belonged to Lady Devonlea. She clutched Laurel's shoulders just as the woman in her dream had, giving insistent little shakes to rouse her.

Gradually the knocking of her heart subsided. With a calmer gaze she took in the cozy furnishings of her rented bedchamber. "How did you get in?"

"The chambermaid remembered me from the other day and unlocked your door for me. And a good thing she did." Beatrice released her but searched her face in obvious alarm. "That must have been one devil of a dream."

Yes, a devil of a dream, a horror, yet one in whose grasp she would willingly remain if it meant answering the endless questions it raised. She knew a fire had destroyed Peyton Manor, her childhood home in the Cotswold Hills, and taken the lives of her parents. From what Uncle Edward had explained, she understood that she and her governess had escaped through the service tunnel that linked the cellars to the carriage house.

But what had caused the blasts she had heard?

That question and others had dogged her for most of her life. Why had her governess vanished from Laurel's and her sisters' lives? Why hadn't she entered into Uncle Edward's employ and continued raising the girls at Thorn Grove? Did the woman continue to live somewhere in the Cotswolds?

Uncle Edward had always been vague in his answers, and Laurel had never been satisfied with his assertion that the blasts had been the result of glass and masonry exploding from the fire's intense heat. She had seen and heard something else that day, something she believed in her very bones explained the tragedy of her parents' deaths, if she could only remember.

The figure in a black cloak—had he been real or imagined, an intruder or merely a shadow cast by the flames?

Beatrice perched on the edge of the bed and studied Laurel with a shrewd expression. "You have suffered this nightmare before."

"Since I was a child," she admitted. "Our home in the Cotswolds caught fire. My parents died." She had been six at the time, and in all the years since then, the dream had never varied. Until this morning. This time it had begun with Laurel safe and happy in Lord Barensforth's arms.

What did that mean? That even her erstwhile protector could not save her from danger? Or that he was no true protector at all, but someone she must take pains to shield herself from?

With shaky fingers she combed the tousled hair from her face. "What time is it?"

"Nearly half past ten."

"So late?" She pushed up onto her elbows. "I have slept away nearly the entire morning."

Laughing, Beatrice placed her hands on Laurel's shoulders and eased her back onto the pillows. "How delightfully country bred you are, my dear! And here I was about to apologize for rousing you with the chickens."

"If you don't mind my asking, why *are* you here?"

Beatrice laughed again. "To see if you might wish to accompany me to the Pump Room this morning."

Remembering the rancid taste of the famous Bath waters from when she had visited the Pump Room the other morning, Laurel wrinkled her nose. While others had hurried to fill their glasses in the interest of boosting their health, she had happily moved away from the foul-smelling fountain. "I hadn't planned to. . . ."

"Oh, do come. There is to be a special presentation. All of Bath's most notable residents and visitors will be there, including Lady Fairmont and . . ." She gave a mischievous wink. "My brother will be there as well, and he is so hoping to see you again. It seems you made quite an impression on George last night."

"Did I?" Laurel pushed to a sitting position.

"You know you did. He came by my place in Queen Square an hour ago and made me promise to procure you any way I might. Thus, being a good sister, here I am."

Laurel swung her legs over the side of the bed, letting her hair fall forward to veil her face. Victoria would be pleased with how quickly Laurel had insinuated herself into George Fitzclarence's life. But her experience at the ball had left a bitter taste in her mouth when it came to her mission, and grave doubts about how to proceed.

She had danced with Lord Munster several more times during the evening. Half into his cups and none too steady, he had held her uncomfortably close until she'd been forced to poke him repeatedly with her fan. He had trodden on her feet until her toes shrieked with pain.

Once, he had gone so far as to suggest, in a whisper that had made her skin crawl, that she ride home with him in his carriage, though whether to his home or hers had remained a mystery, for he never clarified his intentions. She had handled the matter by turning it into a jest, as though she quite believed he had not just insulted her but had intended only to make her laugh.

In truth, the affront she should have felt had been tempered by how quickly he had retreated from his impertinence and joined in her mirth, making her wonder if he *had* been joking after all. At that moment, indeed during all their moments together, terms like *villain*, *scoundrel*, and *rabble-rouser* had grown too grandiose for such a man. He had instead revealed himself as imprudent and biddable, as easily led astray as under other circumstances he might have been guided toward decency and respectability.

Was it the Earl of Barensforth's fault?

She shoved her feet into her slippers, but before she stood, Lady Devonlea placed a hand on her forearm. "You would be good for my brother, Mrs. Sanderson. A steadying influence. Dare I hope you might return his regard?"

Startled by the question, Laurel hesitated. The truth would never do—that she found him piteous at best and repulsive at worst. But neither, she discovered, would her conscience allow her to make convenient use of another human being's feelings. Not even for queen and country. Lines must be drawn and not crossed, or Laurel might find herself mired in dishonor.

For the first time she found herself wishing that Ivy or Holly *had* accompanied her to Bath. As the eldest, she had always set the example for the others, had always espoused honesty and respect and simple good breeding. Now she discovered that old habits died hard. Ivy and Holly, while good girls both, had never held themselves to quite so rigid a code of conduct. When a situation called for it, they saw no harm in cheating.

If ever a situation called for it, this one surely did. Still . . .

"I am afraid, Lady Devonlea, that while I found your brother perfectly charming"—a small lie couldn't hurt too much, could it?—"we are not well acquainted enough to know whether or not we would suit."

"Yes, but just the fact that you would attach the word *charming* to George says something, doesn't it?" Springing up from the bed, the woman crossed the room and swung the wardrobe doors wide. "What shall you wear today? There is a bit of a chill. . . . Let me see. . . . Ah, *this*!" She drew out a periwinkle serge walking ensemble trimmed in braided black velvet.

The maid brought in Laurel's breakfast tray. Returning shortly after, she carried in a ewer of hot water and laid out a fresh chemise and petticoats. When she left, Beatrice laced Laurel into her corset, jerking on the ribbons with an enthusiasm that cut her breath short.

"Perhaps you are uncertain of my brother because of all the other choices presented to you last night," the viscountess teased. "Rather like a buffet, was it not?"

Laurel peeked over her shoulder at the other woman. "While I would agree I experienced no shortage of partners, most happily quit my side after just one dance. I am afraid I did not live up to your generous assessment of my ballroom skills."

"You are too critical of yourself. Of course, I could not fail to notice that the one man with whom you did *not* dance never took his eyes off you all evening."

A tingle whispered across Laurel's nape. "Oh?"

The viscountess spun her about. "Why *didn't* you dance with him? Was he such a cad that he never asked you?"

"Whom do you mean?"

"How coy you are. The Earl of Barensforth, of course. He is devilish handsome, isn't he?"

"I suppose," she murmured, turning away to hide her flushed cheeks.

With a knowing grin, Lady Devonlea helped Laurel on with her skirt and bodice, fastening the tiny buttons up her back. "They may decide to fight over you. I've seen them go at it before. Aidan ... Lord Barensforth ... typically wins, though occasionally he steps aside and allows George the conquest."

"Why, you sound as though I am a trophy, or a piece of territory to be claimed."

Lady Devonlea came around her and placed cool fingertips beneath Laurel's chin. "My dear Mrs. Sanderson, as a widow of independent means, that is exactly what you are."

"But I am not looking to marry again. Not this soon, at any rate."

"You darling thing, you continue to enchant me. Surely you do not think I am speaking of marriage. My brother is already married. Aidan Phillips has sworn not to wed until the last possible moment. As for myself, you cannot imagine that I intend to spend the rest of my days in the company of one man only."

"Oh, I . . ."

"I see that I have quite shocked you." The viscountess placed a palm against Laurel's cheek. "I've turned you pale as a ghost, and for that I am sorry."

"No, no. How silly of me." Suddenly finding something distasteful in the woman's touch, Laurel drew away and lifted her jacket from the bed. "I fear I have too long been sequestered in the country, too long out of touch with the ways of society. I have grown naive and gauche."

Lady Devonlea's indulgent smile brought such beauty to her countenance that Laurel half believed she had somehow misunderstood the woman's meaning, that they were not speaking of adultery and disgrace.

The viscountess's next words proved that conjecture wrong. "We must reeducate you. As always, discretion remains an utmost necessity. Arthur and I have a perfectly civilized understanding that neither of us shall ever make the other look foolish. But think about it, my dear. As a moneyed widow you have the freedom to determine the course of your life. How young and raw you must have been when you married your squire. Have you not earned the right to enjoy the years ahead?"

Good heavens. Laurel wondered what Lady Fairmont would think of Lady Devonlea's tutelage. Would she approve, or be as horrified as Laurel privately felt?

"Never fear, Mrs. Sanderson, I have no intention of tossing a lamb such as you to any of our masculine wolves." Lady Devonlea helped her on with her fitted jacket. "It is your very innocence that I find so refreshing, and why I believe your influence would work as such a tonic on my brother. But come along, or we'll miss today's presentation."

Minutes later, Laurel gazed out the carriage window at the Lower Town's attractive lanes, where hints of medieval influence could still be seen. Even overcast skies and dampened storefronts could not diminish the city's charms. Bath was a place of spires and turrets and grand proportions, a progression of styles from Romanesque to Gothic to the stately Palladian, all clad in the honey-warm tones of the region's distinctive limestone.

In the short time she had been there, Laurel had fallen in love with the city. How she wished she were here with her sisters on no graver business than an early spring holiday.

The carriage rolled to a stop in front of the Pump Room's colonnaded portico on Stall Street. As a porter opened their door, Laurel felt the cool slap of rain-tinged air against her cheeks.

"Lady Devonlea, you never did tell me what was so special about today," she reminded the other woman.

"Ah, yes. Monsieur Rousseau is to explain the healthful benefits of a new elixir he has developed, and he has promised to offer samples to all present at the Pump Room this morning."

As the viscountess stepped down from the barouche, a frisson of alarm shot through Laurel. "Monsieur Rousseau?"

"Yes, the eminent scientist. Perhaps you've heard of him?"

Victoria had mentioned a man named Rousseau, an aristocratic turncoat responsible for countless deaths during the wars with Napoleon. He, the old king, and Victoria's father had traded correspondence even as Rousseau had condemned fellow Frenchmen to the guillotine.

This scientist, of course, could not be the same Rousseau, for that evil man had eventually dangled from the end of a rope. But Laurel knew better than to discount a connection. George Fitzclarence stealing his father's papers and coming to Bath at the same time that this man, Rousseau, was here seemed too convenient to be a coincidence.

Last night she had achieved the important goal of winning the Earl of Munster's regard. Today, however, she would begin her investigation in earnest, and learn all she could about this Rousseau and his elixir.

"Barensforth," came a wheezy greeting as Aidan entered the Pump Room's main hall. "Wouldn't have expected to see you taking the waters so early today. Cleaned up rather tidily in the cardroom last night, did you?"

Aidan regarded Major John Bradford's florid face and sagging mouth, the corners of which disappeared into a pair of outrageously bushy muttonchop sideburns.

"I made out passing well," he said. He shook the man's sausage-fingered hand, at the same time scanning the faces of those promenading up and down the lengthy room.

Was Laurel Sanderson here?

"No need to be modest," Bradford said. "Devonlea's been pouting all morning."

He lifted his ebony cane to point across the way, where the slick-haired Devonlea stood filling a glass at the fountain. The gushing waters glittered against the backdrop of the surrounding floor-to-ceiling windows, and for a moment Aidan became entranced by the jets streaming into the mouths of the leaping bronze fish.

It seemed a simple thing, that fountain, not unlike many others he'd seen. But Bath was an ancient city, with more than a millennium's worth of civilization buried deep under dirt and rock. The fountain and bathhouses were the most recent adaptations of facilities first built by the Romans, and many of their secrets had yet to be revealed.

Nothing should be taken at face value, including his less-than-productive trip to the Cross Bath. Somewhere beneath a facade of apparent innocence lay a crime. He felt it in his bones.

Just as he sensed, instinctively, that beneath Laurel Sanderson's guileless exterior a sultry mystery begged to be solved.

"I hear his luck has turned south lately," the major continued, still speaking of Devonlea. "His wife must be positively overset with him, though of course she's never one to show it. I expect he's here to try and recuperate, if not recoup his losses."

Aidan snapped his attention away from the gleaming waters. What was this? He'd known Devonlea for a spendthrift, but between his and Beatrice's yearly incomes they had always maintained an affluent lifestyle without plunging too far into debt.

Had that changed?

"Surely the old boy can't be doing as bad as all that," Aidan said in hope of prompting further disclosures about the viscount.

Bradford rewarded his effort by lowering his voice. "It was rather hard luck on Devonlea, Babcock's expiring as he did."

Aidan's nerve endings vibrated. Injecting a modicum of boredom into his voice, he raised his brows and remarked, "Oh? How so?"

"Seems the two had run the gambit of London's hells, with Devonlea seeing Babcock several hundred to cover his losses. Now it is Devonlea going bust and unable to collect what Babcock owed him."

"No promissory note?"

"None, and the widow professes no knowledge of the matter."

"Where'd you learn this?"

"Your friend over there." His breath rasping deep in his throat, Bradford used his cane to indicate Fitz, standing in a group of their mutual acquaintances beneath the musicians' gallery. Near them, a dais had been enclosed in black curtains in preparation of Claude Rousseau's presentation.

Aidan didn't see the Marquess of Harcourt among them. This was a disappointment; he had hoped to pose some carefully worded questions to the man about his grievance against Roger Babcock.

Then he remembered that Major Bradford here belonged to all the same clubs as Harcourt, and their wives cosponsored numerous charity balls throughout the year.

"I understand Babcock owed Lord Harcourt money as well," Aidan said, shooting in the dark.

"Did he? Odd. I've never known old Harcourt to lend anyone so much as a shilling. Good man, but decidedly parsimonious."

Damn. "I must have heard wrong."

"You must have." The major tapped his fob. "Rousseau's presentation should begin any moment. Are you on the list?"

"Ah, the famous list." He shook his head. "No. You?"

Bradford nodded vigorously. "Enjoyed my first sample last Tuesday, thank you. But never fear. I hear tell all present this morning shall enjoy a small portion."

"What did you make of this potion? Do you believe it works?"

"Works?" Bradford pulled up as if affronted, his muttonchops bristling. "My dear sir, I'll have you know I have never felt so hearty, not even in my youth."

Taking in the major's labored breathing and pallid complexion, Aidan found ample reason to doubt his claims of restored youth. "Are you investing in the new spa, then?" he asked.

"I'd be a fool not to," the man replied. "And so would you be, should you pass up such an opportunity."

They moved off in separate directions.

"This is the third delay in as many months. This city's aldermen seem to feel they need answer to no one."

Geoffrey Taft's complaints carried through the room, prompting the turning of many heads.

"Now, Captain, I'm sure it all work out splendidly." A crease of anxiety scored Margaret Whitfield's brow as she tried to soothe the man into lowering his voice.

In a conservative walking dress of russet wool and a white lace cap securing her dark hair beneath a silk bonnet, she presented the very picture of a respectable and devoted wife. She reached out several times to touch her lover's shoulder, only to retract her hand at the last minute as his grievances escalated in volume and vehemence.

Aidan stopped at her side and bade her good morning. She returned the greeting with a curtsy and a shrug of apology.

"Trouble?"

Taking Aidan's offered arm, she walked with him a little away from the others and confided in an undertone, "Oh, Lord Barensforth, I am worried about him. He has always been of such an agreeable nature and now . . ." She gestured toward the red-faced Taft, perspiring despite the coolness of the room.

"I tell you, gentlemen, my patience has been pushed to the limit," the retired captain insisted. "Time is money, after all."

"Surely you can't mean to pull out now." A scowl marred Julian Stoddard's youthful good looks. Aidan noticed that he was still using a walking stick to aid his injured ankle. He thumped it now against the floor in a show of annoyance. "These delays are but minor setbacks and to be expected in a project of this scale."

Fitz nodded his agreement. "Stoddard is correct. R-rushing in headlong could spell disaster for all of us. I, for one, applaud the c-corporation's prudence." Fitz was referring to Bath's board of elected officials, which granted licenses and oversaw all building within the city limits.

Giving Mrs. Whitfield's hand a reassuring pat, Aidan stepped forward to join the men. "Perhaps it is time to put the corporation's shoulders to the wall with a few direct questions," he said.

"I had my solicitor do just that yesterday," Devonlea said as he, too, joined the group. "He met with the architects and Mr. Henderson of the corporation and subjected the project to rigorous scrutiny. He assures me all is progressing nicely."

A brittleness in Devonlea's tone set Aidan speculating. Had the viscount wagered a dwindling fortune on this one last chance of success? What if the pavilion failed? How much of Beatrice's fortune might the viscount have put at risk?

Taft looked unconvinced and grumbled his continuing doubts.

Devonlea's lip curled with no small amount of condescension. With glittering black eyes, wide forehead, and pointing chin, his was a face designed for arrogance—enough to shield any desperation that might be hiding beneath. "With the right vision and the finances to back it, there is no reason why Bath should not once more shine as brightly as the resorts of Weymouth or Brighton or Cheltenham."

"I agree." Fitz raised a glass of mineral water as though it were champagne. "Aidan, b-be a good fellow, do, and g-give us your opinion on the matter."

"Sounds like a glorious opportunity for anyone with funds to spare and an appetite for adventure." He looked pointedly at the viscount. "You've always been a gambling man, Dev, and I'm going to trust your instincts on this. If you judge it to be a solvent enterprise, that is good enough for me."

As he might have predicted, a flicker of doubt darkened Devonlea's gaze; a muscle in his cheek twitched.

"But of course," Aidan went on, "that doesn't mean I don't intend giving the property and the books a thorough going-over myself."

Fitz clapped his shoulder. "You'll find the views to be s-superior to any in the area. Indeed, we shall m-make an outing of it. A p-picnic, and invite that jolly good Mr. Henderson to c-come along and explain the plans."

Fitz's spirits rose even higher as he peered down the length of the room. "Ah, my sister has f-finally arrived."

Beatrice stood in front of the fountain, the rainy daylight from outside silvering her profile as she tipped a glass to her lips. Fitz craned his neck like an excited child watching for the arrival of a gift-bearing relative. "Do you see who she is w-with . . . ?"

Aidan did not. He was too busy observing Devonlea's reaction to his wife's arrival. His mouth having thinned to a sullen thread, the viscount visibly seethed. Aidan felt, even more than he saw, the clash of his and Beatrice's gazes, a silent collision of her disdain and his pride. Without a word, Devonlea pivoted and headed for the exit.

Experiencing a swell of outrage on Beatrice's behalf, Aidan resolved to discover the extent of Devonlea's losses and whether he had jeopardized her inheritance.

"Bea k-kept her promise after all. There she is."

"Who?" But Aidan needn't have asked who put the effusive grin on Fitz's face. Peering over heads, he spotted Laurel Sanderson wearing rich blue edged in black, a high-collared, multilayered affair that showed off her figure to even better effect than last night's ball gown. The allure arose now from what Aidan could no longer see, from what her tiered skirt and tailored jacket hugged to such tantalizing effect: her tight waist, slim hips, and the firm, high contour of a pair of breasts that seemed made for the size and depth of his palms.

And his palms alone.

He widened his stance and continued observing her.

Chapter 8

Laurel found something oddly soothing about this morning's ritual at the Pump Room. As she and Lady Devonlea fell into line with the myriad groups promenading up and down the room, she felt swept up in a dancelike pattern similar to last night's quadrille or minuet, an instinctive choreography that turned chaos into social accord, set to the music of a cheerful hum of voices.

She would miss certain aspects of this false life once she completed her mission. Was it very wrong of her to almost dread returning to the musty little Emporium, where nothing exciting ever happened?

She loved her sisters. She missed them. If only she could *be* the wealthy and independent Laurel Sanderson and bring the other girls here . . .

"Why, Lady Devonlea and my dear Mrs. Sanderson, how delightful that you both could make it this morning." The Countess of Fairmont embraced them and drew Laurel aside as a group of ladies bade Lady Devonlea good morning.

"I thought perhaps after last night's festivities, you would wish to spend your morning quietly," the countess said with a raised eyebrow.

"Lady Devonlea was kind enough to come by my lodging house and collect me."

"Did she?" Lady Fairmont linked her arm through Laurel's. "Take a turn about the room with me and tell me your impressions of our Bath society. I noticed you dancing with a certain earl. . . ."

Laurel's moonlit waltz with Aidan Phillips nudged like a guilty little secret, an imprudent pleasure she should never have allowed. What if someone had seen them, alone outside in the dark together? What if Victoria learned of it?

And what of the woman beside her? Laurel had yet to ascertain the nature of Lady Fairmont's connection to Lord Barensforth . . . Aidan, as she could not help thinking of him.

They had traded given names, another familiarity that, like their private dance, exceeded their scant acquaintance. Just as she should never have set her hand against his, allowing their bared palms to touch, she should not have heeded his impertinent request to divulge her Christian name. Heaven help her, he possessed an allure that, like his arms, had swept her up and left her giddy.

She shook the thought away as she and the countess fell into stride with the others circling the room.

"There is to be a concert soon at the Guildhall," Lady Fairmont said. "If you found our Assembly Rooms elegant, you will be no less astonished by the splendor of the Guildhall's banquet room. Nothing anywhere compares."

"I shall look forward to it." Laurel didn't bother mentioning that she had little experience on which to base her opinions. She briefly wondered why that should be. Surely the villages near Thorn Grove must have included assembly rooms, but Uncle Edward had never taken her and her sisters to a function. Had he disdained society as much as that? Even if that was so, why had he begrudged them the pleasure of mingling with others of their own age?

"Good morning, Mrs. Whitfield," Lady Fairmont called across the way. "I do so like her," she said to Laurel in an undertone. "Many people find her shocking, being so much younger than Captain Taft and of slightly mysterious origins, yet I find her plain honesty refreshing. Rather like yourself, my dear."

The woman's candor brought to Laurel another twinge of guilt, and a wish that she could simply be herself, rather than a ghost of a person who would eventually vanish without a trace.

Laurel swallowed a gasp as Aidan Phillips came into view. Beneath the curving gallery at the end of the room, he stood shoulder-deep in a group of gentlemen, his dark hair falling over his brow with a carelessness that remained just this side of dishevelment.

Like many of the other men, he wore the daytime country attire of breeches, boots, and riding coat. But while the pale complexions and urbane manners of the others reduced such fashion to mere affectation, the earl's broad-shouldered confidence breathed truth into the image of a dashing cavalier. Physically speaking, he simply *was* what the men around him aspired to be.

Ah, that was the dazzle, the blazing brilliance, of the man. But what of his actions?

Lady Devonlea said he and the Earl of Munster often went head-to-head to determine which of them would win the right to lead a woman astray. A conquest, the viscountess termed it. Once more unable to resist comparing the two men, Laurel had no trouble believing Lady Devonlea's claim that Aidan typically emerged the victor.

Had he considered her that way last night, as a con-

quest? Did he believe he'd emerged victorious from
their clandestine encounter? The notion should have
outraged her. Instead, deep inside her most feminine
core, something warm and eager fluttered to life.

"Mrs. Sanderson, is something wrong? You look suddenly perplexed."

"Not at all, Lady Fairmont. For a moment I believed I
recognized an acquaintance." Blast her eyes for skitter-
ing in his direction one last time, and blast the countess
for noticing.

"You mean the devilishly handsome brute standing
head and shoulders above the rest? That, my dear, is
Aidan Phillips, ninth Earl of Barensforth. I don't doubt
that you have heard of him, but you mustn't allow rumors to influence your opinion. I wished to introduce
you at the ball yesterday, but you seemed always engaged elsewhere. Come, it is high time you made my
godson's acquaintance."

"Really, my lady, you mustn't trouble yourself. . . .
Godson?" *That* was the tie between Lady Fairmont and
Aidan Phillips?

"Of course. Surely you saw me dancing with him last
night. Did you suppose I'd set my cap for the fellow, an
elderly matron smitten with a dashing young buck?"

"My lady, you are hardly elderly."

"Lady Fairmont, Mrs. Sanderson, good m-morning
to you both." Stepping into their path, George Fitzclarence thrust out a hand. Even through Laurel's glove, his
meaty fingers encased hers in disagreeable dampness.
Hiding her aversion, she smiled up into bulging, mottled
eyes that spoke of too little sleep and too much brandy
the night before.

"Lord Munster. How pleasant to run into you this
morning, sir."

"Indeed, madam, for though but a handful of hours
have p-passed since we parted, the time has stretched
with the unendurable t-tedium of an eon."

Oh dear, Laurel thought as he raised her hand to his lips. She could have done with a smidgen less enthusiasm on his part.

Near the fountain, Aidan came up behind Beatrice and placed his hand lightly at the small of her back. "Do but say the word, and I shall send someone to break his kneecaps."

She laughed without turning around to look at him. "You saw that, did you?"

She referred to the enmity that had darted between her and her husband a few minutes earlier. That neither of them needed to elaborate further spoke volumes about the nature of their friendship, as did the fact that they had never, in all the time they had known each other, slept together. One night a couple of years ago they had found themselves alone in Fitz's London drawing room. With a look and a touch, a sensual possibility had sparked between them, only to become suspended by indecision that had ended, abruptly, with an outpouring of mutual laughter.

At that moment Aidan had realized they would always be friends, no more, no less.

"Sorry," he said, "but yes. What's he done? It isn't another woman, is it?"

"I wouldn't mind that nearly as much as his sudden recklessness at the gaming tables." She stared up at the streams of water arcing from the fountain and sighed. "He's grown as bad as my brother. Just to make a point, I've even banished him from the house. He's staying at his club, but if he runs out of money and comes knocking at your door, you'll know why."

"Want me to talk to him? Rough him up a bit?"

"No. At least not yet." Smiling, she turned to face Aidan. "But thank you. Arthur and I have weathered worse storms than this."

When she failed to offer anything more, Aidan realized the subject had been closed. One thing about Beatrice, she could not be pushed for information. Better to bide one's time and remain available in the event she chose to confide. For now it was enough to have confirmed the gossip relayed by Major Bradford. In future, Aidan would keep alert to Devonlea's actions.

"I see you have brought the enchanting Mrs. Sanderson with you today," he said. "By the way, her name is Laurel. Coaxed it out of her last night. Damn, but I wish we'd laid a wager on it."

The corner of her mouth curled in a cunning smile. "But, darling, how could I know if you cheated? You might have learned her name from any one of a score of people."

"Upon my honor, I had it from the lips of the widow herself."

He caught the mischievous spark in Beatrice's eyes. "I do hope that is the extent of what you had from her lips."

"Alas, yes. But then, I never have been one for rushing a woman."

"True. Then again, what would you do with the likes of Mrs. Sanderson?" She prodded his chest with the tip of her gloved finger. "Do not dare be so impudent as to answer that question. Really, Aidan, she is a sweet, lovely woman. Just the sort who would prove a dreadful bore to you. Mrs. Sanderson is nowhere near as worldly as you or I."

"And yet she has managed to captivate your brother." He gestured with his chin to where Fitz was strolling with Melinda and the widow. Fitz looked downright exultant. His stature seemed to have lengthened. He held his back straighter and his shoulders wider than Aidan had ever seen them.

Watching them, he suddenly felt his own good humor begin to curdle, and when his friend leaned closer to Laurel to murmur in her ear, a red-hot haze clouded

Aidan's vision while his fists hardened around an overwhelming desire to yank the man from her side and throttle him.

He looked quickly back at Beatrice and found her studying him with that same cunning conjecture of moments ago. "Is it so astonishing that Mrs. Sanderson and George might enjoy a mutual fancy for each other's company?" she asked.

"Not astonishing," he lied with an offhand shrug. "Simply . . . unexpected."

"Really." Her nostrils flared as her grin became less good-natured.

"Really," he parroted, while thinking it both odd and regrettable that there should be anything approaching antagonism between them. He nonetheless added, "Need I remind you that your brother has a wife?"

"How tediously bourgeois of you. Shall we count how many of your mistresses have had husbands?"

"That is different. They came to me. I was never their first, and each knew exactly what she was bargaining for."

This met with a burst of laughter that tinkled like the bells of a trained hawk taking flight. "Darling, Mrs. Sanderson is in Bath to take her pleasure in any form it comes, but she is certainly not here to find a husband."

His anger kicked up. The very notion of the widow with Fitz galled him. While Aidan for the most part feigned his excesses, Fitz did not. He drank immoderately, gambled recklessly—not to mention disastrously without Aidan's help—and shirked every responsibility expected of a man in his position.

Poor Mary Wyndham Fox had proved inadequate in bringing her husband to heel, but Aidan had always hoped that the right woman, a woman of single-minded resolve and sufficient devotion, could perhaps set Fitz on a more productive road.

But not *this* woman. Not Laurel Sanderson, who—

He broke off in midthought, baffled and appalled that he should feel so protective of a woman he hardly knew, he didn't quite trust, and who, as Beatrice had obligingly pointed out, was simply not his type.

Perhaps his defensive instincts toward her were merely an extension of the same impulse that had propelled him through a London crowd to prevent her from being crushed. He certainly didn't regret his actions, but he must remember that, guileless though she might seem, the widow presented a shapely bundle of contradictions. It was time he set about unwinding the skein and discovering what lay nestled inside.

First he needed to get past Beatrice, who was still staring at him, still assessing him. "By that brooding look on your face," she teased, "I'd say the gloves are about to come off with regard to you and George wrangling over the desirable Mrs. Sanderson. Perhaps this time you'll lose."

Aidan placed his fingertips beneath her chin, raised it, and smiled down into her face. "Watch me," he said, and strode away.

Walking between Lady Fairmont and Lord Munster, Laurel gestured toward the curtained dais at the end of the room. "Pray, sir, do tell us more about this presentation we are awaiting. Are you at all acquainted with Monsieur ... er ..."

Well enough did Laurel know the scientist's name, but her strategy today was to coax as much information as possible from George Fitzclarence. Last night's ball had taught her that holding her own tongue encouraged others to fill the silence, and most did so eagerly.

Lord Munster did not disappoint. "His name is C-Claude Rousseau. He is a Frenchman, but I hope you will not h-hold that against him."

"I would not dream of doing so," Laurel said with a

laugh that felt as forced as water through a rusty pump. "Though I have heard the name Rousseau in relation to the wars. Is he—"

"He is, madam. His father was a t-traitor. But *this* Rousseau has m-made a distinguished career for himself here. He lectures at Oxford, d-did you know?"

"I did not. How admirable. It sounds as though you are well acquainted with the gentleman."

After exchanging a glance with the countess, he said, "N-no, not well at all. Our acquaintance is recent, and I am eager to hear what he has to s-say today."

"What exactly is the significance of this invention of his . . . this formula . . . ?"

"Rousseau's *elixir*," Lady Fairmont clarified. "It is a stupendous development using Bath's thermal waters combined with alchemical properties and curative herbs."

"And what maladies it is purported to cure?"

"Oh, a full range of infirmities from gout to d-dyspepsia to sluggishness of the blood to consumption." The pride in Lord Munster's face suggested that he, and not Monsieur Rousseau, had developed the magical cure. "And more," he added with a sweep of his pudgy hand. "M-much more."

Laurel looked from one to the other. "Have either of you sampled this elixir?"

The very air resonated with their hesitation. Lady Fairmont cleared her throat. "As a matter of fact, I have. Monsieur Rousseau was kind enough to allow me to be one of the first to try it."

"And how did you find it?"

"Wonderfully restorative."

Laurel experienced a sudden concern for her new friend and benefactress. "Surely you have not been experiencing ill health, my lady?"

"Not at all, rest assured." Lady Fairmont gave Laurel's wrist a pat. "But this elixir is as beneficial to the vigorous as to the infirm. It brings on renewed energy and vitality."

"How extraordinary." Laurel turned to Lord Munster. "And you, sir? Have you tried the formula?"

"I, madam, was lucky enough to be at the t-top of Rousseau's list."

"List?"

"Tell me, how the blazes does one go about securing one's place on this illustrious list?"

The sound of Aidan Phillips's rich baritone raised a shower of tingles on Laurel's skin. Coming up from behind them, he nimbly squeezed between her and Lord Munster.

The four of them halted. Aidan exchanged greetings with Lady Fairmont and a few words with Lord Munster before turning his piercing regard on Laurel. His crisp blue eyes surveyed her with a speculation that left her unsettled, puzzled.

"What an enchanting vision you present today, Mrs. Sanderson."

She felt her cheeks heat. "Thank you, sir."

"I must say, that shade of blue suits you splendidly." He continued to hold her in his gaze until her blood rushed through her veins. "You must find it a tremendous relief to finally shun crepe and bombazine. How long were you hidden beneath such drapery, a year?"

Laurel bit back a gasp. Beside her, Lord Munster murmured something low in his throat, between a hiss of censure and a nervous chuckle.

"Aidan, really . . ." With a frown, Lady Fairmont gave a critical shake of her head.

"It was two years," Laurel said without blinking, though the leading question had left her not a little discomfited. Her fingers trembled; her knees felt wobbly.

"Yes, of course, two years of mourning for a departed husband." A casual twitch of Aidan's eyebrow issued a challenge. "Tell me, for I am curious, in that time were you ever tempted to don something cheerful? A summer-fresh yellow, perhaps?"

"I . . ." Laurel's answer died in her throat while her eyes widened in direct proportion to Aidan's growing smile.

Good heavens, he knew. He must, or he would never have uttered such a question. Lord Munster and Lady Fairmont remained mute, dumbstruck by his blatant display of ill manners. Would he reveal her to them, here and now, or continue baiting her until she gave herself away?

Unless, of course, she managed to confound him with his own game . . .

"Whatever can you be about, posing such a question?" Lady Fairmont scolded. "I've never in my life heard such impertinence. Apologize at once."

"No, Lady Fairmont." Laurel clenched her fists to still her shaking fingers and raised her chin. "That will not be necessary, for I fear that Lord Barensforth is correct in his assumption. However could you have guessed, my lord?"

Lady Fairmont assumed a shocked expression, Lord Munster rather less so. In fact, his eyes twinkled with amusement. "D-do tell," he urged.

"Yes," Laurel continued, shaking her head sadly, "I confess that once or twice, within my second year of mourning, I did cheat by slipping into a cheerful frock in the effort to recapture, in some small way, the contentment of the life I'd shared with my dear Mr. Sanderson. How lonely I was . . . and still am."

She produced a visible tremor across her shoulders, and was rewarded by a pat on her arm from Lady Fairmont and a sympathetic murmur from Lord Munster. Aidan's eyes darkened with an emotion that bordered on dangerous. She swallowed and raised the stakes of her gamble.

"One of those occasions happened to be on the day

of the queen's procession from Kensington to Buckingham. Oh, how I wished my Edgar could be there to share in the excitement of that day, in the glory of the new queen's ascension. . . ." She looked up, her lower lip trembling. "It was a day of such unbridled optimism, you see."

"And you were nearly trampled by an overly enthusiastic crowd," Aidan said.

Laurel braced herself, looked directly into his flinty eyes, and shook her head. "No, sir. I experienced no such mishap, near or otherwise."

"Oh, but you poor dear." Lady Fairmont slipped an arm around her waist and gave a squeeze. "No one could possibly fault a delicate young thing like you for harboring such tender sentiments."

A muscle in Aidan's cheek worked ominously; his eyes shot veritable sparks in her direction. "Forgive me, Mrs. Sanderson, it would seem I have confused you with another young lady who had become separated from her sisters that day."

"That would indeed be a mistake on your part, sir, seeing that I have no sisters. Would that I did." She found herself startled at how easily and swiftly the lies came as she warmed to her role. Why, her hands were quite steady now, her legs as sturdy as oaken branches.

Ah, but she had right on her side. She had not embarked upon a mean-spirited deception, but a justifiable pretense necessary to the service of her queen and friend. Surely that was forgivable.

Would Lady Fairmont forgive her? Would Aidan?

For now it must be enough that they accepted her story. Lady Fairmont did so unequivocally. Lord Munster, too. Laurel perceived their trust in their open expressions and, especially in Lady Fairmont's case, her eagerness to persuade Aidan to stop haranguing her. But then they, like most people, saw what they wished to see and delved no further.

What of Aidan? Did he believe her? Oh, indeed not, though she would wager that he would neither expose her nor confide his suspicions to the countess, whose sympathies Laurel had fully engaged. They both knew that Lady Fairmont would only berate him for a scoundrel. He had no proof of wrongdoing, nothing but a vague memory—she hoped—of her wearing a marigold walking dress when she should have been in mourning. At this point it was his word against hers, and who knew but if she stuck doggedly to her story, he might begin to doubt his own conviction?

So yes, she had won this round . . . but how long would her triumph last?

Chapter 9

I n knee breeches and a forest green waistcoat, a Pump Room attendant moved to the center of the room and gave three strikes of the brass bell he held. "Ladies and gentlemen, if you please, the presentation is about to begin."

Excitement rippled through the crowd. The assembly made its way down the room to converge in front of the curtained dais.

Aidan stepped between Laurel and the countess and offered an arm to each of them. "Ladies, shall we?"

That forced Lord Munster to follow, his cheeks sucked into the sides of his mouth in a clear display of petulance.

"Fitz, old boy," Aidan said, his mood suddenly improved, "you never did explain how you achieved a place on Rousseau's list."

"One must show enthusiasm for the project," Lady Fairmont answered before Lord Munster had the chance. "And lend one's support."

Laurel felt Aidan's response immediately in the bunching of the muscles inside his sleeve. Interesting, she thought. The reaction, though perhaps merely an involuntary movement, hinted at a more than cursory interest in Rousseau and his elixir.

"And how might one do that?" he asked.

Did the others hear the subtle derision roughening the otherwise velvet glide of his voice?

Lord Munster fidgeted with his neckcloth. "By making a n-nominal investment. Can't expect the man to f-fund his experiments out of thin air, after all."

"You never mentioned this."

"Didn't think you'd b-be interested."

Aidan didn't challenge the claim, but in the jut of his chin and the crease in his brow, Laurel perceived his ruminations. As they reached the gathering at the dais, he rounded on Lady Fairmont. "And you've given the man money as well?"

"Dearest, do not look like that. I offered a trifle, merely. Monsieur Rousseau's daily needs are few, and as Lord Munster said, he cannot be expected to work and live on nothing. But hush now! The curtain is opening."

Attendants stationed on either side of the dais tugged the drapery cords, drawing the black curtains in a dramatic sweep to reveal a table stacked with a dazzling array of glassware. A maze of copper tubing connected narrow glass cylinders with beakers, funnels, and flasks, the apparatus extending some two feet into the air. At one end of the table, an assortment of jars and bottles was clustered beside a mortar and pestle. At the other end was what appeared to be a punch bowl, only fashioned from the same pale stone as many of Bath's buildings.

At the center of the table, a bracketed pole held one end of copper tubing suspended above a cauldron that rested on an odd sort of brazier. Made of brass, the heater's half of a round belly was perched on four curved legs, its bowl glowing brightly. What drew Laurel's curiosity, however, were the crank and gears attached to the brazier, and the metal coils that spiraled out from the burning core to connect with the cauldron itself.

Standing behind this peculiar display was an individual

of such modest stature that Laurel had at first overlooked him. A receding hairline emphasized a dome of a forehead that dwarfed the rest of his features, except for his eyes. From behind a pair of thick spectacles, his black eyes seemed to float disembodied from his face, staring out at the audience with a disconcertingly unfocused look.

His ill-fitting coat of shabby tweed momentarily won Laurel's sympathies, until she remembered his background—his father's unspeakable crimes during the wars—and his own potential threat to Victoria. Until she discovered the truth of Claude Rousseau's intentions, she must not let herself be swayed by appearances. Like her, he could be playing a part designed to deceive.

All around her, the audience applauded, all except Aidan, whose expression had turned stony.

"Welcome, and thank you for coming," Claude Rousseau said. Despite his myopic appearance, his strong voice carried through the room. As he launched into an explanation of his elixir, his light French accent became apparent.

"The ultimate goal of alchemy is to unlock the mysteries of transformation within every individual, bringing their unique life rhythms into resonance with the universal forces of the natural world and thus promote a longer, more rewarding, and disease-free life."

He gave the crank on the brazier half a turn, sending the gears for a quick spin. The coils glowed brilliant orange, and steam spurted from the cauldron. "My elixir, as you will see, is designed to purify the imbalances which occur within the body and the mind, thereby bringing the physical, cognitive, and philosophical elements of being into a state of harmony and clarity."

"Good Christ," Aidan swore under his breath.

In contrast, Lord Munster looked on eagerly, echoing the audience's murmurs of appreciation and gasps of surprise, depending on the turn Rousseau's narrative took.

"My research, spanning the ancient writings of such men as Jabir ibn Hayyan, Wei Boyang, Albertus Magnus, and England's own Roger Bacon, has led me here, to this grand city, where the Romans once came to cure their ills."

He gestured to the stone font. "Through my excavations, I have discovered a source of thermal waters far purer than those that flow from the fountain in this room, or that fill the city's bathhouses." He drew his fingertips across the surface of the liquid in the font. "This water has not been contaminated by traveling through ancient rubble and piping. It has been siphoned directly from the natural springs that flow beneath Bath via the majestic hills to the north of us."

"Where is this source of your water?" a man in the crowd called out.

Rousseau smiled like a cat with its whiskers in the cream. "That, sir, is the strictest secret. For, you see, my laboratory is located deep beneath the city, below the sacred chambers of the Roman goddess Minerva. To reveal the location would not only jeopardize my research but also expose others to the dangers of possible subterranean collapse. I alone will risk the hazards, but you shall all reap the benefits."

Appreciative murmurs fanned through the assembly until Rousseau once more called for their attention.

He selected a beaker and dipped it into the font, filling it and then pouring the cloudy water into the flask perched highest on his scaffolding of copper tubing. Next, he opened several earthenware containers, took a pinch or two from each, and ground the mixture with the pestle. The scraping sound set Laurel's teeth on edge.

Next, selecting a slender bottle, he poured a thin stream of amber liquid into the ingredients he had just crushed. "This, ladies and gentleman, is a fusion containing tincture of purple coneflower, a powerful curative used for centuries by the native peoples of the

Americas." He added this to the water in the elevated flask.

Rousseau turned a knob and the mixture vanished, only to reappear and disappear several more times as the tubing brought it in and out of the various containers. The man added more water and tincture at intervals. Finally, the liquid splashed into the cauldron. With another turn of the crank, the brazier sizzled and the coils lit up. The contents of the cauldron began to bubble.

Laurel wrinkled her nose. "Such a dreadful odor."

"Like rotting eggs with a touch of seasoning," said Melinda.

"And perhaps no more worthwhile," Aidan mumbled. He shifted impatiently, and for a moment Laurel thought he would stride away.

"You seem rather vexed, Lord Barensforth." With a slant of her chin, she issued a challenge. "Are you afraid to stay and listen? Afraid Monsieur Rousseau might curb your skepticism?"

"He is by n-nature a skeptic," the Earl of Munster whispered. "A leopard who c-cannot change his spots."

Laurel doubted that. If anything, she suspected Aidan Phillips of being a master of deception, a man capable of assuming a vast array of personae as the situation warranted. Yet like the leopard, he seemed to her a sleek and cunning hunter, one that moved through the shadows with precision and stealth to seduce his unwitting prey.

Had she let herself become his inadvertent quarry last night?

He appeared not to have heard his friend's comment, or perhaps he chose to ignore it. "I've no intention of going anywhere, Mrs. Sanderson." His cool smile caused her nape to prickle. "I wouldn't miss this demonstration for the world."

Lady Fairmont gently shushed him.

"The formula is almost ready," Rousseau declared,

peering down into his steaming, gurgling mixture. "But not quite."

Selecting three vials, he removed the stoppers. He held one up. "Now for the strengthening properties. First, the quickness of mercury." He added a drop of a shining substance to the formula. "Then . . . the luster of silver." Tilting a second vial, he gave it a tap, sprinkling in tiny gleaming flecks. He held up the third vial. "Lastly, the shimmering warmth of pure gold—the most precious of alchemical elements."

The audience heaved murmurs of appreciation.

Aidan's scowls deepened.

Laurel experienced doubts of her own. "Can ingesting metals truly improve one's health?"

"Indeed, Mrs. Sanderson. The c-confluence of alchemical principles with herbal medicines boosts the benefits of the m-mineral waters," Lord Munster explained with an air of self-importance. Several people standing nearby overheard and nodded, as though they had all been well versed in Rousseau's process.

She strained on her tiptoes to see into the cauldron. The water had turned a curious pale mossy shade. Tiny specks flashed as they caught the light.

Aidan whispered in her ear, "You aren't putting stock in any of this, are you?"

Everything about his manner said she would be a fool to believe Rousseau's claims. She shrugged. "I neither believe nor disbelieve. But I am willing to be persuaded by the evidence of a positive outcome."

A team of waiters carried in trays of glasses already filled with the elixir. Apparently Rousseau's demonstration was exactly that, designed merely to illustrate how he prepared his formula.

"Will it cure indigestion?" came a query from somewhere to Laurel's right.

"What of my chest pains?"

"Headaches? I suffer dreadfully from migraines."

"I'd give half my fortune to ease my rheumatism."

Rousseau patiently addressed each query. "And now, ladies and gentlemen, please form a queue if you wish to sample my elixir. So small an amount cannot cure your ills, but you should feel remarkably invigorated."

Within minutes, those at the head of the line began to exclaim their delight with the elixir's effects. Smiles broke out, followed by laughter and cries of astonishment.

"Good heavens, I do believe the fellow is on to something!"

"Did I not tell you as much?"

Lady Fairmont and Lady Devonlea stood before the dais, each being handed a sample. Curiosity overcoming even her aversion to the acrid odor, Laurel moved to take a place in line.

Aidan seized her wrist and turned her about. Behind the clear blue of his eyes, white-hot anger flared. She flinched at his intensity, instantly convinced that, whatever his objections, they had not arisen merely from today's demonstration. His ire seemed the result of a much older, more deeply rooted apprehension.

He leaned close, his warm breath like a streak of fire across her cheek. "Don't."

That was all he said—*don't*—too low to be heard by anyone except her, but emphatic, razor sharp.

"Please unhand me, Lord Barensforth." Despite the alarm etched on her face, the widow spoke with composure. Her lashes swept shadows over her flushed cheeks as her gaze lit on the hand he held clamped around her wrist. "You are hurting me."

He barely heard her through the pounding in his ears. It was all too familiar, Rousseau with his tinctures and procedures and promises. Empty, perhaps even dangerous promises, all too reminiscent of his mother's death, his father's despair.

Laurel gave a tug that thrust him back to the present.

The fingers wrapped about her wrist trembled with tension and anger. He released her, fisting the hand even as he muttered an apology.

Her lips tightened, likely from holding back the reprimand he deserved. She only said, "That is quite all right. Excuse me."

She started to walk toward the dais, where the waiters continued to pass around Rousseau's mystery elixir—a mystery because Aidan was not so naive as to believe the man had just divulged the secrets of his patented formula.

Ah, Rousseau was skillful, damn him. For all his humble and myopic appearance, he possessed a practiced flair for the dramatic. This rubbish about secret laboratories and ancient temples lent just the right aura of mysticism to delight the gullible.

Was Laurel one of them?

He reached out, tempted to catch her shoulder from behind, until he realized he'd exhibited enough inappropriate behavior for one day simply in seizing her wrist. It wasn't as though they were alone on a night-darkened balcony. Here, people would talk.

"Laurel." He hissed her name, and like an arrow the summons hit its mark. She halted and turned. "I'd still rather you didn't."

Her head tilted; the dimple beside her mouth flashed as her lips plumped. "Why?"

How should he answer? What proof did he have that Rousseau was attempting to swindle anyone, or that his elixir might not actually possess a benefit or two? As Wescott had said at the outset, medical advances were made in this manner.

But so were bankrupt estates and broken hearts. "It is too new. Who can say whether his formula might cause an adverse reaction?"

He half expected her to demand why he should care what she did. He demanded that of himself and didn't like the answer: that after a single waltz beneath the stars, this perplexing woman had begun to matter to him. That he had begun to care about her.

"No one else seems unduly concerned." Her gloved hand made a sweep of the line extending out from the dais. Aidan saw the familiar faces of Julian Stoddard, the recently arrived Lord and Lady Harcourt, even the doubtful Geoffrey Taft and Mrs. Whitfield, and a host of others awaiting their turn. "Frankly," she said, "I do not see the harm."

"Then you are as biddable as the rest of these bleating sheep."

Her breath came sharply, but she held her ground. "That is rather harsh, don't you think? Look there, Lady Fairmont and Lady Devonlea are about to enjoy a taste. I see Lord Munster up ahead as well."

With that, she stalked away, and he let her, raking a hand through his hair and expelling an oath through his teeth. Yes, his friends and acquaintances were in line to ingest a hodgepodge of God only knew what. And the truth was, while he didn't relish the thought of these people risking their health, he had not come here to stop them. He hadn't come this morning intending to prevent anything, but rather to scrutinize the demonstration, search out inconsistencies, and sample the elixir himself. How else to determine the truth of its effects?

A sound plan. Yet what had he ended up observing? Laurel Sanderson. What had he sampled? The spark of her gutsy valor as she stood up to him time and again.

Was she the woman from Knightsbridge Street? He *knew* she was. Then why did she have him half disbelieving his own certainty?

Because she had somehow engaged his emotions in ways other women did not, leaving him open, susceptible, distracted—

His thoughts broke off. His mind went utterly still,

then began sifting through everything he knew about flimflam artists.

They often had partners, planted among the potential targets to act as . . .

Distractions. To draw attention away from the trickery of the scheme, and to provide seemingly innocent encouragement to those clinging to their skepticism.

Is that why the lovely and engaging Mrs. Sanderson had suddenly appeared on Bath's social scene? How convenient that she should arrive only days before Rousseau offered his elixir to the general public.

Aidan shook his head at the unlikely stride his logic had taken. Yes, he believed she had lied about being in mourning and, yes, he believed she continued to hide . . . something. But being in collusion with a man who happened to be a respected member of his profession, who had never committed so much as a misdemeanor in all his years in this country?

When he thought of it that way, his suspicions seemed ridiculous. Yet suspicion continued to creep along his nerve endings, raising an irritable itch between his shoulders.

In the past few minutes, the line had grown considerably shorter while the chorus of voices praising the formula filled the room. Fitz reached to accept two glasses from a waiter. He handed one to Laurel. Nearby, Melinda and Beatrice were sipping theirs.

Aidan moved to the dais. "I say, can a bloke procure himself a dram?"

Laurel's glass paused partway to her lips. "But you said . . ." She trailed off, eyebrows angling inward. "You were dead set against it," she charged. "You implied there might be . . . danger."

"Did I? How dramatic. Mrs. Sanderson, you must have misunderstood me. Odd how our perceptions can sometimes confound us." He winked, wagering that she would have no trouble comprehending the gesture.

Her indignation held another instant, then dissolved into a moue of capitulation. She had read his meaning perfectly. If she said nothing more about his objections to Rousseau's elixir, he would not bring up London again.

However much their individual intentions might conflict, for now it seemed the very act of harboring secrets had rendered them unwitting accomplices. The notion should not have made him grin, but grin he did as he clinked his glass against hers and prepared to take his first taste of Rousseau's magical elixir.

Laurel wanted to shake the grin from Aidan Phillips's lips and the glass from his hand. Why put up such a fuss about not sampling the formula if he had intended trying it all along? The man was impossible. Was he deliberately trying to exasperate her?

He was doing a first-rate job.

And his reference to "confounded perceptions" could not have been any plainer. Tit for tat. Blackmail, really. Either she stopped questioning his sudden change of mind, or he would harass her about the color of her dresses and whether she had nearly been trampled in a crowd last summer.

Blast the man and his inconvenient memories. Thank heaven Lord Munster had been too far away that day to have gotten a good look at her.

But the question remained: why *had* Aidan changed his mind after so vehement a protestation, and why did he not wish to discuss the matter in front of the others?

"Drink up, Mrs. Sanderson," Lord Munster urged. "I g-guarantee you shall be impressed."

Snapped out of her ruminations, Laurel started to comply when the clatter of shattering glass stopped her short. She spun around to discover Lady Fairmont holding a hand to her brow and looking as pale as the gloomy sky beyond the windows. Shards of glass glistened on the floor at her feet.

"My lady!" Hastily she placed her own sample on Rousseau's demonstration table before hurrying over to the countess. "Are you ill?"

The broken glass crunched beneath her boots. Her concern escalated to full-scale alarm when the countess's eyes rolled back in their sockets and her legs collapsed beneath her.

Lady Fairmont sank heavily, dragging Laurel down with her onto the hardwood floor. She managed to grasp Lady Fairmont's shoulders, preventing the woman from hitting her head. Then she propped the insensible countess against her. Reaching for the fan attached by its cord to her reticule, she waved it over Lady Fairmont's face.

"My lady? Lady Fairmont? Someone, please help us."

A ring of concerned and shocked faces formed around them. Startled speculation whizzed like arrows over Laurel's head.

"She's fainted!"

"Do you think it was the elixir?"

"Is anyone else feeling ill?"

"Someone should summon a doctor."

From beyond the circle, Lady Devonlea was calling Laurel's name. As though she were suddenly conveyed through time to that summer day in Knightsbridge, she felt breathless, hemmed in, drowning in a sea of people. Her fear for Lady Fairmont mingled with a sudden if irrational dread of being trampled.

And then, just as on that day, a hand, broad and strong, appeared between the press of bodies, followed by a muscular arm, a solid shoulder, and finally Aidan's handsome features.

He paused for a brief assessment of the situation and took charge.

"Fitz," he called over his shoulder, "have the porter summon Dr. Bailey at once."

Relief poured through Laurel as Aidan knelt at her side, bringing with him a sense that all would be well. "What happened?" he demanded.

"I don't know exactly. It came on so suddenly."

He laid a gentle hand on Lady Fairmont's bloodless cheek. "Melinda? Can you hear me? It is Aidan."

"We must get her off this chilly floor," Laurel said. "Can you lift her?"

"Easily."

He slipped an arm around the countess's back, and for a heart-stopping second that arm also lay across the front of Laurel's jacket. The world seemed to begin and end at that small place of contact just above her breasts; her nipples tightened in response, and all her awareness converged on the heat infused by his forearm, so that the room and the people filling it might not have existed.

It was over in a moment, leaving her unnerved and bewildered that her reaction to him could be so powerful. He eased Lady Fairmont away, gathering her securely in his arms before pushing to his feet.

The countess stirred; her eyelids fluttered.

Laurel stood and reached to grasp her hand. "Lady Fairmont, can you hear me?"

"Mrs. Sanderson?"

"Yes, my lady. You fainted. No, do not try to move. Not just yet."

"Who has got me . . . ? Oh, Aidan, it is you." Blinking, she gripped his coat sleeve. Looking up into his face, she produced a saucy grin, albeit an unsteady one. "Ah, if only I were twenty years younger and not your godmother."

"If I weren't your godson, I shouldn't care about those twenty years." The hearty declaration had a warming effect on Laurel's heart and made her smile. Aidan gently lowered the countess's feet to the floor, but he kept a steady arm around her. "Do you think you can walk? If not, I shall carry you out and set you before me on my horse."

The countess laughed weakly. "You will do no such thing. The loan of this formidable arm shall suffice."

"You're a stubborn old she-goat," he murmured with a shake of his head. His arm tightened when she swayed slightly. "Steady, now."

Lady Devonlea pressed through the crowd to reach them. "Lady Fairmont, thank heavens you are on your feet again. Such a fright you gave us."

"Yes, how tiresome of me. I simply cannot fathom what came over me."

Aidan's warnings about the elixir sent a chill through Laurel. Yet no one else appeared to be experiencing ill effects. She glanced over her shoulder; Rousseau was no longer behind the dais. The man was nowhere to be seen.

She eased closer to Aidan and the countess so she would not be overheard. "How much of the elixir did you drink, my lady?"

"Hardly a drop. The glass slid from my grasp before I'd taken more than a sip." With a rueful shake of her head, Lady Fairmont regarded the glass shards littering the floor.

"Too little breakfast, perhaps." A handsome young man, whom Lady Devonlea had introduced to Laurel last evening as Lord Julian Stoddard, limped forward with the help of a cane.

With wheat blond hair and aquamarine eyes that contrasted brightly against his tanned complexion, his were just the sort of looks over which Willow would have sighed and mooned. Despite his walking stick, Laurel perceived a cavalier swagger in his stance, making him seem like a younger, lighter-haired version of Aidan.

"Yes, Julian, now that you mention it, I did set out this morning without a proper breakfast." The countess lifted a hand to her brow. With the other she clung to Aidan's arm. "Yes . . . that must be it."

"Lord Barensforth," Laurel said quietly, "perhaps it would be best to bring Lady Fairmont home now."

He nodded. "Stoddard, be a good lad and ask a porter to secure us a hansom."

The younger man hesitated, regarding Aidan with a sardonic tilt to his lips before setting off. Laurel supposed he didn't appreciate being called a "lad." Or perhaps his injured ankle made the task an arduous one.

Lady Fairmont took a faltering step at Aidan's side and then stopped, extending a hand. "Mrs. Sanderson, you'll come, too, won't you?"

"Of course, my lady, if you wish me to."

Laurel bade good day to Lady Devonlea and thanked her for the ride there earlier. Darting a glance at Aidan's and Lady Fairmont's receding backs, the viscountess whispered, "Remember what I said earlier. Aidan is on the prowl, and you, my dear, are the prey he covets. If I were you, I would be on my guard."

Chapter 10

"Oh, do stop this infernal fussing, all of you." Propped on pillows whose linen cases rivaled the ashen tone of her skin, Lady Fairmont scowled at the servants bustling in and out of her elegantly appointed bedchamber.

Their arrival here at Fenwick House, perched on a hillside north of Bath, had tossed Lady Fairmont's household into a veritable uproar. She lay at the center of the oak and wrought iron four-poster that dominated her bedchamber, her disapproval tempered by the tremor of her fingertips against the satin counterpane and a quiver she could not quite clear from her voice. Yet she insisted, "There is not a thing wrong with me that a strong cup of tea won't remedy."

Laurel dearly hoped she was right. Had Rousseau's elixir caused her swoon? Lady Fairmont claimed she had ingested only a small sip. Laurel's own sample had gone untouched, but no one else in the room had seemed adversely affected.

"Mrs. Prewitt is bringing up tea directly, ma'am," said a short, stout maid whose red curls reminded Laurel of her sister Holly. The girl bobbed a curtsy and deposited a stack of linens onto the commode beside the brass and porcelain washstand.

Laurel perched on the edge of the bed and took one of Lady Fairmont's icy hands between her own. "Do allow them to fuss, my lady. However unnecessary their attentions may be, it helps them to feel needed. Believe me, I know. I . . ."

Barely in time, she clamped her mouth shut. She had nearly mentioned having nursed her three sisters through countless illnesses, but not an hour ago at the Pump Room she had professed to having no sisters.

Lady Fairmont laid a sympathetic hand over Laurel's. "I believe I know what you were about to say, my dear. Did you spend many hours at your husband's bedside, during his final days?"

Laurel discovered that the ease in lying she had experienced at the Pump Room failed her now, but she was saved from having to spin another tale by the appearance of Mrs. Prewitt, the housekeeper Laurel had met upon arriving at Fenwick House. Younger than most housekeepers, the woman had dark brown hair drawn back into a severe knot and thin, rather plain features that Laurel found nonetheless pleasant.

With quick, efficient movements, Mrs. Prewitt set a tray holding a teapot and covered dishes on the nightstand. "Will there be anything else, ma'am?"

Lady Fairmont thanked her and waved her away. The other servants trailed the housekeeper into the corridor.

"Well, now, something certainly smells heavenly." Laurel lifted silver covers to reveal a platter of steaming scones and an array of finger sandwiches.

The countess broke a corner off a scone and popped it into her mouth.

"How do you like your tea?" Laurel lifted the teapot.

"Two lumps and a spot of cream, thank you, dear."

Placing the cup and saucer carefully in Lady Fairmont's unsteady hands, Laurel found herself holding her breath and hoping the woman didn't burn herself with the hot liquid. As she looked on, it struck her as immeasurably sad that there was no one better suited to care for the ailing woman than servants and she herself, who had met Lady Fairmont only a few short days ago.

"Have you any family nearby?" Laurel asked gently. "Someone we can send for?"

Lady Fairmont shook her head. "I have two daughters, both presently abroad with their families. My son died a year ago, and my five-year-old grandson, Joseph, has assumed the Fairmont title. Fenwick, however, belongs to me," she added with emphasis, as if someone might suggest otherwise.

Her teacup clattered as she set it on its saucer. "Of course, I've always considered Aidan a second son. He and his mother spent many happy days here with me. I do miss her dreadfully. . . ." Her eyes misting, she stared into the steam rising from her cup. When she looked up again, it was with a resilient grin. "Oh, the stories I could tell you. Such an unruly scamp, that boy was, and such a daredevil, too. You never saw the like. One time, he decided to play tightrope walker on the stone balustrade outside my dressing room. Good heavens, I thought we were going to lose him that day."

"Oh, what happened?" Laurel was no stranger to childhood accidents. Of all her sisters, Holly had been the daredevil, climbing trees too high, riding her pony too fast. Laurel's blood chilled as she recalled one of Holly's more harrowing injuries, a gash across the knee that showed the bone. "Did he fall? Was he terribly hurt?"

"Your concern for my younger self is touching, Mrs. Sanderson."

Aidan leaned in the doorway, watching them with a smile. He had shed his coat, exposing the charcoal sheen of a waistcoat that emphasized impressive shoulders and the tapering lines of his torso. Beige riding breeches hugged slim hips and powerful thighs. Laurel's insides fluttered at the sight of him, at the thought of all that hard, barely contained muscle. She tried to look away and found she could not.

His gaze softened in return. "I was not hurt that day," he said. "My mother very patiently coaxed me down to safety. She then had Lady Fairmont's groom introduce my backside to the flexible end of a riding crop. I believe I was six at the time."

"Yes, and very little good that whipping did you, as I recall," the countess said.

"Oh," Laurel said a little weakly. She struggled to picture this very large, very solid man as a small, naughty child. She could not manage it, could not see him as anything but the vital, commanding earl he had become.

The notion curled with delicious—and forbidden— warmth inside her.

"I came to tell you that Dr. Bailey has arrived," he said. "Shall I tell him to come up?"

"Pshaw." Lady Fairmont scowled. "Who the blazes summoned him?"

"I believe it was Lord Munster," Laurel told her, "but at our insistence. Just a precaution, of course."

"Indeed." Aidan straightened, filling the doorway. "You aren't going to be a stubborn goat about it, are you?"

The countess heaved a sigh. "Send him up."

Minutes later, a soft knock at the open door announced Dr. Bailey's arrival. With his well-tailored suit, thinning hair, and silver spectacles, he brought a sense of reassurance that Lady Fairmont would receive the care she needed.

The countess apparently did not agree. "Humph. I assure you there was no need to disturb your morning on my account. As you can see, I am being perfectly well looked after."

"Em, Lady Fairmont," Laurel whispered, "remember what I mentioned about allowing others to feel needed?" From the corner of her eye, she caught Dr. Bailey attempting to hide a grin as he waited to be invited closer to the bed.

The countess released a breath and relaxed deeper against her pillows. "All right, but do not dare prick me with any of your pointy instruments, Doctor. And no leeches. I cannot abide the disgusting creatures."

"I thoroughly agree." Laurel stood up from the bed. "With your permission, Lady Fairmont, I shall wait in your drawing room."

The countess nodded, then snatched Laurel's hand with a surprising burst of determination. "I should prefer that we not be so dastardly formal. Do call me Melinda, if I may call you Laurel."

The gesture flooded Laurel with surprising warmth. A vague memory sifted inside her. A gentle hand around her own, the scent of sweet perfume, the reassuring sound of a calm voice. Her mother? An ache in her throat pushed tears into her eyes.

"I would be delighted." Laurel patted the countess's hand and promised to return the moment the doctor was finished prodding and poking.

In the heavy silence of the drawing room, she stood before the tall, arched windows overlooking the front park. The weather had worsened and a light rain fell, driven by a restless wind that rattled the oaks marching single file on either side of the drive.

Where the hillsides sank into the wide valley hugged by the River Avon, the rooftops of Bath mirrored the sky. Laurel fingered the fringed swag of window curtain and contemplated the medieval layout of the Lower Town compared with the spacious and modern Upper Town. Without success she tried to pick out the peaked slate roof of her boardinghouse in Abbey Green.

Beneath the window stood a marble-topped table cluttered with an array of cherubic figurines fashioned of jade, alabaster, bronze, and porcelain. Each winged fellow played a flute or tiny mandolin, or aimed a minuscule bow and arrow. She regarded the bland smiles and sightless eyes and wondered if the collection represented a fondness for innocence and whimsy, evidence, perhaps, of a softer vulnerability hidden beneath Melinda's self-sufficiency.

With a sigh she turned back into the room, wishing she had asked the housekeeper to light a lamp or two. Only a few short minutes ago it hadn't seemed necessary, but the sky had darkened to a cold iron gray. How quickly things could change.

"How is she?"

With a hand at her throat, Laurel spun about. Down the room's murky length, Lord Barensforth's outline took shape as he stood up from a wing chair. Shadows concealed the better part of his face, but even so her pulse leaped at the sight of him, at the thought of being here with him, alone in the storm-induced dusk.

"You startled me." Her hand slid to press her heart, her palm absorbing the erratic beats. "I thought you were downstairs. Why did you not speak when I entered the room?"

"You seemed lost in thought. I didn't wish to disturb you." He came toward her. The dull light from outside deepened the lines of his face, accentuating prominent cheekbones and the high curve of his brow, while turning his eyes and mouth into caverns of mystery. "How is Melinda?"

Laurel didn't immediately reply. She couldn't think, couldn't find her voice. The rain hitting the panes tossed a dappled reflection onto his torso that made him seem less than corporeal, otherworldly. Until now she had seen him only in society—polished, polite, refined. Even last night, despite the seductive nature of their encounter on the terrace, she had still felt a semblance of . . . safety. Refuge.

As well there should be now. They were standing in a countess's drawing room, in a house full of attentive servants who could at any moment enter the room to inquire after their comfort.

But no footsteps sounded in the corridor and the countess lay in her bed many rooms away. And here, *here* was this man emerging from the shadows with a power hinted at by the bulky sway of his shoulders beneath his linen shirt and silk waistcoat.

He passed the harpsichord with its painted panels depicting satin-clad gentry in pastoral settings. He might be an aristocrat, but he was nothing like *them*, not pretty and well-mannered and . . . tame. He was not a man to be controlled or managed, not by rules or mores or customs. No, beneath his restrained surface, she sensed a dangerous undercurrent, along with a nature as solitary and sensual as the leopard to which Lord Munster had compared him.

A shiver ran hot and cold down her back as she remembered what Lady Devonlea had said about his being on the prowl, and her, Laurel, his coveted prey.

His fingertips tripped lightly over the instrument's ebony keys, sending a trill through the air. She flinched, her stomach tossing in rhythm with the dissipating notes, her racing heart vibrating the whalebone stays of her corset.

"Is she feeling any better?" he asked, his voice as low and lulling as the rain against the windows.

She groped for control over her spinning thoughts. "I am concerned about her. I do not believe she is at all well."

"Then you don't believe a lack of breakfast brought on her weakness?"

No, she did not. She had nursed her sisters through enough illnesses to recognize the signs of infirmity when she saw them. "I can only hope the explanation is that simple," she said. She hesitated, then asked, "Did you taste the elixir?"

"No. I was about to when Melinda fainted. You?"

"The same. But it could not have been that. No one else seemed out of sorts. Which would mean . . ."

"That Melinda may truly be ill." His throat twitched and fear entered his eyes. "Dr. Bailey is well respected hereabouts. She will have the very best care."

He seemed desperate to convince himself. The depth of his concern took her aback, and for the second time today she rediscovered the man who had once defied a squad of policemen to rescue her. Suddenly tempted to go to him, to offer the reassurance of an embrace, she folded her hands at her waist and gripped them tight. "Yes."

He nodded and gestured at the streaming windows. "It appears you are trapped here for the time being,"

Instead of gazing out at the rain, she focused instead on his hand, not soft and white like an aristocrat's, but the hand of a man who took action, who commanded . . . who would be neither intimidated nor disconcerted by a woman who led when she should follow.

She tore her eyes away and stared at the watery windowpanes. "I've no intention of leaving. Not until I see the color restored to Melinda's cheeks."

"First names. You two get on well."

"She is very kind."

"No." He laughed, a baritone note that raised a private little quiver across her shoulders. "Be assured, Melinda is anything but. Ah, she's the most fair-minded individual I have ever met, but cross her, annoy her, or simply bore her and she will promptly erase you from her social register."

Laurel couldn't help smiling. "Yes, I can believe that, and I do think that is one of the qualities I like most about her. No pretensions."

"None whatsoever. Tell me, Mrs. Sanderson, are you a woman without pretensions?"

The look in his eyes, half conjecture, half amusement,

made breathing difficult and sent her to the refuge of the closest settee. Her reprieve proved all too short when he came and sat beside her, his thigh brushing hers, his masculine scent enveloping her.

"I sense a mystery in you, Laurel. Why is that?" His devilish grin suggested how large her eyes must have grown, how plainly the truth must be swimming in them. From this close she could see a light shadow of facial hair his razor could not quite conquer. "I wonder . . ."

"I assure you, my life has been singularly uneventful." The words came too quickly, too emphatically. Blast her speeding heart; surely he could hear its wild patter. She swallowed, pulling her gaze from his chin and jaw, trying to ignore the contrast they presented to his sumptuous mouth. "There is little about me that warrants wondering."

"Ah, but there is. For example, I've known Melinda all my life, but not once did she ever mention you. So tell me, how *are* the two of you acquainted?"

"We were not, previous to my coming to Bath." The truth came easily. She paused, seeking strength in the formidable outlines of the room's furnishings before embellishing her story. "My mother served at Kensington Palace as a lady-in-waiting to the Duchess of Kent. Melinda—"

"Yes, I know, she was a companion to Princess Sophia, also at Kensington. So your mother and Melinda met there."

"Not exactly. They were at the palace at different times."

Beneath the tumble of his dark hair, his brow creased in confusion. Silently Laurel damned the man for his inquisitiveness and wished she had never left Melinda's side to venture into the dusky, perilous trap the drawing room seemed to have become.

If only Victoria had devised a more straightforward story, but they had needed to account for the fact that no one in Bath, or anywhere in polite society, had ever heard of Mrs. Edgar Sanderson.

"At Kensington, Melinda and my mother both became acquainted with Mrs. Lehzen, the queen's former governess," she explained, praying this would satisfy him. "It was Mrs. Lehzen who arranged for Melinda to introduce me into society here in Bath."

"But why Bath?" His mouth quirked in a maddening show of enjoyment. "There are so many more agreeable places to visit nowadays."

"But Bath is lovely. Besides, you are here."

An infinitesimal twitch of his eyebrow revealed how her statement must have sounded, not as the countercharge she had intended, but as though *he* were the very tie that bound her to the city.

As if she had come here seeking him.

"Wh-what I mean is . . ."

"I understand." He smiled again, faintly, pensively. "I myself came to Bath in pursuit of an investment."

The upward note on which he concluded implied it was now her turn to elucidate. Before she did, a figure appeared on the threshold.

Laurel jumped to her feet. "Dr. Bailey, how is she?"

The despondency in his eyes, magnified by his spectacles, caused her pulse to stumble.

"Good heavens . . . ," she whispered. Her hand went to her throat.

But in the next instant whatever emotion she had perceived in him vanished. His furrowed brow conveyed only professional benevolence. "Lady Fairmont is well on the road to recovery. I have persuaded her to eat more and spend the remainder of the day resting. She should be restored by tomorrow, although I have prescribed extra rest for the next week or so."

"Thank you, Doctor. I shall see that she gets it," Aidan said, sounding relieved.

Had he also anticipated sorrowful news from Dr. Bailey? Perhaps Laurel hadn't imagined the turbulence in the man's expression.

She turned back to the doctor. "Do you know what caused her to faint?"

"Fatigue and a touch of hunger, as best I can tell." Gripping a lapel, the man strolled farther into the room. "I've been advising her ladyship for some time now that, despite appearances, she is not the young woman she once was. Charity work, her involvement with the Bath Corporation, social functions . . . I fear the countess is running herself ragged."

"Lady Fairmont is involved with the corporation?" Aidan asked. "In what way?"

Dr. Bailey made an apologetic gesture with the flat of his hand. "I am afraid you shall have to ask her ladyship, for I know little about the matter. Only, please leave it for a few days, Lord Barensforth. As I said, Lady Fairmont needs her rest."

Promising to return the next morning, the doctor made a hasty retreat, leaving Laurel with the impression that he could not quit Fenwick House fast enough.

"I'm going to check on Melinda. Care to join me?" Aidan started past her.

Without thinking—or she would never have done so—she reached out and closed her fingers around his sleeve. A shock of awareness, of the stony vitality of his maleness, shimmied through her, through him as well. He flinched, stopped, and turned. Their gazes met, sparking with sentiments that were both illicit and reckless.

In the power of that moment, Laurel yearned to know how his chest would feel against her cheek, how the swells and hollows of her body would fit against the planes and sinew of his.

Those same desires flickered in his eyes with a need that frightened her. Unlike a fleeting kiss or a stolen dance, or the duel of wits they had played in the Pump Room, this attraction suddenly threatening to ignite between them was no longer a game. Neither moved a muscle, as if each feared the consequences of doing so.

That he didn't press his advantage said something surprisingly contrary to everything Victoria had told Laurel about him, something she would consider at a later, quieter, safer moment. For now . . .

She snatched her hand away.

"What is it?" he whispered, the sound heavy in the silence.

"I'm sorry, I . . . It's just that . . ."

Gathering himself to his full height, he moved back a step, opening space and allowing cooler air to rush between them. "Tell me."

"Dr. Bailey," she said, fighting past the roiling clash of her thoughts. "I do not believe he is being entirely forthcoming about Melinda's condition."

He searched her features. "Why would you say that?"

Because it took a liar to know one? "I cannot explain exactly, but every instinct tells me he has left out something important."

Chapter 11

Three nights later, Aidan rapped softly at the door of a one-room flat located at the dodgy end of Avon Street, close to the wharves. Rife with drunkards, prostitutes, and cutthroats, it was not an area men of his rank typically frequented, but at least here he would not stumble upon any of his acquaintances as he met with his Home Office contact.

Without waiting for an answer to his knock, he turned the knob and walked in. Phineas Micklebee was expecting him. Grinning with one side of his mouth, the man motioned Aidan to take a seat at the oak table that filled a good portion of the room. In the corner, a brazier sat cold and dark. Beside the door, a narrow bed filled an entire wall. A rickety wardrobe and a few teetering cupboards completed the room's furnishings, while the single window looked out at the moldering wall of the tenement next door.

Micklebee had taken the tiny room for convenience's sake. Cheap and discreet, the place provided the secrecy they required to trade information.

Aidan scraped back a spindle-backed chair. Straddling the seat, he huddled into his cloak. "Christ, doesn't the Home Office cover heating expenses?"

Scratching his unfashionably bearded chin, Micklebee chuckled. He pushed a tin cup in front of Aidan and poured a generous measure of whiskey into it.

"This'll warm your cockles. Straight from Ireland. Only the best."

Aidan tipped his cup in Micklebee's direction, waited for the other man, thin almost to the point of gauntness, to do the same. Tilting their heads back, they drained their cups and smacked them on the tabletop.

Micklebee poured another round. It was an established ritual between them. Then the agent leaned forward and said in his Manchester drawl, "What've you got?"

"Paid a visit to the City of Bath Corporation yesterday."

"About time. And did our good aldermen reveal anything useful?"

"The name of the investment firm backing the Summit Pavilion is Bryce-Rawlings Unlimited. They've an office in London on Red Lion Court, just off Fleet Street."

"Hmm." Micklebee's hand returned to his whiskers; he gave a scratch and a tug. "Never heard of 'em."

"Neither have I."

"I'll send word to Wescott to have someone track the place down." Micklebee held his cup close to his nose, closed his eyes, and inhaled deeply. "Anything yet about Roger Babcock's death?"

"A beginning." Aidan swirled his whiskey, staring into the tawny liquid. "Contrary to the information the Home Office had on Babcock, he apparently owed money to Arthur Steele, Viscount Devonlea. Sounds like it had been a relatively recent development. I'm told Devonlea covered some of Babcock's gambling debts for him, although the more I think about it, the more unlikely that sounds."

"How so?"

"I know Devonlea. He's a gambler, yes, but generous?" Aidan shook his head. "My guess is old Dev extended the MP a loan for a venture that guaranteed a lucrative return on his investment."

Micklebee narrowed his eyes. "Like what?"

"Perhaps this Summit Pavilion everyone is bursting to sink their money into. But I doubt it. It's too easy an answer and besides, Devonlea is putting his own money into the project. Why help Babcock? No . . . it must have been something only Babcock had access to. . . ."

He sipped his whiskey, a silken flame that glided down his throat to warm his gullet. "And then there's the Marquess of Harcourt. Apparently he and Babcock had locked horns, although over what I don't yet know."

"You don't know much," Micklebee pointed out. He'd been listening closely, though. He always did.

Once, early on in their acquaintance, Aidan had demanded the man take notes. Micklebee had merely laughed and told him notes were dangerous. Later, Wescott had explained that, like Aidan, Phineas Micklebee possessed his own unique talent. He never forgot a face or a fact. Never. Which made him the perfect go-between, relaying Aidan's reports to the next link in the chain, someone who remained nameless and faceless to Aidan himself.

"Damned, but you're right." Aidan drained his cup, placing his hand across the rim when Micklebee once more lifted the bottle. "There's something else I need investigated. *Someone* else, I should say."

He explained about Laurel—Mrs. Edgar Sanderson— suddenly showing up in Bath seemingly out of nowhere, having connections to prominent people yet never actually having made their acquaintance previously. "I tell you, there is something about the lady that fails to tally. I don't believe she's even a widow."

He knew he wasn't giving the agent much to go on, leaving out a host of details that supported his suspicions concerning her. For instance, he didn't mention her tendency to lead during a waltz, or how innocent she—a formerly married woman—had felt in his arms, or how ingenuously she had gasped when he'd kissed her that day in London.

Or how the slightest touch of her fingers around his wrist could stir up an explosive desire in him.

By his own design, he had barely seen Laurel in the three days since Melinda had fallen ill at the Pump Room, despite the fact that he had stayed at Fenwick House, inhabiting his old guest chamber and ensuring that Melinda got the rest Dr. Bailey had prescribed.

Aidan had observed Melinda closely in their time together, and was unable to decide whether traces of her illness continued to plague her or she had simply begun to show her age. She had always seemed so animated to him, so eternally youthful. He had tried questioning her about her health in recent months, but she had responded with good-natured scowls and a hasty change of subject. In accordance with Dr. Bailey's orders, he had not yet asked her about her involvement with the Bath Corporation.

Laurel usually arrived in the afternoon, bringing Melinda thoughtful gifts of books or flowers or tea cakes. Each time, Aidan had found excuses to absent himself from their company. He wouldn't go far. Out to the terrace, into the next room, close enough to observe without falling prey to the truth—that he burned to see her, to be alone with her, to touch her again in the hopes of discovering whether that lightning-sharp zing he'd experienced had been real or imagined.

Precisely because he could not get her out of his mind, he knew he must avoid her, at least until he discovered more about her. There were still too many questions that needed answering, too many reasons he could not—did not—entirely trust her. He dared not let himself become distracted from the task he had come to Bath to accomplish, and investigating Laurel Sanderson had become an integral part of that task.

Micklebee studied him with an amusement Aidan chose to ignore. He pushed to his feet. "Find out what you can about her and that deceased husband of hers."

"*If* he existed."

"Yes, *if*. In the meantime, I've arranged to spend tonight in the company of an individual who might unwittingly provide some of the answers we need. Wish me luck."

Some ten minutes later, he descended from his cabriolet outside the graceful arches of the Theatre Royal in Beaufort Square. Inside, Aidan relinquished his greatcoat and beaver hat to a cloakroom attendant and made his way into the lobby, greeting acquaintances as he went. An obliging servant offered a glass of champagne, which he accepted.

A group milled at the foot of the grand staircase, and he spotted familiar faces: those of Fitz, Beatrice and Devonlea, the Marquess and Marchioness of Harcourt. Not far away, Geoffrey Taft and Margaret Whitfield chatted to Claude Rousseau. Once again, Mrs. Whitfield might have been mistaken for a respectable wife, clad in a pale rose hue that brought out the richness of her dark hair. Diamonds winked from around her neck and wrist. Taft apparently treated his mistress well.

That thought made Aidan pause as he remembered Taft's display of frustration in the Pump Room three mornings previous. He had decried the delays in breaking ground for the Summit Pavilion, and implied he was having second thoughts about his investment.

Perhaps the retired captain found himself short of funds these days.

Continuing his perusal of the group, Aidan noted that tempers between Beatrice and Devonlea did not appear to have cooled. Oh, any stranger would have thought them happily at ease as they smiled, greeted friends, and exuded the flair of a sophisticated, aristocratic couple.

But further study revealed their disinclination to exchange a word or even a glance. Side by side they stood, separated by a wall of icy discord. Aidan guessed they were still residing under separate roofs. Presently, Beatrice was making a show of being charming to Captain Taft and Mrs. Whitfield, a woman Aidan knew incurred Beatrice's acrimony merely by being younger and prettier.

Aidan often wondered why Beatrice bothered to include Margaret Whitfield in her circle. True, Captain Taft belonged to all the same clubs as Devonlea, but that didn't make them friends. Perhaps Beatrice enjoyed vexing her husband, who was enough of a prig to deem the captain's mistress beneath his notice.

Bea and Dev were not the only two out of sorts tonight. Standing a little apart from the others, Julian Stoddard leaned on his walking stick and peered sullenly from beneath a shock of blond hair. Occasionally, his gaze raked over Devonlea as if to flay the man. Even more unusual for the youth, he failed to acknowledge the numerous young ladies in the room who were attempting to catch his eye.

When Henri de Vere greeted him, Stoddard made only a curt reply, nearly a cut direct in Aidan's estimate. He wondered briefly what could be fueling Stoddard's ill humor, then dismissed the young man as his attention switched to de Vere.

Aidan had not seen Henri de Vere since the Assembly Rooms ball, but he had made certain the Frenchman would attend tonight's performance by inviting him to share a box on the mezzanine level. As a former spy, de Vere undoubtedly noticed subtle details others typically missed. Aidan hoped he might shed light on the former strife between Lord Harcourt and Roger Babcock.

As Aidan made his way toward his acquaintances, his thoughts turned to Laurel. Had she come tonight, or had she perhaps opted to spend a quiet evening with Melinda, or attend a different social affair? He searched for her amid the glittering finery, and a disappointment he should not have felt descended like a stale mist. He told himself it was because he wanted the chance to observe her interactions with the others.

Then why the jolt to his pulse when he suddenly spotted her across the lobby? Her golden hair had been piled high, with a single, spiraling tendril falling to tease the curve of her shoulder. She wore cinnamon silk, low-cut, shoulder baring, and waist cinching to an impossibly tempting degree. Simple pearl earbobs and the jet mourning brooch she always wore completed a look that far outshone even Beatrice in elegance.

How on earth had he missed her?

He watched as she politely retreated from the group and made her way, smiling with obvious enjoyment, in his direction. Heads turned in admiration as she crossed the room, the men displaying glints of avarice, the women envy. Aidan's chest alternately swelled and constricted as he watched her, as he traced the sway of her hips and the swing of her thighs beneath her shimmering gown.

Her gaze met his, and with recognition came an abrupt change in her demeanor. Her smile vanishing, her displeasure bored into him like the bullet he had once taken in a London gambling hell. His shoulder ached with the memory; his loins throbbed with wanting her. He suddenly wished he hadn't asked Micklebee to investigate her, that he had simply been able to trust her.

Reaching him, she curtsied with arctic correctness. "Lord Barensforth."

"Mrs. Sanderson." Never mind that they had been on a first-name basis only three days ago. Tonight they reverted to formal reserve, much like Beatrice and Devonlea. He did not reach for her hand, and neither did she offer it.

The last time they had spoken, she had all but accused Dr. Bailey of lying about Melinda's condition. Aidan had responded with incredulity first, then condescending denial. A respected physician would never offer false information about a patient, he had insisted. Dr. Bailey might withhold the facts at the behest of his patient, but he would never risk the integrity of his reputation with blatant dishonesty.

But the truth was that he, too, suspected Dr. Bailey, not only of lying about Melinda's health, but also of divulging more than he had meant to when he mentioned her involvement with the Bath Corporation. Aidan intended getting to the bottom of both matters, but he didn't want Laurel Sanderson involved. Not unless he knew beyond a doubt that she could be trusted.

"Mrs. Sanderson, there you are," Beatrice called to her. "We are all about to go up to our seats."

"Yes, one moment," she replied. Concern creased her brow as she stepped closer to Aidan, bringing her warm, sensual scent to scramble his senses.

So near he saw, too, that she had worn the delicate chain again, the one he had noticed at the ball. It disappeared into the plunging V of her beribboned bodice, and he yearned to follow its glimmering length, to discover what secret charm might lie hidden between her breasts.

He shook away the thought and raised an eyebrow. "What may I do for you, Mrs. Sanderson?"

"Melinda seemed well when I visited her today," she said after a moment's hesitation. "But you know her far better than I. Does she seem . . . herself?"

"Dr. Bailey assures me she is recovering nicely."

"That is not what I asked you."

"That is all I can tell you."

"No, it is all you *will* tell me," she countered with sudden passion. "Whatever you may think of me, however much you believe you know about me, please do not ever doubt the sincerity of my affections for Melinda Radcliffe. To do so would be a grave injustice, sir, and one I do not deserve."

In a flurry of cinnamon silk, she whirled and hastened to the steps.

Lady Devonlea and the others waited at the bottom of the grand staircase, but a crowd of people pressing to make their way to their seats cut Laurel off from them. As she tried to squeeze her way through, the sting of tears increased her frustration, forcing her to acknowledge that she did not so much wish to catch up to her new acquaintances as to flee—from Aidan, and from a powerful attraction she could no longer deny.

Damn and double damn. She should *not* be entertaining romantic notions about the man even if he *had* once ridden to her rescue. That was precisely the illusion about which Victoria had warned her. She had told Laurel not to be fooled by genteel appearances.

Making her foolishness so much more pitiable, he did not return her feelings. Good heavens, such a gross understatement, that. He apparently found her company so odious he continually took great pains to avoid her. And now this glaring show of mistrust.

Mistrust she deserved, despite her self-righteous claim to the contrary. Only, not where Melinda was concerned. Despite her necessary and often regrettable deceptions, Laurel would never do anything to harm that amiable lady.

A mutinous tear splashed hot on her cheek. She swiped it away on the back of her satin glove and circled an elderly couple, rather rudely, she must admit, but it couldn't be helped. Just to regain the ability to breathe freely, she needed to put distance between herself and Aidan's devastating good looks and his quelling lack of regard.

She must not let it hurt, *could* not let it. She had a job to do, and by the time she reached Lady Devonlea and the others, she had regained her composure, or at least a semblance of it.

"Goodness, are your seats in the heavens?" she jested as they mounted the stairs.

"The view from our box is well worth the climb," the viscountess assured her.

Reaching a landing, they followed the curve of a carpeted hallway until Laurel became quite lost and overwhelmed by the rich damask wall coverings, the glittering, gas-fed lights, and the crimson velvet draperies tied in fringed swags in the entrances of the box seats.

She soon found herself clutching the arms of her seat as she took in the theater's towering heights, the dizzying sweep of the orchestra seats below her, the impossible length of the stage. Other than the Christmas pageants at church in Thorn Grove, she had never attended a play there, and of course the London theaters lay far beyond her limited finances.

Lord and Lady Devonlea sat to her left. Behind them, Captain Taft, Mrs. Whitfield, and Lord and Lady Harcourt settled in. Raising the lorgnette an usher had handed her, Laurel perused the mosaic of boxes on either side of her. She saw no sign of Claude Rousseau.

And no sign of Aidan, either.

The Earl of Munster took the empty seat to her right. "I apologize for the p-provincial n-nature of the Theatre Royal, madam. One can only hope the performance exceeds expectations."

Laurel's mouth dropped open. Had this man no appreciation for the wonders around him? Yet before she expressed her incredulity, another thought occurred to her. She was here to assess his behavior and ascertain whether he posed any threat to Victoria, and he had just provided her with the perfect opening to pry into his life.

"You must remember, sir, that my experiences have been limited," she said. "This theater far exceeds in grandeur any of those near my home in Hampshire."

He sniffed. "That, m-madam, is m-most regrettable."

"Perhaps, but that is why I find such excitement here in Bath. I feel like a child at a sweetshop window, filled with admiration for all I see and everyone I meet."

"Everyone?"

She did not mistake the innuendo in his question. "Oh, indeed, sir. For instance, one can only imagine the notable places your lordship has been, and the illustrious individuals with whom you are acquainted."

"You allude, of course, to m-my relations." His peevish shrug acted as a warning that she trod on sensitive ground. Well enough did she appreciate the turbulent nature of Hanover family relations.

"Not at all, my lord. Oh, certainly His Majesty, your dear departed father, left you with an invaluable legacy." She paused to gauge his reaction, and wondered if his pensive smile meant he was thinking about the documents he had stolen from among his father's possessions. Now if only she could coax him to talk about those papers and what they held . . .

"My m-mother was an actress, you know," he said unexpectedly.

Disappointed, for she had no wish to discuss this aspect of the man's past, she nodded. "Yes, Dorothea Jordan. I am afraid I never had the pleasure of enjoying any of her performances."

"You would have been f-far too young. She was one of the best of her day. A p-pity Papa had to set her aside. His royal d-duty dictated that he attempt to m-make suitable heirs with a suitable wife. For all the g-good it did him."

His quiet words dripped with bitterness, reminding Laurel that his grievances were not entirely without cause. It could not be easy being the firstborn son of a king while knowing that, as an illegitimate child, he could never claim his birthright.

"And yet as the new queen's aide-de-camp, you do

hold an esteemed place in Her Majesty's court," she gently pointed out.

His snort suggested that he derived little satisfaction from the post. Laurel decided she needed a change in tactic; speaking of his family only increased the man's melancholy.

"Still and all, a man in your position must enjoy connections to all sorts of fascinating individuals. Lawmakers and intellectuals, men of vision and"—she searched for the right word—"innovation . . . of the sort that could so benefit our society."

His head instantly swiveled. His features alight with enthusiasm, he half turned in his chair to face her more fully. "You, madam, strike me as a woman of r-rare perception."

"Why, thank you, sir. That is singularly the most welcome compliment I have received in quite the longest while. I do happen to pride myself on my powers of discernment."

"And you see the necessity for ch-change in this country."

"I believe one would term it progress, yes?"

His palm slapped the arm of his chair. "Precisely, Mrs. Sanderson. P-progress is the key to England's future. That is something my young c-cousin fails to comprehend."

That unfair assessment raised a prickly ire in Laurel, yet she managed to nod in feigned agreement and produce a fawning look of encouragement. "What sorts of progress do you feel would lend the most modernizing advantages?"

"Political change, my d-dear Mrs. Sanderson." He thrust a finger in the air, and Laurel's eyes widened. Was he about to reveal his involvement with the Radical Reformers? His next words brought disappointment. "Coupled, m-most importantly, with scientific discovery."

"I see. Then would you consider yourself more a man

of science, or of politics?" She hoped he would choose the latter and expound upon his views.

He declared without hesitation, "The two go h-hand in h-hand." Crossing one plump leg over the other, he angled his torso closer to Laurel, and she had to remind herself not to lean away. "With the advent of science comes a p-purity of rational thought and the b-banishment of pointless traditions. That is why I seek to surround myself with individuals like Claude Rousseau, m-men intent on leading the way into the m-modern age."

At the sound of the Frenchman's name, Laurel went utterly still, remembering how, at the Pump Room three days before, George Fitzclarence had professed not to know Rousseau at all well.

"Oh?" was all she said, and waited for him to fill the silence.

"Humble though he m-may seem," the earl continued, "the man is fearless, a veritable p-pioneer of scientific advancement. His elixir will revolutionize m-medicine. And I, madam, shall be at his s-side when he does."

"How exhilarating." She decided to gamble all. "Then you and Monsieur Rousseau might be termed Collaborators of the New Age."

"A c-capital way of phrasing it, my dear."

"Are—" Her throat hitched with excitement. She coughed, then plowed on. "Are there others? I would be most delighted to meet them and . . . and learn more."

She wondered if she would discover Aidan Phillips to be among those collaborators. The thought filled her with dismay.

But what of Claude Rousseau? Did *his* aspirations extend beyond the scientific into the political? She found it hard to believe that of the unassuming, bespectacled man. For the first time, she wondered if the old king's documents had anything to do with the elixir. If they did, then perhaps she could ease Victoria's fears of Lord Munster using them to undermine her reign.

"Tell me," she said, "does this New Age allow for the participation of women?"

"Indeed, when the w-women are as astute as you, Mrs. Sanderson . . . or"—he leaned closer still, face bright with an eager hope that caused her to flinch a little away from him—"m-may I call you Laurel?"

The drawn-out whisper of her first name raised gooseflesh down her back. In his lingering gaze she saw a disconcerting jumble of wistfulness, fear, expectation, while in the accompanying puff of air she received a cloying whiff of brandy.

That might explain the loosening of his tongue and his contradiction concerning his acquaintance with Rousseau.

Before she could answer him, the gaslit sconces throughout the theater began to dim. Behind them, an usher released drapery cords and the velvet curtains fell closed.

"D-damn." Fitzclarence rubbed a hand across his chin. "I find myself f-far more interested in the present company than in the c-coming performance. I should certainly enjoy continuing our c-conversation at a later time . . . Laurel."

Oh dear. Had she encouraged him too far? She had only meant to further his confidence, but too late did she realize that what others would take for simple cordiality, George Fitzclarence perceived as flirtation.

Still, she now had an invitation of sorts, and she must not let him forget the offer he had extended.

Was she about to enter into the political intrigues of the Radical Reformers? Butterflies filled her stomach as she continued to tempt fate. "I should like that very much as well, my lord."

Lady Devonlea leaned around her husband to shush them both. "The curtain is opening."

From the orchestra pit, the first chromatic chords of the overture burst through the theater, sending a vibration through the very walls. Laurel shuddered, but not in response to the ominous music. Having raised her opera glass again, she glanced across the open expanse above the orchestra seats to discover Aidan Phillips leaning on his balcony rail, staring straight at her.

Just before the lights went down, Aidan learned something that left his senses abuzz.

His box sat mostly empty, for much to the disappointment of several marriageable young ladies and their mamas, he had invited only two guests: Henri de Vere and Julian Stoddard.

Stoddard seemed all too eager to discuss the particulars of Roger Babcock's death. The gorier the details, the greater the pleasure Stoddard seemed to derive from them.

But Aidan most wished to question de Vere. Knowing the former spy would recognize even the subtlest interrogation techniques, he proceeded with the utmost care. Aidan must appear to have no interest in the matter other than an appetite for lurid gossip.

He put Stoddard to good use, manipulating the conversation until the young bounder raised the subject of Babcock's death himself. So far Aidan had little to go on, only hearsay that the MP had owed Devonlea money, and Lord Harcourt's own inflammatory condemnation: *I shall waste no energy mourning a rapscallion like Babcock.*

As Aidan had done with Major Bradford at the Pump Room, he again raised the possibility of Babcock having been indebted to Lord Harcourt, or perhaps vice versa.

"I heard Babcock died owing considerable sums his widow refuses to acknowledge," he improvised. "Even old Harcourt has cause for grievance."

"Harcourt?" Stoddard gave a laugh. "That old miser?"

Looking thoughtful, de Vere leaned back in his chair. "If anything," he said in a French accent that was noticeably lighter than Claude Rousseau's, "it was that property by the river that came between them."

"Property?" Aidan raised his brows and feigned mild interest when in fact his pulse points rapped with the thrill of finally uncovering a worthwhile morsel.

"A warehouse on Broad Quay." De Vere twitched an eyebrow. "Falling to ruin. I cannot comprehend why either of them wanted the place."

"Which of them ended up with it?"

"Couldn't say. Perhaps neither. Supposedly a third party intervened with a higher bid."

"Whoever the bloke is, he'll more than likely lose his knickers in the bargain," Stoddard put in brightly, his mood apparently much improved since he had stood brooding in the lobby.

A warehouse on Broad Quay . . . Aidan would look into it tomorrow. Satisfied for the time being, he relaxed into his seat as the lights began dimming, only to snap back to attention just before the theater plunged into darkness.

Across the way in the Fitzclarences' box, Laurel sat next to Fitz, their heads close together. Aidan pushed forward, leaning his arms on the railing in front of him and wishing he could steal close enough to hear what appeared to be an animated conversation.

Happening to raise her lorgnette and peer in his direction, she saw him and went still. Then her hand fell away from her face, leaving her eyes uncovered. Their gazes connected in the instant before the theater fell dark, and as the first dramatic, D minor notes rose from the orchestra, a strange but pervasive foreboding filled him. He sat back again, his hands tightening around the padded velvet arms of his chair even as his stomach clenched around an irrational fear of impending danger.

Perhaps Mozart had simply done his job too well. *Don Giovanni* had never been one of Aidan's favorites.

Its theme of the Commendatore avenging his own murder by dragging Don Giovanni down into hell hit far too close to home for his comfort. Neither of his parents had been murdered, but they might as well have been: his mother by a ravaging illness and his father by a villain who had all but pressed the pistol into his hand and squeezed the trigger.

His skin continued to crawl with a nameless anxiety. Raising his glass, he resumed his distant perusal of Laurel, visible again now that his eyes had adjusted. The stage held her riveted interest as the floodlights flared and the curtain opened upon a dusky courtyard scene. Clutching the handle of her opera glass, she flinched each time the orchestra hit a crescendo. When the actors entered the stage, she seemed swept up in the drama of Giovanni's relentless pursuit of the innocent Anna.

Suddenly Aidan's mind filled with images of Fitz pursuing Laurel in similar fashion, and like an arctic wind, animosity spread a bitter frost through his chest. But he had no hold on Laurel Sanderson. No obligation. If she chose to involve herself with the likes of George Fitzclarence, what business or concern was it of his?

Unless, of course, she had an ulterior motive, which would make anything and everything she did very much his business.

Was he hoping for that? Hoping she would give him a reason to interfere in her life, make demands of her, and insist she answer his questions? He looked over at her again, tracing the upsweep of her hair, the curve of her neck, the swell of her bosom.

Yes, he could not deny that he would very much like to make her his business.

Chapter 12

During the intermission, Lord Munster's attentions toward Laurel heightened to an uncomfortable degree. Not only did he continue to address her as Laurel, but he added endearments—*lovely* Laurel, *sweet* Laurel. She enjoyed a moment's respite when he went to procure her a glass of champagne punch and a plate filled with marchpane cakes, but soon enough he planted himself at her side, so close that each breath she drew came laden with the sharp redolence of spirits.

All of that might have been bearable had he been inclined to continue their earlier discussion. She very much wanted to hear more about these world-altering aspirations of his. Were his goals limited to scientific advancement and the betterment of society, or did they include toppling the monarchy? When he had spoken of pointless traditions, the traces of peevishness in his voice had confirmed her suspicion that sentiments other than altruism drove his ambitions.

Bitterness toward his cousin?

She would not find an opportunity to question him in the lobby, for the noise level allowed for little more than occasional shouted comments. At the earliest possible moment she sought her escape.

Placing her glass and plate on the tray of a passing waiter, she excused herself. "Lord Munster, I believe Lady Harcourt presently wants for a companion."

"G-George, if you please."

"Now, Lord Munster, we are hardly well-enough acquainted for that." She raised a hand to gesture across the lobby. "But see there, Lady Harcourt is standing alone."

"I d-don't see her."

"Near the pillar. Lord Harcourt seems to have abandoned her, and that will never do. Please excuse me."

"B-but—"

Laurel swept away, squeezing through a crush that quickly closed behind her and cut her off from Lord Munster's sputtering protest. She lost sight of Lady Harcourt as well, and when she finally arrived at the pillar, the woman had disappeared. Within the confusing tableau of silks, jewels, and tailored black evening wear, she took a moment to reorient herself. She finally spotted Lady Harcourt ascending the staircase with Lady Devonlea and Mrs. Whitfield. Rather than rejoin Lord Munster, Laurel hurried in their direction.

She never caught up to them; there were too many people in the way and one in particular stopped her in her tracks, one foot poised on the riser in front of her. Several steps above, Aidan climbed the stairs flanked by a pair of willowy young blondes, one on each arm. Dressed in the height of fashion and remarkably similar in appearance, they could be only sisters, and barely out of their adolescence. Their giggles carried over the general din, and as Laurel watched through narrowed eyes, one of them turned her cherubic face toward Aidan and touched a finger to her bottom lip in a blatantly suggestive manner.

A sense of utter wretchedness filled the aching hollow beneath Laurel's breast. Raising her skirts, she hurried on blindly and hoped he would not see her. Or if he did, that he would not notice the moisture clouding her vision.

Minutes later, she came to a halt as the house lights dimmed and the corridor emptied. Looking about, she discovered nothing familiar, not the runner beneath her feet nor the damask covering the walls. Even the wall sconces were of a subtly different shape from those she remembered outside Lord and Lady Devonlea's box. Had she climbed too far?

Turning, she began to retrace her steps. From behind the closed velvet curtains, a low drone of conversation drifted from those who had resumed their seats. As Laurel approached the corner, someone came hurrying around toward her. A hooded cloak flew out to tease the shadows.

She let out a gasp at the same time he pulled up short. He lingered several yards away, his face unfathomable but for the dull gleam of his eyes. As his black cape sifted into place, a treble note of fear trilled through her.

She shook her trepidation away. He was merely a man hurrying to find his seat, as she must do.

"Excuse me, sir." She attempted to sidestep around him. He shifted to block her way.

"Simone?" His voice was a rough whisper. He hissed several more words that sounded French to her. He pressed closer. Laurel caught a brief glimpse of his features—hooked nose, thin mouth, craggy chin. His dark eyes sent shivers down her back.

She retreated a step. "Please, I don't speak much French. Are you lost?"

He repeated the first word: a name—Simone? Laurel felt sure it was when he added another to it: de Valentin.

Her throat gone dry, she shook her head. "I do not know whom you mean. Now let me by."

"Non, mon Dieu." He came closer still, his stride urgent, angry. *"Vous n'êtes pas Simone. Vous êtes Lissette."*

His hand came up. She recoiled, filled with bone-numbing dread and an inexplicable sense that she should know him. Relief poured through her when two ladies and a gentleman rounded the corner. The man brushed the stranger's shoulder.

"Terribly sorry," the gentleman said. The trio continued on, passing through a set of velvet curtains into a box.

As if from far off, Laurel heard the heavy rhythms of *Don Giovanni* rise from the stage as the second act commenced. The notes burrowed inside her, warning of danger. This man in his hooded cloak could well have been the ill-intentioned Don and she his victim. She considered darting into the nearest box when footsteps along the corridor heralded another approach. The stranger jerked his head toward the sound, spat an incoherent word, and pushed past her.

Her heart careening, Laurel whirled to watch him until the blackness at the end of the passage swallowed his form. The music built to a crescendo that spread ripples of unease through her, though she could of think of nothing as unsettling as the stranger's cold stare, his harsh words. . . . What did it all mean?

Without being able to recall how or why, the rhythm of his stride, the set of his shoulders . . . even the vehemence of his incomprehensible oaths, seemed uncannily familiar.

But from where?

The name he had spoken echoed in her mind. Simone de Valentin. A quiver began at her core and trembled outward to the tips of her fingers and toes. In her mind's eye, flames raged—the flames of the dream that had haunted her since her earliest days, her dimmest memories. She felt suddenly small and helpless and terrified as her mind filled with the shrill sound of a woman's scream, the crack of an explosion, and a figure draped in black speeding toward her down a corridor.

"Laurel?"

The whisper from behind her sent her spinning into panic. She tried to cry out, but an arm like an iron band went round her and a hand covered her mouth.

"Laurel, it's me, Aidan. Stop struggling, and for heaven's sake, don't scream."

For several seconds fear held her rigid against him. Gradually the resistance drained from her limbs and he turned her to face him. Lingering panic glinted in her eyes.

He pulled her close, feeling the hammer of her heart through their clothing. From far off, the opera gathered force with deep harmonies driven by the lower register of violas, cellos, and basses. Laurel's hands clutched convulsively around his coat sleeves. Her body melted against his. With a tremulous sigh she burrowed her face into the side of his neck with a sweetness that silenced his suspicions and imprinted a burning desire on his soul.

No sooner had the thought formed than he felt her strength returning, her shaking subsiding. As she pulled away, it was with painful reluctance that he let her go.

Relief lent a wraithlike quality to her beauty. "Thank goodness it's only you."

"Whom were you expecting? And what the devil are you doing up here?"

"I became lost and . . ." Her expression turned instantly wary. "Did you follow me?"

The accusatory note propelled him back a step. "I saw you miss the landing on the staircase. I tried to catch up and stop you."

"You could not have."

"You're calling me a liar?"

She thrust her chin forward. "I am saying I have been standing in this corridor a sufficient length of time for you to have reached me long before this."

"I was waylaid by well-meaning acquaintances wishing to inquire after Melinda's health."

"Oh." Her stance lost something of its stubborn heft, but only momentarily. As a solo baritone filled the theater with menacing tension, her eyes narrowed within their halos of golden lashes. "If you ask me, they had an odd way of showing their concern."

The statement sparked with rancor. With a huff she started past him. He caught her arm and stopped her. "Are you speaking of the Lewes-Parker twins?" He couldn't help grinning at the thought.

"You may wipe that smile off your face. Do you not find them a trifle young for you?"

Now he laughed outright, albeit beneath his breath to prevent the sound from carrying into the nearby boxes. "They are distant cousins whose father and brother happen to be next in line for the Barensforth title—a title the family would very much like to acquire. But in the event I do not meet my demise before producing an heir, their next preference would be for one of the twins, Edwina or Emily, to become my countess."

"I see." One bare shoulder lifted in a show of indifference belied by the crease above her nose and a blush even the shadows could not conceal. "So which is it to be?"

"Neither." He didn't elaborate, didn't bother to explain that he would rather leap off Pulteney Bridge into the Avon than endure a lifetime chained to either of his vain, impossibly shallow cousins.

Instead he stepped closer and said, "What I cannot help wondering is why it should matter to you. As it so clearly does."

"It doesn't. Not at all." But the protest sounded forced, halfhearted. Her gaze locked with his, and her eyes grew large and liquid, swimming with fathomless desires that mirrored the carnal images racing through his mind.

Putting a hand beneath her chin, he tilted her face up and bent his head, touched his lips to hers, and experienced an inferno of pleasure that spread havoc through his loins. When she didn't resist and, in fact, released a purring sigh against his lips, he put his arms around her and deepened the kiss, prodding his tongue past her lips. She met the gesture shyly, tentatively, but no less thoroughly as her tongue swept his and entered his mouth.

Their surroundings melted away, leaving only satiny heat and licking flames of mutual desire. Somehow they had swung about until Laurel's back was against the wall. She didn't seem to notice or care but clung to him, her arms wound tightly around his neck, her lips pressed urgently to his, until an abrupt burst of applause broke them apart with a jolt.

An aria had ended; which one, Aidan couldn't say. His thoughts were heavy, drowning in lust, yet at the same time spinning with the shock of how readily they had lost control and in such a public place, where anyone might have exited a box and witnessed their display.

The same sense of alarm held Laurel's eyes wide. Her kiss-reddened lips fell open. "Oh, I . . . Good heavens."

He took her hand. "Let's go."

Her skirts raised a hiss as she let him propel her to the stairs. She seemed dazed, as disconcerted by their brief passion as he felt. It was more than the mindless urgency of the moment continuing to affect him. It was how she had felt in his arms, how her lips had responded to his kisses. Like Virgo, ablaze and glorious in the night sky . . . and a virgin.

Was it possible that this widow had never been kissed? Never been loved as a woman was meant to be?

Partway down the stairs, he brought them to a halt. "Laurel, I'm sorry. I didn't mean for that to happen."

"Please, let us not discuss it." She looked everywhere but at him. "It was a lapse, nothing more. I must find my way back to Lady Devonlea's box. They all must be wondering what happened to me."

"Will you answer one question first?"

Fresh panic washed over her features; he half expected her to bolt. "How can you kiss me like that, and return to George Fitzclarence? What do you see in him?"

She shook her head, looking half-guilty, half-bewildered. "Nothing. I am not returning to Lord Munster. He simply happens to be occupying the same box as I."

Apparently, not all of tonight's acting was to be confined to the stage. Aidan pushed out a breath. "I see."

They continued down. As they turned onto the lower level, his curiosity once more took control of his tongue. "Then answer me this. When I found you, you were ready to jump out of your skin. Why? What frightened you so?"

"I had become lost."

"Yes, you already said that." Detaining her at the foot of the stairs, he refused to give ground. He placed his fingertips beneath her chin and raised her face to a nearby circle of gaslight. "Why not tell the truth—for once?"

Laurel's heart swelled to clog her throat even as her stomach plunged in dismay. She wanted to launch herself back into Aidan's arms and give in to every temptation ... to kiss him, to trust him.

To tell him the truth.

What truth? What had been real about her encounter with the stranger, and what distorted by her imagination? Because he had spoken French, her suspicions had immediately turned to the scientist Claude Rousseau. But no, this man had not worn spectacles; his features were different from Rousseau's and his stature greater.

No, it could not have been Rousseau.

And now she considered it, perhaps the stranger's agitation had arisen from his being lost, and when his attempt to communicate with Laurel had met with in-comprehension, his frustration had surged.

With tonight's performance conjuring images of murder and ghostly vengeance, was it any wonder she might perceive a threat where none existed? And the name he had spoken—Simone de Valentin. Perhaps here, too, she had been mistaken in what she heard. Her proficiency in French had never been much to boast about.

"Well, Laurel?" Aidan's query caressed her cheek like a warm summer draft, but his fingers held firm beneath her chin. He seemed prepared to wait the rest of the night rather than let her evade his question.

"There ... was a man."

He startled her by lurching closer and tightening his hold on her chin. "What man? Did he hurt you? Insult you? Tell me what happened."

His sudden fierceness unnerved her. His eyes blazed with it. His lips became pinched and drained of color.

"He did nothing," she hastened to assure him.

His piercing gaze held her for another moment, then softened. His hand fell away. "He must have done something to leave you so distraught."

She shook her head, trying to remember exactly what *had* happened, and why the brief incident had filled her mind with the horrific images of her recurring nightmare. "He wore a cape with the hood up, and I could not see him properly. I believe he might have been lost as well. He seemed overset, but when he spoke to me, I could not understand the words."

"Why not?"

"He spoke in French. It is not a language I mastered as a child."

"Then what happened?"

She thought back. Footsteps had sent the stranger scurrying away. An instant later, Aidan had whispered her name. "Then you came," she said, suddenly filled with the conviction that whenever she most needed him, somehow Aidan would be there to rescue her, just as he had been on that day in London.

He studied her for several pulse-tripping moments, his gaze lingering over her lips before sinking lower. Surely he witnessed the labored rise and fall of her bosom as she struggled to breathe. But each gulp of air filled her with his scent, his taste. Her lips burned with the imprint of his kisses; her mouth tingled for the return of his tongue.

His hand rose, and with his forefinger he traced the gold chain hanging around her neck. At the heat of his touch against her bare skin, her heart thrust wildly against her ribs; her nipples tightened to peaks straining to be touched.

"Come," he murmured. "We'd best get you back before people begin to talk. Before I give them more reason to talk."

Those words left her feeling giddy and slightly afraid . . . afraid she would not have had the strength to resist temptation. Reluctance and relief warred within her as they arrived outside Lady Devonlea's box, and she stepped alone through the velvet curtains to endure the remainder of the night without him.

Laurel rose early the next morning, dressed in a walking outfit, and set out from her lodging house in treelined Abbey Green to nearby Stall Street. From there she took a hansom to Milsom Street, looking for the confectionary shop Lady Devonlea had recommended the night before. She wanted to purchase an assortment of marchpane treats like those served at the theater last night, to bring to Melinda later in the day.

Before going to Fenwick House, she would attend a luncheon at Lord and Lady Devonlea's home in Queen Square. George Fitzclarence would be there as well, and after last night Laurel felt certain that with careful persuasion she could obtain more information about his activities. Victoria had been correct; the man responded with singular zest to flattery. With any luck, Laurel might even guide him into revealing what he had done with the missing documents.

She hoped they would be joined today by the sort of individuals to whom the earl had alluded last night. Collaborators of the New Age, she herself had dubbed them. As then, a swarm of butterflies crowded her stomach at the thought that she might be plunging in over her head.

The morning sunlight stung her eyes. She had tossed much of the night, plagued by fitful nightmares that had begun with her happy and secure in Aidan's arms, but soon gave way to the cold fear of fleeing down an endless, inky black corridor.

Again and again, cloaked figures had jumped out to terrorize her and shout incomprehensible threats. Awakening in a cold sweat, her fists balled around the crumpled bedclothes, she had wondered if such dreams were dredged from events in her past, or if they signified present-day fears . . . such as her unreasonable attraction to a man she had been warned not to trust.

Upon reaching Milsom Street, she exited the cab. The sun lit up the painted storefronts and flashed its cheerful reflection in the windows. Continuing on foot, she read the colorful signs as she went and stopped to admire a silk bonnet here, a lovely cashmere shawl there, only to find her enjoyment of the day diminished by lingering anxiety, like an ill-intentioned presence hovering at her shoulder.

Having located the confectioner's shop, she purchased a package of marchpane and another of almond puffs for Lady Devonlea and tucked them into the straw basket she carried. With more than an hour yet before luncheon, she strolled southward on Milsom, continuing to peek into the shop windows in an attempt to dispel her worries.

Near the corner of Quiet Street, she peered into the tidy confines of an office space and gasped. Pulling back, she considered hurrying away, then shaded her eyes with her hand and looked inside again.

Seated in an armchair before a sturdy mahogany desk, Aidan leaned comfortably back, one leg crossed over the other, what looked to be an open ledger book balanced on his knee. He seemed to be studying whatever lay written on the pages, while across the desk, a young man in spectacles and a severe black suit coat spoke rapidly. Occasionally he reached across the desk to point out some detail in the ledger.

Laurel now noticed the stack of ledgers occupying the desktop between the two men. Across the room from them, a wooden counter topped in marble stretched along the wall. A group of patrons consisting of several smartly dressed gentlemen and a woman in mourning crepe waited in the open area at the center of the room.

Laurel stepped back. The sign above the window read BARCLAYS BANK.

Minutes passed while Aidan flipped through the first ledger, then chose another. He scribbled notes on a writing tablet and occasionally spoke to the clerk without glancing up. As he leaned over the book, Laurel's gaze was drawn to the strong angle of his neck and the set of his shoulders, to the determined lines of his chiseled profile....

The sun growing warm on her back, she pondered what could snare the fascination of this known gambler, drinker, and womanizer. An investment? The Summit Pavilion, perhaps?

He snapped the book closed and stood. The clerk stood as well, nodding a brisk bow. They exchanged a few words, and Aidan turned to the door.

Backing away from the window, Laurel stepped into the path of a pedestrian. Waving at the curt advice to look where she was going, she whirled and scurried across the street, nearly colliding with a wagon pulled by a lumbering draft horse.

"Are ye blind or just daft?"

Waving off the driver's shouted expletives, she stepped into the recessed doorway of a milliner's shop, taking no notice of the bonnets displayed in the window.

As she watched, Aidan exited the bank, glanced up and down the street, and walked the short distance to the corner. A moment later, a handsome cabriolet pulled up and blocked her view of him. When the vehicle pulled away, he was gone.

Laurel took no time to analyze the impulse that had sent her hurrying to the corner. Seeing no sign of Aidan walking on Quiet Street, she deduced that the cabriolet must be his and he had climbed inside. A little way down the street, the carriage came to a stop where an overturned cart had spilled its burden of empty milk pails across the road.

At that moment a hansom rumbled down Milsom Street, stopping to drop off a pair of ladies at the same milliner's shop where Laurel had sought refuge. She flagged the driver as he maneuvered back into traffic.

"Follow that cabriolet," she said, pointing. She rummaged in her purse for a sovereign. Wondering if she was offering too much, she held it up for the driver to see. "Mind you, keep well behind. Don't let on you're following them."

The man didn't ask questions. When Aidan's cabriolet turned south, the hansom did also. For the first several minutes Laurel felt exhilarated, like an adventurer, a true spy on a secret mission. Gradually, however, doubt took hold. What could she hope to accomplish by following a man on his daily errands? Why had she run for cover as he had left the bank? Why had she not simply bidden him good morning and continued on her way?

Because time and again she glimpsed qualities in

this man that contradicted both Victoria's and society's views of him. In the brief course of their acquaintance, she had observed courage and audacity, flirtation and sincerity, and, at times, undeniable kindness in him. Today, the manner in which he had pored over those ledgers at the bank suggested that there was a good deal more to Aidan Phillips than the world suspected.

And she burned to know it all.

Chapter 13

"Apparently Babcock and the Marquess of Harcourt wrangled over the purchase of a Broad Quay warehouse here in Bath," Aidan told Phineas Micklebee when he arrived at the man's Avon Street flat.

He didn't typically meet with his Home Office contact during daylight hours, but he had information to convey that couldn't wait. To make himself less conspicuous in Bath's poorest neighborhood, during the carriage ride he had removed his cravat and changed into a coat, waistcoat, and boots purchased secondhand in London especially for occasions like these. His driver had let him off some distance away so the expensive cabriolet would not attract attention, and would collect him later at a prearranged location.

"I'm heading down to the wharf as soon I leave here to see if I can determine which warehouse it is," he added. "I'm told it's in quite a state of disrepair."

Due to the earliness of the hour, the agent poured him a cup of coffee rather than whiskey. "Why would two men fight over a decrepit warehouse?"

"Three men. Someone else bought the place out from under them both."

Micklebee gave a thoughtful harrumph. "I'll see if our people can find out who."

"That's not all our MP was up to." Aidan blew into his coffee and took a sip that burned on the way down his gullet. "I just came from the bank where an account has been set up for the Summit Pavilion investors. It appears Babcock was a member of the board of directors of Bryce-Rawlings Unlimited."

"Do you think he might have been double-dealing?"

Aidan shrugged. "It's hard to say. But I've a gut feeling based on the records I studied this morning and my past experiences with this sort of thing." Hunching forward over the table, he leaned on his elbows, the coffee cup warm between his hands. "An unnamed individual formed Bryce-Rawlings and purchased the land for the Summit Pavilion under the company name. I'm guessing that in order to make the company appear legitimate, some London stockbroker's clerk was paid a generous fee to sign the appropriate deeds and checks."

"Or was bribed, more like. Finding him won't be of much help though, will it?"

"No," Aidan agreed. "I don't expect such a clerk would have been told anything useful."

Micklebee stared out the grimy window at the equally filthy brick wall beyond it. "You think there's a slew of bogus shareholders as well?"

"I'd stake my life on it. The best way for a charlatan to encourage legitimate investors is to present a well-padded but phony stockholders' list."

"Another way is to set up an impressive board of directors. One that includes an MP or two."

"Precisely. Babcock might have been duped into buying enough shares to put him on the board. And if so, if I'm right about everything else, his widow may find herself in disastrous financial arrears when the Summit Pavilion project comes tumbling down."

"Maybe Babcock was murdered because he discovered the truth." When Aidan nodded his concurrence,

Micklebee shook his head. "You pieced all this together just from staring at numbers this morning?"

Aidan grinned. "I did. You have everything we've discussed committed to memory?"

"I do, mate." The man tapped a forefinger to his temple. Then he sobered. "What about Fitzclarence? What's his role?"

The name put a sour taste in Aidan's mouth. He hadn't liked seeing Fitz and Laurel sitting so close together at the theater last night. She had claimed they were merely friendly acquaintances, and certainly the sweet pressure of her lips against his own had supported that assertion. Even so, he could discern no good reason for this supposed friendship, not unless she had some ulterior motive.

"So far I've found nothing with which to incriminate Fitz."

Micklebee studied him for a moment. A grin dawning, he extended his hand, curling and uncurling his fingers to prompt Aidan to proffer further information. "Except . . ."

"Yes, all right. Except that I've a nagging sense Fitz is rather too enthusiastic about the Summit Pavilion and this elixir Claude Rousseau has cooked up." Indeed, thinking back, he realized Fitz had been the one to encourage Laurel to sample the elixir at the Pump Room. Only Melinda's fainting spell had prevented her from doing so. "He's also been more reserved around me lately, and that worries me as well."

"You think he's hiding something."

Without answering, Aidan pushed back his chair and stood. "I'm headed down to the wharf now. I've a strong intuition that if I can discover who bought the warehouse, we'll have the name of Bryce-Rawlings's founder. And perhaps the culprit who murdered Babcock, if indeed he *was* murdered."

"Long shots, these hunches of yours."

"I thrive when challenged." At the door, he hesitated. "Speaking of challenges, I don't suppose you've uncovered anything about Laurel Sanderson?"

"Since last night? No."

"Just thought I'd ask." He let himself out. Downstairs, he pushed through the street door and stepped into a situation that raised his alarm.

Most people might have overlooked the subtle details that alerted him. The two ruffians crouched in a doorway halfway up the street might have been passing the hours in dicing or some other idle pursuit. One of them might have been waving off a fly, rather than signaling the stooped beggar approaching from the south corner. And the scruffy, towheaded youth who crossed the street whistling might have been only ... whistling ... and not calling the others to attention.

Aidan shot a glance toward the north corner and immediately identified their likely mark: a hansom clearly not from this part of town. The relative cleanliness of the vehicle spoke of the posher side of Bath, and the nervous fidgeting of the driver suggested he didn't often drive his rig down Avon Street.

Now that Aidan thought of it, he realized the hansom had pulled up as he had arrived at Micklebee's tenement. What were the odds of two affluent visitors—himself and the occupant of the cab—arriving in the same derelict vicinity at the same time on the same day?

Had someone followed him?

A movement inside the vehicle caught his eye just as the shabby youth's whistle turned shrill. Recognition thrust his heart into his rib cage. He dashed diagonally across the street as the two men crouched in the doorway jumped out and the stooped vagrant straightened and pulled out a knife.

The hansom driver hovered in his box like a plum ripe for the plucking, too flustered to understand what was about to happen. Aidan let go a shout for no other reason than to disconcert the attackers and perhaps buy a second or two in which to escape them. Reaching the hansom an instant before the pair from the doorway would have, he vaulted up onto the seat beside the driver, seized the reins, and snapped them above the horse's back.

The vehicle bolted forward. Inside, a feminine voice, one Aidan recognized, let out a cry. Snapping out of his stupor, the driver reached behind the seat and drew out an iron bar but appeared undecided as to whom to strike, Aidan or the men pursuing his rig.

The vagabond ran alongside the hansom. Slashing out with his knife, he grazed the horse's flank. In his red-rimmed eyes, pitted skin, and rotting teeth, Aidan caught a vivid glimpse of frothing bloodlust. The bounder heaved closer, a claw of a hand snatching at the reins. The driver swung his iron and missed. Aidan shoved a bootheel into the bastard's shoulder. The attacker stumbled, and at the driver's shrieked command, the nag picked up its pace nearly to a gallop.

The other assailants fell behind the speeding vehicle, but Aidan didn't slow down until they reached the river. Audible *oomf*s and whimpers issued from inside the carriage. Aidan set his teeth and ignored them. His plans for the remainder of the morning had been brought to a crashing standstill. Not only must he delay his plans for investigating the riverside warehouses, but Micklebee's location had been compromised.

Damn, *damn*. How could he have been so careless?

Veering east, he maneuvered the vehicle through the bustling Broad Quay district. The odor of river muck hung heavy in the air, mingling with the smells of the coal and lumber being transported along the Avon.

Finally, he brought the rig to a halt and tossed the reins back to the driver. Still panting from the excitement, the man turned to him and gaped. "God's teeth, where the devil did you come from?"

Aidan peeled his lips back in his best approximation of a cutthroat's sneer. "Never mind. If you know what's good for you, you'll bloody well forget you ever saw me. And from now on, stay the blazing hell away from Avon Street."

Jumping down, he swung open the door, reached in, and pulled out Laurel Sanderson.

"Good heavens," Laurel cried as the hansom door opened. Glittering sunlight hit her full in the face, blinding her. Blinking, she felt herself being hauled across the seat until her booted feet made contact with a packed dirt road. Her involuntary gasp filled her lungs with the pungent scents of the river. "What on earth happened back there?"

"What happened?" Aidan shouted her words back at her. He thrust his face close, and the blackness of his anger frightened her—truly, *truly* frightened her in a way she would never have believed possible, not with this man.

Yet back on Avon Street, she *had* begun to suspect him of all manner of illicit activities. After having seen him emerge from his cabriolet transformed as if . . . as if he was in disguise, she had naturally imagined the worst when he had entered that hideous building.

Though she loathed the possibility, she had wondered if he might be attending a secret meeting of the Radical Reformers, for wouldn't such militants choose just such a location? She had kept a sharp eye out for Lord Munster's arrival as well. She never saw him, but that might have been because he had already arrived and was awaiting his friend inside with others of their ilk.

Then, without warning, the hansom had burst into motion. Fear had sliced through her, only to dissipate at the sound of Aidan's voice coming from the driver's box. She had recognized its rich timbre immediately, and while his urgent shouts had indicated some sort of crisis, she had been certain he would rescue her from harm.

He always did.

Now, however, she shrank in the face of his seething rage. "You needn't take that tone," she said. "I am not a child." But oh, she suddenly felt like one, a child caught at some inexcusable naughtiness.

"What you are, madam, is a snoop. And a damned shameless one at that."

That wasn't completely true. She *was* rather ashamed at the impulse that had prompted her to follow him. However . . . she glanced down at his attire, steeled herself, and met his gaze. "One might venture to question why you, sir, are wearing those ridiculous clothes and skulking about such a disreputable neighborhood." Awaiting his answer, she raised a self-righteous eyebrow.

His reply came in the form of a tug on her arm—albeit a gentle one—in the direction of the very cabriolet in which he had first set out from Milsom Street. His steel grip persisted until they were both seated inside the luxurious leather interior. Though little separated them from the driver, the man faced forward and paid no attention to the goings-on behind him. He apparently already had his instructions, for the carriage pulled assertively forward to find its place with the northbound flow of traffic.

With no small measure of longing, Laurel peeked out at the passing sidewalks. She felt trapped, crowded by Aidan's long, muscular limbs and broad shoulders.

Her stomach sank at the sound of his rumbling exhalation and grinding teeth. He was furious.

As if only then becoming aware of his grip on her arm, he abruptly released her, then turned toward her and grasped her shoulders between his hands. His chest heaved. "Why were you following me? What were you hoping to discover?"

"Discover? I . . . ?" A notion filled her with dismay. "My confections! I left them on the seat of the hansom."

"Your *what*?" He removed his hands from her, but

his presence continued to overwhelm her until she felt hot and breathless.

"My m-marchpane and almond puffs," she stammered in confusion. "For Melinda and Lady Devonlea. I forgot all about them and now I'll never get them back."

"Damn it, Laurel." His husky tone, part warning, part caress, spread shivers through her like ripples in a pond. "Don't you know you might have been killed?"

"I . . . I still don't know what happened."

"Then let me enlighten you. Four vagabonds had the carriage surrounded and were about to close in on you. If I hadn't exited the building when I did, they would have attacked. Fiends like that would slice your throat for the buttons on your jacket."

"Oh, dear Lord . . ." Ensnared by his blazing eyes, she shook her head. "No. You wouldn't have let anything happen to me. You didn't."

"Pure luck. You'd be a fool to think otherwise. Interfering in my life is a dangerous endeavor, Laurel. You will never do it again. Understand?"

He spoke with the sternness of a schoolmaster, in a tone even Uncle Edward had never taken with her. It produced quite the opposite effect from what he must have intended. Once more taking in his obvious attempt to disguise himself, she found the courage to counter his commands. "Then tell me what you were doing at that place, and in those clothes."

His scowl filled her vision, making her regret her query. "Just as you told me why you once donned yellow when you should have been in black?"

He had a valid point. She stared back, mute.

"This is not a game, Laurel. What you did was both reckless and devious. You owe me an explanation. Not to mention an apology."

Yes, perhaps she did. Only, she herself couldn't quite explain why she had set out after him. Victoria had sent her to Bath to investigate Lord Munster's activities, not

Aidan's. Earlier, she had observed him in the middle of conducting his banking business, and there was nothing sinister in that. But even with a window and a closed door between them, she had sensed a difference in him as he'd pored over those bank ledgers, a serious, studious quality that contrasted sharply with his reputation.

Had that difference truly raised her suspicions . . . or her fascination?

Leaning forward, he shrugged off his tattered suit coat. Next he removed his faded waistcoat. Flinging both into a corner of the floor, he reached with one powerful arm around Laurel. For a moment she thought he meant to embrace her. Heat shimmied through her as their shoulders touched, and her breasts ached at the light contact with the side of his forearm.

But he only seized a small pile of garments that had been folded on the seat beside her. Straightening, he slid his arms into the brocade silk waistcoat he had worn earlier.

As he fastened the silver buttons, Laurel exhaled a shaky breath and wondered if he could hear the slamming of her heart as it gradually slowed to a normal pace.

"Laurel—"

"You are right," she said. "I do owe you an apology and an explanation." She shifted to face him. "I'm very sorry I followed you."

His eyes narrowed. "My forgiveness is contingent upon your explanation."

"Not very Christian of you," she murmured. When he opened his mouth to speak again, she thrust up a hand. "Very well. I followed you because you are Lord Munster's friend."

Not entirely true, at least not at first, but after arriving on Avon Street and seeing him transformed from aristocrat to workman, she had based her suspicions about his intentions on her conversation with Lord Munster at the theater last night.

He said nothing. After donning his proper coat, he crossed his arms over his chest and tilted his head in a condescending fashion. He looked very much amused. "Explain."

Laurel sighed, a ruse intended to steal another moment to gather her thoughts. "Last night, he raised a rather startling subject. He spoke of political changes and scientific advancements, and how the two together would propel our society into a new age of . . . reform."

The term hadn't actually come up, but she ventured to use it now to see how—or if—Aidan might react.

He studied her for a lengthy, uncomfortable moment. "And what has that to do with me?"

She threw up her hands. "As I said, you are his friend. I thought perhaps . . . well . . . that you might share his views."

"Is there something wrong with his views?"

The question raised her indignation along with her concerns for Victoria's future. Her spine stiffened. "That depends on his intentions, doesn't it?"

"Fair enough . . . for the moment. But should Fitz's intentions prove less than honorable, what on earth do *you* intend doing about it?"

Oh, dear. He had arrived at the crux of the matter and once again she had no answer, at least not one she could share. What she intended was reporting back to Victoria about potential threats posed by Lord Munster or anyone else. Even . . . so help her . . . Aidan.

She hoped not Aidan.

She gripped one gloved hand with the other, squeezing until her fingers ached. She forced her hands to relax, and then saw that he had noticed.

"Humph," he said, looking down into her lap with a roguish curl of a smile.

She gathered her courage and took a chance. "Do you know what Lord Munster might have meant? *Is* he involved in activities or with individuals that might hurt the queen? You must remember that my mother served Her Majesty's mother, so naturally I feel a certain . . ."

"Responsibility toward her?"

"Yes!" Laurel smiled broadly. "That is it exactly. She is so young and—"

"More than adequately supported by a cabinet full of devoted ministers, an entire Parliament of capable peers and MPs, and a palace filled with servants and guards. Yet you feel the queen needs *you* to champion her?"

His condescending laughter piqued her ire. If only he knew the truth!

"Then you will not ease my mind concerning your friend?"

The question brought about a sudden change, banishing all trace of his amusement. "I cannot."

The soft admission startled her; she had expected him to flatly deny her allegations. His next words rang with haunting sincerity. "He worries me, too, at times. I wish to believe he is all bluster and bitterness and nothing more, but lately . . ."

He trailed off, gazing out the window at pedestrians and passing shops. "He is not as open with me as he usually is." Even with his face turned mostly away, Laurel could see the tension working the muscles in his neck. "And that makes me believe he may be hiding something. And if he is, I may not be able to help him."

"Do you often help him?" she asked quietly. She could easily imagine him—sophisticated, quick-witted, physically fit—coming to the rescue of the gauche, often inebriated Earl of Munster. Odd, but rumor held that Aidan often shared in Lord Munster's debauchery, yet Laurel had yet to encounter him in his cups.

"I try to." His murmured reply warmed her. For better or worse, he sought to be a good friend to Lord Munster, and that made her want to reach out and caress that little expanse of neck visible above his collar, made her yearn to put an arm around him and lay her cheek against his shoulder.

Abruptly, he turned back around, pinning her with a harsh glare. "Should you continue keeping company with Fitz, and if he *is* playing with fire, there is every chance you will find yourself scorched. And I may be unable to help either of you."

Disconcerted, she sought refuge by glancing out the window as the carriage slowed. Stately mansions lined a lush sward. "Where are we?"

"Queen Square. You *are* expected at Beatrice's luncheon, are you not?"

"How did you know that?"

"Because after the performance last night, when we men gathered for brandy in Fitz's drawing room, he boasted to everyone who would listen that he would be lunching with you today."

Again that accusing tone. It obviously irked him that she should associate with the Earl of Munster, even, perhaps, made him jealous. Suppressing the smile evoked by that thought, she said, "I am lunching with Lord and Lady Devonlea. I did not presume to ask who else might be on the guest list. Are . . ."

She stopped, not wishing to ask, not wishing to appear as if she cared either way. But she could not help herself. "Are *you* on the guest list?"

"I am."

Her spirits brightened like the midmorning sun, spreading a glow throughout her that must have shown on her face, for she felt the heat of it on her cheeks.

"However, I have sent my regrets," he went on. "I have business elsewhere."

"Oh." Her mood deflated. She shook aside her disappointment and attempted one last time to glean insight into today's events. "I don't suppose you'd care to share the nature of that business?"

"No."

"Or why you went in disguise to that deplorable place today?"

"No." His mouth tightened.

He reached up, intending to rap on the ceiling, a signal for his driver to come down and open the door for her. She caught his wrist to stop him.

"Wait."

He lowered his arm to his knee. She looked up at him, at the lushness of the mouth she had tasted and wished to taste again. So close, so tempting, yet, for all her longing, so forbidden.

Kiss me. Touch me, touch all of me. . . . Unfettered desire pounded through her. She gasped, then pressed her lips together and stared at him, horrified by her own inexplicable loss of composure.

"Yes?" he murmured.

Once again her racing heartbeat slowed but never quite achieved its natural rhythm. "I . . . I . . . er . . . that is, may we please return to Milsom Street first?" When he frowned in bafflement, she explained, "For marchpane and almond puffs."

Chapter 14

The day after Aidan visited the bank and officially became an investor in the Summit Pavilion project, he drove his own cabriolet up a hillside to the north of Bath to view the future building site.

Fitz sat beside him. Behind them were the Lewes-Parker twins, Emily and Edwina, accompanied by their brother, Sanford, a pimply, petulant seventeen-year-old who tended to view Aidan with an air of conjecture, as if contemplating how best to dispose of his inconvenient, titled older cousin.

Yet the springlike weather thawed even Sanford's chilly demeanor. With the vehicle's oiled canvas roof folded down, the warmed breezes hit them full in their faces and raised their spirits. Fitz had babbled nonstop since Aidan had collected him at his home in King's Circus, the twins had yet to spark an argument, and Sanford joined the conversation without his usual nasal whine dragging at every word.

Their parents rode somewhere up ahead, part of a long procession of carriages snaking into the Bath countryside. Laurel, Aidan knew, was two carriages behind his, in Melinda's phaeton.

It was all he could do not to keep glancing back. He would not give her the satisfaction. Yesterday she had

trailed him, discovered his contact's general whereabouts, and impeded his investigation of a warehouse
that might provide key evidence in financial fraud and
murder.

He'd had every right to drive off and leave her
stranded on Broad Quay, yet what had he done? He had
complied with her wide-eyed request that they return to
Milsom Street for more bloody marchpane. God help
him if Laurel Sanderson didn't bring about his and the
Home Office's complete downfall.

He had returned to Broad Quay later that evening,
although damned if he didn't peer out the back of his
carriage every few minutes to make certain no one followed. Once more in his workman's guise and armed
with a dagger in his boot, he had tramped along the
wharf area inspecting structures and asking questions.

"Lookin' for work," he'd told several dockworkers ranging in inebriation from mildly tipsy to stinking,
staggeringly drunk. "Hear tell of a new owner needin'
lumpers?"

One of the more coherent of the bunch had sized Aidan
up, judging his potential as a cargo loader by the bulk of
his biceps. Then the man had challenged him to an arm-
wrestling match that had ended in a draw. With a shrug
that seemed to indicate Aidan had passed muster, the
dockworker had told him, "Ain't heard nuthin' 'bout new
owners lookin' for blokes, mate. Try over at Peabody's."

"What about that place?" Leading the man out of
the tavern, Aidan had pointed to a warehouse across
the way whose silvering plank walls and crumbling roof
best fit Henri de Vere's description of "falling to ruin."
Could that be the property over which Lord Harcourt
and Roger Babcock had clashed?

The dockworker had recoiled a step backward. "Keep
away from there. Right peculiar goings-on, over there."

"Like what?"

"Chaps sneaking in and out all hours of the night

and . . ." Huddling between his massive shoulders, the worker had leaned closer and lowered his voice. "Ol' Will Shyler wandered over there one night to take a piss and never came back. Someone found 'im next morning with his face all smashed in."

Aidan had come away fairly certain he had found his warehouse. Further investigation would have to wait until after today's outing, a picnic sponsored by the Bath Corporation to familiarize investors with the plans for the Summit Pavilion and entice others to join the venture. Rousseau would be there, too, giving out more samples of his elixir. This time, Aidan intended to partake of his share.

At the crest of the hillside, the scalloped edges of three brightly striped, open-sided pavilions flapped in the breeze. Nearby, the sun flashed on tables laden with platters, silverware, and rows of tumblers and goblets. Earlier, a veritable army of servants had set out from town, armed with blankets, baskets of food, kegs of wine and ale, and barrels of lemonade.

Within minutes Aidan's cabriolet reached the wide summit and he parked amid a dozen other carriages. He and Fitz helped the Lewes-Parker twins down. A soft breeze ruffled the lace edging their collars and cuffs and sifted through their glossy blond curls.

"Oh, Cousin Aidan, such a villain you are. You haven't said if you liked our dresses today," one of the twins—he was forever confusing them—observed with a pout of her rosebud lips.

"That is because I find them too elegant for words." He escorted the girls beneath a pavilion where blankets had been spread out. Hands stuffed into his trouser pockets, their brother trailed them. Fitz had already set out for the food. Claude Rousseau worked his way along the buffet table as well, picking and choosing judiciously from among the many selections.

Aidan looked for Laurel, and saw her strolling

through the next pavilion, stopping to chat and greet acquaintances as she went. She wore cream and rose stripes today, with a wide straw hat covered in tiny silk flowers and a broad velvet ribbon tied beneath her chin.

An ache grew in his chest as he watched her. In full daylight, she dazzled him as she had on that day in London despite her dishevelment and the dirt streaking her face. Ever since, he had only encountered her by candlelight, in the dim interior of his cabriolet, and beneath a starry sky. In each circumstance she had blazed with unequaled radiance, but here, with her golden curls spilling out from beneath her hat and her porcelain skin fresh and glowing, he found her as luminous as sunlight slanting through a garden.

The comparison drew a silent groan. Had he really just waxed poetic for a woman who threatened everything he was trying to accomplish here in Bath?

"Truly, Cousin, could you *be* more preoccupied?" one of the twins griped in an octave that set his teeth on edge.

"I am no such thing." Finding an empty blanket near their parents, he bade all three of his cousins to sit, then flashed a teasing grin and tweaked one of the girls' corkscrew curls. "I am merely baffled as to which of you is the more lovely."

Sanford rolled his eyes as the sister to his right exclaimed, "Me, of course. Everyone declares it to be so."

"Oh, Edwina, no one makes any such claim." Ah. Now that Aidan knew which was which, he saw that Emily's dissatisfied scowl deepened as she peered out at the latest arrivals to reach the crest of the hill. "So many people here today. How will everyone fit?"

"Don't be absurd," Sanford retorted. "This hilltop is adequate and then some, or we would not have come. Father said the Summit Pavilion is to be Bath's grandest facility yet. But then, as females you cannot understand the complexities of such matters."

While the siblings argued, Aidan contemplated the party dispersed beneath the three canopies. Many had already visited the buffet tables, returning to their blankets with plates piled high with cold meats and slices of pigeon pie, fruits, cheese, pastries, and tarts.

Laurel and Melinda had settled with Fitz, Beatrice, and Devonlea beneath the largest of the canopies. At Fitz's encouragement, Laurel held her cup out to the stream of wine flowing from the footman's pitcher.

Fitz had also encouraged her to sample Rousseau's elixir at the Pump Room. Did he hope to render Laurel inebriated in order to take advantage of her? It wouldn't be the first time Fitz had relied on liquid persuasion to have his way with a reluctant woman.

"I do say, the view of Fenwick House is splendid from here," Edwina mused between sips of the lemonade a footman had just handed her. "A pity Lady Fairmont lives there all alone. A waste of such a grand estate, in my opinion."

Sitting straighter, Aidan twisted round to follow his cousin's gaze. Surprise went through him. He had not realized how close this property lay to Melinda's. So close, in fact, he surmised that the parcel of land intended for the Summit Pavilion had originally lain within Fenwick's eastern border.

His mind raced with what he knew about the estate. Unentailed to the Fairmont title, the house and surrounding land belonged outright to Melinda, bequeathed to her long ago by her maternal grandparents. He also knew that while originally the property did not extend this far east into the Cotswold foothills, Melinda's husband had purchased all the land within two miles of the house for the purpose of safeguarding the pristine views.

Melinda's involvement with the corporation—was this what Dr. Bailey had alluded to the day she took ill? Why in God's name would she have sold this parcel of land? She could not have needed the money. Aidan knew for a fact that her annuities paid over eight thousand a year.

Or had those annuities somehow proved insolvent?

Turning back around, he snatched Edwina's hand and brought it to his lips. "Thank you, my dear. You are most astute."

"Am I?"

"Is she?" Emily's nose wrinkled indignantly.

Sanford's lips twisted in disdain.

"If you will all excuse me." Their protests hot on his back, Aidan set off, ducking as he stepped out from beneath the canopy.

"Such breathtaking scenery," Laurel exclaimed. Having finished eating, she was walking with Melinda and Lord Munster beyond the pavilions. The hilltop's grassy ridge commanded spectacular views in all directions.

To the south, the city's spires, turrets, and domes lay sprawled like the pieces of an intricate puzzle. To the north, a lush, rolling landscape tumbled to the edge of a hazy horizon. "You say these enchanting hills are the Cotswolds?"

"The southern Cotswolds, yes," Melinda said with an indulgent smile. She seemed to derive great pleasure from Laurel's enthusiasm.

Laurel had worried that this afternoon's activities would overtire the countess. She had even suggested that they spend a quiet day together at Fenwick House instead, but Melinda had insisted on coming. Looking at her now, with the silk flowers trimming her bonnet complementing the rosy hue of her cheeks, Laurel had to admit that the past days' rest had done wonders to restore the woman's youthful vitality.

Reassured, she gazed out at the panorama before them. "I had not realized how close the Cotswolds are to Bath."

"B-but a stone's throw away." Lord Munster picked up a pebble and sent it skipping down the hillside. He went on to describe the limestone aquifer that ran beneath the hills, channeling the mineral waters that had made Bath famous.

Laurel barely took note as she stared out over the blue-green hills stretching as far as she could see. However little she remembered of her early childhood, she did know that her life had begun somewhere in this region.

Uncle Edward had provided only the vaguest details about Billington, the village the Sutherlands had called home. Assuming he had found it painful to dwell upon memories of the sister he had lost, Laurel had eventually stopped pressing him for information. Now he was gone, and the answers were forever sealed with him in his grave.

Unless she discovered something on her own . . .

Lord Munster droned on as she continued gazing out at the knolls and vales she had once called home. Why could she remember nothing of that life? Every part of her, down to her fingertips, trembled with a desire to touch something of her past.

Melinda took Laurel's hand in her own. "Is something wrong, dearest? You look pale and . . . and your hand has grown quite cold."

That was because her heart had clenched around a painful longing, yet in all those idyllic miles, nothing struck a chord of recollection. How could that be? True, she had not glimpsed these hills for many years, but should she not feel some connection? Some twinge of belonging here?

She managed a smile for Melinda's sake. "The breeze has grown chilly. Let's return to the others now."

"Another g-glass of wine will warm you, Laurel."

She felt Melinda's reaction to Lord Munster's use of her given name in the slight tightening of her fingers.

Laurel met her gaze and quirked an eyebrow as if to say, "It is not my idea," and hoped the other woman understood.

They returned to the bustling activity of the footmen circulating through the pavilions collecting the tableware. Everyone else had come to their feet.

"Mr. Giles Henderson of the Bath Corporation is addressing questions concerning the Summit Pavilion," Lady Devonlea informed them. "Then he will conduct a tour to show us where each wing of the facility will stand."

Lord Munster pressed a goblet of wine into Laurel's hand. She thanked him absently, her attention captured by Aidan's easy, long-legged stride as he came into view. He halted at the edge of the crowd gathering before the alderman.

His neighbors politely shifted to grant him a place in their midst. Women curtsied; men bobbed their heads. Several exchanged a few words with him before returning their attention to the speaker.

Laurel experienced a welling of emotion at how readily Aidan commanded a crowd, how easily he could command her with a mere word or gesture, if she let down her guard. She already *had* yielded to temptation, once when she allowed him to kiss her at the theater, and again yesterday when she had followed him to Avon Street. She had done so to learn more about him, and what she had discovered had given her more reason than ever not to trust him.

Will you tell me what you were doing at that place, and in those clothes? she had asked him.

Just as you told me why you once donned yellow when you should have been in black?

Thus they had reached a stalemate. What now?

Beside her, Lord Munster misconstrued the focus of her interest and offered his arm. "Come, Laurel, let us m-move closer and hear what Mr. Henderson has to say.

The S-Summit Pavilion and Rousseau's elixir are intricately intertwined, for each shall ensure the success of the other. Are you interested in investing in the s-spa?"

She almost said no, that she had no resources for luxuries such as investing in resort facilities. But as a wealthy widow, she would most certainly possess such funds. Not only that, but expressing an interest in an endeavor that held such importance to him was guaranteed to keep him talking.

At yesterday's luncheon at his sister's home, much of the talk had centered around politics, as Laurel had hoped, yet her expectation of finding herself surrounded by Radical Reformers had met with disappointment.

The group around the dining table, Lady Devonlea included, eschewed many of their new queen's policies. They felt that as a woman, Victoria allowed her Whig ministers too much freedom, and that soon the influence of the landed classes would give way to a system in which even the poorest workman had a voice in the government.

Laurel had wondered if that would be so dreadful, but she knew better than to voice such a sentiment. Lord Devonlea in particular seemed to fear that loss of power would lead to loss of wealth. Lord Munster had merely grumbled about the consequences of placing a crown on the head of a naive young chit.

Though disparaging, the talk had hardly been treasonous. These were traditionalists, Tories, not radicals, and Laurel was beginning to wonder if Victoria had been wide of the mark concerning her cousin. Then again, perhaps George Fitzclarence had wisely concealed his revolutionary opinions from his sister and mutual acquaintances.

Perhaps he and his fellow rabble-rousers met in secret . . . say, in derelict parts of town where people such as Lord and Lady Devonlea would never dare tread.

Where Aidan had gone yesterday, in disguise . . .

"Are you, Laurel? Interested in investing, I m-mean?"

The repetition of Fitzclarence's question snapped her out of her reflections. She blinked. "Why, yes, I am most interested. Perhaps you might advise me as to the proper course to take in such a venture."

His chest visibly swelled. "I should be d-delighted to. This project is of vital importance to me. I have invested m-much into its success."

Mr. Henderson began leading his audience from place to place on the hilltop, describing the future layout of the facility. As Laurel and Fitzclarence followed, he took her hand and placed it in the crook of his arm. Given the uneven terrain, the gesture would not be considered improper, except that George Fitzclarence had a wife. Laurel continually thought of poor Mary Wyndham Fox, at home with the children while her husband pursued affairs with other women.

With Laurel, at present.

She resisted the urge to pull her hand away, or to use it to smack sense and prudence into the man. "I have no doubt," she said evenly, "that the Summit Pavilion will prove highly profitable."

"Oh, but my d-dear, this means infinitely more to me than mere m-money. I wish to contribute to this city, to help create a thing of c-consequence. A legacy, one m-might say."

He looked out over the distant spires, his face suddenly younger, animated, filled with dreams.

Her heart gave an involuntary squeeze. "A most noble goal, sir. I do believe the venture will prove a great credit to such aspirations."

"Do you expect they'll erect a p-plaque in my name somewhere on the p-property?"

Good heavens, were those tears in his eyes? Did a slight tremor accompany his words?

Was this vulnerability to be believed, or had he inherited his mother's acting talents? Smoothing a frown of puzzlement, she replied, "I am certain of it. Given your partnership with Monsieur Rousseau, you are certain to succeed."

Beneath her hand, his forearm tightened. From the corner of his eye, he stole a peek at the French scientist standing by Lord and Lady Harcourt, Julian Stoddard, and several others. "Partnership? Ah, you m-mean my investment in his elixir. You will have a s-second chance to sample his formula before we leave here today."

Laurel gazed up into his protruding brown eyes, grown heavy-lidded with wine. He had forgotten their talk at the theater, she realized, when he had admitted to collaborating with Rousseau, and others like him, to usher in a "new age."

He had been in his cups then, too, and could not keep his stories straight. Which was the truth? If his interests truly lay in establishing a meaningful legacy, why would he lie about his relationship with Rousseau?

"Are you certain you're feeling better?"

While Giles Henderson explained the system of cisterns, piping, and pumps that would redirect the thermal system running beneath the hillside into the Summit Pavilion's future bathhouses, Aidan walked beside Melinda at the edge of the crowd. "If you're tiring, I'll accompany you home."

With a coquettish gesture, she tossed her head. "Don't be silly. I feel glorious. Who would not on such a day?"

Aidan glanced out over the western sky where somber clouds were gathering. "As long as those thunderheads keep their distance." He looked back at Melinda, taking in the brightness of her eyes and the restored glow to her complexion. "You do look exquisite, and young enough to tempt a man half your age."

"Perhaps more of those will return to Bath once the Summit Pavilion is built."

"Perhaps," Aidan said. Then a sharp male voice drew

his attention to the front of Henderson's audience. "But it appears not everyone shares your exuberance."

"Would it not be easier to place the spa at the base of the hill?" Geoffrey Taft was complaining again. "Perhaps with simpler engineering the project would not have suffered repeated delays."

"But in so doing, we would lose this unparalleled view." Henderson swept an arm out wide.

"I shall admit to having entertained similar qualms," Devonlea spoke up. "But our Mr. Henderson is correct. If mere facilities sufficed, Bath would not have ceased flourishing in recent times. Nowadays people prefer to spend their leisure in exceptional surroundings."

"What do you think?" Melinda whispered to Aidan. "Were they wise to pick this location, or will these feats of engineering prove impossible to achieve?"

"Good questions both." He offered his arm, and with a fond smile she leaned lightly on him as he led her farther from the crowd. "But what most sparks my curiosity is what possessed you to give up this land."

Melinda went still, her features frozen in chagrin. "How did you know?"

He raised an eyebrow in answer.

She pursed her lips. "Even as a small child, you were far more observant than anyone ever gave you credit for."

"A person learns a lot simply by being quiet, and one can never be sure what knowledge will prove useful in the future." He brought them to a stop, removed her hand from the crook of his arm, and held it between his own. "So . . . the land. Why did you sell it? Surely your finances are not—"

"Dear me, no, I am in no financial difficulty. And I did not sell the property. I donated it."

It was his turn to be dumbfounded. "You *gave* it away?"

"*Traded* would be the more precise term, in exchange

for a sizable share in the Summit Pavilion. Oh, don't look like that. Bath is my home, and I believe in this project. Its success will ensure a great future for the city."

"Melinda, it is a risky venture at best. Why didn't you seek my counsel? Did you at least have one of your sons-in-law look over the records?"

Anger sharpened her expression. "Need I remind you I am no child, and Fenwick House and all its property belongs to me outright, to do with as I see fit."

He studied her. So this was the business she had been conducting with the Bath Corporation, the donation of the land upon which the Summit Pavilion would be built. *If* it was built.

And she had clearly not intended for him to know.

"Why didn't you mention this?" he asked. "Don't you trust me?"

"Of course I do. I suppose I didn't wish to be dissuaded. As I said, I am of independent means and perfectly capable of making decisions for myself. Do you seek outside validation once you have made up your mind? No. Then why should I be expected to simply because I am female?"

"Ladies and gentlemen, if there are no more questions," Giles Henderson announced, "we may now all sample more of Monsieur Rousseau's elixir."

Spurred to action, the footmen hauled a barrel beneath the largest of the striped canopies and pried open the top. Using a ladle, Rousseau himself began filling cup after cup with the foul-smelling water. All around him, excitement eddied through the company.

It was all Aidan could do not to knock the cup from Melinda's hand. How many sham remedies had his father held to his mother's lips in those final months, her body nonetheless wasting away and the family fortune falling to ruins? But he bit his tongue as Melinda tipped her head back and drained her cup. A cup found its way into his own hand.

Across the way, he watched as Laurel also sipped a sample. Her nose wrinkling, she tossed a glance over her shoulder, another to the side. Was she considering pouring the brew into the grass? He wished she would. Fitz placed his hand at the bottom of her cup and gave a nudge of encouragement. Laurel raised the brim to her lips, shut her eyes, and drank.

Something inside Aidan's chest tightened painfully. The woman perplexed him, raised his suspicions, angered him . . . yet all he wished to do was protect her. Yesterday, she had nearly brought a Home Office operation to ruin, yet his foremost instinct had been to ensure her safety.

Moments like these reminded him that his position with the Home Office often rendered him powerless to safeguard those he cared most about. He could not confide in any of them: not Melinda, Beatrice, Fitz . . . not Laurel, either. He could not explain why he suspected this elixir and the entire Summit Pavilion were fraudulent. He could only go on pretending ignorance until he stumbled upon enough evidence to bring the perpetrators to their knees.

Had Melinda been swindled out of valuable acreage? Were they all now ingesting poison? He had no choice but to remain silent, keep watching, and hope he found the answers before any real harm was done.

He raised his cup and drank.

Chapter 15

L ike fine brandy, the elixir spread warmth and a pleasant tingle through Aidan's body. He felt no ill effects, nothing that would lead him to suspect the water
held anything but the ingredients Claude Rousseau had
claimed.

What had he been so worried about? That the past,
his mother's wretched ordeal, would repeat itself? Or
that Melinda's illness at the Pump Room had been
caused by the elixir? Around him, he saw no evidence
of that being the case, nothing but high spirits and lively
conversation punctuated with laughter.

He could not deny the elixir's immediate positive effects. He felt buoyant and energized, as though he could
easily sprint a mile or go several rounds in the wrestling
ring.

Now, there was a thought. He hadn't wrestled since
university. What on earth made him think of it?

Melinda studied him as a half smile played about her
lips. "Well?"

"Perhaps there is something to this after all." The
breath he drew deep into his lungs sent a quivering rush
of vitality to his muscles. "I feel extraordinary."

"And now you understand the excitement that has
taken hold here in Bath."

"The list," he said. "You have been on it all along, meaning you've taken regular doses."

"Yes, and except for a bout of fatigue brought on by overexerting myself, I have never felt better."

Aidan nodded, deciding to dismiss the tiny, nagging doubt that persisted in a far-off corner of his mind.

A crack of thunder ripped across the hillside. Melinda jumped. Several ladies cried out in alarm, followed by nervous laughter.

"Thunder in March? How very odd." Lady Harcourt waddled to a corner of the pavilion and peered out at the sky. Her several chins jiggled in urgency. "Good heavens, it is time for us to take our leave. I fear the storm is nearly upon us."

The company fell to disorder as people scrambled for their belongings and shouted orders for their drivers to raise the folded carriage tops. As the first fat drops fell, Melinda's footman came running with an umbrella.

"Ye don't want to be catchin' your death, milady."

Melinda ducked under the umbrella. "Where is Laurel? I don't see her."

Aidan didn't see her, either. In the confusion, he spotted his three cousins climbing into their parents' sturdy brougham. Fitz handed his sister into her barouche, then climbed in behind her. Devonlea followed him in and shut the door. Margaret Whitfield let out a screech as she and Captain Taft made a dash for his curricle.

The rain fell heavier, slashing at an angle across the hills. Water slid off the striped canopies in sheets, while gusts of wind threatened to upend the steel and canvas structures.

Aidan turned back to Melinda and raised his voice to be heard. "You go. I'll find Laurel and see that she gets home safely."

She hesitated, seeming about to argue the matter. Then she nodded and hurried off with her servant beneath the umbrella.

Heedless of the rain, the dripping footmen continued packing away picnic supplies and dismantling the pavilions. In the midst of their activity, a figure in dusty rose stripes appeared. Like a flower tossed along by the wind, Laurel ran, or tried to run, fighting the drag of her skirts through the grass.

Aidan hurried to her. "I sent Melinda on ahead." He took her hand. "My cabriolet is this way. I'll take you home."

Hunched against the driving rain, she frowned at him from under her sodden bonnet. Assuming how wretched she must feel, he moved with her as quickly as possible across the saturated terrain.

His vehicle stood alone on the empty plateau, abandoned by the others, though he could hear the creaking descent of the last few making their way down to the road. He was relieved to discover that someone had obligingly raised the canvas roof of his cabriolet and the seats had remained relatively dry. The horse stood quietly, oblivious to the change in the weather.

"Would you like to sit in the back?" he asked Laurel, reaching to open the door for her.

She shook her head and climbed up into the front seat. He slid in beside her.

Untying the velvet ribbons beneath her chin, she removed her dripping hat and tossed it onto the seat behind them. "I fear for your upholstery. We are quite soaked through."

"Never mind the upholstery." He struggled out of his coat and draped it around her shoulders. "Sorry it's wet, but it's at least another layer between you and the draft."

"No, it's lovely, thank you. Quite dry inside, actually." Wiggling her arms into the sleeves, she hugged the garment tighter around herself.

Watching her snuggle inside his sleeves proved oddly arousing, sparking protective, possessive instincts. He wished she were in his arms instead of inside his coat. Hunkering low on the seat, she gave a little shiver, and he felt a nudge of shame. How could he entertain such notions when his first concern should be to whisk her somewhere warm and dry?

"Are you all right?" he asked as he set the horse in motion.

Instead of the brave but quivery reply he expected, she surprised him by turning a beaming face to his. "I feel splendid. You?"

He grinned. "Damned if I don't feel splendid, too, now you mention it."

"Thank goodness for the rain, for I'd become most eager to see the end of that picnic. I'd grown intolerably weary of the entire affair."

The statement piqued his curiosity, and he wondered where she'd been. Needing all his concentration to maneuver the carriage down the rain-slick hillside, he kept the question to himself. When they reached the bottom, the rear panel of Geoffrey Taft's curricle could be seen lumbering away down the road ahead. It rounded a curve and disappeared from view, leaving him very much alone with Laurel on the rainy, darkening country road.

The branches of the trees on either side of them meshed above their heads, creating a shadowed tunnel that provided a measure of shelter from the rain. Still, breeze-born moisture found its way beneath the oiled canvas roof. Laurel tilted her face and smiled as occasional drops splattered on her cheeks.

Even bedraggled by the wind and rain, she was beautiful, all the more for being so unconscious of it . . . and of the effect she had on him. Her golden hair had fallen from its pins and spilled in damp, unruly spirals down her back. Her lips were parted and moist, her teeth white and gleaming. At that angle, her chin jutted in a show of pert, pretty defiance of the elements, firing in him a swift desire to touch her. *Kiss* her.

He brought the horse to a standstill and dropped the reins on the seat beside him. Claiming Laurel's chin between his fingers, he turned her head and brushed his lips across her wet ones, darting his tongue over their Cupid's bow curve. She tasted of rain and heaven, a sweetness he could never grow tired of.

At her sigh of permission, he pressed deeper, losing himself in the suppleness of her lips, in the swirl of their tangling tongues.

His senses came alive with a keen awareness of everything around them: the tapping of the raindrops on the leaves, the luscious fragrance of Laurel's skin mingling with the dampness of silk and linen, and most of all the fiery heat generated at the juncture of their lips, coursing through him in wave after intoxicating wave of pleasure.

He wanted more of her, yearned to peel away clothing and mold their naked bodies even as their mouths molded one to the other. Yet he found this mere act of kissing, of not touching any other part of her but her lips, intensely erotic. It heightened his anticipation and sharpened his hunger for her to a painful degree.

For now, though, he gently eased away. At first she didn't move, but sat with her hands folded, her eyes closed, and her swollen lips parted. Then very slowly her golden lashes swept upward and she met his gaze with a look of astonishment.

A perplexed frown followed. "*He* tried to do that, too," she said. "But it's an entirely different experience with you."

Although he'd had every hope of keeping the interlude between kisses a short one, her speech took him aback. "Who tried to do what?"

"Your friend Lord Munster. He tried to kiss me. Can you imagine the cheek?" She gave a soft laugh that made the dimple beside her mouth dance. Looking down at her hands folded primly in her lap, she murmured, "Then again, I suppose you can."

Abrupt anger sent the blood rushing in his ears. "*When* did he try to kiss you?"

"After we sampled the elixir, just before the rain began. That's why I walked off. He made me so angry. Such presumption!" She shuddered and drew herself up taller. "Was Melinda worried about me?"

"Yes, but I told her I would find you and bring you home. This does explain why you disappeared." He scowled at the puddle-dappled road and swore under his breath. "I ought to snap his damned neck."

It was more than a sentiment. Aidan believed that if Fitz appeared before him, he would indeed wrap his hands around the man's neck.

He drew a breath. Good God, from where had that notion arisen? He well understood Fitz's tendencies, which was why he so often stepped in to prevent his royal friend from ruining respectable women. Aidan did so as a matter of course. Rarely did Fitz's indiscretions pique his temper this way.

Laurel's hand closed over his wrist. "You'd thrash the man for doing exactly what you just did?"

A teasing light twinkled in her eyes, while her moist lips tantalized him. His loins tightened. Wishing he hadn't chosen such formfitting breeches that morning, he took up the reins and hoped she wouldn't notice his body's response to her nearness.

"You're quite right. Don't know what came over me." He clucked the horse to a walk. "I'll take you home now."

She recaptured his wrist, her grip strong and decisive. "No. Not yet. Just drive." Her lips widened in a mischievous smile. "Or better yet, hand those reins to me."

Laurel didn't know what instinct prompted her to make such a brazen request. Talk about cheek! It was one thing for a widow to ride with a man in an open carriage in plain view of a dozen other carriages. It was quite another to set off down a deserted country road with him. But she could no more have swallowed the impulse than she could have stopped breathing.

With his shoulder pressed against hers and his taste still fresh on her lips, she felt effervescent, slightly feverish, tingly . . . and, heaven help her, reckless, as though she were riding the crest of a tall wave racing toward an unknown shore.

For an instant his gaze smoldered over her, his sculpted features as majestic as the hills surrounding them on all sides. His own rogue's grin blossoming, he faced front, guided the horse in a wide half circle, and passed the reins into her hands. Then he reclined against the seat, propped an ankle on his knee, and crossed his arms over his chest. "Well?"

She tipped her chin. "Do you trust me?"

"Implicitly. Do you trust *me*?"

At that moment, she did. With a laugh she clucked the horse to a trot, quickly widening the distance between them and the outskirts of Bath. Soon they entered the vast, sloping patchwork of the southern Cotswold Hills, where the pale greens of early spring sprouted in the sheltered river valleys.

His question echoed in her mind. *Do you trust me?*

The true question was, did she trust herself with him?

She urged the gelding faster, harder, and the animal responded with an eager burst. The road streaked beneath them while the countryside blurred on either side. Laurel laughed again as the wind sent her hair streaming out behind her. Her sodden skirts adhered to her legs, the hems fluttering to reveal her tasseled boots and silk stockings.

Did Aidan notice?

A quick glance confirmed that her ankles commanded the better part of his attention, a circumstance she found immensely satisfying. Still laughing, she gave the horse full rein. They rumbled along the dirt road, the wheels raising splashes, until they hit a bump that sent the vehicle bucking into the air and jolting down hard.

Laurel's teeth clacked together, sending stars dancing before her eyes.

"Whoa there!" Aidan's arms instantly encircled her. His hands closed over hers and he pulled back on the reins to slow the horse to a walk. He didn't remove his arms from around her, but continued to hold her, wrapping her in a delicious cocoon of masculine sensuality. "Are you all right?"

"Yes, fine. I'm sorry I lost control. . . ." She couldn't resist sinking back against those massive shoulders, that hard chest. He felt so warm and heavenly and made her feel so safe. . . .

His lips nuzzled her hair with a tenderness that triggered a firestorm of yearning. Her body suddenly straining to be touched, she twisted half around and raised her face to his. His arms tightened around her middle as he bent over her and took her mouth. He ravaged her lips, his tongue parting them with an intimate demand she had no power or wish to deny.

And his hands . . . oh, with her side pressed to his chest, his hands roamed the front of her bodice, molding to the shape of her breasts through her corset before plunging lower and gliding over her waist and abdomen and hips.

Inside her, taut cords stretched to snapping, tugging mercilessly at her female places until her nipples hardened to sensitive peaks and aching heat claimed her lower regions. A tiny caution warned that as easily as she had lost control of the carriage, she could lose control of this rising passion . . . and of herself.

Rather than heeding that voice, she placed her hands over his to guide him in the pleasure he brought her, sliding them down over her skirts to trace the lines of her thighs, and then back up again.

The reins having fallen, the horse ambled to the side of the road and ducked its head to graze on the coarse weeds. As he munched, his motions rocked the cabriolet in a lulling rhythm. Her skin on fire, her passion inflamed, Laurel turned in Aidan's arms until her breasts came flush against his chest.

A cool draft grazed her calves, then her knees. Her heart stood still as Aidan tunneled a hand beneath her skirts, his palm and splayed fingers igniting a blaze along her leg. Her heart lurched to a hammering pace. As when she had urged the horse to a near gallop, she felt breathless, ecstatic, filled with giddy anticipation.

In some corner of her mind, she noted that the sun had dipped behind the hills and the rain had stopped, its steady hiss replaced by the chirping of the evening's first crickets. Soon night would descend to cloak them in darkness. If they tarried much longer, how far might this go?

She did not wish to leave.

Aidan's hand abruptly stilled and his mouth broke away from hers. The startled look on his face brought Laurel up short. "What's wrong?"

With a frown he tipped his chin at the horse. The animal had abandoned its roadside feast and stood with its head high, ears pricked and alert, nostrils quivering.

"Someone is coming." With deft motions Aidan disentangled himself from her skirts and seized the reins from off the floorboard.

An instant later a rumbling heralded the approach of a carriage from the north. With the skill and speed of a master horseman, Aidan turned the animal sharply about and set him at a brisk trot toward Bath.

"Your hat," he said.

Laurel's hands went to her hair, fallen in a tangle down her back. Twisting, Aidan reached to the seat behind them and managed to catch the brim of her bonnet between two fingers. He dropped it into her lap. With

trembling fingers she coiled her hair in a knot at her
nape, set the bonnet on her head, and tied the soggy ribbons beneath her chin.

"Presentable?"

"Give your skirts a shake."

As she complied, he straightened his coat and
smoothed a hand over his hair.

Moments later, a barouche overtook them. As the
vehicle swung around to pass them, a gentleman inside
peered at them through the window and waved a greeting. Laurel and Aidan waved back, then faced forward
as though nothing scandalous marked their outing.

The skies darkened to purple during the ride back
into the city. Aidan said nothing, his jaw tight, arms
tense, eyes intent on the road. His silence threw Laurel
into a misery of confusion and embarrassment. Did he
think her loose, a trollop? What had possessed her to
behave in such a rash, untoward manner?

But a single glance at his powerful physique and taut
features raised an echo of the passion that had driven
her into his arms, and she knew that at the slightest sign
from him—a word, a look, a touch—she would be back
in his arms.

"I asked you if you trusted me," he said suddenly,
startling her. He continued to face forward, his profile
rigid and grim. "It was a question I should have asked
myself." He glowered at the road. "I cannot trust myself
with you, Laurel. I am sorry."

Knowing full well that the blame for what had happened rested as firmly on her own shoulders, she looked
down at her trembling hands. "You have been called a
rogue in my hearing, but what sort of rogue apologizes
for living up to his reputation?"

"Even a rogue follows his own set of rules."

She shook her head. He was as much a villain as she
was a widow.

What was he, then?

Even the way he had maneuvered the horse, with such urgent precision, led her to conclude that he was not like other men of his class. She remembered the disguise he had worn yesterday when he'd gone to Avon Street, raising her suspicions that he was a member of some radical political faction. But she also thought of how he had questioned her about her past, how he had questioned others about the new spa, the elixir. . . . A memory flashed in her mind of his vehemence when he had attempted to dissuade her from sampling Rousseau's elixir.

Suddenly she understood, at least partly. Like her, she was investigating . . . something. Something to do with the Summit Pavilion. But for whom? And why?

She said nothing of her realization as the pitted country road gave way to the paved streets of the Upper Town. Questioning him would have only invited further interrogation about herself and the circumstances she had sworn not to reveal. The crown had yet to rest securely on the new queen's head, and Victoria could ill afford to have her family difficulties aired publicly.

Where Walcot Street turned into Northgate, Aidan slowed the carriage to accommodate the pace of the other vehicles on the road. Bath's thoroughfares were filling with evening traffic as the inhabitants set out for balls and fetes and theaters.

They continued south, nearing Laurel's lodging house in Abbey Green. Soon she would have to leave him, and spend the remainder of the night alone with the mystery of who and what he was.

And why his merest touch sparked her uncontrollable passion.

As they swung past the Grand Parade overlooking the river, she could not resist one last touch before they parted. Reaching up, she stroked the curve of his cheekbone with her fingertips.

He flinched, but she refused to pull away. Instead

she grasped his chin and turned him to face her. "You mustn't blame yourself for what happened. I was just as much at fault."

He said nothing, but drove the carriage onward with a steely resolve that left her bewildered. He seemed so angry. At her? Himself?

They came around York Street, then Stall, and on treelined Abbey Great Street, the approach to Abbey Green, he brought the carriage to a halt.

Though Laurel continued to hear other horses and buggies bumping along Stall Street, all lay quiet and dark on Abbey Great Street and on the green up ahead.

Aidan grasped her face in his hands. "I lost control back there."

"So did I."

The scowl that had not eased during the ride now deepened. He pressed closer, not intimately, but relentlessly. "You do not understand. Make no mistake, Laurel, I want you. Were you any other sort of woman we would not now be sitting a stone's throw from your lodging house. We would be at *my* house, in my bedroom. In my *bed*. We may end there yet, but not this night."

Her breath caught, and her insides quivered at the images evoked by his stern assertion. "Oh, I—," she began, but he cut her off.

"Don't speak. Listen." He released her face and lifted her hands in both of his. "You are *not* the sort of woman I take to bed. You are the sort whom I make a point of avoiding. Always. As I said, even a rogue follows certain rules. Except today. Today, I lost control. Damn it, Laurel, I might have pulled you into my lap and taken you right on this very carriage seat. And that, by God, is no way to make love to a lady."

His vehemence drew a gasp from her lips. The images conjured now were stark, coarse, infinitely shocking. To lose her virginity on a carriage seat, exposed to the elements . . . oh, but silently, shamelessly, she continued to wonder if she would have stopped him.

His jaw clenching, he gave her a shake. "I swear, I do not understand it. All I know is that you are not safe with me. This is no game, Laurel. Because with you, I simply cannot be trusted."

Of all the lies either of them had told, that was the most dishonest. She did not believe for a moment that he would harm her. Honor would compel him to turn her away long before that ever happened, just as he did now, when he prompted the horse forward and brought her to the steps of her lodging house.

He descended from the carriage and offered his hand to help her down. Barely looking at her, he stood like a soldier at attention, his features tight and pained and angry. Distance, murky and immeasurable, yawned between them.

She wanted to span that distance and put her arms around him, kiss him, reassure him, and convey the depths of her confidence in him. The closed look on his face prevented it, and sent her silently but swiftly up the steps, where she fumbled with the latch, obscured by the tears burning in her eyes.

Chapter 16

His feet propped against the cupboard that held his few kitchen provisions, Phineas Micklebee rocked gently to and fro on the back legs of his chair. For the past few minutes, he had listened without comment to Aidan's account of the previous day's picnic: the attendees, the details provided by Giles Henderson about the Summit Pavilion, and, most significant, the sampled elixir.

To this Aidan added the phenomenon he had observed this morning when Barclay's Bank on Milsom Street had unlocked its doors. A line had immediately formed in the lobby, one made up of a good two dozen of yesterday's picnickers. While Aidan had watched from a recessed doorway across the street, he had surmised that they had come to purchase shares in the Summit Pavilion.

He had confirmed that assumption with a visit to the bank himself once the initial rush had tapered off.

"It is extraordinary how bearing a title grants me access to all manner of official documents. Being an earl proves highly convenient," he said.

Micklebee rolled his eyes. "I wouldn't know."

Aidan ignored the man's mocking tone. "People all but shoved one another out of the way to be first in line to invest. Even those previously invested in the project came out to sink more funds into it. People like the Marquess of Harcourt, Major Bradford, and my own relations, the Lewes-Parkers. Even cynical Geoffrey Taft seems to have miraculously overcome his misgivings, for he arrived eager to empty his pockets."

"That rather does take suspicion off the man," Micklebee interrupted.

"Yes, and I managed to sidle up to his mistress as she spent her time window-shopping up and down the street. The poor woman had circles beneath her eyes but a smile on her face. Do know what she said to me?"

"I'm on the edge of my seat, milord."

Again, Aidan disregarded the sarcasm. "That due to the elixir, both she and Taft arrived home from the picnic in such high humor that neither of them were afforded much sleep last night."

"Good God." The agent studied him. "Did it have a similar effect on you?"

When Aidan didn't answer, the front legs of Micklebee's chair hit the floor with a thwack. "It did, didn't it? Who was she? Some debutante fresh for the plucking? Or . . . a certain young widow, perhaps?"

"Unless you want to be found floating facedown in the river, you'll discontinue that train of thought. Besides, *she* wasn't anyone, because unlike Taft and pretty Margaret Whitfield, I didn't act on the impulses brought on by Rousseau's elixir."

A partial lie. Yet he continued to wonder whether his ill-advised actions last evening had been caused by the elixir, or if he had simply lost all control when it came to Laurel Sanderson. Yesterday hadn't been the first time. At the Theatre Royal, he had pressed her up against the corridor wall where anyone might have seen them, and had kissed her breathless.

But as he had lain awake last night, it had occurred to him that stolen kisses were understandable. Initiating sexual relations on an open carriage seat bordered on inexcusable, and would have been unforgivable had matters gone any further. Clearly, Rousseau's elixir held more than curative properties.

"The high spirits Taft experienced seemed to have been shared by the others, myself included," he told Micklebee. "Except for an initial warming sensation, the effects were subtle, not like being drunk or drugged. One felt . . . happier . . . and capable of performing extraordinary feats."

"A kind of euphoria, but without any physical disorientation."

"Yes."

"So the same energy that kept Taft and his mistress awake last night might have sent all those others to the bank this morning."

"Precisely what I think."

Micklebee's brows converged, all trace of humor gone from his manner. "So what's in this formula to produce such enthusiasm?"

Aidan pushed out a mirthless chuckle. "I don't expect Rousseau will offer up his secret recipe, and the whereabouts of his lab are strictly hush-hush."

"Then you'll have to find it on your own, won't you, mate?"

Aidan answered the question with one of his own. "Anything on Laurel Sanderson yet?"

A glint of amusement sparked in the agent's eye, but he shook his head. "Give it time. If your lady is hiding something, we'll find it."

"She is not *my* lady."

Micklebee just smiled.

On Friday evening, Laurel learned the true meaning of opulence. She had thought the Assembly Rooms grand, the Theatre Royal ornate. Both paled beside Bath's Guildhall, situated on High Street around the corner from Abbey Green, but worlds away in terms of sheer magnificence.

She had come with Melinda to attend a reception followed by a concert, and as they ascended to the Aix-en-Provence Room on the first floor, it was all she could do to keep from gawking at the carved ceilings and the expansive arches, the gilt-encrusted columns, and the intricate friezes.

"The city's aldermen of the last century had wished to astound their guests with their Guildhall," Melinda said, observing Laurel's stupefaction. "This building stands as a monument to their collective pride."

"It certainly does that," Laurel agreed, having to remind herself not to let her mouth drop open.

Glittering with bejeweled women and silk-clad men, the reception room held a close-packed throng of some two hundred people. Along the walls, refreshment tables offered every tempting treat imaginable. A fountain in the corner captured Laurel's attention.

"Why, it's just like the one at the Pump Room, only smaller!"

"Yes, but this one dispenses champagne," Melinda told her. "Is that not Aidan I see filling a glass for his cousin?"

"Oh . . . it is. . . ." It hurt Laurel to gaze upon him, to see him surrounded by friends and family and looking so handsome in sapphire tails and dove gray knee breeches, his intricately tied ivory cravat set with a diamond pin. He seemed . . . happy.

It had been two days since the picnic, and she had neither seen nor heard from him since then. Would he ignore her tonight? Yes, they had gone too far on the front seat of his cabriolet, but his abrupt retreat had been more than physical; it had been prompted by more than propriety. The emotional wall he had erected between them had been guilt-ridden. He had effectively stifled any chance of intimacy between them, and left her suspecting that he had scrambled to protect his solitary life.

Why?

Not that he appeared in any way solitary tonight. Acquaintances and admirers vied for his attention, including the two young cousins who each coveted the title of Countess of Barensforth.

Jealousy pierced Laurel's side as she regarded the stunning twins, as she begrudged them their place at Aidan's side, a place forbidden to her.

"Laurel, dear," Melinda whispered behind her fan, "you must learn the rules of the game. To stare so openly at a man is to publicly wear your heart on your sleeve, and certain to set tongues wagging."

Disconcerted, Laurel quickly looked away. The countess smiled tolerantly and linked arms with her, and they began a circuit of the room. They greeted Lady Devonlea and Julian Stoddard. Lord Munster kissed her hand but to her relief made no further overtures. For a few minutes they joined a group that included Claude Rousseau, who was discussing his elixir.

Laurel had learned from Lady Devonlea that the scientist would be attending tonight's concert, and she herself had come for the specific purpose of observing the Frenchman and Lord Munster together. She hoped their actions might provide further hints into the nature of their relationship. Were they casual colleagues, or fellow conspirators?

At present she could determine little, and as the man answered questions about his formula, she allowed Melinda to draw her away from the group.

"You know, Laurel, I sense there is more to you than meets the eye."

Laurel received this observation with a frisson of alarm. Was Melinda beginning to see through her masquerade? "I cannot fathom your meaning."

"Then I shall enlighten you." Melinda exchanged a

greeting with an acquaintance, then continued. "I have known my godson all his life, and I can assure you that no quiet country widow has ever attracted his notice before. I am sorry to confess that his assignations are typically of the secretive sort, with socially unavailable women."

"But Lord Barensforth has sought no assignation with me, nor I with him." That might not have been quite true, but Laurel felt certain there would be no future trysts between them.

"Ah, but he is partial to you, Laurel. I see it in his eyes whenever he looks at you. I see it at this moment, for here he comes."

His approach brought on a wave of astonishment and a smidgen of panic. What could he possibly want after the deplorable way he had left her outside her lodging house? Perhaps he was crossing the room with another destination in mind. Perhaps . . .

"Good evening, Melinda. Laurel. I trust you are both well?"

"Quite well, thank you, dearest."

Aidan kissed Melinda's offered cheek, and raised Laurel's hand to the slightest graze of his lips. "I called upon you this afternoon," he said to Melinda, "and was told you were not at home."

"I must have been at the dressmaker's. Why? Had you come to ask me more impertinent questions?" Melinda snapped her fan open and closed and said to Laurel, "Aidan has appointed himself champion of my affairs, and seeks foremost to protect me from the folly of my own ways."

Sensing a private argument between them, Laurel didn't know how to respond. She stole a peek at Aidan and was surprised to encounter a covert flicker of frustration, as if he sought her assistance in appealing to the countess.

"I wished to speak with you," he said. "It is important."

"I'll wait with Lady Devonlea." Laurel started away, but Aidan reached out, almost but not quite touching her arm.

"I'd like to speak with you both," he amended. "But not here. Somewhere private. Tomorrow perhaps?"

"So inscrutable." Melinda tapped his shoulder with her fan. "Come by for luncheon, and you may air whatever matter has turned you so somber tonight. You come, too, Laurel, since this appears to involve you as well."

A quarter of an hour later, they proceeded into the next room, where rows of seats fanned out in a semicircle from the musicians' platform. Laurel and Melinda found seats about a third of the way back and were joined by Lady Devonlea, Lady Harcourt, Mrs. Whitfield, and Lady Penelope Lewes-Parker, the mother of Aidan's hopeful cousins.

Emily and Edwina sat farther along the same row in a group that included Aidan, Lord Munster, Lord Devonlea, and Claude Rousseau. Julian Stoddard sat a row behind them, and for a moment Laurel wondered why the striking young man seemed always to attend these social functions alone. Enjoying his time as a bachelor, she supposed.

She faced front as a chamber ensemble took to the stage and began warming up their instruments. The performance began with a Purcell sonata. Laurel found the nimble speed of the harpsichordist's fingers over the keys a delight to watch. When the piece ended, she turned to Melinda beside her to convey her appreciation. That was when she noticed the empty seats at the end of their row.

Lords Munster and Devonlea, Monsieur Rousseau, and the bright blond head of Julian Stoddard were nowhere in sight. Other seats were empty as well, although she could not remember who had occupied them.

Aidan's cousins were busily whispering and attempting to include him in their discourse. He nodded absently but turned his attention to the doorway leading into the Aix-en-Provence Room. The opening notes of the next piece filled the hall. Aidan spoke to his cousins, adjusted his coat, and made his way out of the row. He, too, disappeared into the next room.

The music faded beneath Laurel's speculation. While it was likely the men had grown bored with the entertainment and had gone somewhere to play cards, her instinct prodded suspicions to the contrary. What about Aidan? Had he left to join them, or to follow them? Once again, her instincts supplied an answer, one that precluded any wrongdoing on his part.

She came to her feet, bending over to avoid blocking the view of those behind her. "Excuse me, Melinda. I'll be right back."

"Is something wrong?"

"No, no. A loose stay is poking my side. I am sure a minor adjustment will set all to rights."

"I'll come with you."

"No need, truly. Enjoy the performance. I shall return presently."

With that, she sidestepped to the end of the row, hoping her instincts weren't about to lead her into the biggest blunder of her life.

From the gallery, Aidan heard the drumming of footsteps retreating across the marble hall below. He moved quickly to the landing and caught a glimpse of the backs of a half dozen men exiting through the street door.

Without retrieving his cloak and top hat, he burst out upon High Street to see the group striding briskly northward. A fog as thick as gruel crawled along the storefronts, swallowing their forms and muting their footsteps.

Darting from doorway to doorway and hugging the building fronts, Aidan trailed after them. He recognized the flash of Julian Stoddard's blond hair, not to mention the walking stick he carried. Recently he seemed to be using it less, and some of the spring had returned to his stride.

From the silhouettes of their flapping cloaks, he also made out Devonlea and Fitz. A snippet of a French accent confirmed that the short one was Rousseau. Aidan strained to discern the other two. Taft? Perhaps. And possibly de Vere, but the mist made it difficult to be certain.

At the corner of Bridge Street, two of the group broke off from the others and headed east. The rest continued north. Aidan knew Stoddard had leased a town house farther along Northgate, and it appeared that four of them would be adjourning there, probably to drink brandy and play a few rounds of whist.

It was the direction that Fitz and Rousseau had taken that interested Aidan most.

Swiftly they made their way past the north entrance to the Grand Parade. The street was deserted. Between the shops lining Pulteney Bridge, the rumbling of a carriage echoed. A barouche came clattering over the cobbles, emerging onto Bridge Street to veer sharply south onto High Street. Fitz and Rousseau hastened their steps, all but disappearing into the viscous fog rolling over the river's steep banks.

Crossing the road, they proceeded beyond the mouth of the bridge to the staircase that led down to the boat slips. The mist engulfed them, but Aidan heard their heels echo against the stone steps. Slipping from the concealment of the Grand Parade, he sprinted diagonally across the road.

He could see nothing down below, but pricking his ears, he thought he heard the swish of paddles maneuvering a craft beneath the one of the bridge's wide arches.

"Spare a shilling, mate?"

He spun about. From out of the mist a beggar took

shape, his hulking form swathed in tattered layers, his face concealed by a threadbare scarf. Menacing eyes peered at Aidan from within deep, shadowed sockets. The man extended a begrimed hand.

"I haven't got any money on me, no." Aidan spoke harshly, hoping his bark of authority would sent the beggar packing. Injecting a disdainful gleam in his eye, he started to push past him.

"You sure about that, mate?" The beggar stepped in his way. A malevolent leer revealed blackened stumps of teeth. A waft of fetid breath striking him, Aidan tensed, ready to defend himself. "Mayhap I should shake you upside down to be sure, eh?"

Shoulders bunched, the footpad moved closer. Aidan didn't wait but sprang forward, propelling his fist into the man's nose. The blow produced an audible crunch. Blood spurted. With both hands cradling the injury, the villain roared and stumbled backward. Aidan made to bolt past him, but a crippling blow from behind struck between his shoulder blades. Pain exploded a second time as a booted foot hit the backs of his legs and sent him to his knees.

Before he could wrestle his feet beneath him, the second attacker, still unseen, thrust a stinking woolen sack over his head. Aidan threw punches blindly, hoping against hope to make contact. His lungs seized at the foul stench clogging his airways. A cold dread seeped through him. Would his assailants toss him in the river to drown?

Through the pain, he half wished they would empty his pockets and get on with it.

A kick sent him face-first into the street. He immediately rolled and by some miracle maneuvered his feet beneath him. A shuffling beside him warned of another attack. He spun, lunged, and made contact with his knuckles against a solid form. There came a grunt of pain, the thud of someone hitting the ground. Reaching with one hand, he tore the sack from his head and prepared to swing again.

A club emerged from the misty darkness. He tried to lurch away, but the weapon slammed into his shoulder. Agony radiated down his arm and across his back. Blackness rose up to swallow him. The attackers, the bridge, and the cold breath of the fog receded into a nightmarish void.

As the crack of an explosion shook the walls of the bridge, he felt himself hitting the ground and crashing into the oblivion of a final thought: he might never see daylight, or Laurel, again.

Chapter 17

Attempting to keep Aidan in her sights, Laurel came around the corner onto Bridge Street. The fog made the task of following him a difficult one, as did the need to stay well behind him so as not to alert him to her presence.

She had almost continued straight onto Northgate, following the four figures who were talking and laughing and making no attempt to conceal their presence on the street. But then she had spied Aidan—mist or no, she would recognize the cut of his figure anywhere—slipping from the shelter of a doorway and rounding the corner toward Pulteney Bridge.

She could not see his quarry, but she knew he would not be wasting his time, as she had almost done, pursuing the wrong suspects. If she could only creep close enough to observe the evidence he managed to gather. He, of course, need never be the wiser. If he knew what she was doing, he would undoubtedly send her straight back to the Guildhall.

She lost sight of him in the swirls of fog. Up ahead, a man's voice drifted on a wisp of breeze. "Spare a shilling, mate?"

The rasp of that voice chilled her through, and goose bumps swept her back. Sharp with defiance, Aidan's reply followed. The first voice came again, spilling words of murderous intent thinly veiled in amusement.

She could not see the men, but she heard a series of thuds and grunts that twisted her stomach in knots of dread. Breaking into a run, she struggled to open her reticule. In her haste she nearly dropped the beaded purse, then managed to tug it wide. She shoved a hand inside, rummaging to the bottom.

Aidan's shout of pain filled her with a terror that nearly immobilized her. She only just managed to close her shaking fingers around the item she sought, the gift Victoria had given her back in London, on the night she had appealed to Laurel for help.

Raising the sleek silver percussion pistol, she fired high into the air.

From within a haze of pain, Aidan felt his shoulders being tugged from the pavement. A moment ago the report of a gun had pierced his eardrums.

Had the bloody bastards shot him?

God, it felt like it. Every muscle in his body, every limb, and every rib shrieked in pain. He wished they would leave him to die in peace, wished they would cease pulling and pushing at him. He supposed they were harvesting everything of value on his person before they let the rushing river current erase the evidence of their crime.

He suffered bone-shuddering misery when he was unceremoniously rolled onto his back. But when he expected a pair of rough hands to grab him beneath the shoulders in preparation of hauling him over the bank, cool, petal-soft fingertips swept across his brow instead.

"Aidan . . . Aidan? Oh, please, can you hear me? Be alive. Oh, God, please let him be alive."

A gentle weight pressed against his chest, followed by a butterfly's touch against his throat. A soothing, flowery scent mingled with the metallic taste of blood at the back of his throat.

"Laurel?" Her name came as a croak. He swallowed and drew a painful breath. "Go. Not safe. They . . . may . . . be back."

"They ran away. But don't speak. I'll . . . I'll go and find help."

He raised a hand, closing his fingers around the first thing within reach—a fold of her dress, he thought. "Stay. Have I . . . been shot? Do you see—"

"No," she insisted before he could finish the thought. "It was my gun you heard. I fired into the air and frightened them off."

What? A *gun*, in Laurel's possession? No, he was delirious. "Help me up," he said.

"Do you think you should?" She sounded desperate, distraught. He must look ruinous.

Releasing whatever fabric he'd latched on to, he tried again and this time grasped her arm. She in turn managed to get a firm grip on him. She let him use her for leverage as he sat up. He tried but couldn't quite suppress the groan that accompanied his effort. Releasing her, he dropped his head into his hands.

"You need a doctor."

He shook his head and reached for her again. No matter her reassurances that the fiends had run off, he wanted her gone from there straightaway. "Help me to my feet."

She got her own feet beneath her and encircled him with her arms. "This is foolish."

"Can't . . ." A stab to his side momentarily cut off his words. "Can't sit here all night."

But when she attempted to help him up, a realization held him immobile where he sat. He regarded his hand, then felt inside his coat.

"My ring." The faceted sapphire on his smallest finger flashed darkly in the lamplight. "My watch." He tapped the fob across his waistcoat, then felt for his diamond cravat pin. "They didn't steal them."

"No, I told you, I frightened them away before they had time to pilfer anything."

That might have been true, yet another theory came to mind: that they weren't thieves at all, but hirelings charged with guarding the entrance to the boat slip . . . employed, perhaps, by the men Aidan had followed there.

The next minutes were a blur of fog and darkness, of the sudden glare of streetlamps, of leaning his weight on Laurel, an arm slung across her shoulders, and attempting to walk a straight line.

At times nearby voices sent his thoughts swimming in panic. Had his attackers returned? But even as his pulse threatened to pound through his wrists, she whispered assurances.

"Only people on their way to their next engagement, and they appear more in their cups than you do. I doubt very much they'll remember us."

Her observation made him laugh in spite of himself, an act made regrettable by the spear apparently twisting in his left side.

God, how he hated broken ribs.

"We're here. Hold on to this while I fetch the key from my purse." Her arms slipped from around him, and she guided his hands to the cold length of an iron railing.

His surroundings whirled in his vision, a kaleidoscope of creamy building fronts, a bright red door, and the rattling, night-blackened reach of a sizable oak. They all seemed familiar. . . . "Where are we?"

Her arm returned to his waist. "Abbey Green. My lodging house. Be very quiet. If anyone happens to see us, you are my brother newly arrived from Fernhurst. And perhaps we should say you have been in a carriage accident."

"I feel as though a carriage ran me over."

"*Shh.* Steady, now. Mind the steps."

Minutes later, his body bathed in icy sweat from the effort of mounting the stairs to her room, he collapsed across her featherbed. His eyes fell closed. He must have slipped into an immediate doze, for the next thing he knew, a cool, moist cloth draped his brow. Another dabbed at his lip, and Laurel's sweet scent surrounded him with the comforting knowledge that he had survived, that he had not merely dreamed of her coming to his rescue.

"You saved me," he murmured.

He heard a soft chuckle. She continued pressing the cool compress to his lips and cheeks; her warm fingertips grazed his skin.

He risked the pain of a smile. "I like that."

He drifted off again, and was awakened suddenly by a nudge at his shoulder and the whisper of his name. "I have to leave for a while."

No. Not safe out there. Realizing he had only thought the words, he tried again. "You can't . . ."

"I must. Melinda will be frantic if I don't return to the Guildhall, and it is only a few minutes' walk from here. Besides, I must see that Dr. Bailey is summoned."

He caught her hand. "No doctor. Tell no one what happened."

"But—"

"I'll speak to Melinda myself when I see her. No one else must know what happened."

She shook her head, her beautiful face hovering temptingly close. If only his own face didn't hurt so devilishly. "I don't understand," she said.

He smiled again, feeling the sting where his bottom lip was split. "Yellow dress, remember?"

Wariness and exasperation warred across her features. Yes, that yellow dress she wore last summer had become a sort of code between them: *Ask me no questions, and*

I'll tell you no lies. It meant they both harbored secrets neither was willing to divulge.

He couldn't be certain, but he believed she swore at him under her breath. Conversely, she laid her palm ever so gently against his cheek. "I'll be back as soon as I can."

Laurel awoke to the prod of dawn through the diamond-paned window beside her and the startling proof that nothing about last night had been a dream.

Aidan lay sprawled faceup in the middle of her bed, his soft snores filling her with an odd sense of content-ment. When she had returned from the Guildhall last night, she had managed to remove his coat, collar, neck-cloth, and shoes and covered him with the counterpane. He had awakened only briefly to catch her wrist and hold it to his lips before tumbling back into a deep slumber.

Rising from the overstuffed chair in which she had slept, she tiptoed across the room to lean over him. She had expected his face to be a mass of welts, but to her surprise, the bruising appeared minimal. A relieved sigh escaped her at the confirmation that his nose had not been broken, that it remained as firm and straight as ever. Purple shadows stretched across a cheek and be-neath one eye, and a swelling protruded above his left temple. A bit of a gouge marred his bottom lip, but with the dried blood wiped away it wouldn't be terribly noticeable.

Of course, that didn't account for all his injuries, and she could only imagine the wounds hiding beneath his shirt. The very notion caused a stirring inside her. The counterpane had fallen to his waist, and unable to resist, she grasped the open neckline of his shirt between two fingers. Gently she lifted the garment and angled a peek lengthwise down his torso.

Her breath quavered. His chest was replete with rug-ged, rippling planes and hollows, a sprinkling of dark hair, and—goodness—two dusky spheres rather like her own, yet nothing at all like her own.

"By that look on your face, my dear, I assume I've passed muster?"

With a cry, Laurel released his shirt as though it were made of hot coals instead of linen. "You might have warned me you were awake."

"You might have warned me you were a Peeping Tom."

"I most certainly am not! I was merely inspecting your injuries for infection."

His grin, however shaky, said he didn't believe a word of it.

Laurel couldn't suppress a rueful smile, either. "How are you feeling?"

"I believe 'like hell' fairly well sums it up. How do I look?"

"Not quite like hell. Like purgatory, perhaps."

He chuckled, a sound cut short by a wince. "I suppose I should send my apologies to Melinda rather than have her see me like this. She had invited us to luncheon, remember? God, how long ago that seems now. Tell me, what happened when you returned to the Guildhall?"

"I made it back during the intermission, and a good thing, too. Melinda had been about to send a brigade out to search for me. I apologized and pleaded an unsettled stomach, whereupon she sent me home in her carriage."

"While you were there, did you notice the return of Fitz or Rousseau, or any of the others who slipped out early?"

She shook her head. "No, and when I remarked on their disappearance to Melinda and Lady Devonlea, their utter lack of concern seemed highly curious to me. Oh, I know gentlemen typically find those sorts of affairs a dreadful bore and are likely to make an escape, but the ladies seemed to want to change the subject as quickly as possible. Aidan, what is this all about? Has it anything to do with the Summit Pavilion? And what prompted you of all people to follow them?"

"Me 'of all people'?" He raised his eyebrows in a show of innocence.

"Yes, you," she insisted. "What is your interest in their actions?"

"I could ask you the same. Do you wish to explain your inclination to follow me, not once now, but twice?"

Oh. Drat him for turning her inquisitiveness around on her like that. "No," she said, then attempted to turn the tables again. "Do you wish to explain why you went to Avon Street in disguise the other day?"

"No. Do you wish to tell me why you wore yellow when you should have been in black?"

She threw up her hands. "That again."

"Yes, the impasse we cannot seem to breach."

They glared at each other. With a groan, Aidan pushed up higher onto the pillows. He grasped her hand and gave it a light tug. "Sit. Please."

Wary, she perched at the edge of the bed.

"Truce?"

She narrowed her eyes.

He destroyed her composure utterly by pressing her hand to his lips, then turning it over and nuzzling her palm. His lips were warm and moist and softly persuasive, with the power to make her fall into his arms and tell him everything he wanted to know.

Almost.

The touch of those lips also delivered a sobering dose of reality. She had secreted a man in her room all night long, a man presently lying in a scandalous state of undress in her bed, with her sitting close beside him. True, she had exchanged her evening gown for a muslin day dress rather than a nightshift, but that would not prevent tongues from wagging should they be discovered. Somehow, she must find a way to convey him away from Abbey Green without anyone seeing. She must....

His tongue swirled over the tip of her middle finger, sending a tingling wave of heat up her arm.

Then, abruptly, he froze, his mouth stilling over her finger. His eyebrows knotted as he breathed in through his nose.

His gaze rose to meet hers. "Powder. I can smell the traces of it. You fired the gun that drove off my attackers."

"Yes, I explained that last night." Laurel pulled her hand away and gripped it with the other in her lap.

"You mentioned it, but you explained nothing." He sat up straighter, until his considerably taller frame loomed over hers. "I don't suppose you'd care to tell me why a lady feels the need to carry a lethal weapon?"

"No." She got up from the bed and retreated to the window, only to hear him in halting pursuit behind her. Although his infirmities slowed him down, by the time she turned around, he was there, inches away.

"I'm afraid denials will no longer do, Laurel." A strange menace rode his murmur and sent a ripple of warning down her back. "The stakes have become dangerous."

"Aidan, I—"

"No more lies." He reached toward her, but his arm dropped as a grimace claimed his features. Laurel gripped his shoulders and guided him into the chair.

"You aren't well. I wish you would allow me to send for Dr. Bailey."

"There isn't much a physician can do for bruises and a broken rib."

"What about the authorities? Will you report the attack?"

To this, too, he gave an adamant shake of his head. "They'll call me a fool for wandering along the riverbank alone at night. And they would be correct."

"So the events must remain cloaked in secrecy."

"Indeed they must." Without warning and with surprising strength considering his condition, he spanned her waist with his hands and pulled her down onto his lap. He winced again. Between gritted teeth he said, "I hereby swear you to secrecy."

"Oh, but I'm hurting you." She started to stand up, but he wrapped his arms around her. As though she were balm for his injuries, he held her in place and leaned his forehead against hers.

"Will you swear?"

In his condition, how could she deny him anything?

"Of course, if you wish it. I swear." Reaching her arms around him, she held him close and gently rocked him as she had once rocked her sisters.

But no, this was vastly different. Mingling with the heat of the rising sun against the windowpanes, the heat of their contact filled her with contentment edged with a sensual promise . . . a promise to be kept once he had recovered. For now, however, this closeness was enough. It made her happy as she had never dreamed possible.

Outside, only the birds twittering in the massive oak broke the silence of Abbey Square. From the streets beyond the square came the thumps and jangles of shops opening for business. Laurel wished the city would never awaken, never intrude upon their quiet, pleasurable companionship. She wished she could remain in the circle of Aidan's arms, against his formidable chest, forever.

I believe I am beginning to love him.

Aidan's head came up, his eyes holding her in their indigo depths, his generous lips parting. "What's wrong? Why did you just flinch?"

"Did I?" She knew she had. Heaven help her, she was tumbling irrevocably in love with the Earl of Barensforth, and the knowledge shook her to the core.

It was knowledge she would hold close to her heart, to

hoard and protect as she did all her other secrets. Though Aidan might not be the rake Victoria had warned her of, and while she believed he desired her, love was another matter entirely, one wrapped in vulnerability and uncertainty. She could afford none of those risks, at least not until she had fulfilled her promise to Victoria.

Seizing upon a change of subject, she said, "About today's luncheon with Melinda. You had something important to speak to us about. Do you wish to tell me what it was?"

His shoulders bunched beneath her hands, and his expression turned somber. "The elixir, Laurel. I believe it is dangerous, capable of making people do things they ordinarily wouldn't. And shouldn't."

A blaze climbed to her cheeks at the memory of their carriage ride following the picnic. A sinking dismay filled her that he would attribute their passion to unnatural influences, rather than mutual desire. No outside force could have propelled her into his arms if she hadn't wished to be there.

He, apparently, believed differently. Thank goodness, then, that she had given no hint of the direction her thoughts had taken moments ago.

Breaking free of his arms, she slipped from his lap. She began pacing the room, pretending to tidy up by opening drawers needlessly and shutting them again. All the while, she fought a quelling disappointment that pinched her throat. "And to what properties do you attribute our untoward behavior?"

She felt his gaze upon her. "Are you angry? I thought you would be relieved to discover there *was* a cause, and that we hadn't simply lost our heads."

"Relieved. Yes. Wildly so." She slammed a cupboard door. The sharp sound fractured the tension that had built up in the room and made her realize how absurd she was being. The tidings Aidan had imparted were vital in nature and deserved her focus.

She paused to collect herself. "I am not angry with you. But if your suspicions are correct, then Rousseau has been deliberately drugging people."

"To help persuade them to part with a sizable portion of their money, yes."

"How beastly. But if it is true, the Earl of Munster is in on it. He all but admitted to me that he and Rousseau are in collaboration." Excitement sent her back across the room to stand before him. This might not be the treason Victoria feared, but a crime of fraud perpetrated by a member of the royal family against prominent citizens would cause the queen untold embarrassment and perhaps significantly weaken public support of the monarchy.

Aidan watched her intently. "He admitted his complicity with Rousseau?"

"Yes . . . well, more or less. He was in his cups at the time and later denied it, but his actions last night seem to confirm it. Where do you think he and Rousseau were going? Do you believe Lord Devonlea and the others who left the Guildhall are involved? If so, we must find proof of their guilt. Perhaps if we—"

Aidan startled her by pushing himself out of the chair. Though pain tightened his countenance, he didn't miss a beat as he grabbed her, drew her against him, and pressed his mouth to hers. His kiss forced her lips open and his tongue entered her mouth, submerging her in a sensual abyss that blotted out the room and all but the pleasure he sent sizzling through her.

Breaking the kiss suddenly, he left her breathless and trembling with desire for more of him. That was clearly not his plan, for he turned away and retrieved his collar and cravat from the bureau upon which she had placed them.

His nonchalance as he fixed his collar to his shirt put her out of sorts. Frowning, she ran her fingertip over her tingling bottom lip. "What was that for?"

"To shut you up, of course." He threaded his neck-cloth beneath his collar. "If there is any proof to be had, *I*, and not *we*, shall see to it. Sneaking about is dodgy business and no task for a lady, not even one who wields a gun."

"I did save you last night, didn't I?"

"You did indeed, and while I am exceedingly grateful, I see no reason for you to continue putting yourself at risk."

"I believe that is for me to decide."

"Is it?" In two long strides he returned to her and kissed her again until the floor seemed to fall away from her feet and she felt in danger of plummeting. Steadying her with a hand at her elbow, he smiled down into her eyes. "Here is a bit of intrigue for you. If anyone else in the house is up and about, go and create a diversion so I can slip away on the sly."

"You are going home to rest, I trust."

"Ah, it is not important that you know where I am going, Laurel." The pad of his thumb made a sensual sweep of her lower lip, while the simmer in his eyes set her skin aflame. "As long as you understand that you have not seen the last of me."

Chapter 18

His ribs protesting, Aidan sucked the sharp morning air into his lungs. He had made it out of Laurel's lodging house undetected, thanks to her asking the maidservant to prepare her morning tea and toast a half hour earlier than usual.

But for the delivery carts, the streets were still relatively empty. He had attempted to restore respectability to his appearance by camouflaging his bruises with a bit of Laurel's dusting powder, but he still garnered a few looks from shopkeepers sweeping their front stoops. Ignoring them, he headed back to the bridge, convinced that last night's attack had been no random occurrence. Even with the firing of Laurel's gun, any experienced thief would have managed to grab his victim's watch fob or cravat pin before scrambling away.

So if they hadn't been thieves . . . what *were* they?

Last night, the fog had swallowed up Fitz's and Rousseau's forms, and they might very possibly have proceeded across the bridge to the other side. For all Aidan knew, Rousseau lived somewhere on the river's eastern bank.

Every instinct, however, sent him back to the steps that led down to the boat slips. An assortment of small river craft bobbed up and down in the current. Aidan made his way along the narrow pier, questioning the boatmen as he went. Had any of them conveyed two gentlemen downriver last night? If anyone had, no one admitted as much. But that didn't mean Fitz and Rousseau hadn't hired a craft to meet them here at a specified time, just as those ruffians might have been hired to ensure that no one followed them.

He remembered the words of the dockworker he'd met down on Broad Quay. *Ol' Will Shyler wandered over there one night to take a piss and never came back. Someone found 'im next morning with his face all smashed in.* That suggested that someone had been guarding the place.

A guarded warehouse and a guarded entrance to a pier were too much of a coincidence for Aidan's comfort. Micklebee had told him to find Rousseau's secret laboratory, and every instinct told Aidan he would find it inside, or somewhere close to, the derelict warehouse on Broad Quay.

A coal ferry, small enough to navigate this section of the river, appeared ready to put out. Aidan hailed the helmsman.

"Going on to the quay?"

"That I am, sir."

"May I hitch a ride?" He flashed a silver coin.

His face shadowed by a low-slung cap and a dark growth of beard, the man eyed him curiously but shrugged. "As you like, sir."

The ferry navigated beneath the bridge's middle arch and then skirted wide around the horseshoe weir that controlled the river levels. Along the way, Aidan considered what he had learned so far.

He had come to Bath expecting to yet again exonerate the man who had been both quarry and friend these past several years. Time and again, the Home Office had suspected George Fitzclarence of conspiring against his country, and time and again Fitz had proved them wrong.

Oh, he engaged in the usual run of victimless crimes such as the illegal purchase of smuggled brandy and tobacco, or fueling rumors to help drive up the price of specific stocks.

This time however, the subterfuge involved more than money. A member of Parliament lay dead and the well-being of some of England's most notable citizens had been put at risk, both their purses and their health.

For Aidan this case went deeper, had become more personal, than any before. Melinda had been coerced into giving away valuable property. And Laurel . . . his chest tightened. Laurel might have been killed last night.

He still couldn't claim to know much about her, not who she really was or why the blazes she owned a pistol. But from everything he had observed so far, he was pretty damned certain she posed no threat to anyone except for unwitting thieves and . . .

Himself. His heart. His work for the Home Office.

A woman like Laurel made a man susceptible in more ways than one. She distracted him and turned his priorities upside down. She brought out fears and furies he never knew existed inside him. The thought of her following him last night, of being in the same vicinity with fiends who would have spared her no mercy, wrenched his gut into knots and made him itch to commit murder.

In his line of business, emotions such as those could prove deadly liabilities, for they robbed a man of his perspective and ran roughshod over his ability to think rationally.

Yes, with Laurel, logic took a backseat to desire.

Broad Quay bustled with morning activity as steady streams of workers scrambled between the warehouses and the docks to load and unload freight from the river barges. Aidan weaved a circuitous path among them, keeping well out of the way. He hadn't dressed the part of a laborer, but at this time of day it didn't seem to matter. These roustabouts were too busy to take much notice of him, and besides, he didn't intend asking questions and therefore had no need to fit in or gain anyone's trust.

Locating the warehouse with the rotting timbers and crumbling roof, he examined the structure from several vantage points before making his approach. His conclusion corroborated the hunch he'd had, that like the boat slips beside Pulteney Bridge, the property went unguarded during daylight hours.

Circling the building, he discovered that the front and rear loading bays were secured with chains and padlocks. The shutters on the building's few windows seemed not merely latched but barred from the inside. Those facing the secluded alley were a good ten feet off the ground. Finding a gap in the building's timbers, he attempted to peek inside. Dusty shafts of light speared through holes in the roof, illuminating a few rectangular shapes shoved into one corner. Otherwise, the place seemed as decrepit and abandoned as the exterior would lead one to believe.

In a rear corner, he found two broken planks. Crouching, he grabbed hold and tugged. The warped wood groaned but gave barely an inch. He would need more than his bare hands to break through.

He found that interesting. This warehouse was sturdier than appearances suggested.

Not wishing to push his luck, he left the quay, continued over to Dorchester Street, and climbed into a battered hackney. He stopped home briefly to freshen up and have his valet, Phelps, bind his ribs and help him change his clothing, as well as further conceal the bruising on his face.

By early afternoon he set out again, returning first to the bank, where he gathered the latest investment figures on the Summit Pavilion. The records confirmed his suspicions that, since the picnic, investments in the project continued to burgeon.

He pressed on to an impromptu meeting with the members of the Bath Corporation. His unexpected and unannounced appearance threw the aldermen into a bit of a panic, but once they calmed, they were able to assure him that construction on the pavilion would commence within the next few weeks. Whether that would prove true or not, Giles Henderson and his associates seemed genuinely convinced of it.

His next stop brought him back to the Cross Bath, where the MP Roger Babcock had died. His visit here served two purposes. While he casually questioned patrons about poor Babcock's misfortune, he also immersed himself in the thermal waters. He left with no new revelations but with fewer aches from last night's beating.

Last, he headed to Avon Street to confer with Phineas Micklebee. Together they considered the previous night's events.

"So, four of them," Micklebee said, "Devonlea, Taft, de Vere, and Stoddard, all went on their way up Northgate."

"Probably to Stoddard's to play cards. I don't consider any of them as suspects. Not even Devonlea. It's Fitz's and Rousseau's actions that garner my suspicion."

"Not surprising. However, don't let your suspicions begin and end with them, milord. I've got a bit of news for you."

"Go on."

"Our man in Hampshire checked with the local parish and found no records of any Sandersons having been born, married, or interred in Fernhurst within this century. Furthermore, there are no deeds registered anywhere in the area on an estate owned by anyone of that name. Sorry, mate, but either your lady is lying or she's a ghost."

Evening had settled over the city by the time Aidan arrived back at his Royal Crescent residence. There he discovered an invitation on his post salver, one that proved as cryptic as the "ghost" who had sent it.

Across town, Laurel stood at her bedchamber window and opened the locket pinned to her bodice. Ten minutes after nine. Swinging a black velvet cape around her shoulders and pulling up the hood, she scampered down the lodging house stairs and out to Abbey Green. A hackney cab flagged by the maidservant waited at the curbstone.

"The Circus," she told him.

Just before she stepped up, footsteps thudded across the green. She peered into the skeletal shadows cast by the old oak growing on the sward. Like a phantom, a figure cloaked in black from head to toe, as she was, darted to the southwest corner and disappeared into the street beyond.

A chill swept her shoulders as she thought of the hooded stranger at the theater. Had he somehow found her? Perhaps he had been at the picnic, or the concert at the Guildhall. The lights at the Theatre Royal had been dim and she had not gotten a good look at him. She might have passed right by him on another occasion, even knocked elbows with him at a buffet table, without recognizing him.

Had he been standing beneath the oak tonight, watching for her?

"Goin' or stayin', ma'am?"

She gazed across the square for another moment, then shook her fears away. How silly of her. Hers was not the only residence lining the square; any one of a number of gentlemen might have been crossing to Abbey Great Street on his way to his evening's activities.

"Sorry," she said, and climbed in.

They traveled north, their progress hindered by the

snaking procession of carriages, horse riders, and pedestrians zigzagging across the city to their sundry social engagements. The congestion thickened as they entered the Upper Town. Laurel's confidence began to plummet. When she had conceived of her plan earlier today, it had seemed a sound one. Now doubts darted through her mind with the menace of cloaked figures.

She had spent the afternoon with Melinda and had come away more determined than ever to find the evidence needed to either incriminate or absolve George Fitzclarence. Armed with Aidan's words of warning, she had tried to deter Melinda from consuming another drop of Rousseau's elixir. To her consternation, the countess would not be dissuaded. Melinda had laughed at the notion of the elixir containing a mind-altering drug, or any properties other than the herbs and minerals that Rousseau claimed made up his formula.

"Dearest, if people behave differently," Melinda had insisted, "it is due to the elixir's restorative properties. A touch of audacity is the natural result of renewed vitality. Blaming brash deeds on the elixir is rather like blaming a murder on the gun."

Despite her animated protestations, the countess had looked decidedly peaked to Laurel, renewing her concerns for the woman's health. She supposed fatigue could still be to blame. Perhaps Melinda hadn't been sleeping well. But if indeed she owed her pallor and pinched appearance to the elixir, then all the more urgent that the formula's true nature be exposed. Laurel had left Fenwick House with a new resolve and a drastic plan that meant breaking part of her promise to Victoria.

She prayed she wouldn't be making a mistake.

At the Gay Street entrance to the Circus, she rapped on the ceiling. The carriage rolled to a stop and she glanced out the window, looking for Aidan. Earlier she had sent a note to his home asking him to meet her here at precisely nine thirty.

She saw no sign of him anywhere along the circular sweep of Bath's most exclusive residential enclave. Few people were about, although bright lights shining from windows and carriages parked along the street indicated that several house parties were under way. Two carriages clattered past hers, raising startling echoes against the elaborate facades of the town houses. A third vehicle exited by the northeast route onto Bennett Street, likely conveying its passengers the short distance to the Assembly Rooms.

Surely Aidan must have received her note. Laurel slid closer to the door, straining to see into the shadows. A low fog swathed the cobbled street, but the mist was nowhere near as dense as on the previous night. The columned facades of King's Circus, divided into four quadrants of attached town homes soaring three stories high, loomed fortresslike and forbidding. Her misgivings mounted.

In her lap, Victoria's silver pistol was a solid weight inside her reticule. She considered removing it and holding it at the ready, but this was not some thief-infested expanse of riverbank. It was King's Circus, home to Bath's finest nobility. The worst adversity she could expect was a show of indignation on Aidan's part once he learned of her plan.

A personal invitation from George Fitzclarence had sent her here, and had earlier prompted her to deliver her entreaty to Aidan. Lord Munster was holding a supper party for a number of intimate guests, and Laurel had decided to seize an opportunity that might not come again.

She now knew that, for whatever reason, Aidan, too, was investigating the earl, the elixir, and the Summit Pavilion. And while she'd had every reason to distrust him when she had first arrived in Bath, enough had changed since then to convince her they were not at cross-purposes.

He had been the first to suggest a truce. Why, then, should they not work together?

Footsteps and the abrupt opening of the carriage door sent her heart thrashing in her throat. Aidan had arrived, but would he agree to her plan or call it daft and send her home?

"I feared you might not come," she whispered as he leaned into the vehicle.

His gloved hand gripped her upper arm. She was hauled along the seat and yanked out of the carriage. A cry escaped her, ricocheting along the building fronts. In the blur of images assaulting her, she glimpsed a black cloak, and a face hidden by a hood with a scarf wrapped high to cover the mouth. Only the eyes were visible. Cold as steel, they sliced through her.

She knew those eyes. This was not Aidan—it was the man from the theater.

Before she could scream for help, his arm came around her, facing her away from him while he clamped a palm over her mouth. The bitter tang of leather made her stomach roil. She raised a desperate gaze to the coachman. Why didn't he help her? The man gaped back in mute fear. Her assailant shrieked unintelligible but nonetheless threatening words. The driver swore and cracked his whip, spurring the horse to a canter and leaving her to fend for herself.

She thought again of the gun in her purse and fumbled to reach inside, but the man slapped the bag from her grip. Panic fractured the last of her hope as he dragged her along the street and forced her into the cave-dark gap between the western quadrants, where the streetlamps didn't reach and where no one would see her.

The hands released her arm, only to grip her shoulders and spin her about. A shove brought her up against a wall. One hand returned to her mouth. The other hovered in front of her face, the leather-encased fingers curled around the hilt of a blade that flashed reflected moonlight in her eyes.

A whimper of terror rose from deep inside her as his hand slid from her mouth to enwrap her throat. Her breath cut short, she didn't dare move, not even to blink. His hot breath chafed her skin. "Lissette . . . Lissette de Valentin?"

"Please." Her voice was a feeble rasp. "I don't . . . understand."

His fingers tightened around her throat. The hiss of his words made no sense until her mind seized upon one she understood—*flamme*—French for "flame."

Did he mean the fire that killed her parents and destroyed her home? When she didn't respond, he drew back. The flat of his palm whipped across her cheek. Her head snapped back against the stone wall behind her, but through her terror she barely felt the sting of the blow.

From within her fright, determination to survive surged. With a strength she hadn't known she possessed, she swung her fists upward, connecting with her assailant's jaw. The shock of it thrust his head back. Laurel lashed out with her knee. A solid thud sent the man staggering backward. He cried out, but just as quickly launched himself at her again.

She screamed and jumped back as his blade slashed through the air in front of her; closer, closer it came, filling her vision. She slid along the wall, trying to evade him. He caught her shoulder and swung the knife. With a loud rent the blade tore through her velvet cloak.

Then, from somewhere beyond the building, a shout echoed. Impossibly, she heard her name being called. Her attacker flinched, went rigid. She seized the opportunity to rush at him, shoving him with both hands. Together they toppled, landing on shrubbery, rolling into soft grass and then onto the cobbled walkway. The stones tore at her elbows and knees. The dagger flashed at the edge of her vision, then suddenly receded as she felt herself being gripped from behind and hauled to her feet.

"Laurel, go!"

Aidan's command sent her to the corner of the building, but the knowledge that he was now grappling with her attacker halted her retreat. The dagger swung between them, flashing in the light of the streetlamps. The tangle of limbs and billowing cloaks cast a gyration of grotesque shadows.

A grunt of pain set Laurel into motion again. She must run to the nearest doorstep and plead for help. As she started for the street, a clanking close behind her brought her up short. She turned back around to behold the dagger bouncing end over end across the pavement. An oath rang out, and Aidan said, "De Vere?"

In the next instant the attacker shoved him against a wall. Aidan sprang instantly forward, but the cloaked figure turned and fled, blending into the inky gloom to the rear of the town houses.

His shoulders heaving, Aidan clenched his fists and stood poised to run. On wobbly legs Laurel scrambled to his side and wrapped both hands around his arm.

"Let him go. Please, don't go after him," she begged.

Aidan turned and caught her in his arms. "Did he hurt you?"

"No, I . . . I think I'm all right."

He raised a hand; his fingers were clenched around a glove. "This slipped off him as we wrestled for the knife."

Anchoring an arm around her, he started to walk her out from between the buildings. A glimmer on the ground caught Laurel's eye. "What is that?"

Aidan released her long enough to retrieve the item. When he straightened, he held up a man's weighty signet ring for her to see. "This must have come off the bastard's finger along with his glove." He stared down at it for another moment, and dropped the piece in his coat pocket.

Beneath a streetlamp, he cradled her face in his hands and raised her cheek to the light. His fingers stiffened, and his expression turned dangerous. "Good Christ, he hit you."

Her eyes misting, she covered his hands with her own. "I suppose he did."

"I wish I'd killed him."

The words chilled her soul. She trembled beneath his fierce regard, and at the thought of what might have happened if he had not arrived in time to save her—again.

A recollection made her gasp. "You called him by name. You knew him."

His hands slid to her shoulders. "No. I only thought I did. He resembles a man by the name of Henri de Vere. But it could not have been him. This devil is taller and leaner." He hugged her close before drawing back again. "This did not have the look of a random theft. Laurel, what did he want?"

She began stammering an explanation that even to her ears made no sense. He set his fingertips against her lips.

"Not now. Let's get you home. Can you walk?"

Only now did she become aware of the pain in her knees and elbows, still throbbing from her fall. But she nodded.

They found her reticule lying in the gutter, and after retrieving the attacker's knife and tucking it into his waistband, Aidan enfolded her against his side and swept the edge of his cloak around her. Grateful that her legs cooperated, she depended on his strength to guide her. Some minutes passed before she realized they were hurrying along Brock Street. When he had spoken of bringing her home, he had meant, not her lodging house in Abbey Green, but his own home in the Royal Crescent.

*   *   *

Aidan believed Laurel's assurances that she had not been physically hurt, at least not seriously, but the bewildered glaze in her eyes frightened him, as did the way she clung to him. Such passivity was unlike the Laurel he had come to know.

Yet what *did* he know about her? Only that the Fernhurst village records listed no such person as Mrs. Edgar Sanderson, and that men with concealed faces dragged her into corners and threatened her life.

Within minutes they emerged from Brock Street and crossed the Royal Crescent to his front door. After pausing to make a few requests of his manservant, Phelps, Aidan brought Laurel up to his private rooms on the second floor. He removed her cloak and settled her onto a sofa close to the hearth, then set about lighting the fire. By the time Phelps arrived with brandy and a steaming pot of tea, Aidan had coaxed a respectable blaze to life.

Pouring tea and mixing into it a generous measure of spirits, he pressed the china cup into Laurel's hands. "Drink this. It will help."

She sipped absently, seeming unaware of what she consumed. Meanwhile he poured more brandy into a snifter and tossed back the contents in a single gulp. Now that the danger had passed, the sting and throb of his own injuries from the night before revisited him with breath-stealing vigor. His ribs especially plagued him. He had determined they were not broken, but one or two might bear hairline fractures.

Even here, where they were safe, he could not banish the sickening images of what might have happened if not for the lucky kick that had dislodged the dagger from the assailant's hand. Before that moment, Aidan had felt his strength fading, a strength that, in his present condition, had sprung solely from determination.

Pouring another draft of brandy, he returned to the sofa and crouched at Laurel's feet. He had so many questions he wanted—*needed*—to ask, so many mysteries to unravel. For now, though, all but the simplest would have to wait.

"Are you certain you weren't hurt?" When she nodded, he placed a hand on her thigh. "I got your note earlier. What were you doing there?"

"Waiting for you." Shaking, her voice held but a wisp of its natural timbre. "I had a plan, you see, for both of us to attend Lord Munster's supper party. I wanted to search his rooms, or rather suggest that you do it. He trusts you...."

"Search for what, Laurel?"

"Documents. Stolen letters that link . . ." She hesitated as if unsure whether she should confide in him.

"You sent for *me*," he reminded her. "So why not trust me?"

"I do trust you." Fingers spread, her hand went to his cheek. "But there are certain things I've sworn to tell no one." She lowered her hand, holding it with the other around her teacup.

If he didn't know better, he would swear that she, too, worked for Lewis Wescott. Of course, he could think of no good reason why the Home Office would have sent another agent, much less a woman, to run roughshod over his own investigation. But she was obviously working for *someone*, which meant his best course for now was not to push her beyond her boundaries, self-imposed or otherwise.

"Very well, then," he said, "leave out what you must and tell me what you can."

She clenched her jaw, continuing her inner debate for another several seconds. Then she said, "It is believed that George Fitzclarence is in possession of letters dating back to before the wars . . . which link his and Claude Rousseau's fathers."

"William and André Rousseau?" Stunned that she should have such information, Aidan sat back on his heels. The Home Office had suggested a sinister aspect to the link between Fitz and Claude Rousseau, and now Laurel all but confirmed it.

Good God, the French traitor and England's former king? What brand of mischief could Fitz be planning with such inflammatory documents?

His eyes narrowed as he regarded her. "Did Lewis Wescott send you?"

She frowned and shook her head. "Who?"

For some odd reason he believed her denial. But how did tonight's events figure into the larger picture?

"What about this villain who attacked you?" he asked. "What does he have to do with what you just told me?"

"I wish I knew. I've never seen him before. At least, not before that night at the opera."

"You mean when I found you in the corridor outside the boxes?"

Fresh fear glazed her eyes as she nodded.

Suddenly remembering the ring they'd found on the ground at the Circus, he fished it out of his coat pocket. "This might give us a clue to his identity."

Laurel took it from him and held it to the firelight. The heavy gold band held an onyx stone, with an inlaid golden crest that depicted a shield divided by a bar sinister, with a fleur-de-lis on one side and a crown on the other.

Laurel went rigid. "I know this design."

Before he could question her, she tugged a delicate gold chain—the very same that on more than one occasion had piqued his curiosity—from inside her bodice. At the end dangled what appeared to be a gold button bearing an insignia identical to that of the ring. "I've had this for as long as I can remember. It is a memento, you see, from my early life."

"What does it mean?"

Her expression became anguished. "That's just it. I don't know. I have never known . . . or I don't remember.

When I was a child, I kept it hidden away as if it were a precious treasure, thinking it connected me to my past and to my parents. How could that man bear a ring with the same design?"

"Do you remember anything he said to you?"

"No. He spoke in French. I never learned French well. Uncle Edward did not deem it a priority in our education. Oh, we all spoke Latin and, of course, German and a smattering of Greek, but—" She broke off, shivering, her frightened gaze darting about the room.

Aidan slid up onto the sofa beside her, took her teacup from her hand, and set it on the side table. Gently he gathered her in his arms. "It's all right, Laurel. I'm here. You're safe." He stroked her hair and pressed kisses to the crown of her head. "You've nothing to fear, I swear."

But he burned to know the meaning of her jumbled response. Who was this Uncle Edward, and the "we" she spoke of?

That she insisted the assailant spoke French brought his thoughts spiraling back to Henri de Vere. De Vere was French, though over the years his English had become almost perfect. Before the bastard had turned and fled, Aidan had glimpsed enough of his face to assure him it was not de Vere, but there had been a resemblance. . . .

"Whoever that man is, he knows me," Laurel said, her voice stronger, her eyes clear of confusion. "He knows things about my past."

"What things?"

"The fire. When I was young, a fire killed my parents and destroyed our home." Her features tightened in concentration. "He said something about flames. He . . . was so angry." She trembled and her teeth chattered, but when Aidan moved to hold her close again, she drew back. "I know him, Aidan. I remember him, or things about him."

"From where?"

"My nightmares."

Setting the ring aside, he pulled her back into his arms, chafing his hands up and down her back to warm her. Despite the proximity of the fireplace, her skin felt like ice. Reaching for her tea, he held the cup to her lips and coaxed her to drink. It wasn't physical discomfort making her shiver, he knew, but a bone-deep fear that gripped her, and he felt helpless to do anything other than hold her and continue to whisper reassurances.

Finally she seemed to relax, burrowing her cheek against his shoulder in a childlike gesture that squeezed his heart. Just as quickly, her head snapped up. Her eyes were large, filled with alarm.

"What if he had hurt *you*? You chased him off this time, but you had the advantage of surprise. It might not be that way next time." She began to pull away from him. "I won't risk that."

"Stop." He tightened his hold on her until she stilled. "I can take care of myself. It was rather more than surprise that frightened him away."

The resistance drained from her limbs, and her lips curled in something approaching a smile. "Yes . . . yes, I believe that. Even last night, those footpads got the best of you only because there were two of them." She studied him, her parted lips glistening in the firelight. "You are no ordinary gentleman, are you?"

"About as ordinary as you are, Mrs. Sanderson."

The tip of her tongue darted over her trembling lower lip, and like a wall crumbling stone by stone, the artifice in which she had cloaked herself fell away before his very eyes, leaving a vulnerable, frightened young woman who needed him, who stirred his every protective instinct and thoroughly claimed his heart.

"Aidan," she whispered, "I—"

He dipped his head and kissed her, intentionally silencing anything she might have confessed. It wasn't that he didn't wish to know. He most certainly did. He just didn't need to hear it then, while he held her so close that he could feel the beat of her heart against his chest. For however long he might preserve the moment, he would not for the world interrupt the hissing of the fire, the rasp of her rapid breathing, and the light smack of her lips against his as he kissed her again and again.

Her shudder brought him to his senses. He broke away, disgusted by his actions and by a desire he could not control. From the start, he had not been able to resist her, not when it was in his own best interests to do so and not now, God help him, when it was in hers.

His eyes fell closed. "I'm sorry. I shouldn't have done that."

Her silence seemed to confirm how much of a cad he had been, but the touch of her fingertips beneath his chin and brush of her lips against his own nullified the charge. He opened his eyes, only to close them again as Laurel combed her fingers through his hair and drew him down for a long, heated kiss that held nothing of fear or confusion and everything of an insistent, mutual hunger that must be sated.

"Yes," she said. "You should have."

Desire came on like a storm across an open plain, with nothing to hinder it—not secrets or fear or social barriers. He hardened with need, with wanting her more than he'd ever wanted any woman. His affairs since he'd joined the Home Office had been part of the persona he'd invented, a necessary deception. For all her duplicity, Laurel was the first woman who filled him with the conviction that neither of them belonged anywhere but with each other.

Yet even as he drank in the taste of her, he felt as though he could never have enough of her, never know all of her. Through her parted lips he swept his tongue, exploring her mouth and savoring the vibration of her moans against his teeth. He filled his hands with her breasts, finding the nipples through her bodice and teasing them until they puckered between his fingers.

Needing more, he smoothed his palms down her corseted sides to the softness of hips and thighs and the firm, mind-consuming curve of her bottom. Lifting her, he molded his hands to the shape of those high, rounded buttocks and wondered how anything could be so perfect, so delightful.

The release of a few pins brought down her hair, a silky cloud of spun gold. He buried his nose in it, dragging her long legs across his own until she sat perched in his lap, her arms tight around his neck, all of her his for the taking.

Dare he?

He slipped his hand beneath her skirts, gliding along the silky skin to her knee and allowing his fingertips the pleasure of tracing its shapely bend. Insatiable, he dragged his lips across her face, her throat, down the fragrant curve of her bosom. His free hand followed, fingers sliding into the sweep of her neckline.

"Laurel, I want you. You know I do, but I want more than kisses and a few stolen caresses. My only question is what, and how much, do *you* want?"

Her bosom trembled against his lips. "I want your hands on me. Everywhere."

"Are you quite certain?"

"Oh, yes."

He brought her hands to his lips and kissed them, turned them over, and suckled her palms. "And will you put your hands on me, in return, or are you afraid?"

A mingling of uncertainty and joy brightened her eyes and daubed her cheeks with fevered patches of color. Her bottom lip slipping between her teeth, she slowly set about unbuttoning his waistcoat, working the knot free from his cravat, opening his shirt.

With each light touch his lust for her mounted, yet he sat motionless against the cushions, tensed but passive, giving himself up to her ministrations and the dark, enveloping bliss of erotic pleasure. When at last she peeled the layers away and leaned to press her mouth to his bare skin, his chest muscles quivered; his blood raced.

Tenting his trousers, his sex throbbed visibly. Laurel saw it, and the candid wonder in her eyes nudged a part of his conscience that was fast turning numb. How innocent she seemed. Indeed, he had even compared her to Virgo, the virgin. Yet at the shy touch of her fingers closing around him through his trousers, his breath hitched and he dismissed all lingering notions of guilt.

He grabbed her in his arms again, swiftly, roughly, making her yelp and grin and arch her neck in an open invitation for him to set his mouth against it. He suckled her skin and slid his tongue along the underside of her jaw, making her squirm and laugh and press herself more tightly to him. God, she was beautiful. Innocent, yes, and at the same time wickedly loose, a fallen angel that had landed smack in his lap.

What on earth was he to do with her?

He hesitated for the duration of two ticks of the mantel clock before reaching a decision that felt as inevitable as breathing. Scooping her up in his arms, he gritted his teeth against the pain in his side and carried her into the next room.

His bedchamber.

Chapter 19

Laurel knew where Aidan was bringing her, and knew she should demur, should put an end to this madness before it spun wildly out of her control.

Too late. Thought and desire meshed into a sensual conviction that silenced Victoria's warnings and any admonishments society might have made, leaving only her body's desperate plea to feel him, know him, join with him in that most intimate of acts.

The fireplace opened onto this room, too, and rich, tawny light bathed the walls, draperies, and hulking four-poster. Aidan stopped beside the bed and lowered her feet to the floor. He held her, kissed her, slid both hands to her bottom, and pressed her to his arousal.

His hands moved higher to undo the buttons down her back. Layer by layer he stripped her clothes away. She felt the fire's kiss on her arms and shoulders . . . her ankles and thighs . . . on her naked belly and finally her breasts. All the while he held her close, keeping her within the circle of his arms so that though she stood naked before him, she felt covered and protected and unafraid.

His lips played tenderly against her own, hot, feathery kisses that lit a blaze at her core. He raised her chin, kissing his way along her neck and lower. She shivered as his tongue traveled between her breasts, as he held each mound in his palms and kissed, sucked, leaving them heavy and tight with longing.

His mouth closed around a nipple, and suddenly her entire world felt delineated by the texture of his tongue and lips. At the light scrape of his teeth, her womb contracted. Her knees threatening to buckle, she let out a soft cry.

Straightening, Aidan stepped back. The flickering firelight caressed his features, smoothing the planes and deepening the hollows. Gilded and shadowed, he was beautiful, breathtaking. Though her limbs trembled with the desire to propel herself into his arms, she waited, spellbound, as he removed his boots and set them aside. Then his hands went to his trousers, his eyes piercing her through the shadows as he undid each button.

He kicked away the last of his clothing. The room around her spun in her vision while he became the center of her focus, her existence. Solid and firm, he was the only fixed image in an otherwise whirling universe. Her gaze dipped to his hardened length standing proudly and imposingly away from the rest of him. Such power, such strength. Her body ached to have him inside her.

A feral glint lit his eyes as he came forward, and her body pulsed with the anticipation of his touch. His chest muscles twitching, his features rigid with pent-up emotion, he framed her face and kissed her. No other parts of their bodies touched but their lips and the faintest brush of his chest hairs across her nipples.

Taken unawares by a surge of passion, Laurel cried out again. All at once Aidan swept her into his arms and dropped her, without ceremony, onto the downy center of the bed.

In a fluid motion he levered himself on top of her. The heavenly weight of his body pressed her deeper into the mattress, compressing the feathers into a snug nest around them.

"Frightened?"

"Not anymore," she said, and meant it. Tonight she had experienced the most frightening moments of her life, but Aidan had saved her, as he had saved her before. Grabbing the chain that still hung around her neck, she yanked it free and tossed it to the bedside table. The treasure she had coveted all her life now seemed defiled, seemed a lie, and she wanted no further part of it.

She wanted only this, only Aidan. "How could I ever be anything but safe in your arms?"

"Oh, but I assure you, madam, there will be no safety for you here tonight." His wicked grin sprinkled goose-flesh up and down her body. "Prepare to be ravished . . . very, *very* slowly."

He began at the tips of her fingers, suckling each into his mouth with tantalizing swirls of his tongue. He nuzzled a moist path along her arm to her shoulder, her nape, then turned her to tend to each beaded ridge of her spine, lower and lower, all the way down to the cleft of her bottom. He touched her in places that tingled and tickled and shocked, that reduced her to shivering delight and made her beg him to stop and then plead for more.

Smoothing her hair away, he eased his body over hers. His mouth worked shimmering magic at her nape while his shaft nudged between her legs and teased her entrance from behind until she throbbed painfully and whimpered her longing into the pillows. Ah, but he didn't torment her for long. Rolling her onto her back, he reached a hand between them, seeking and finding the sensitized flesh between her legs. A finger slipped inside her.

Her cries this time came longer, louder, as bursts of ecstasy hurtled through her body. Bucking against his palm, she clenched and unclenched her fists while her surroundings dissolved into rippling pleasure.

"Laurel, look at me."

She opened her eyes. Her senses felt heightened. Even the fire's glow seemed overly bright, its crackle sharp in her ears.

The beauty of Aidan's smile brought tears to her eyes. "Laurel, darling, this is your first time."

A tear spilled over. Her throat closing around the truth, she could only nod.

"Why didn't you tell me?"

Yes, why hadn't she?

Because she had been deceiving him all along, weaving falsehood into falsehood until even she could barely discern between truth and lies. And because she feared how he would react when he learned the depth of her deception, how he might push her away and turn his back on her . . . forever.

"I am sorry, I—"

He held his fingers to her lips. "You've nothing to be sorry for. Just tell me what I should do, either stop or go on, because, so help me, at this moment I don't know what is right."

No more than she did. She knew only what she wanted. "Please, don't stop."

He hesitated as if still uncertain, still debating. Then with a gentle thrust, he entered her. There was the glide of his length, then a raw, stabbing pain. He retreated, then eased himself deeper inside her, stretching her inch by inch, each time waiting for the discomfort to subside before advancing again.

"So tight," he murmured. "So luscious . . ."

She felt his restraint, the postponement of his release, however excruciating, until he had satisfied her. Retreating and surging, he filled her, became part of her, her body, her being. Pain faded, leaving only his thrusts to carry her headlong into a breakneck passion as exhilarating as it was frightening.

An overwhelming energy built and burst and rippled inside her. He swallowed her cries and lunged, seeking fulfillment by sheathing himself fully and sealing their bodies. The heat of his seed as it pumped into her sent her soaring again, and she shouted against his shoulder, unaware that there should be any reason to hide her rapture, her delight.

Her love of him.

When at last the rapture receded, he draped himself over her. His lips moved across her eyelids, her cheeks, her lips. His body covered hers for a long moment. Then she felt him begin to ease away.

Her hands closed over his shoulders. "No. Stay."

"I'm not going far. I'm heavy, Laurel. I don't wish to hurt you."

"Stay. You feel, oh, heavenly."

He relaxed against her, his muscular weight filling the contours of her body. "As long as you wish," he whispered.

Forever. She didn't say it out loud. But it was a hope that filled her heart, her soul.

With her cheek pillowed on his chest, Laurel dozed while Aidan held her. His thoughts raced as he stared into the fire beyond the foot of the bed.

He had once claimed to her that even a rogue followed his own rules. Well, he had just broken the most cardinal of those rules, for if this had been a first for Laurel, it had been equally momentous for him.

Married women of less-than-spotless virtue, widows who had sworn off marriage, high-class courtesans, and honest, workaday whores—these had been the focus of his sexual exploits since he'd joined the Home Office. All had been women who asked no questions and demanded no commitments.

Would Laurel? He would bet his life she wouldn't. If he had learned anything about this woman, it was that her actions were dictated by pride and a strict code of integrity.

The latter notion brought him up short. Why would he assign such an attribute to a woman who had lied to him at every turn?

But hadn't he done the same? Should he assume that she had done so for reasons any less noble than his?

No, and that made his actions tonight all the more irresponsible, not to mention reprehensible. His work for the Home Office precluded his allowing a respectable woman into his life. Men like him didn't have wives and families. Attachments were a liability and made a man of his occupation vulnerable. Despite appearances, he existed on the fringes of society, observing and analyzing but never truly belonging. People only supposed they knew him, and that made his job both easier and safer, for him and for them.

Was it time to quit?

That such a thought would even cross his mind shocked him . . . and demonstrated the extent to which this particular woman affected him. The prospect wrapped its allure around him as he pictured the two of them retiring to one of his country estates, occasionally visiting Town with their several children in tow. . . .

The idyllic images were shattered by the remembered crack of a pistol and the ghastly sight of his father slumped across his desk six years ago.

With a silent groan, Aidan threw an arm across his eyes and attempted to blot out the blood and gore and the hopelessness of his younger self squeezing his hands around his father's shattered skull, desperately trying to undo the horrific act.

He'd been too late then, just as he had been too late in detecting the financial scam that had driven a broken Charles Phillips to load his gun that day. He could never bring back his father, but now that he understood his talents for rooting out financial fraud, he *could* save countless others from a similar fate.

Would he abandon them in pursuit of his own happiness?

Laurel stirred, her soft exhalation across his chest a stark reminder that the question was not an easy one to answer. What of *her* happiness, *her* needs?

If he had only adhered to his damned code of ethics . . .

Little would be different now if he had. He had to admit that. It wasn't simply making love to her that had thrown his future into a shambles. It was having met her, touched her, held her . . . loved her.

God help him.

Laurel shifted again, the movement ending with a twitch of her shoulders. Her breath caught, rasped. She began to mumble.

"No . . . no. Holly. Danger . . . run. No . . . not safe. Don't speak. . . . Not safe. Ivy . . . go, go through the garden, through the garden. . . ."

Aidan held her tighter, remembering someone once telling him that it was best not to wake a person in the middle of a nightmare. Such dreams usually passed quickly and were instantly forgotten, unless the dreamer awoke suddenly. He kissed her hair and lightly stroked her back in an attempt to soothe the dream away. She startled him by crying out and lurching upright.

From within the tangles of hair that streamed around her face and over her breasts, she stared wildly about the room. Aidan sat up and reached for her, but she lurched out of his arms. Then she seemed to bring him into focus.

"Aidan . . . ?"

He gathered her to him. "You were having a nightmare."

"Oh, God, it was awful." She leaned her cheek on

his shoulder and raked her spiraling hair back from her face.

"Tell me," he whispered. An ache gripped his throat as he wondered if he would ever be strong enough to let her go, to continue in a life without her that now seemed as empty and dismal as a winter's famine. "It might help to dispel the images."

"He came back," she murmured against his shoulder. "He chased me with his dagger and cursed me. He said . . ." Frowning, she lifted her head.

He took her hands in his. "Yes?"

"He shouted at me in French, but I understood him. I should not have been able to, but I did, only . . . it wasn't quite me."

"What do you mean?"

"I was younger, a child. He demanded to know how I'd survived the fire, why I hadn't died as my parents did. He said only a witch could have evaded the flames, and that witches must be made . . ." Tremors racked her body. Her fingers clutched at his hands. "Must be made to suffer and die."

"Good God." The thought of Laurel in such danger, of coming under the threat of so vile a fiend, filled him with an unspeakable, trembling rage, but one masked by the calm of a simple decision. He would commit murder before letting harm come to her.

He looked deep into her eyes. "Are you certain you aren't confusing your dream with reality?"

Her expression adamant, she shook her head. "No. I remember distinctly that he said those awful things to me tonight—those very words. In French. I don't understand how, but in my dream I came to understand him. He is someone from my past, and he abhors my very existence."

Her certainty iced Aidan's soul. Leaning back against the headboard, he drew her beside him and into the shelter of his arms. "I can protect you, but only if you tell me everything, Laurel. *Everything.* Can you do that? Can you trust me enough to finally tell me the truth about the woman in the yellow dress?"

The question seemed so simple, so straightforward, as though it would not derail every promise Laurel had made to Victoria. As though it would not strip her bare and lay her greatest vulnerabilities at Aidan's feet.

Did he even realize how his fingers grazed back and forth across her bare breasts, showering her flesh with tingling goose bumps, or how the tip of his forefinger now circled her nipple with an inferred propriety that cut through all the layers of deception and rendered her defenseless to resist him?

Perhaps he did. Perhaps each seductive nuance served as a tactic of persuasion. Regardless, she owed him the truth, insofar as that truth did not put Victoria, and the monarchy, in jeopardy.

"My name is Laurel Sutherland," she said, looking up at him to gauge his reaction. "There is no Mrs. Sanderson."

He gave no outward sigh of reproach, but gently stated, "Then you have never been married."

She shook her head. "I made that up in order to—"

"No," he interrupted. "We'll save that for now. Let us instead begin at the beginning."

"But I don't know the beginning." As disapproval claimed his features, she hurried on. "I'm telling you the truth. I have no memories prior to my sixth year. That was when our home burned to the ground and my parents were killed. I only know what my uncle has told me about my early life."

"Your uncle Edward raised you?" When she nodded, he smiled faintly. "You and those sisters who may or may not exist, depending on your mood?"

"I have three, all younger. Holly, Ivy, and Willow."

His eyebrows went up. "I heard you speak of Holly

and Ivy in your dream. You also mentioned a garden, which led me to believe you were speaking of running through the foliage."

"We did run through the garden the day of the fire. Nurse brought me out through a tunnel that ran from the wine cellar out to the carriage house. Other servants brought my sisters out."

"Then you do remember the fire?"

"Only vaguely, and only because it is part of a nightmare that has plagued me ever since."

"Again this blending of dream and reality," he mused. "Where were you living at the time? Surely your uncle would have told you that?"

"Yes. Peyton Manor was not far from here, actually. Twenty, perhaps thirty miles to the north. Near a town called Billington."

"In the Cotswolds. Have you never gone back?"

"There was nothing to go back to." An ache of loss spread across her heart—for her home, her parents, and the part of herself she had lost that day. "There would only be the foundation and the charred remains of the outbuildings."

He must have heard the sorrow in her voice, for he held her closer and pressed his lips to her hair. "It is time, then."

Despite the heat of his body against hers, an unnamed dread blew coldly at her nape. "Time for what?"

"To return. Perhaps your past holds the key to the danger in your present. I propose that we set out first thing in the morning."

The prospect terrified her. Returning to her home meant facing her nightmares, meant facing death.

For the first time, it struck her that Uncle Edward's reticence through the years might have been due to more than his sorrow over losing his sister. Perhaps he had believed there were things in the past that Laurel and her sisters were better off not knowing. *Safer* not knowing.

As of tonight, she could no longer afford the luxury of ignorance. If a threat had reemerged from her past, her sisters might be in danger as well.

She pulled up straighter. "You are right. This is something I must do. But can you make time for such a journey? I realize there are vital matters keeping you in Bath, and—"

"I believe vital matters brought us *both* to Bath," he interrupted. "And soon enough, you and I shall come to terms with those matters."

However quietly spoken, the commanding force of that pronouncement wrapped itself around her. Aidan knew she had been lying to him, yet tonight he had gallantly set aside all questions that didn't pertain to the immediate danger she faced. Eventually, however, he would demand more . . . as would she, for he surely kept as many secrets as she did.

Her duty dictated that she safeguard those secrets, though her heart decreed otherwise. But what of Aidan's heart? Would he be forthcoming with her, or would honesty be a one-sided affair between them?

The answers must wait. Wondering where her clothing had fallen, she began to disentangle her legs from the bedclothes.

Aidan's arms held her still. "Where do you think you're going?"

"Back to Abbey Green." At his puzzled frown she explained, "I cannot stay here all night. Already your servants must be abuzz about the woman their master has secreted away in his bedchamber."

He pressed his lips to hers, his kiss punctuated by soft laughter. "Laurel, I have only one servant here, my man, Phelps, who attends to all my needs. I can assure you, I have never known a more discreet soul."

"Oh . . . in that case . . ." She relaxed into his arms, the nudging doubts and even Victoria's admonitions dissolving into the heat of their joined bodies as they stretched out, pulled the covers over them, and made slow, languorous love until sleep claimed them both.

Just as she drifted off, she felt Aidan's lips at her cheek and heard the words *I love you. S*he didn't know whether he had spoken them, or whether she had, or whether they had been merely part of the dream that enveloped her.

Chapter 20

They set out from the Royal Crescent soon after dawn, driving the cabriolet out through the service entrance at the rear of the property to avoid supplying Aidan's neighbors with the seeds of gossip.

By midmorning they arrived at the outskirts of Billington, some twenty-five miles northeast of Bath. Laurel had always considered the countryside surrounding Thorn Grove lovely, but the fairy-tale perfection of these rolling fields bordered by limestone walls and lush woodlands, sweeping valleys, and sudden, breathtaking hills dazzled her.

The villages they passed, built of the same creamy stone as Bath, held similar charm. Yet just as when she had peered out from the proposed site of the Summit Pavilion, she discovered along the neat, winding roads nothing that struck a chord of remembrance. Nothing recognizable stirred in the breezes sifting across the meadows; no scents triggered any deep-rooted childhood memories.

How could she have lived here for the first six years of her life and remember nothing about it?

In Billington, Aidan pulled the cabriolet up beside a tidy coaching inn, freshly whitewashed and thatched. Vibrant flowers lined the path and spilled from window boxes. The signpost bore the image of a bright red fox, and the front door stood open to the brisk morning sunshine.

Entering a cleanly swept public room, they chose seats at a table by a window overlooking a rushing stream. The proprietor brought spiced ale for Aidan, mulled wine for Laurel. She regarded the man's thinning hair and weathered complexion and estimated his age to be some forty-odd years. Old enough, perhaps, to remember a grand estate and the fire that had destroyed it.

"We are searching for a property hereabouts," she told the man. "Peyton Manor. The house is gone, burned to the ground nearly twenty years ago. Have you heard of it?"

"Peyton Manor?" He stroked the grizzled hair on his chin. "Don't strike a bell, ma'am."

"It would have been between here and Chedford, I believe. The owners were called Sutherland," she added, hoping to jog his memory. "They most certainly would have patronized Billington's shops, as well as employed some of the villagers at the manor."

"Sutherland. A common enough name, I expect." The barkeep shook his head. "Still, I can't think of any abandoned properties nearby, nor fires that destroyed 'em, and I've owned the Crimson Fox for nigh on thirty years."

"Does this look at all familiar?" Aidan held out the signet ring for the man to see.

"No, sir." He sauntered into the kitchen, leaving Laurel and Aidan alone.

"Perhaps my parents conducted their business in Chedford," she reasoned, "rather than here in Billington."

Aidan dropped the ring into his coat pocket, then reached across the table and placed his hand over hers. "The house may be gone, but the property won't have walked away. Someone is bound to remember."

"Perhaps, but I wonder if anyone will be able to shed light on why a Frenchman would have any connection with my family." Laurel blew into her wine, waiting for the steam to settle before sampling the fruity beverage. Both spicy and sweet, it tickled her tongue and warmed her on its way down.

"Did your father fight in the wars?" he asked.

"Yes, but that would not explain how the attacker recognized me. Or why he seemed so familiar."

Aidan's hand tightened around hers, and very gently he asked, "Is there any reason to suspect that your parents' deaths were anything but accidental?"

She jolted, nearly spilling her wine. Though she had had a similar thought last night, hearing it spoken so plainly undermined her fragile composure. Setting the goblet down, she drew a breath and forced herself to consider the worst of possibilities.

"Uncle Edward never once wavered in his story. He said the inspectors believed the fire started with a popping ember in the drawing room."

"Could someone have deliberately set the fire?"

Chills shimmied up her spine.

The barkeep returned with wooden trenchers of stewed mutton and hunks of coarse brown bread. They ate quietly, their hands occasionally touching, their gazes meeting across the table. Aidan's presence steadied her, made her feel safe, and yet . . . she felt the presence of an evil specter hovering close by, an unknown entity from her past that was capable of committing acts of unspeakable wickedness.

She feared for her sisters, for herself, and, yes, by association, for Aidan. But she also knew that danger would not frighten him away.

A half hour later, they climbed back into the cabriolet. After stopping to question a handful of Billington's villagers, they continued north. The valleys deepened; the hills became more sheer. In the bend of a river, a watermill churned the currents into a rushing music that echoed across the pastures surrounding a farmhouse and outbuildings. They hailed the farmer, who met them at the gate.

"Peyton Manor? Tween here and Chedford? Can't say as I've ever heard of such a place."

Laurel recounted the directions Uncle Edward had once described.

The man removed his straw hat and passed a sleeve across his brow. "Sounds like the way to Greys Abbey. Not much more'n a pile of stones, the abbey. Very ancient. I can't remember any estate that ever sat near it."

He called to his wife, who had just then exited the barn with a tiny brown lamb in her arms. Her husband explained Laurel's quest. Aidan showed them both the ring.

Like her husband, the woman shook her head. "Chedford . . . you're sure, ma'am? Not farther north, perhaps?"

Laurel combed her fingers through the fleecy warmth of the lamb's coat, then tickled the adorable creature beneath its chin. It gave a weak little bleat and nuzzled her finger. "I'm not sure of anything anymore," she said.

They thanked the couple and drove on. Holding the reins in one hand, Aidan reached an arm around her shoulders and pulled her close. "We'll find your answers. I promise you."

She did not remark that such promises as often as not went unfulfilled.

The day wore on. As the slanting sun stretched golden rays across the rippling landscape, jagged stone walls rose up before them. Tumbling shrubberies and tangles of hawthorn surrounded the roofless structure.

"That must be Greys Abbey," Laurel noted.

They drove past it and continued to Chedford. Again they questioned local residents and shopkeepers. Surely the elderly seamstress would remember Laurel's mother, who could not have ordered *all* her dresses from London. Hard of hearing, the woman cupped a hand behind her ear and urged Laurel to speak up. In the end, she tucked a gray wisp under her cap and shook her head.

Everyone they approached shook their heads. No Sutherlands, no Peyton Manor.

Disheartened, Laurel climbed once more into the carriage and sank back against the plush squabs. "Where do I come from?" she mused aloud.

"There is a simple explanation," Aidan assured her. "But it's growing late and will be dark soon. We should start back to Bath. If you remember anything important, we'll return."

Reluctant to give up, yet knowing he was right, she nodded. Wandering the countryside, especially in the dark, would not magically reveal the details of her past.

When the ruined abbey came into view again, a sense of urgency prompted her to grasp Aidan's wrist. "Stop the carriage, please. I . . . I wish to see Greys Abbey close-up."

"Does it seem familiar?"

She peered at the abbey's remains. "Not exactly familiar, but you see, I've always loved history, and I can only assume I inherited my interest from one of my parents. If we lived nearby, then we would have explored this abbey, perhaps picnicked here on Sundays." Her fingers increased their pressure on his wrist. She could not prevent it; she felt as though she were hanging on for dear life.

In effect, she was.

The breeze felt cool against her burning cheeks, and she realized that hot tears of frustration were trickling down her face.

With the pads of his thumbs, Aidan wiped the trails of moisture away. "Come, then. If we must, we'll spend the night at the Crimson Fox."

"Thank you." She summoned a shaky smile. "Most

men are put off by a woman's tears. Your courage is most commendable, sir."

"Perhaps, but be warned." He yanked her closer and set his mouth against her neck. "My services come with a fee."

The kiss he pressed to her throat smoldered with suggestions and produced in her a tremor of anticipation. She hoped he would not wait long to collect his due.

"There is nothing in this wretched place that I remember. Nothing."

Her lovely features turning stony with pain, Laurel about-faced, swept the length of the sanctuary, and stepped out into the gathering twilight. Aidan followed, wishing he didn't feel so powerless to help her.

They had explored the abbey thoroughly, wandering through the dark and chilly chambers, the echoing passageways and secluded cloisters, the lonely graveyard. They had bent to read the epitaphs scratched into the markers. None bore the name of Sutherland. Little by little, Laurel's eager, hopeful expression fell away until the threat of tears gathered like storm clouds in her eyes.

Her frustration was palpable, but more than that, they shared a rising apprehension to which neither gave voice. Their failure to uncover any link to her past suggested more than a miscommunication between her uncle and herself.

If her guardian had passed on erroneous information concerning Laurel's origins, Aidan suspected he had done so intentionally to prevent her from ever finding Peyton Manor—if such a place existed. And he would wager the man's reasons had something to do with a mysterious, murderous Frenchman.

Laurel stood at the abbey's encircling wall, her hand resting on the curve of the iron gate. Walking up behind her, Aidan slid his arms around her waist. For an instant she resisted as if to pull away. Then the breath whooshed out of her and she relaxed against him.

"I was so certain this abbey would trigger a recollection. If we lived close by, surely I would have played here with my sisters. My mother would have brought us here to gather wildflowers. Or I might have ridden past it with my father. He used to take me riding, you know; Uncle Edward told me so. . . ."

A sob echoed inside her but she fought back the tears. Then she pulled up taller and raised her chin as if scenting the air. "I feel no affinity whatsoever for this place. I wish I'd never come to the Cotswolds."

"Laurel." He closed a hand over her shoulder.

She spun about to face him. "Do not tell me I'll find my answers. Make no more false promises."

He waited for the echo of her resentment to fade into the trees. "I was merely going to suggest that we leave."

Her shoulders falling, she bowed her head and spoke to the gorse sprouting around the gatepost. "Forgive me. This should not be your concern."

"After last night, your problems are mine." His heart pounded against his chest wall. What was he saying? It was one thing to lend his assistance for a day, even two, as he might have done for anyone in need. It was quite another to offer the sort of commitment his words implied.

Too late to take them back. Laurel launched herself into his arms and kissed him full on the lips. His response was immediate and unconditional, drowning out logic and resolve and the best of intentions. With the same need with which the budding leaves overhead would open to life-giving rain, his lips parted to the prodding of her tongue.

"I felt so lost, orphaned all over again," she whispered between kisses. "The desolation that has haunted me for most of my life crept over me again today until I thought I would drown in it." Her lips moved urgently against his. "When your arms are around me, the desolation lifts and I feel as though I am home at last."

Their kisses became frantic, imperative. Together they stumbled through the gate and sank to the springy moss beneath the wide, bare branches of an ancient yew.

Aidan's blood rushed, echoing the current of a nearby stream. Like water over rocks, he felt himself plunging into a maelstrom of sensation. How could this be? After last night, how could lust rise up so abruptly and powerfully, as if he hadn't lain with a woman in weeks?

Laurel wasn't just any woman—not like the others, mere placeholders for what his heart craved. No, she filled the hollows inside him as no other woman ever did or could.

And that could lead them both straight into danger. Him, because she would become his Achilles' heel, his one vulnerability in a life that permitted none; and her, because she would learn too much about him and his business and thus would become a potential target should his double life ever be discovered.

Love was a luxury he'd agreed to give up when he joined the Home Office. At the time, it hadn't been a hard choice to make.

"Confound it, Laurel. Why can't I resist you?"

"I don't wish you to."

"No? You would if you knew what was good for you." He pressed her to the earth, dipping his face hungrily to her throat. Straddling her waist and sitting up, he gripped the edges of her carriage jacket and opened it with a single rending motion.

She had the audacity to smile up at him and slowly, *very* slowly, trace her bottom lip with her tongue.

"Is that so?" He yanked her bodice and camisole down, exposing her breasts to the evening air. Reaching behind him, he dragged her skirts up and burrowed a hand beneath them.

She made pleasure sounds that silenced his twinges of

conscience. Leaning over, he untied her bonnet, tossed it away, and pinned the golden hair that came loose to the ground. "Look at me."

Her eyes were storm-ridden with joy and entirely permissive.

"Another man, a better man, would have walked away long ago."

"I wouldn't be here with any other man."

Her assertion maddened him, filling his heart and lancing his lower regions. The latter spawned an instinct to be a scoundrel and simply impale her.

His heart won out, and he eased off her. When her brow creased, he grinned and lifted a slender booted ankle. Little by little he worked his way up her silk-clad leg, lips first. He spread her thighs as he went, and then he leaned close, tugging her drawers aside and using his lips and tongue to open her.

She raised her hips to meet him, her body undulating with each suckle and prod. The last of the sunlight turned her hair to liquid gold, the glistening down between her legs to threads of amber.

His breath caught. He had never seen her like this, laid out before him in the vivid outdoors, with nothing hidden, nothing shadowed. She was his, all of her, and at that moment there were no secrets or deceptions between them. That he could banish her fears and immerse her in passion heightened his own arousal. He throbbed to be inside her.

His sense of power became explosive as he opened his trousers, covered her with his body, and slid the tip of his sex inside her.

Laurel gasped her pleasure, shattering his control. With a single thrust he sheathed himself. Her inner muscles embraced him, squeezing with a fit so snug he might have been created for the purpose of entering her, and she of receiving him.

With each beating pulse of her response, a conviction grew. Whoever she might be, whatever her history, she was his.

But could he find a way to make the future theirs?

The sun dipped behind the hills with startling suddenness, plunging the countryside into blue-black shadow. Greys Abbey stood ghostlike against the sky, the broken limestone walls reaching as if to embrace the rising moon.

The air turned sharply frigid. Still, Laurel did not wish to move or break the fragile spell that prevented the surrounding world from encroaching on her happiness. In Aidan's arms she felt freed from the burdens of threats and mysteries and even from the promises she had made to the queen.

Her respite proved all too short. He stirred beneath her, tightening his arms around her and sitting up. In the gleam of the half-moon, she saw his rueful smile. "We'll catch our deaths if we lie on this ground any longer."

She clung to him for another moment. "I am almost willing to chance it."

He nonetheless helped her to her feet and helped her straighten her clothing and don her carriage jacket, adding his own coat around her shoulders to ward off the chill.

"No, you'll need it," she protested.

He pressed his forehead to hers and kissed the end of her nose. "Keep it. No arguments."

They circled to the side of the abbey where they had left the carriage. At the sight of the dozing horse silhouetted against the twilight, Laurel came to an abrupt halt. The cold, stark beauty of the hills and the abbey and the emerging stars renewed her earlier impression of having stumbled into a fairy tale. It was an illusion that broke her heart.

"Leaving here will mean an end, you know."

Would he understand? However much she might wish it, she could not continue as they had been. Her life was no fairy tale, nor was she a widow in control of her own fate. She was a single woman who had forgotten the vital importance of discretion . . . and of chastity. She had her sisters to think of, and Victoria . . . Victoria, whose trust she had betrayed simply by taking Aidan into her confidence, much less surrendering her body to him.

Could she convince the queen of his worthiness? Even if she could, Victoria would never condone Laurel's actions these past two days, would never give her permission to take this relationship further.

Beneath her fingers, Aidan's forearm tensed. He looked down at the ground and nodded. "We have been reckless, and I have been irresponsible."

"No—"

"It's true. I knew from the first that I should stay away from you, yet I used every excuse I could think of to be near you." He rested his hands on her shoulders and drew her closer. "Laurel, my life is such that I cannot offer you more. Not now. And it would be selfish of me to ask you to wait, or ask you to accept what I could give you, which would fall miserably short of what a woman like you deserves."

A contradiction sizzled on the end of her tongue but went no further. She had worried that Victoria would not approve of such a relationship, but she hadn't stopped to consider that Aidan himself would deem it necessary— or perhaps desirable—to walk away.

However prettily he worded it, he obviously regarded her as an inconvenience . . . and as a temporary diversion in his life.

Why should that raise her resentment? She had as many reasons as he to end their affair, perhaps more. Better to do it now, before she lost her courage.

She stepped out his warm embrace, refusing to flinch at the cool slap of the breeze against her cheeks. "Let us be off, then."

"Wait." He came up behind her as she reached the carriage. "There is bitterness in your voice, Laurel. Must it be like that? Must we have ill feelings between us?"

"How else shall we part? As *friends*?" She spat the word with all the vehemence she could muster. She didn't want his friendship or his protection, not unless his heart came in the bargain as well.

"I am not suggesting we never see each other again. There are still too many matters to be settled. Do you think I'd abandon you, knowing a fiend lay in wait to harm you?"

"I'll take care of myself, thank you."

His soft laughter infuriated her. How dare he find humor when all she wanted to do was bury her face in the nearest pillow and sob until her chest and throat and eyes ached more than her breaking heart?

It wasn't his fault. He was correct in ending what should never have begun . . . but he seemed intent on making it as difficult and as painful as possible.

Especially now, as he took her in his arms and pressed her cheek to his chest, and the tears she hadn't known were falling began to soak his shirtfront.

"I'm sorry," she said between sobs. "I am not usually like this."

"It's been a long day. But before it ends, I have a request."

She lifted her face and swiped her hands across her cheeks. "Yes?"

"A dance."

"What? Here?"

"What more perfect place? You and I have danced beneath the stars before, Laurel. Don't you hear the music now?"

"Don't be silly. I hear only the breeze." She paused

to listen. "And the stream and crickets and a creaking branch . . ."

"Yes, and there is music in all of it." His hand a warm and steady guide at her waist, he moved her away from the carriage and twirled her. Over the grassy terrain he swept her backward, forward, to the side, and back. At first she stumbled along, but by some miracle they fell into the graceful pattern of a three-count rhythm. He held her close and softly murmured the beats into her hair.

"Listen closely," he whispered. "The strings, pianoforte, now the woodwinds. Let yourself hear it, feel it. Let it flow through you. . . ."

Suddenly the sensuous notes of a waltz drifted through her mind, enveloping her in sound, sensation, a thrilling sense that the world was hers—theirs—to command and shape. She felt alive, exhilarated . . . invincible.

"You hear it, don't you?"

"Oh, yes."

"Now look up."

As he whirled her in dizzying, glorious circles, she obeyed, lifting her face to the twinkling constellations and waiting for the next miracle.

"The stars, Laurel. They're dancing. The bear, the wolf, the hunter. The virgin. Do you see them?"

Oh, they were, whirling and whirling in time to the music, to a beautiful waltz that only she and Aidan and the stars could hear.

And then the whirling stopped and all went still, the music coalescing into one long, beautiful, lingering note as Aidan bent his face over hers. At first she thought he would kiss her, but he only smiled into her eyes with longing and sadness and steely-edged resolve.

Her heart overflowed with all the love they would never share. "Why did you do that?"

"So that years from now it will be what you remember of this day. Not the disappointments or the heartache or my wretched failings, but the glory of commanding the earth to sing and the sky to dance. For you, Laurel. All for you."

And she realized that though he might not be offering her a happily-ever-after, he had already given her more than she had ever imagined.

Chapter 21

They spent the night in separate rooms at the Crimson Fox in Billington. Aidan passed the hours tossing and turning until he finally threw off the bedclothes and went to sit by the window and stare up at the sky.

He would never look at the stars the same way again. In their patterns, he would always see Laurel's beautiful face, the sparkle of her tears, the glow of her smile. Had he made the right decision in letting her go? His chest ached with the dismal prospect of a life without her, but if keeping her safe meant forfeiting his own happiness, he would do it gladly.

Then why did a clawing doubt scrape his gullet raw? Why that niggling sense that it hadn't been noble sacrifice but cold, choking cowardice that prompted him to back away from the first woman who was capable of breaking through the walls he had erected around himself ever since . . . ?

Ever since he saw what love had done to his father.

A burst of fury sent his fist slamming against the wall beside the window. His decision concerning Laurel had nothing to do with his past. The only hold his mother's illness and his father's death had on him now came in the form of his obligation to prevent others from being preyed upon in similar ways. The Home Office needed him. England needed him.

And Laurel needed a man who was free to put her first.

Yet as he stared down at his bleeding knuckles, he once more felt a raw scrape of uncertainty inside him.

He arrived home to alarming news. After bringing Laurel to Abbey Green and extracting a promise that she would not venture out alone, Aidan had returned to the Royal Crescent. There he discovered a note from Mrs. Prewitt, Melinda's housekeeper.

He was needed at Fenwick House immediately.

"Her ladyship did not wish me to alert you, milord," the housekeeper said as she admitted him into the foyer. Taking his cloak, she handed it to a ready footman. Together she and Aidan started up the curving staircase. "She was adamant about it, but with her daughters so far away and you practically being family, sir, it seemed prudent to disregard milady's wishes this one time."

"Yes, you did the right thing. Tell me what happened."

"Her ladyship was attending a meeting of the Ladies' Botanical Society this morning when she fell into a swoon, much as she did at the Pump Room." Her hand poised on the banister, the woman paused on the steps and turned to him. "It isn't like milady to take ill so often. She's always been of such a hearty constitution."

He regarded the worry lines dragging at Mrs. Prewitt's eyes. "Do you mean to say the countess had been ill prior to the incident at the Pump Room?"

They continued up, and Mrs. Prewitt said, "She has been poorly several times since the New Year. And once or twice before that, sir. At first, she wouldn't allow me to send for Dr. Bailey."

"Mrs. Prewitt, you were correct when you said I was

like family. You can trust me with the truth. Do you know what is ailing her?"

"No, sir. Her ladyship insists it's nothing that a strong—"

"Cup of tea won't cure. Yes, I know how the countess can be." He released a breath and smoothed the concern from his face. They had reached the top of the stairs.

Framed by the brocade curtains of her canopied bed, Melinda greeted him with a moue of disapproval. Yet it was to her housekeeper that she expressed her dissatisfaction. "Prewitt, I distinctly remember telling you not to make a fuss."

Undeterred, Aidan gestured for the housekeeper to leave them. He strolled into the room. "Since when do my visits make you snarl so, Melinda?"

"Since they became prompted by pity."

"Don't be ridiculous." He stopped beside the bed. "Let me look at you."

It was all he could do to prevent his dismay from showing. Every ounce of improvement Melinda had made since falling ill at the Pump Room seemed to have drained away, leaving her thin and wan, with perturbing smudges beneath her eyes and a downward tug at the corners of her mouth.

He pressed a hand to his chest. "As stunning as ever, still capable of breaking hearts."

"Bah. I am no longer a beauty and I accept that. I suppose it's high time I learned I can no longer flit about like a debutante."

He sat at the edge of the mattress, noting how Melinda seemed to draw farther back against the pillows, as if to escape him—or his scrutiny. "You are about the age Mother would have been. . . ." Dread seeped through him at the thought, until he remembered that Melinda's malady might be more easily explained. "I want you to promise me something."

"How serious you look."

"This is serious. Take no more of Rousseau's elixir. It could very well be what is making you ill."

"Or what restores me so swiftly after one of these spells of fatigue. Tell me, my boy, has anyone else who has tried the formula taken ill?"

He almost wished someone had, if only to gain enough evidence against Rousseau to expose him as a fraud and shut down his operation. But the truth was that, aside from a loss of control over certain impulses, no one else had experienced any detrimental side effects.

So far.

When Aidan failed to reply, Melinda regarded him with a triumphant arc of an eyebrow that fueled his frustrations. He tried several other arguments, including pointing out that if nothing else, the elixir had failed to alleviate her symptoms. Nothing he said could persuade her that Rousseau might be perpetrating a hoax, and that sent him from Fenwick House with a new resolve and a new plan.

He set out for Abbey Green.

At a soft knock, Laurel opened her door to Sally, the downstairs maid. "A gentleman to see you, ma'am. In the front parlor."

Her breath caught with the hope that Aidan had returned—returned to renounce all those hurtful words he had said at Greys Abbey and swear to her that the stars would dance for them for the rest of their lives.

But no, they hadn't said cruel words, merely rational ones, the only words that made sense for two people who hailed from such different worlds, and whose obligations would always send them in different directions. Isn't that what he had meant when he said he could not offer her all that she deserved?

Or had he simply meant he didn't love her, not enough?

Another equally quelling thought occurred to her.

This morning she had received a note from George Fitzclarence conveying his considerable disappointment that she had failed to attend his soiree the night before last, along with his sincere hopes that she suffered from no indisposition that would continue to deprive him of her company.

Oh dear. Had he come to pay his respects?

"Did he give his name, Sally?" she asked.

"No, ma'am. But a right elegant young gentleman he is, to be sure, ma'am."

Aidan.

Laurel stepped back from the threshold and brushed at the muslin day dress she had changed into upon arriving home that morning. "Do I look all right?"

"Pretty as a sprig of fresh flowers, ma'am."

Laurel patted the braids she had coiled around the crown of her head. "My hair?"

"Lovely, too." Sally bobbed a curtsy. "I'll go and fetch tea for you and your visitor, ma'am."

Clutching the banister, Laurel made her way down to the ground floor, where she leaned to peer through the doorway into the parlor. She hoped to have a glimpse of him first, to try to gauge his mood and discern his reason for coming.

He stood with his back to her, a hand raised to grip the mantel as he stared into the cold grate. From merely his stance and the set of his shoulders, she perceived an unease that raised her own apprehensions.

He glanced around and caught her peeking at him. "There you are. Come in and close the door, please."

Her heart pattering, she complied.

"I need you," he said without preamble.

The words echoed inside her and buoyed her spirits. Is this why he appeared so somber and anxious? Because he had come to do exactly as she had hoped? Then she would make it easy for him. Her hands extended, she hurried across the room to him.

"Yes, Aidan? What is it you need?" *Ask me anything.*

He took her hands in his. As though meeting him for the first time, she was struck anew by how strikingly handsome he was, how broad and tapering and masterfully sculpted. At that moment, she would have refused him nothing and yielded everything, oh, positively *everything*, to him.

"Laurel," he said with urgency, "in three nights' time Fitz is holding another affair at his home, a celebration of his sister's birthday. I wouldn't ask this of you if it were not of vital importance. But he is smitten with you, and I believe you have the power to distract him in the way that I require."

"Distract him?" Oh. This was so far from what she had expected that at first his words failed to make sense. A rush of blood to her ears drowned out the rest of his explanation while a crushing disappointment sent her sinking into the nearest chair. It didn't help that he followed and knelt in front of her, or that he reached to reclaim one of her hands. Like a proposal. Except that it wasn't. Her fingers trembled against his. With a supreme effort of will she held them still.

"I wish to search for those documents you spoke of, and I'll need Fitz occupied long enough so that he won't notice my absence from among his guests. This was your idea, Laurel, remember?"

"Oh . . . yes. Of course." It seemed an eternity since she had devised her plan to bring Aidan into her confidence and work with him as a team. But then she had been attacked . . . and so much, so *very* much, had occurred in the aftermath.

For her, perhaps, but apparently not for him. For him it was business as usual. He hadn't come to give voice to the fanciful wishes of her heart. He spoke rationally, clearly, relying on plain, hard logic to guide his actions.

Through the incessant clamor in her ears, she only half listened to the part he wished her to play in his scheme, until something he said sliced through her wretchedness.

"You wish me to flirt with him?"

"Only enough to give me time to go through the two rooms in the house, his study and bedchamber, where he would likely keep such papers."

A bubble of laughter escaped her, a harsh, brittle note. It appeared she had come full circle, then, right back to the night of Victoria's extraordinary request. Except that so much had changed since then. No longer was she the naive, sheltered girl she had been. Her time in Bath had dispelled notions of black and white, good and evil, and taught her that human beings were a complicated mingling of virtues and vulnerabilities and flaws. She had learned, too, that flirtation was neither an art nor a game, but an often cruel manipulation of feelings, including her own.

And now the person who embodied her most heart-felt hopes wished to toss her into an arena where she would be forced to raise and then dash the hopes of another man. Thus the game played round and round again, spinning her to the point of dizziness.

The irony of it made her turn her face aside as a torrent of emotion threatened to reduce her to uncontrollable laughter and unstoppable tears.

"If you do not wish to do this, I'll understand." His fingertips scorched the flesh beneath her chin. "But I believed you'd not only want to but would insist upon helping. You were sent here to investigate Fitz, and while I will not ask you for whom, I am willing to help you complete the task."

Of course he wouldn't ask. To do so would only prompt her to raise similar questions about him, and then he would be obligated to take her into his confidence and reveal the same sorts of details.

And that, it appeared, was something he was not prepared to do.

"I came here directly from Fenwick House," he said. "Melinda is ill again and continues to put her faith in Rousseau's elixir as a cure."

At the mention of Melinda, Laurel blinked away an errant tear and turned back to him. "She is ill? I must go to her immediately."

"You may. I'm sure she will be glad to see you. But you will better serve her by finding hard evidence against Rousseau. Even if it is not the elixir causing her illness, it may be preventing her from seeking an effective treatment. You know how she shuns Dr. Bailey."

Laurel nodded, her own concerns dissipating beneath her worries for that kind and generous lady. "You believe the letters Lord Munster stole from his father might provide that evidence?"

"Think about it. First he steals those letters, and soon after, he establishes close ties with Claude Rousseau, ties to which he first admitted but later denied. Both men are heavily involved in the Summit Pavilion, a project that smacks of fraud."

Rising from the chair, she sidestepped him and stumbled past the hearth. Her back to him, she searched deep into her soul, drawing on the strength she had cultivated through all the years of serving as the mother her sisters had never had, when time and again she had put aside her own needs and concerns in order to focus on theirs.

She drew a breath of conviction. "Whatever you require of me, I will do . . . for Melinda's sake if nothing else. I would not for the world see her victimized in any way."

"I'd hoped you would say that. But I must be honest with you, Laurel. More is at stake than money and people's good health. An MP named Roger Babcock might have forfeited his life in pursuit of the elixir's false promises. If I can find the link between the elixir, the pavilion, and a warehouse on Broad Quay, I believe I will learn the identity of the killer."

He came up behind her, so close the heat of his body permeated her back in a way that was nearly torturous. "I had rather cut off my right arm than believe it, but that man might be Fitz."

Laurel spun around. "No, I don't believe that. Financial fraud, scientific trickery, yes, he is capable of both. But when it comes to the pavilion, he is passionate and sincere. He sees the project as his legacy to the world. He truly wants it to succeed."

"He told you this?"

"Yes, he was most adamant and . . . vulnerable."

"Then that means he has even more to lose should his plans fail to reach fruition. And having much to lose, Laurel, is often an irresistible motivator when it comes to murder."

George Fitzclarence, a murderer? When she had first come here, he had been a faceless entity and a thorn lodged deep in Victoria's side. It had been easy then to despise him and wish for his downfall. Now that she had come to know the man—the brother, the friend, the king's disappointed son—she pitied him and felt even a certain fondness for him.

No, she did not wish him to be a murderer.

"I hope you are wrong," she said.

"I hope I am, too. Perhaps in three nights' time, we'll know one way or the other."

"You still hobbling, old man?" Aidan clapped his hand on Julian Stoddard's shoulder and gestured at the silver-handled walking stick the young man was presently thumping up and down on the Aubusson rug in Fitz's drawing room.

"Frankly, I've rather grown a liking for the thing." Stoddard gave the cane a deft twirl between his fingers. "Adds a touch of sophistication, wouldn't you say?"

Even standing as close as they were, they raised their voices to be heard above the din of the crowd filling the room. A teeming crush packed Fitz's town house, over-flowing into the central hall and the two smaller salons that opened onto the drawing room.

Upon arriving, Aidan had made a circuit of the rooms. He hadn't seen Laurel and he wondered whether she had arrived yet, or would come at all. Perhaps at the last minute she had balked at the plan, albeit it had originally been her own. In the interim she had been attacked and then forced to face the ambiguity of her own background. Perhaps she had decided she'd had enough of uncertainty and danger.

He wouldn't have blamed her. Yet even given all the rational arguments why she should avoid tonight's conspiracy, he would be greatly surprised if she broke her promise to come. She didn't strike him as a woman who left matters half undone.

He continued scanning the faces. The absence of one piqued his curiosity. "I haven't seen de Vere here tonight."

"No, you won't," Stoddard said. "Didn't you know? He left Bath the other day."

Aidan's senses pricked. "Which day?"

Stoddard shrugged. "Yesterday? The day before? Not sure, really."

Aidan had ruled out de Vere as Laurel's assailant, but the Frenchman's sudden departure from the city coinciding with the attack set him wondering again. If not the actual culprit, could de Vere nonetheless be involved? Both were French, and Aidan had thought he perceived a resemblance between the two men. . . .

He would make inquiries via the Home Office, but for tonight the question would have to wait. Seated on an ornate Louis Quinze settee at the east end of the drawing room, Beatrice held court, greeting friends and well-wishers with all the aplomb of the royal princess she might have been if not for her father's indiscreet lifestyle.

"She's in her element tonight," Aidan commented.

"Ravishing. One would never guess her age to be above thirty." Stoddard's enthusiasm caused Aidan to give the youth a thorough looking over. Was the poor chap smitten with Bea? But the youth's attention quickly wandered to a passing servant who held a tray of champagne glasses high in the air. "I wonder if there might be something a trifle more potent to be had. Care to join me in my search?"

"I think I'll pay my respects to our guest of honor." He set off down the room.

"Aidan, you naughty thing. Where have you been?" Beatrice beamed up at him and offered a satin-gloved hand for him to kiss.

"Here and there," he murmured as he leaned over her. "I never stray far from wherever you are, my dear."

"Oh, hush, or people will suspect us of conducting an intrigue." By the way she used her full voice and laughed, it was clear she didn't take the notion the least bit seriously, nor did she expect that the ladies sitting near her would, either. To have done otherwise, to have lowered her voice and issued a stern warning, would have set tongues wagging before the footmen carried in the next round of hors d'oeuvres.

Still, standing a few feet behind the settee, Devonlea's face turned away from the group of men surrounding him. A gaze simmering with derision settled on the back of his wife's bejeweled coif, then flicked to Aidan. Over the glass of champagne the viscount raised to his lips, his eyes narrowed.

It was all Aidan could do not to laugh outright. Did Devonlea truly suspect him of trifling with Beatrice?

Though she could not have seen her husband's enmity, she seemed intent on fueling the fire in the man's gullet by coming to her feet and grasping Aidan's arm. "Come take a turn about the room with me. Though with so many guests, one hardly has space to breathe, much less walk."

"It would seem, my dear Beatrice, that you are all the rage here in Bath."

"Hmm. Yet it appears I am not the only one." As they passed the grand piano, Beatrice raised a finger to point.

Silhouetted by the torchlight bathing the terrace beyond the French doors, Laurel cut a dramatic figure in wine red silk.

The air slid from Aidan's lungs as he took in the daring neckline, her bared shoulders, the wicked tilt of her breasts beneath the shimmering fabric. He had never seen her look more sophisticated . . . intoxicating. A garnet teardrop teasing the inch or two of cleavage visible above her bodice, her creamy skin glowed. And her hair . . . it had been piled high with tendrils plucked artfully free to float like curling sunlight about her shoulders.

"You may stop staring," Beatrice said with a chuckle that held little humor. "Goodness, but you're as infatuated as on that first night at the Assembly Rooms. Oh, but look what has happened. It appears my brother has reined this filly in, at least for the moment."

If anyone had been reined in, it was certainly Fitz, who stood close at Laurel's side looking hopelessly awestruck. She in turn appeared thoroughly charmed by his attentions, and did not so much as blink when he stumbled over the edge of the rug in his haste to procure her a glass of champagne.

So far, their plan showed every sign of success.

"Mrs. Sanderson, how good of you to come." Beatrice embraced Laurel and kissed her cheek, but Aidan sensed restraint in the gesture and caught the envious flare of Bea's nostrils. She didn't like being upstaged, especially by someone who accomplished the feat with little apparent effort.

"I wouldn't have missed it for the world. Happy birthday, my lady." Laurel dipped a graceful curtsy, then slipped a hand around the forearm Fitz offered to help her rise. In that instant she communicated a message to Aidan from beneath her lashes. She was here, ready to assume the role he had assigned her, and she would utilize every alluring weapon in her arsenal to play her part to perfection.

He should have been grateful. Instead, a fist closed around his heart, squeezing tight around a galling sense of his own stupidity.

How had he ever believed he could bear to watch her entice another man?

Chapter 22

Aidan had been gone for nearly half an hour before he turned up in the drawing room again, a lean hip propped against the curve of the grand piano, a brandy in hand, and a carefree expression lightening his chiseled features. For a moment Laurel pondered how he had managed to slip away so entirely unnoticed and then reappear, taking up as though he had never been gone with the finesse of an accomplished spy. Where and why did an earl learn such skills?

His cousins the Lewes-Parker twins stood one on either side of him. With a wistful expression their mother looked on from nearby. The girls, as elegant as ever, were laughing, clearly flirting, and he just as clearly seemed to be enjoying their repartee.

Laurel quickly reminded herself that they had come to playact tonight, and that his flirtations were merely a form of camouflage. Before he had disappeared, they had exchanged a few brief words at the punch bowl. "I'm going now to search the study. Be sure to keep him in the drawing room."

"I shall not leave his side."

His departing look had acknowledged what she had not been able to prevent: the sardonic edge to her voice. She had little liking for this night's work, and even less for how easily Aidan had requested her assistance, as though he had not at the same time asked her to compromise her integrity.

He wished her to distract George Fitzclarence? Then she would do so to the very best of her ability, and she hoped each simpering smile and each coquettish touch struck Aidan's conscience as sharply as it did her own.

No, she didn't mean that. She wasn't angry, not really. She was hurt, though not so much by him as by the circumstances in which she found herself ensnared.

Now, over the swarm of feathered and beribboned headdresses and the gleam of the men's pomade, he caught her eye. The signal he sent her came with a nod and a lift of his glass.

Without hurrying, she extricated herself from between Lord Munster and Lady Harcourt.

"But where are you g-going, my d-dear?" the earl said as he reached out to clasp her hand. He nearly missed, catching the tips of her fingers and dislodging her elbow-length glove from its snug fit around her elbow.

An excess of alcoholic spirits had sent his aim awry, and Laurel inwardly shuddered to consider what fate she would meet in his drunken arms had she intended to follow her flirtations to their logical conclusion. If only the man would temper his vices, how much more agreeable he would be.

She searched the crowd for her excuse. "Why, there is Margaret Whitfield, sir, and I have not yet had a moment to speak with her."

He released her with obvious reluctance. "D-do hurry back."

"Indeed I shall, sir."

Lady Harcourt's sly chuckle followed Laurel as she started away. "She is a delight, Munster. A pity you aren't unattached. . . ."

Aidan, too, had managed to escape his cousins. He and Laurel met in the center of the room and walked several feet together before parting and moving in separate directions. In those brief moments he said in an undertone, "I searched all the probable places in his study and turned up nothing."

Earlier, she had relayed to him Victoria's description of the documents, including a depiction of the old king's seal while he had yet been the Duke of Clarence. "Did you search thoroughly?"

"I know his hiding places, including which picture frames to look behind. I'll search his bedchamber next, during the entertainment following supper."

Without another word they parted, and Laurel slipped an arm around Margaret Whitfield's waist and bade the woman walk with her. "I understand you were with Lady Fairmont when she took ill the other day. . . ."

Supper stretched on interminably. In breach of etiquette, Laurel found herself seated at George Fitzclarence's right at a dining table reserved for the highest-ranking guests, while those of lower status were dispersed among smaller tables set up in the corners of the room and the adjoining antechamber.

Her cheeks burned at the low twitter of speculation that bore her name. Lord Munster seemed oblivious or perhaps indifferent, but Laurel felt the brand of numerous furtive stares. This, she realized, was what it felt like to have one's reputation compromised, and she was suddenly grateful for her assumed identity and the obscurity to which she would eventually return; grateful, too, for the arrival of the soup course—a rich seafood concoction—which subdued the whispered gossip.

That did not, however, make the situation much easier for her. Diagonally across the table Aidan laughed and flirted openly with the ladies on either side of him, at the same time carrying on a disdainful if silent discourse with the icy blonde Laurel had met earlier, Lady Amanda Beecham, who happened to be seated directly opposite him.

She tried to ignore it all—the gossip, Aidan's dalliances, even the ankle Lord Munster attempted to rub against her own beneath the table. He had been drinking heavily all evening, evidenced by the increased stutter in his speech and his unsteadiness in handling his fork. Though he might not remember much in the morning, her success in capturing his regard for the remainder of the evening seemed all but assured until, during dessert, the splatter of a bit of raspberry florendine on his neckcloth threatened to undermine her and Aidan's plans.

What if he happened to pass a mirror and saw the violation to his snowy cravat? Might he rush upstairs to change it at just the precise moment Aidan tore through his bureau or clothespress or bedside table?

"Do you c-care for s-sailing, my dear?" the man asked her a second time, and Laurel realized that in staring so intently at that small but conspicuous stain and pondering its significance she had neglected to respond.

"Oh . . . I cannot say." She affected a neutral expression. "I've never sailed."

Perhaps she should mention the stain herself, but when? Supper was ending. In another moment the ladies would adjourn to the drawing room for tea while the men remained here for brandy and cigars. Lord Munster might not care about the state of his neckcloth without the ladies present, and wait until just before the entertainment began to visit his bedchamber. Laurel might not be able to warn Aidan in time. . . .

Too late. The gentleman all came to their feet and held the ladies' chairs as they rose to leave the table. Laurel found herself swept along in the tide of rustling silks and excited giggles. Apparently the Countess of Rockingham, newly arrived from Brighton, had a scandalous morsel to report and had been waiting to have the women alone to impart the tale. Laurel tried not to think of herself as the future topic of such accounts.

When the men rejoined them some twenty minutes

later, Aidan was not among them. Several footmen brought extra chairs into the drawing room, and people began finding seats. Lord Munster drew Laurel to his side on a settee placed close to the doorway.

"Do you p-play, madam? Or s-sing?" he asked her.

"Not well enough for this gathering," she replied honestly. She began to relax. He had apparently not noticed the raspberry stain, leaving Aidan free to conduct his search.

Amanda Beecham went to stand beside the piano while an older woman took a seat on the bench. They conferred for a few moments, then appeared to reach an accord, and the first notes were struck. Amanda Beecham's clear soprano floated through the air.

Sitting across the room, Lady Devonlea sent a solicitous gaze around the room, undoubtedly making certain that each guest had found an agreeable place from which to enjoy the performance. Her eyes lingered on her brother, and then she made a face. Her hand came up, moving over her neck as if, like him, she wore a cravat. She waggled her fingers in the air.

"Whatever is she c-carrying on about?"

"I cannot imagine," Laurel said. "Lady Amanda's voice is superb. Wouldn't you agree, my lord?"

"My n-neckcloth? Is that what she is s-signaling about?" He fingered the starched linen and attempted to angle his chin so he could peer down at the knot. "Oh, d-damn me, I've s-spilled something."

"Did you, sir? I hadn't noticed."

"If you'll exc-cuse me, my d-dear."

Before she could protest, he stood up and disappeared into the hall. Laurel came to a swift decision. Scurrying after him might ruin her in the eyes of all present—and all of Bath society by tomorrow—but she could not abandon Aidan when he needed her.

"Lord Munster . . ."

Laurel arrived at the foot of the stairs in time to witness a small miracle. Lord Munster had ascended half-way up when his butler came hurrying out from the service corridor.

"Milord, a word if you please."

The earl looked quizzically down at Laurel, then flashed an impatient frown. "Yes, R-Rimsdale, what is it?"

"It appears the champagne is running low, milord. Would you like us to serve wine with Lady Devon-lea's birthday cake or shall we delve into the reserved stock?"

Lord Munster expelled a breath. "No, Lady D-Devonlea would not like it if we s-switched to w-wine."

On his way back down the stairs, he fished a small set of keys from his coat pocket and with a jingle dangled them between his fingers. "S-some things one should not trust to one's s-servants," he said to Laurel, "and re-serves of f-fine champagne is one of them."

At the base of the stairs he stopped and grazed her chin with the backs of his fingers. "Whatever sent you out after m-me, my dear, d-do hold that thought. I shall r-return shortly."

Laurel waited until he had retreated into the servants' domains before she lifted her skirts and raced up the stairs.

At the faint click signaling a turn of the doorknob, Aidan extinguished his candle, dashed into the dressing room, and slipped behind the door. Damn! How maddeningly inconvenient. He'd had time only to scan the first of the sheets of parchment he had discovered in a small, leather-bound portfolio tucked at the bottom of a bureau drawer. His pulse rattled in his impatience to continue his scrutiny.

The page bore the seal of the Duke of Clarence.

The door opened long enough to admit a few high notes of Amanda Beecham's distinctive voice accompanied by the pianoforte. With another soft click the sounds were shut out of the room. The approach of footsteps across the rug in the outer sitting room prompted him to hold his breath. Holding his ear close to the gap between the door and the lintel, he heard those steps come to an uncertain halt. He tucked the map and the portfolio into his waistband and drew his waistcoat down over it.

A whisper darted through the shadows. "Aidan?"

He rushed out from behind the door and traced a swift path through the darkened rooms to her. His hands closed over her bare arms, her skin warm against his fingers. He was at once happy to have her back with him, away from Fitz, and apprehensive about what had brought her. "Laurel. What are you doing here?"

"He's coming. A shortage of champagne sent him belowstairs, but soon enough he will be here to change his neckcloth."

"The raspberry florendine."

"Yes, you noticed it, too? I thought we were free and clear until his sister pointed it out to him from across the drawing room."

"Drat Bea for her keen observations." He drew out the parchment he had been studying. "See here, Laurel, I've found something."

With no light to aid her, she squinted to make out the writing. "But this isn't a letter. It appears to be . . . why, a map."

"Indeed."

Frowning, she shook her head. "We are supposed to find correspondence between the Duke of Clarence and André Rousseau. Victoria never said anything about a map."

Aidan's insides went still, his thoughts silenced by the echo of the name Laurel had uttered. She realized her mistake, for her eyes went wide and a hand flew up to cover her lips.

"Victoria *who*?"

She grabbed his wrist and tugged. "Aidan, he'll be coming shortly. We must go."

"Victoria the *queen*?" He felt as if the shreds of a tapestry had suddenly mended themselves to reveal an astonishing landscape he could never have imagined. "The *queen* sent you?"

She looked over her shoulder at the door and gave another tug. "Aidan, please."

Outside, footsteps thudded across the upper landing. Laurel gasped. "It's him! We must hide."

"No time. Come here." Shoving the map back beneath his waistcoat, he seized her in his arms and crushed his mouth to hers.

A muffled sound of protest vibrated against his lips as she struggled to break free. He held her fast and lifted his lips a fraction. "We've no choice. Play along."

The door opened, throwing a rectangle of candlelight across the floor. Turning Laurel to the right, Aidan glanced up through her hair to see Fitz's ungainly hulk silhouetted in the doorway.

"Who's h-here?"

Fitz reached for the candle burning in the sconce beside the door and held it in front of him to illuminate the room. "By God, B-Barensforth, you b-blackguard!"

The candle went out, thrusting them all into darkness, as Fitz pounded into the room. Clamping Aidan's shoulder, Fitz hauled him away from Laurel. The force of Aidan's back hitting the wall sent pain radiating through his already injured ribs. In another instant Fitz was on him again. Gripping a lapel, he dragged Aidan forward and at the same time raised a fist.

Aidan ducked the blow, pulling out of Fitz's grasp and darting around him. Fitz swung around and staggered, then grabbed the back of a chair to catch his balance.

"She b-belongs to me, you s-swine," he ground out between clenched teeth. "How d-dare you?"

Head down, he released the chair and charged. Again Aidan moved out of the way, then gave Fitz a shove from behind that sent him reeling. "I beg to differ, old boy. The lady's with me."

"Stop it, both of you!" Laurel yelled as Fitz struck a side table and stumbled hard to his knees. A lamp teetered, but lurching forward, Aidan caught it before the crystal piece hit the floor and shattered. "Good heavens, grown men behaving like schoolboys. And making such impertinent assumptions, not to mention insulting advances. I have never experienced the like."

Frozen in place, both Aidan and Fitz gaped at Laurel—Fitz in somewhat inebriated confusion, Aidan in consternation. What had she not understood when he had commanded her to play along?

Her admonition called for a quick change of course and he pretended to see her—truly see her—for the first time. "*Mrs. Sanderson?* Good heavens, how embarrassing."

"Indeed, sir. Whom *were* you expecting?"

He shot his cuffs. "A gentleman doesn't like to say."

"Laurel, d-darling," Fitz said from his semiprone position on the floor, "then you d-did come up here to w-wait for me?"

Her hands snapped to her hips. "It is Mrs. Sanderson, sir, and no, I most certainly did not. Nor did I expect to be manhandled by Lord Barensforth. Had I known these were your private chambers, Lord Munster, I should never have set foot inside."

"Then . . . wh-what *are* you doing here, m-madam?" Fitz struggled to his feet, accepting the hand Aidan offered to help him up.

"I had merely sought an empty room in which to"— here she paused, drew herself up, and gave a dignified sniff—"to right an article of clothing that seems to have come loose. And that is all I shall say about the matter. A lady does not discuss the particulars of her wardrobe in mixed company."

With that, she whirled and swept from the room, leaving Fitz looking thoroughly dejected and Aidan filled with new admiration for a woman with the ability to take on two rogues and trump them both.

As her footsteps receded down the staircase, Fitz murmured, "W-well, old boy, it seems we've b-both lost this one."

An hour later, having left the party in separate carriages, then rendezvousing at his town house, Laurel and Aidan sipped strong tea in the proper environs of his downstairs parlor. Sifting through the documents strewn among their teacups and soda cakes, they made their plans.

From what they had been able to piece together, they learned that before the wars Lord Munster's and Victoria's fathers had been part of an intellectual society dedicated to the advancement of the alchemical sciences. The French traitor André Rousseau had been among the group's members.

"This is not at all what I believed I would find," Laurel said, lifting one of the letters signed by André Rousseau and holding it to the light beside her. "Can they truly have believed in the transmutation of base metals into gold? Or that immortality could be achievable through an elixir created with this so-called philosopher's stone?"

"It's been my experience that the promises of wealth and eternal youth often make the ridiculous seem sublimely plausible." Aidan gave a waggle of his eyebrows. "Both the dukes of Clarence and Kent lived lifestyles that exceeded their incomes. It isn't hard to imagine them seeking miracle cures for their financial woes."

She fell to studying a diagram that outlined the alchemist theory on the connections between wisdom, morality, bodily harmony, and salvation. "It's rather like a religious doctrine, only without God." She chose another page. "Rousseau seemed initially skeptical that the basic properties of the stone could be extracted from the minerals in Bath's thermal waters."

Aidan nodded. "Until the Duke of Clarence produced this map. That appears to have finally convinced the others."

She reached for the parchment he had briefly shown her in Lord Munster's bedchamber. The rendering of Bath's Lower Town depicted all the significant landmarks, among them the Pump Room, Bath Abbey, and the Guildhall. But superimposed against the city's streets, bold black lines stretched from the west end of Pulteney Bridge to the docks south of Avon Street. "What do you suppose these signify?"

"I have my theories."

"Yes?"

Silence stretched. He took the map from her and laid it aside. Evenly he said, "You work for the queen."

She sighed. "Yes."

His eyebrow arcing, he aped Micklebee by rolling his fingers in a gesture that meant he wanted more from her than a one-word reply.

"Oh, all right. I am here at Victoria's behest to discover whether George Fitzclarence is plotting treason against her, most specifically with Claude Rousseau."

"And how in God's name are you connected to the queen?"

"Actually, I have known her nearly her entire life." Laurel couldn't help smiling at a quick memory of the toddler Victoria, and at the way Aidan's features grew taut as he took in her words.

"You see, my father was once an officer under the Duke of Kent in Canada and Gibraltar," she explained. "My uncle Edward as well. They remained friends afterward, and after their deaths Victoria's mother and her uncle Leopold were frequent visitors to Thorn Grove, usually the only visitors we saw for months on end. Uncle Edward was a decidedly reclusive gentleman and—"

"*Why*, Laurel? Why the devil would the queen send you to investigate when she might simply have made her suspicions known to her ministers or the Home Office or the police or, for heaven's sake, any number of individuals who would have made a great deal more sense than sending *you*?"

"I beg your pardon. I believe I've made a rather first-rate job of things. We have the documents, do we not? And happily enough, they do seem to exonerate Lord Munster of treason, if not of some odd and perhaps illegal behavior."

His lips thinning, Aidan grabbed a decanter off the table beside him, pulled the stopper, and poured a generous measure of spirits into his tea. He drank and then ran a hand through his hair.

"What was the queen thinking, sending you into a potential powder keg? Does she not realize that she has armies at her command? It so happens *I* have been investigating Fitz, and I must tell you, your interference might well have compromised my position." He tugged at his open collar. "In fact, once or twice it did."

"I'm sorry, but it couldn't be helped. Victoria wished this matter handled as quietly as possible. The scandals surrounding her grandfather's and uncles' reigns have left a bitter taste in many mouths. There are those who would end the monarchy once and for all, and another disgrace to the Hanover name might be just the thing to tip the scales against her. In a way, although her cousin might not have been plotting overt acts of treason, his involvement in fraud and . . . and *this*"—she pointed to the documents—"could still prove damaging to Victoria's standing."

She reached for his hand. "Oh, Aidan, she is so young

and so determined to lead this country to the best of her ability. She deserves the chance to do so."

He brought her fingers to his lips, kissed them, and held them there for a moment. "I agree, even if I heartily protest her methods."

Silence fell. Laurel drained her tea and resolutely set the cup aside. "Now that you are privy to all of my secrets, isn't there something you should like to tell me?"

"Not particularly, no."

"Aidan!"

He shut his eyes and pinched the bridge of his nose. "The Home Office. I work for the Home Office and have ever since I recognized a diamond-mine scam a few years back that would have fleeced a good number of England's distinguished citizens out of their life's savings, including some of those you've met right here in Bath."

"Well. I cannot say this comes as a shock. I figured out quite a while ago that you were no ordinary noble-man."

"And you, madam, are no ordinary lady." His arm snaking around her, he pulled her to him for a kiss.

She couldn't help grinning when he broke away. Savoring the lingering heat of his lips on her own, she leaned across him to retrieve the map.

"We need to focus. So far we've learned that André Rousseau and the dukes of Clarence and Kent knew one another before the wars, and that together they explored the properties of alchemy as they pertain to the legend of a life-renewing elixir." She raised her brows and shook her head. "It seems more of a hobby to fill their leisure time than an act of treason, to be sure."

"That depends on their intentions. Were they merely dabbling for sport? Were they foolish enough to believe in the promise of an ancient alchemist recipe? Or were they planning to separate a number of wealthy individuals from their fortunes, as their sons appear to be doing?"

"A pity Uncle Edward is no longer with us. As a friend to both dukes, he might have been able to shed light on the matter. Now we may never know the truth."

"Not the truth of decades ago, perhaps, but I won't rest until I discover what Fitz and Claude Rousseau are cooking up together."

"What do you intend to do?"

"At his demonstration, Rousseau claimed his laboratory is hidden deep beneath the city. At the time I took the assertion as mere dramatic folderol to entertain his audience, but . . ." He took the map from between her fingers. "If these lines represent a tunnel system beneath the Lower Town, they might lead me to the answers I've been seeking."

"Good. When shall we go?"

"Oh, no, my dear. I am returning you to Abbey Green posthaste."

"But—"

"But nothing. I want you out of harm's way. That is an order."

Laurel paused to gather her courage and a convincing veneer of bravado. She had promised Victoria to investigate George Fitzclarence's actions, and she would not be left behind at such a critical juncture in her mission. She possessed a pistol, and as she had discovered that night by the bridge, she had no qualms about firing the weapon when necessary. "You say you work for the Home Office?" she asked lightly.

"Yes."

"Then you cannot issue orders to me."

Scowling, he pressed his face close to hers until it was all she could do not to flinch away. "You think not?"

"Oh, I know not. My orders come straight from the queen, and the queen's authority supersedes that of the Home Office. You, sir, are now working for *me*." She gave his cheek a little tap, then held her hand there, enjoying the scrape of his evening whiskers against her palm. "We either do this my way or you shall find yourself in a great deal of hot water. Scalding, in fact."

His mouth opened and then closed. In his indignation he glowered, until the greater portion of her bluster began to falter and she fully doubted he would let her have her way. Without visibly moving, he became taller, broader, a virtual wall of defiance. He would flat-out refuse and there would be nothing she could do about it.

The release of an audible breath robbed the steel from his posture. "Damn."

She smiled. A mistake.

"You impossible minx." Catching her hand and sliding it to his lips, he traced a heated trail from the base of her forefinger to the pulse in her wrist.

Then he pulled her closer and dipped his head. The hungry suckle of his mouth on her neck evoked instant ripples of desire, and the respectability of sipping tea in a downstairs parlor spiraled into oblivion. She could not resist the strength of his arms as he turned her and tilted her face up. His exploration of her flesh continued as his lips traveled over the expanse of bosom bared by the low cut of her evening gown. He reduced her to shivers when his tongue delved between her breasts.

His head came up a fraction and, as he spoke, the motion of his lips tickled her skin. "A trickster does not relish being tricked, my dear. If I cannot command you, I will nonetheless ask you to listen to reason and remain somewhere safe while I follow the map."

"No, Aidan." Her breath came in gasps while her heart threatened to burst through her stays. He seemed well aware of his effect on her, adding the caress of his fingertips along her calf for good measure. "Victoria . . . sent me to do a job," she insisted, "and I must see it through. She is counting on me."

"And you may count on me."

His wondrous touch tempted her to give in, to yield her royal obligations to him. Only the knowledge that together they had learned more than either would have managed alone kept her resolute. "You know I am right. You need me—you have all along. If not for me, you would never have discovered the map. I am coming with you, and there is an end to it."

His lips returned to her bosom. Through her dress and chemise, his teeth closed over her nipple, the sharp pleasure of it prompting her to cry out in helpless delight. It was his turn to smile. "That, madam, is a promise for later, when I am no longer bound by the queen's authority."

Chapter 23

The mud of the riverbank sharp in Aidan's nostrils, he proceeded alone across Bridge Street to the top of the steps that led down to the boat slips. Because of the map he had discovered, he now suspected that Fitz and Rousseau hadn't boarded a boat and traveled downriver the night of the Guildhall concert.

Back at the entrance to the Grand Parade, Laurel waited with Phelps in the cabriolet. Aidan had left his manservant with a pistol and strict orders to shoot should a pair of ruffians holding clubs or any other weapons leap out of the shadows.

A fine mist drifted off the river, but for the most part the air remained clear and sharp and provided nowhere for a footpad to hide. Besides, Aidan suspected the henchmen were hired only on nights when Fitz and Rousseau intended venturing down to their subterranean lair. He doubted they would do so tonight. When he and Laurel left the fete, Fitz had already been too inebriated to go anywhere.

Still, with a pistol of his own ready in one hand and a lantern in the other, he made his way down the steps. From the boat slips he was able to peer beneath the closest of the bridge's arched supports to where the massive struts met the river's high walls. As pictured on the map, a rectangular opening in the wall emitted a thin stream of water, part of the old drainage system for the thermal baths.

A narrow ledge ran the length of the wall. Heedful of the muck and slime, he stepped up onto it and made his way to the drainage duct. It stood some three feet high and about six inches wide. He set down his lantern, tucked his pistol into his waistband, and placed his hands on the stonework.

The map had told them what to do. Press the third and fifth stones from the top on either side, then the second and fourth. He had only to apply the slightest pressure before he heard a clink and a grind. Like the mechanism of a puzzle box, the framework slid inward and opened to either side. A waft of musty air hit him full in the face. The opening now granted access to a culvert that was large enough to accommodate him if he bent over slightly.

His heart picked up its pace. Stepping in, he examined the system of gears and pulleys on either side of the opening. The arrangement was ingenious, and he wondered who had originally engineered it and why. Perhaps merely to facilitate the draining of the bathhouses. But such questions were of little concern to him tonight. His job was to proceed to wherever the map led and gather his evidence.

Should he go on without Laurel, and leave her waiting in the cabriolet with Phelps to protect her? Every instinct but one told him he should. It would be safer for her and perhaps even for him, for should he meet with any form of trouble, it would be easier to fight his way clear if he was alone.

But within a chorus of common sense, mutiny cried out. He wanted her with him. It had nothing to do with her being invested with the queen's authority. She was smart and quick on her feet, and if tonight had proved anything, it was that they worked well together, operating like a single agent capable of being in two places at one time.

He needed her. . . .

The thought wrapped itself around his throat and nearly choked him. With something approaching desperation he amended the sentiment. He needed her perspective, her unique point of view, in order to complete his assignment.

Beyond this mission there would be others, leaving him no time to devote to a wife or family, no chance to surrender his heart to circumstances that came without guarantees, where each day he ran the risk of losing everything, *everything* that mattered. . . .

"Aidan?"

Laurel's whisper echoed against the underbelly of the bridge and brought him up sharp. Wrapped from head to toe in the black velvet cape she had mended following her attack, she appeared phantomlike at the base of the steps.

"I thought I asked you to wait in the carriage."

"You were taking so long, I became concerned."

And to think he had considered proceeding without her, as if she would have stood for that. "Where's Phelps?"

"Just there." She pointed to the top of the steps.

"Signal him to go."

The manservant knew where to meet them later. Aidan only hoped he and Laurel would emerge at the appointed place. Moving back to the end of the ledge, he helped her step up, holding the lantern to guide her footing. "Careful, it's slippery."

At the mouth of the culvert her eyes shut tight and her hand flew up to cover her nose, an understandable reaction to the stale reek of more than a thousand years' worth of subterranean decay. At his prompting, she hesitated another fraction of an instant, then braved a stride inside. Aidan followed her in and closed the framework of the aperture, in effect sealing them in.

"Ready?"

"I *loathe* dank places."

"You should have thought of that earlier."

The fear in her eyes made him realize her remark had not been a complaint, but a show of distress.

"Do you wish to leave?" It would compromise his plans, perhaps even put off his investigation for another night. He also would run the risk of Fitz discovering that the documents were missing and raising the alert.

But if Laurel wanted out of here, he would take her home.

She shook her head.

His relief mingled with pride in her courage. By God, they did make a damn good team. Grinning, he pressed his lips to her cheek in a kiss of camaraderie that somehow meant as much to him as all the others they had shared. "I'll be right here beside you."

He held the lantern out in front of him. The culvert, constructed of cemented stones, sloped upward and wound out of sight. Shallow water ran its length, at least at the moment. If any of the baths in town were being drained, the water would engulf them. But he had no intention of pointing that out to Laurel.

"We should have stopped at Abbey Green for you to change," he said instead. "Those satin slippers won't survive this jaunt, and your cape and gown won't fare much better."

"Victoria will understand."

The statement took him aback. The exquisite red dress was not hers. Even having learned of her double life, he hadn't stopped to consider that everything about her, even her clothing, was part of the charade.

That she was gently born he did not question, but did having to borrow her fine clothes signify that she and her sisters had been left without a proper income? Like so many women without family, were they forced to stretch each penny and go without the niceties they should have taken for granted? Had this uncle of theirs failed to provide for them?

Galled by the thought, he formed a resolve to check into the Sutherland sisters' finances at the first opportunity.

They started forward.

At a scratching noise, Laurel came to a sudden halt that raised a splash. She clutched his arm and pressed herself to his side. "What was that?"

"I couldn't say. It was beyond the lamplight."

"You know very well it was a rat. Oh, I heard it again. This place must be teeming with vermin."

True, but he savored the feel of her against him and was silently grateful for scurrying creatures. "Try thinking of them as fat squirrels with long, skinny tails."

She swore beneath her breath in a most unladylike manner.

Up ahead, the culvert split in two directions. One offshoot sloped away to the right. To the left, debris-cluttered steps led up to a higher level.

Reaching into his waistcoat, he consulted the map. "Left it is."

He helped her over fallen rocks and masonry. At the top of the steps, the passage tapered to the unsettling width of a grave. Laurel clung tight to his free hand, her fingers clamping his painfully. They were no longer traversing one of the ancient drainage pipes, but a tunnel, one that had undergone recent repairs by the looks of it.

Releasing her hand for a moment, he raised the lantern and smoothed a palm along a ceiling joist. "See the paleness of this wood? This passage has been recently fortified."

Pushing on, he steadied Laurel as she stepped over the rubble. She kept up without a word of complaint, and the lump of pride lodged beneath his breastbone swelled. They passed three more forks, each time consulting the map.

"A person could become hopelessly lost in such a maze. I do hope the lantern oil holds out."

Aidan hoped so too.

Light suddenly burst from the darkness ahead, stopping them dead in their tracks. His heart crashing against his chest, Aidan shoved Laurel behind him and reached for his pistol. As he moved, so did the light up ahead.

"Bloody hell. It's just a reflection," he whispered, his voice shaking with relief as once more he wondered—if they were caught down here, would he be able to protect Laurel?

From behind him, she rested her chin on his shoulder to peer over him. "What is it?"

A dozen yards farther along, they stepped through an archway. Laurel came up beside him, her eyes growing round as she took in the chamber that opened in a cavernous expanse before them. "My word."

Overheard, vaulted ceilings soared, braced by arches adorned with broken tiles that had once formed elaborate borders. On the wall opposite the entrance, a crumbling mosaic reflected the beams from their lantern. Niches that must once have held statuary flanked the artwork on either side. Throughout the room, chunks of stone and plaster littered a marble floor that had buckled in places and sunk in others. Masonry and shards of pottery glittered in the light.

Her mouth agape, Laurel started into the chamber. Aidan held out an arm to stop her. "Careful. The walls are half collapsed. We don't want to cause a cave-in."

She lifted a wary gaze to the ceiling. "What do you suppose is above us?"

Again he consulted the map. "According to this, we are practically beneath the Pump Room."

"My goodness, Aidan, do you realize we must be

standing in part of the original Roman bathhouse?"
Wonderment sent her voice several notches higher.

"Couldn't be. The Roman complex would have been
crushed beneath the newer construction centuries ago."

"But look at the tile work." She took the lantern from
him and carefully picked her way across the chamber.
She shone the light on the mosaic. "I've seen art like
this in books. And Uncle Edward had a nearly identical painting. The image depicts Minerva, the goddess of
healing. Rousseau claimed his mineral water came from
beneath Minerva's temple. This must be it." She cocked
her head. "Listen. Do you hear that?"

From somewhere beneath them, a faint pulsing
tapped out a rhythm.

"This way," she urged.

In a wider passage that branched off from the first
chamber, the ruins of what must have once been a
magnificent arcade impeded their progress. The columns were cracked and shattered, some having toppled
across the floor, their scrolled capitals crushed. Laurel
and Aidan crawled over, ducked beneath, and stepped
around the devastation. Overwhelmed by the awe of
their discovery, Laurel seemed to have lost much of her
earlier trepidation.

As they went, the rhythm became louder, no longer
a tapping but resonating like a steam-driven piston, like
those Aidan had once seen while touring a coal mine
he'd invested in.

The arcade opened into another chamber, and again
Laurel gaped in astonishment. Near the center of the
floor, the giant head of a fallen statue, some three feet in
diameter, lay on its side, its blank eyes peering at them
askew.

"This must be a temple dedicated to Minerva," she
whispered as if she feared disturbing the goddess.

Aidan rapped on the tarnished statue's surface.
"Bronze. This place is a treasure hunter's dream."

To his surprise, Laurel shook her head. "There is much of historical value, to be sure, but only such treasure as a museum would covet. When the Romans abandoned their outlying colonies, they took with them everything of value they could carry. Remember, they departed Britain because the empire had begun its decline and funds had run short." She pointed through the next archway. "That way?"

He glanced at the map and nodded. Another set of steps took them deeper beneath the ruins. The rubble became denser, the way more arduous, and they saw none of the embellishments of the other chambers. The resonating thumps, accompanied now by gurgling sounds, drew them on.

The map led them to a threshold shored up by timbers resembling those in the earlier tunnel, standing out garishly new against the ancient stonework.

"I'd wager my fortune that *this* wasn't left behind by the Romans." Aidan raised his voice to be heard above the echoes of the watery pulsations coming from close by.

Through the doorway, they discovered a trestle table covered with laboratory equipment—flasks, cylinders, beakers—while shoved into a corner at the back of the table was the very same brazier Rousseau had used during his demonstration at the Pump Room. It was plain to see that the contraption, with its impressive coils and gears, wasn't much used for anything . . . other than beguiling would-be investors.

A larger, quite conventional brazier hugged another of the walls. Beside it stood an assortment of casks, undoubtedly for storing the formula. A familiar sulfuric odor permeated the air.

"Rousseau's secret laboratory," Aidan murmured. Part of him itched to leave now, both to make his report to Micklebee and to get Laurel to safety. But they still had much to learn.

"The noise is coming from in there." Holding a hand over her nose, she pointed across the chamber. Wisps of steam drifted through a low archway. Exchanging a glance, they ducked and continued on through.

Aidan had expected to discover some sort of mechanical pump, which would have explained the pulsations. Instead, a single structure dominated the space, a basin carved into the limestone bedrock. At the center of the pool, steaming water heaved upward as if forced from deep within the earth, forming a massive bubble that burst on the surface and spread in frothing ripples. Each bubble sent up a spray of hissing steam and resonated with the throbbing rhythm they had heard.

"The thermal spring must be directly beneath us." Excitement quivered in Laurel's voice. She even lowered her hand from her nose, though the stench here was nearly unbearable.

"Rousseau's source of unsullied water." Aidan swung the lantern in a slow arc to illuminate the walls and corners of the chamber. Seeing nothing but rough stone, he ushered Laurel back into the adjoining room. "Now let's see if we can discover what makes perfectly reasonable individuals lose their heads."

As Aidan began opening the containers lining Rousseau's laboratory table, the echo of his words held Laurel immobile. They had lost their heads the day of the picnic. Did he view their subsequent lovemaking in a similar light? With blunt honesty he had confessed his inability—or was it unwillingness?—to offer her more than they had already shared.

Oh, but he had also made the stars dance for her.

Yes, to give her a fond memory with which to warm herself as she grew old without him.

Except for the bubbling waters in the next chamber, the room grew quiet, and Laurel snapped out of her broodings to find that Aidan had stopped rummaging through Rousseau's supplies. He peered intently at her.

"I just realized what I said." A stride brought him to her. His arms went around her. "Damn. I didn't mean it as it sounded."

Standing tall, she refused to yield to his embrace, or to her own unquenchable desires. "Yes, you did and you are correct. Rousseau's elixir did cause us to lose control."

"Ah, but not every time, Laurel."

She looked at the ground. "Once unleashed, passion tends to take on a life of its own. That is why society adheres to such strict rules. We should not have broken those rules."

"I don't believe that—" He stopped short, tension coursing through his body and into hers. He lowered his arms and stepped back. Very softly, he said, "Perhaps you are right."

She nodded, the constriction of her throat too great to allow for words. Blinking moisture from her eyes as she walked past him, she went to the table. Choosing a vial at random, she held the vessel beneath her nose. The odor made her whisk her head aside. "Oh, that's bitter! What is it?"

He took the vial and ventured a whiff. "Wormwood."

"I don't remember Rousseau naming that as one of the ingredients."

"He didn't." Aidan selected a flask. "Smell this."

"Licorice?"

"Aniseed. There is also juniper, fennel, dittany . . ." He hefted a jug from beneath the table, pulled the stopper, and sniffed. "Alcohol." His nose pinched, his lips whitening with anger, he said, "I know what the bastard is doing."

"Then please enlighten me—"

Muffled voices reverberated along the tunnel walls. A cry lodged in Laurel's throat but went no farther.

"Quickly!" he urged. They replaced the containers in their original positions. Reaching for Laurel's hand, Aidan hurried her back out into the main passage.

There he paused to lower the lantern's wick until only a droplet of orange lit the way.

"We can't go back the way we came," Laurel whispered.

"I never intended to."

She started to question him, but he shushed her with a look that warned her not to make an unnecessary sound. When she expected them to make a hasty retreat, he instead turned into the first doorway they came to.

Here, the floor sloped sharply upward, and as Laurel climbed into the tunnel, she realized this was due to the partial collapse of the ceiling. Her scarlet silks and rich velvet cape snagged on the jagged rubble. With a hand at her bottom Aidan assisted her progress, and together they crouched and crawled along the debris. When they could go no farther, they wedged themselves among the rocks to keep from tumbling back down into the central corridor, perhaps into the path of the intruders.

Aidan drew out his pistol and blew out the lantern.

The profound blackness threatened to suffocate her. Upon entering the culvert tonight, she had nearly begged him to take her back out into the cool, open air. It had felt too terrifyingly similar to the tunnel in her nightmare, when the crackling flames had driven her and her governess to the tunnels beneath the house and the horror of being buried alive had dogged her every step.

For Aidan, she had shoved those fears aside. Now, only the press of his body as he settled beside her anchored her senses.

"Not a sound," he breathed.

She nodded, understanding. Echoes traveled far in this place. As easily as they had heard the others coming, so would they have been heard making their escape.

Perspiration stung her eyes and trickled maddeningly down her sides. In vain she attempted to close her ears to the creatures scampering among the ruins. When something tickled its way across her hand, she bit the sides of her mouth to keep from crying out.

A glow wavered on the ground outside in the main passage. The sound of footsteps rebounded along the walls, along with a curious rapping. Every few steps it came. *Rap*, *rap*, like something striking the wall. They were close, so very close, only yards away. The voices came intermittently, garbled by their own echoes and the thump-thump of the thermal spring.

Yet through the distortion, Laurel perceived the drawl of a French accent.

Against her, Aidan went rigid.

Though they could still hear the voices, the footsteps stopped. Whoever it was must have reached the laboratory. Laurel and Aidan waited, then waited some more. Then, slowly, Aidan began to move. First he struck a lucifer, the sound so loud in the silence that Laurel thought surely they would be discovered. He relit the lamp, turning it as low as it would go without extinguishing the flame. Making his way over the rubble with painstaking care, he helped Laurel down as he went.

"They must be in the lab," he whispered against her ear when they once more stood in the main tunnel.

Taking her hand firmly in his, he led her, creeping step by silent step, along the tunnel until they reached another fork. Aidan checked the map and chose a direction that led them into another series of drainage ducts. Here, he began to breathe more easily. Taking his cue, Laurel allowed some of the tension to drain from her stiffened limbs and sore neck.

"We must be near the Cross Baths," he murmured. "According to the map they drain to the south of the city, and that should put us where we'll want to be."

Though puzzled by his words, she held her questions in check. Her body ached. Her feet and hems were soaked, the shoes, gown, and cape ruined as he had predicted. His evening wear hadn't fared much better. But bother their clothing. They had narrowly escaped being apprehended by possible murderers.

For all that, she would not have wished herself elsewhere, not unless Aidan were there as well. Soon enough they would part; he had made that much clear. Until then, she would savor every moment, however cold or wet or dangerous.

They stopped frequently so Aidan could pinpoint their location on the map. While the drainage system curved away to spill out beneath the Broad Quay wharves, a tunnel led them into a tiny, damp cellar. In one corner, a narrow wooden staircase climbed to a trapdoor in the ceiling.

Aidan started up. "Let's hope this is it."

Chapter 24

With a shove, Aidan dislodged the trapdoor from its frame. He laid aside the wooden planking and poked his head up through the opening. "Hand me back the lantern."

When Laurel passed it to him, he reached up to set it on the floor above him before climbing the rest of the way. Pewter light peeked through gaps in the wooden walls around them, signaling the arrival of dawn.

He helped Laurel up, then drew her into his arms and kissed her soundly. "Thank God we made it out of there in one piece. I'd never have forgiven myself if . . ."

Her arms around his neck, she smiled broadly. "Don't think about what might have happened."

How could he not? There had been a terrifying moment when his thoughts had slipped out of his control. His mind had run amok with fear, and he had pictured Laurel dying at the hands of those men back in the tunnel.

Rousseau? He believed so. Fitz? He honestly couldn't say. All he knew was that while time had hung suspended like a sojourn in hell, he had finally comprehended the despair that had prompted his father to place a pistol in his mouth and pull the trigger.

He didn't wish to ever feel that way again. The pain was

too great, too crippling. He had made a grave mistake in bringing Laurel with him and he would die before he made the same error in judgment again. He had his life; she had hers. It was time they accepted that those lives were never meant to intersect, and must not do so ever again.

Outside, the air gradually filled with shouts and rumbles and hammering, the sounds of the dockworkers beginning their day.

"Come, we'd better be fast before it gets any lighter out." After closing the trapdoor, he made his way past barrels and crates to the nearest window. The shutters were fastened tightly, secured with brackets and a metal bar, just as he had suspected the morning he had first visited this warehouse.

Behind him, Laurel asked, "Shouldn't we see what Rousseau is storing here?"

It was his turn to smile. They hadn't discussed what this place could be, but apparently she needed no explanations.

"If we don't leave now, someone will see us exiting the place." Looking about, he spotted a small crate and dragged it over to the window. Sliding the bar from the brackets, he cracked the shutters and peered outside. "Good, it's the alley and not Broad Quay. I'll go first and help you out."

He stepped onto the crate, levering first his torso and then his legs over the sill. It was a good ten feet to the packed-dirt alleyway below. Lowering his body, he hung by his hands for a moment and then dropped. When his feet hit the ground, he bent his knees and rolled to his back to absorb the impact.

The sun not yet up, deep shadow draped the alley. Though the clamor of morning activity continued to resonate from beyond the buildings, here all lay still. Nonetheless he huddled close to the wall, listening and searching the immediate darkness for movement. Seeing none, he stood up and faced the window.

Laurel's features stood out small and moonlike in the surrounding gloom. He held out his arms. "I'll catch you."

"What about the lantern?" she whispered back.

"Leave it, it doesn't matter." He would have preferred leaving no trace that they had been here, but it couldn't be helped. There was no way for them to reinsert the bar over the window shutter.

She threw her cape down to him first. Wrestling with her skirts, she managed to swing her legs over the sill. She lowered herself and hung by her hands as he had done, only longer.

"I promise I'll catch you."

She let go. Her skirts ballooned, and then her body struck his chest. His arms closed around her and together they fell. His back struck the ground, cushioning her fall but sending bolts of pain through his side.

Laurel must have heard his grunt, for she instantly rolled off him. "I'm sorry!"

If his ribs hadn't been broken previously, they almost certainly were now. "Just help me up."

Holding an arm to his side, he crept to the mouth of the alley. Laurel followed close. His back flat to the wall, he inched his head around the corner of the building. A welcome sight sent relief pouring through him.

On the street, the cabriolet stood waiting. Though the horse appeared to be dozing, Phelps sat alert in the driver's box. In plain sight, he held his pistol across his thigh as a warning to any who would be tempted by the sight of the costly vehicle.

"Laurel," Aidan said, "run."

Laurel still hadn't caught her breath when, some five minutes later, they climbed to the third floor of a tenement building on Avon Street—the same tenement to which she had followed Aidan that day she saw him at the bank.

He knocked on the door of a flat, sending chipped paint sprinkling the floor at their feet. After some moments a husky voice from inside demanded, "What d'you want?"

"It's Barensforth."

"Do you know what bloody time it is?" The door opened to reveal an individual who clearly had just dragged himself out of bed. His nightshirt askew, his hair standing up in a dozen different directions, he attempted unsuccessfully to stifle a yawn. Yet the sight of Laurel brought a spark of clarity to his eyes. "What the devil?"

"Don't worry, she's working for us," Aidan said as he pushed past the man and into the room.

"What he means," she explained calmly as she, too, crossed the threshold, "is that at the moment you both work for me." She extended a hand. "I am Laurel Sutherland. How do you do?"

"Phineas Micklebee, at your service." He shook her hand, then scratched his head. "I'm clearly still asleep."

"This is no dream, and what we discovered last night was no illusion." Wasting no time in launching into an explanation of their exploits beneath the city, Aidan shrugged out of his evening coat and sank into a kitchen chair.

His groan sent Laurel to him. She crouched beside his legs and gently laid a hand against his side. "He was injured in a fall," she said over her shoulder to Mr. Micklebee. "Have you anything with which we might bind his ribs?"

"Never mind that, I'll be fine." Aidan silenced her protests with a finger across her lips, though a lingering hint of longing in his eye told her he would rather have used his mouth instead.

"So you believe you heard Rousseau in the tunnels," the Home Office agent said, working through what they had told him so far. "Are you certain there was only one other individual with him?"

Laurel took a seat beside Aidan at the table. "Yes, as far as we could tell, but sounds can be deceiving in those tunnels. We only recognized Rousseau because of his accent."

"Rousseau has a particular inflection that distinguishes his speech patterns," Aidan said. "But as far as the other voice, it could have been any Englishman. The echoes made it impossible to differentiate. Although it couldn't have been Fitz."

"How can you be certain?" Mr. Micklebee asked.

"That stutter of his. I'd recognize it anywhere, even with the echoes."

"All right, for now we have identified one participant." Mr. Micklebee set about lighting his cookstove and readying a pot of coffee. "What did you find in the laboratory?"

Aidan pushed out a mirthless laugh. "Rousseau is brewing absinthe. That's the secret of his elixir, the reason people feel invincible and behave recklessly but have no sense of being intoxicated."

Laurel questioned him with a frown.

"Absinthe," he repeated. "Also known as the Green Lady or the Green Goddess. Far more potent than any wine or even whiskey. Yet for reasons no one quite understands, the mixture of alcohol with wormwood and the other herbs we found produce what's been termed a 'euphoric clarity of the mind.' People under the influence of absinthe are certainly intoxicated, but in such a way that they are fooled into believing their mental capacities have been enhanced, not hindered."

"Alchemy of the mind, I've heard it called." Mr. Micklebee joined them at the table while the coffeepot began to hiss aromatic jets of steam.

Aidan nodded. "Based on the effects Laurel and I experienced, I'd say Rousseau has been lacing his mineral water with just enough of the stuff to bring on a state of exhilaration, without allowing the taste to raise suspicions."

"Enough to persuade them of the elixir's magical qualities," Laurel added, "and send them straight to the bank to invest in the spa, the only place Rousseau's elixir will be available."

"Except that in the end there will be no such place," Aidan said. "Only a great deal of disappointment and many depleted finances."

"And, of course, a handful of individuals with heavier pockets than they had at the outset," Mr. Micklebee said in conclusion. Rising, he rummaged up three earthenware cups, filled them with coffee, and passed them around.

At a knock at the door, the three of them jumped. After last night's events, Laurel would rather they remained silent until whoever it was gave up and went away, but Aidan and Phineas Micklebee exchanged a guarded look before the latter man rose.

"Who is it?" he said gruffly through the closed door.

"Ben, sir."

Micklebee opened the door crack. "What've you got?"

"A message, sir."

Standing on the threshold was a lad of about seventeen. Laurel caught a quick glimpse of tousled brown hair, ragged clothing, and a pair of faded old boots. A dirty hand extended a folded missive. Mr. Micklebee snatched it and examined the seal before fishing a coin from a pair of trousers slung over the foot of the bed.

"Thanks, Ben. Come back before noon. I'll have outgoing for you."

"Yes, sir." With that, the boy turned and left.

"He's worked out well for you?" Aidan asked.

"Ben finds being a courier preferable to life in Marshalsea." Micklebee used a kitchen knife to slit the seal. "This will take a few minutes."

Laurel found his next actions puzzling. Taking a quill and inkpot from a cupboard, he moved nearer to the light seeping through the window and began scratching out words between the lines of the message.

"May I ask what you are doing?"

Without looking up from his task, Mr. Micklebee replied, "Code."

"What?"

"It's written in code," Aidan said. "Micklebee is making the words coherent."

Several minutes later, the agent said, "You were right about the investment firm. Bryce-Rawlings seems only to exist on paper. Our people found nothing at the address on Red Lion Court."

"Not surprising." Aidan stood and went to peer over the man's shoulder. "Do we know yet who established the company?"

"No, but . . ." Mr. Micklebee set down his quill. Even in the dim light, Laurel saw the color drain from his face. "You'll want to sit back down for this, mate."

Laurel started at Aidan's abrupt movement, and in the time it took her to blink, he had taken possession of the letter. "Why the devil should I sit down?"

He scanned the contents. Then his hand dropped to his side and the paper fluttered to the floor. He turned as white as Micklebee. Whiter.

His distress brought Laurel to her feet. "What is it?"

His mouth worked, but no words came out. His features pulled taut. His hands fisted.

"Aidan, please."

The agent stooped to pick up the letter. He gestured to Aidan. "His theory all along has been that if he could discover who owned the warehouse you were in this morning, he'd learn not only who was ultimately behind the Summit Pavilion scam, but also who murdered the

MP Roger Babcock. This letter contains the name of that person."

"Isn't it Rousseau?"

Aidan shook his head. Mr. Micklebee continued. "Rousseau and his elixir are an essential part of the deception, but another financier lies at the heart of the swindle."

"Lord Munster, then?"

The agent started to reply, but Aidan spoke over him. "The name the Home Office found is Melinda Radcliffe, Countess of Fairmont."

The bells of Bath Abbey struck nine in the morning, startling Aidan out of his thoughts. The carriage listed as Phelps weaved the cabriolet in and out of slower traffic, and every now and then the manservant shouted for vehicles to move out of the way. Though the quality were still abed or enjoying their breakfasts, the streets of Bath were alive with delivery wagons making their way to the back doors of shops and the service entrances of elegant homes.

Sitting beside Aidan, Laurel broke the tense silence that had fallen between them. "Where are you taking me now?"

They had just left Abbey Green, where she had changed her clothes, washed her hands and face, and restored her hair to order. But even Micklebee had agreed that she should not be left alone at her lodging house, not until everyone involved in the Summit Pavilion fraud had been apprehended. And especially not until they learned how Roger Babcock had died. If it hadn't been an accident—and Aidan was certain it had not—then his murderer could be anyone. Anyone at all.

Dear God, even Melinda might bear some responsibility for the MP's death. Aidan refused to believe his godmother could be capable of taking a life, but until he learned the entire truth, even she remained a focus of his suspicions.

"Somewhere you won't be alone," he said. "Not Melinda's."

Under ordinary circumstances, Fenwick House would have been his first choice. Given their situation, he hadn't yet decided where she would be safest. He had merely told Phelps to head north.

"I see no reason why I should not remain with you and see this through." Laurel tilted her chin in a show of stubbornness.

He gripped the hand strap with undue force as the cabriolet turned a corner. "Yes, well, I can cite several reasons. And I don't care whose authority you invoke— from now on we'll do this my way."

"I should be present when you confront Melinda."

He gritted his teeth and said nothing.

"Aidan, don't believe for one moment that she has done anything illegal or immoral. If she purchased that warehouse, it is because she was duped into doing so."

"As she was duped into donating her land to the Bath Corporation for the pavilion?"

Shock turned Laurel's eyes to saucers. "What?"

"It's true." He sighed and angled a gaze out the window. His insides churned with misery and frustration. "That hillside used to belong to the Fenwick estate. So you see, Melinda is waist deep in the mire."

Her hand closed around his chin; she turned his face to hers. "There is an explanation."

He shrugged.

"Aidan, stop it." She framed his face between her palms and set her lips to his, a light, sweet touch that triggered an almost crushing need to pull her into his arms and bury his face in her hair, her neck, her bosom. He kissed her back but resisted the rest.

He drew back and said, "I'm not going to see Melinda. Not yet. It's time for me to end a friendship first."

"Lord Munster?"

"I'm going to get the truth out of Fitz if I have to beat it out of him."

Her cheeks blanched. "You can't go there alone," she whispered. "You said he might have murdered that man."

He leaned back against the squabs and gathered her to his chest despite his resolve to begin distancing himself from her. "The thought may have crossed my mind, but I don't believe it. I've been shadowing George Fitzclarence for over three years now."

Somehow his fingertips found their way to her hair. He stroked reassurances while being careful not to dislodge the newly arranged curls from their pins. "He has trusted me, and I probably know him better than most of his siblings. He may be an unprincipled scoundrel, but he simply isn't the murdering kind."

She slid her arms around him and pressed her cheek to his shirtfront. "Promise me you'll be safe with him."

"I promise." Outside, he recognized the manicured approach to Queen Square. "Turn in," he called to Phelps. To Laurel he said, "I'm bringing to you Beatrice. You'll be safe there."

"What about her husband? He left the Guildhall, too, that night."

"They're estranged, so he won't be at home. Besides, he proceeded on to Stoddard's that night, not to the bridge with Fitz and Rousseau. The only thing I believe Devonlea is guilty of is risking Beatrice's financial well-being with gambling and foolish investments."

"Very well, but what shall we tell her about why I am intruding uninvited upon her morning?"

Aidan hesitated. Beatrice would likely see through any lie they concocted. Could he trust her with the truth? He had always found her to be honest and straightforward, and not once had he ever doubted the sincerity of her concerns for her eldest brother.

"Say nothing about the Home Office or the queen,

nor mention Rousseau's elixir. Tell her only that having detected a discrepancy in the pavilion records, I suspect fraud and have set my solicitor on the trail. We'll tell her Fitz may be involved with dangerous men, and that I am resolved to help him if I can."

"Are you?" Laurel gazed up at him with solemn eyes. "Will you give him a chance to redeem himself?"

It was a question he couldn't yet answer.

Chapter 25

Despite the early hour, Fitz's butler hardly blinked at Aidan's arrival. The main staff, which followed Fitz from residence to residence, had grown accustomed to Aidan's coming and going freely, and at any time of the day or night.

Surprised to learn that Fitz was already out of bed and breakfasting in his library, Aidan saw himself up to the second floor. He would have thought Fitz too hungover to stir before noon, but he discovered him hunched in a wing chair placed close to the fireplace. Like Micklebee's, his hair stood raggedly on end, and though he had donned breeches and boots as if intending a morning ride, he remained coatless and wore neither collar nor cravat.

Chin in hand, Fitz stared vacantly into the coal-fed flames. A platter of poached eggs and a slab of ham lay untouched on the table beside him. Next to his plate, a crystal decanter reflected the firelight. Apparently, breakfast this morning consisted of brandy, and plenty of it, from the way Fitz's head lolled in his hand.

"A bit early for that, isn't it?" Aidan said as he entered the room.

Fitz lifted his face from his palm. "Aidan? What're you d-doing here, old b-boy?"

Reaching into his waistcoat, Aidan withdrew the documents he and Laurel had discovered last night. He slapped the leather-bound bundle against Fitz's chest.

The flap opened, but Fitz caught the papers before they scattered to the floor. The moment stretched, and he raised a red-rimmed gaze weighted by a liquor-induced languor. "So you've f-found me out, have you? C-clever of you. How did you ever m-manage it?"

"*How* doesn't matter, you sodding bastard. Whatever possessed you, Fitz? Why would you do such a vile thing to people who are your friends?"

Fitz's hand came up in a gesture of supplication, then slapped palm down on the documents resting in his lap. "I s-suppose you're right. I've b-been a wretched sh-shithouse, n-not including you."

"Not including me?" Grabbing handfuls of Fitz's shirt, Aidan hauled him from the settee, sending the king's documents fluttering. "You believe I am here for my *cut*?"

Fitz merely blinked and frowned and swayed on his feet. He might have fallen if Aidan hadn't held tight to his sleeves. With a disgusted thrust he returned Fitz to his chair and fisted his hands in the air.

"Haven't I taken care of you? Seen to it you won at the gaming tables? Kept you out of scrapes and supplied you with more than ample pocket change?"

"What *are* you g-going on about?"

"Damn it, Fitz." A current of rage sizzled beneath Aidan's skin. Again he gripped Fitz by the shoulders and heaved him to his feet, venting his fury in a shove that sent the heavier man stumbling backward until he struck the desk positioned before the window. The mahogany piece shuddered on its legs. Fitz collapsed onto the leather-padded surface, his arms flailing. Ledger books, inkpots, and a silver box of quills clattered to the floor.

In his oddly inverted position, Fitz gaped up at the

ceiling. "Have you l-lost your mind? C-could have k-killed me."

The commotion having drained a measure of his anger, Aidan poured more brandy into the snifter and carried it to the desk. He offered his friend a hand to help him up. "Here, drink. It will help."

Perched on the edge of the desk, Fitz used both hands to bring the snifter to his lips. When he'd drained half the contents, Aidan took the glass and set it aside.

"You're up to your ears in hot water, my friend, and this time I might not be able to supply the lifeline to keep you afloat."

Fitz looked thoroughly confused, which might merely have been due to the continuation of his drunken state from last night into this morning. "I d-don't understand. Rousseau and I have m-merely taken up where our f-fathers left off. It's exciting, old b-boy, the p-potential in this elixir. W-we will add y-years to people's lives."

Was he serious? Looking him up and down and finding no sign of artifice in his manner, Aidan very nearly believed so. Could Fitz have been duped by Rousseau? Perhaps, but there was too much at stake for carelessness . . . or for misplaced pity.

"If you and Rousseau meant no harm, why have you denied having anything more than a casual association with the man?"

"That was R-Rousseau's idea. He s-said the f-formula should appear n-new, and not s-something dug up from d-decades ago. He said p-people nowadays want m-modern, fresh ideas, especially in the sc-sciences."

"The elixir is a fake. A fraud," Aidan said bluntly, narrowing his eyes to observe Fitz's reaction.

He gave an adamant shake of his head. "No, no. We f-followed the recipe exactly, except to m-make improvements. The h-herbs, Aidan. The herbs have m-made all the d-difference."

"It was not the herbs, damn it." Frustration again

curled Aidan's hands into fists. He began pacing back and forth to spend the energy rather than vent his anger on the other man again—at least for now. He couldn't promise himself he wouldn't throttle Fitz soundly before he handed him over to the authorities.

He halted near the hearth, temptingly close to the iron poker. "It's the absinthe Rousseau has been mixing into his elixir that has people convinced their ailments have been cured. It's the absinthe that has persuaded them to invest their fortunes."

"Absinthe? N-no, that's im-p-possible. . . ."

Aidan felt himself losing the battle with his rising temper. "You have been bringing the supplies in through the warehouse you swindled Melinda into purchasing—"

"No one has s-swindled Lady F-Fairmont. You h-have this all wr-wrong."

"Oh? And I suppose you'd have me believe she handed over the land for the Summit Pavilion without the mind-altering persuasion of absinthe."

Fitz didn't so much as blink as he replied, "She donated the p-property before the first b-batch of elixir had even been m-mixed."

"Don't lie to me, Fitz. So help me—"

"I s-swear it's true, Aidan."

"Why would a levelheaded woman like Melinda do something so foolhardy and pointless?"

"It isn't p-pointless. The elixir is w-working. Lady Fairmont was m-much more ill before she began t-taking it."

Aidan's insides ran cold. "What are you saying?"

"The elixir is k-keeping her alive."

"Don't, my friend." His steely whisper quivered with fresh rage, this time threatening to erupt beyond his control. "Do not dare use my godmother's name to lie your way out of this."

"She's d-dying, Aidan."

Propelled by a firestorm of indignant fury and stubborn denial, Aidan rushed his friend. A right hook caught Fitz beneath his flaccid chin. Aidan heard the crack and felt the sting in his knuckles. He saw shock and then pain register in Fitz's bloodshot eyes. The man blinked and toppled, taking the desk lamp with him as he crumpled to the floor. The glass shattered, spilling oil onto the parquet floor and soaking Fitz's sleeve.

The ensuing silence filled Aidan with a chilling and undeniable truth.

She has been poorly several times since the New Year. And once or twice before that, sir. Mrs. Prewitt, Melinda's housekeeper, had told him this the last time Melinda fell ill.

"She's dying?"

Blinking away the stupor caused by Aidan's punch, Fitz slowly sat up. With a groan he cupped a palm to his chin. "A d-disease of the blood, according to D-Dr. Bailey."

With his other hand Fitz held the edge of the desk and struggled to his feet, and Aidan realized his friend would not have weathered the blow so well if he hadn't been deep in his cups. That, and the fact that, at the last minute, something had caused Aidan to restrain the force of the blow.

"She didn't w-want you to know, old boy. D-didn't want anyone to know and gave Bailey s-strictest orders to k-keep it hush-hush."

"Good God. Melinda . . ." A sinking helplessness seeped through Aidan. He wanted to shout at the injustice of it, smash things, and destroy the room . . . yet the knowledge that he was powerless to change the situation wrapped around him like shackles and held him immobile.

"That's l-like her, though, isn't it? Plucky old d-duck, Lady Fairmont is. She b-believes the elixir is helping her, and s-so do I." Fitz actually smiled despite the swelling on his chin. "Th-think of it, old man. A miracle cure.

B-bottled longevity. What m-might men achieve with
the extra y-years we provide them?"

"Bloody hell, Fitz . . ." Aidan's bellowed response
shook with the emotion he couldn't contain. Bone-
crushing weariness dragging at his limbs, he circled the
desk and sank into the studded leather chair. His head
fell into his hands. Swallowing, he continued more quietly, "The elixir is an illusion. So is the Summit Pavilion.
The financial records, the initial shareholders, the investment firm—it's all a sham."

When several moments passed and Fitz didn't speak,
Aidan glanced up at him. The change in the man took
him aback. Staring openmouthed into thin air, Fitz looked
crestfallen, beaten . . . crushed.

"That c-can't be . . . ," he whispered. "The p-pavilion
is m-my dream. My l-legacy."

His head sagging between his shoulders, Fitz made
his way back to the wing chair and fell into it. "All we
w-wanted . . . all *I* wanted . . . was to c-continue my father's
dream. To b-build a legacy for when I am g-gone."

His gaze drifted to the flames in the hearth. "D-damn
it, Aidan, my f-father let the dream s-slip through his
hands. When Victoria's f-father died, *my* father gave up.
And now he's d-dead, too. What will he b-be remembered for? An undistinguished reign and a p-passel
of illegitimate brats. As for m-me . . . I'll be n-nothing
more than a smudge in the h-history books. Illegible . . .
b-bloody inconsequential."

Eyes burning, he raised his face. "I am n-nothing,
Aidan. Neither r-royal nor common, neither here n-nor
there. And I am g-growing old. Old and worn-out and
b-broken. And this—" He spread his hand wide, then
bunched his fingers in a fist. "*This* s-seemed a way to
redeem a w-wasted life."

"You went snatching at shadows," Aidan said, sympathy and repugnance at war within him. "Shadows
have no substance, Fitz, only a darkness that sucks you

in and destroys whatever hope there might have been for you."

In a staggering flash of understanding, he realized he might have been speaking of himself. For years now the darkness of his parents' fates had been the driving force of his existence, his work for the Home Office fueled not by altruism but by a kind of twisted, backdoor revenge, both on people like those who had swindled his father and on himself. All these years of putting his own life second, of denying himself a proper home, family . . . love. Had it all truly been in the name of duty, or self-punishment for his failure to recognize a scam and save his father?

His answer came not in words but in the image of a beautiful face framed in wild golden curls. The image wrapped itself around his heart so tightly that a bolt of panic shot through him. To love so deeply, so painfully, meant risking loss, heartache, despair . . . such as his father had known.

Apprehending criminals was easy. Was he strong enough for love?

Fearing the question as he had never feared an adversary, he forced his attention back to the man slumped before him. Crossing the room, Aidan perched on the settee opposite Fitz's chair. "Did Rousseau murder Roger Babcock?"

With a slight shrug, Fitz shook his head. "All I know is that Babcock w-wanted to see me the day he died. His message said it was urgent, but we n-never did meet. He was found d-dead that morning."

"He must have discovered Rousseau's deception. Or he knew of it all along and decided he wanted out. Though I don't quite see Rousseau as a murderer . . ." Aidan considered for a moment, then asked, "When did Rousseau first approach you about resuming the project begun by your fathers?"

"He d-didn't. I approached *him*."

Aidan frowned, not at all liking the implications of Fitz's admission. He would have preferred to fix the blame squarely on Rousseau. "He didn't put you up to stealing your father's documents?"

"I didn't s-steal them."

"Then how did you obtain them?"

"My sister g-gave them to me."

Like a tremor from the ground, the revelation rattled Aidan's bones. "Which sister? Not Beatrice."

"Of course, B-Bea. She d-discovered them when F-Father died. But she is a w-woman. What could she have d-done with them? N-naturally, she gave them to me."

"Beatrice . . . and Devonlea. Good Christ!" Aidan surged to his feet. The answer had been staring him in the face, taunting him, all along, but he had allowed his personal feelings to blind him. He had overestimated Beatrice and underestimated Devonlea.

Even now he hoped, prayed, he was wrong. He clung to the possibility that Beatrice knew nothing about the fraudulent nature of Bryce-Rawlings Unlimited, or of Rousseau's trickery, or if she did, that she had been coerced by that pompous, patronizing husband of hers. Indeed, that must be the source of their current marital discord.

But what if Beatrice *was* involved . . . what if she and Devonlea had only feigned their estrangement in order to deflect suspicion from themselves? Even with the abridged story he and Laurel had agreed upon, Beatrice would know that Aidan had gone to question her brother, and she would easily guess that Fitz would link her to their father's documents and the Summit Pavilion fraud.

How might she react?

He took off at a run, heading for the stairs. "Stay here. Do nothing until you hear from me."

"Where are you r-rushing off to?" Fitz called after him.

From the top of the stairs, Aidan shouted, "Queen Square. I walked Laurel straight into danger."

"My dear Mrs. Sanderson, you mustn't take anything Aidan says seriously. I told you he and my brother would come to blows over you. I simply never imagined Aidan would stoop so low as to invent such ridiculous slander about poor, hapless George."

Having dismissed her maid, Lady Devonlea crossed her boudoir, a room designed explicitly to a woman's taste with its feminine florals and bright striped chintzes. She threw open her wardrobe doors and selected an ivory morning gown, its frilled oversleeves and tiered skirts the very latest rage from London.

"Your brother is far from hapless, Lady Devonlea," Laurel replied as she helped the woman on with the dress, tugging it down over corset and crinolines. The viscountess's hauteur rankled, but then she knew only a fraction of the story and Laurel was not yet at liberty to reveal the rest. "And neither is Aidan inventing tales. In his pursuit of quick wealth, your brother has involved himself with dangerous men and dastardly deeds."

Turning her back to Laurel, Lady Devonlea laughed, a cynical burst. If she had been slightly flustered by Laurel's sudden appearance earlier, she had recovered her aplomb quickly enough. "Lace me up, please. I believe I know both men far better than you. For whatever reason, Aidan has you fooled, just as he has fooled countless other women in the past. Perhaps he seeks to hide his own illicit dealings. Perhaps he merely wishes to coax you into his bed." Peeking over her shoulder, she smiled coyly. "Has he succeeded, my dear?"

Any fondness Laurel had ever felt toward the woman evaporated instantly. She gave the coral satin laces a firm, final tug and tied a bow at Lady Devonlea's nape. "Aidan would never betray my trust."

"I see he *has* seduced you." She waggled a finger

back and forth in her face. "You should have heeded my
warnings. Poor thing. Did he manipulate you into believing the seduction was all your idea? That is how he oper-
ates. Typically, though, he preys upon married women.
That way his affairs are always fleeting, with no threat
of commitment. Congratulations. I do believe you are
his first widow."

A snippet of truth in the woman's mocking words
made Laurel's heart contract. Aidan hadn't manipulated
her into his bed; she had gone willingly, joyfully. But neither had he offered her any form of commitment. In
fact, he had made his intentions perfectly plain. There
would be no proposal, no future together.

He had admitted to wanting her. He cared for her,
perhaps deeply, but not deeply enough to change his life.
Perhaps he loved her, but not as much as he loved his
work.

In the foyer below, the door knocker clanged. The
continuing clamor drove all other considerations from
Laurel's mind. Could Aidan have returned so quickly
from his confrontation with the Earl of Munster?

Over the maid's protests, a man's shouts rose up the
staircase. "Beatrice? Come down here. I demand to see
you this instant."

Lady Devonlea released a breath. "How exceedingly
tiresome he is." But her face blanched as she spoke, and
a kernel of fear sprouted in her gaze. "Wait here."

Laurel lingered long enough for the viscountess's
footsteps to recede down the stairs. Then she hurried
out to the landing in time to hear Lord Devonlea say,
"You are my wife and you'll do as I say."

Laurel tiptoed down the first few steps and leaned
over the rail, straining to hear. She caught a glimpse of
the couple. The viscount had wrapped a hand around
his wife's arm and was towing her none too gently down
the hall, toward the salon adjoining the dining hall. The
maid was nowhere in sight.

The couple's raised voices echoed through the rooms.

"This sort of behavior will get you nowhere, Arthur."

"Oh? Do you not know I could divorce you on grounds of infidelity and leave you with nothing?"

"A lot of good my money will do you while you're swinging from the gallows."

"Me? Why you little . . ."

The next words were lost beneath the tramp of feet and the whack of a piece of furniture being knocked out of place. Porcelain shattered. Lady Devonlea let out a shriek of laughter that sent a chill scurrying down Laurel's back.

She started down the steps but paused when a door above her opened.

"I say, what's all the commotion?"

Laurel turned. Seeing a familiar figure poised on the landing, she gasped. "Lord Julian?"

Nodding his blond head, Julian Stoddard flashed a rueful grin. "I fear they must be arguing over me."

Before the implications of his admission had registered with Laurel, the front door shuddered from a sudden pounding from outside. Aidan's shouts penetrated the heavy panels.

"Laurel? Beatrice? Let me in!"

From the parlor, Lord Devonlea bellowed, "Perhaps I'll simply kill you now!"

"Lord Julian, we must do something!" Laurel raced down the stairs and fumbled to turn the key hanging in the lock. Her fingers shaking, she jiggled it back and forth until the latch clicked. The door burst open, and then she was in Aidan's arms, her face pressed to his shirtfront.

Chapter 26

Relief cascaded through Aidan in torrents as he crushed Laurel to him and allowed each of his five senses to assure him that no harm had come to her. Yet the time for rejoicing passed all too quickly. She pushed out of his embrace, her face a mask of alarm.

"Quickly! He's going to hurt her!" A crash exploded down the hall, followed by the clash of combative voices. "They're in the salon," Laurel cried.

Leaving her framed in the doorway clutching her skirts, Aidan ran through the closest archway and dashed the length of the dining hall to the smaller parlor beyond.

A battle seemed to have taken place in Beatrice's India Blue Salon. Among upset vases and furnishings that had been knocked askew, Devonlea had her pressed up against a wall. His hands were at her neck. Her eyes bulging, Beatrice gripped his wrists and sputtered for breath.

Aidan launched himself at the viscount's back. Latching on to Devonlea's arms, he heaved him away from Beatrice and spun him about. In the corner of his eye he saw Beatrice collapse to her hands and knees, her head dipping between her shoulders as she dragged air into her lungs. Devonlea's face registered surprise, then panic as Aidan drew back a fist.

Devonlea's hands shot up in an attempt to shield his face. "Don't! You don't under—"

Aidan's fist caught the side of his jaw. Devonlea went down, overturning a small marquetry table and a bronze plant stand. The pot smashed and dirt and leaves skittered across the tile floor. The viscount fell onto his back, out cold.

As the sting of the blow radiated up his forearm, Aidan shook out his hand. Laurel swept into the room, stopping long enough to take in the prone viscount and the fact that Aidan was still on his feet before she hastened to Beatrice's side.

"Lady Devonlea, are you hurt?" Laurel wrapped an arm around Beatrice's waist and helped her sit up. "Can you speak?"

"He . . . has gone mad."

On the floor, Devonlea stirred. Crouching beside him to assess the damage his fist had done, Aidan heard footsteps approaching the hallway entrance to the salon. Expecting a servant, he was surprised to discover Julian Stoddard limping through the doorway with the aid of his walking stick.

Their gazes met, Aidan's no doubt filled with questions and Julian's conveying the promise of forthcoming answers. But the young man also had questions of his own.

"What on earth?"

"It's a long story," Aidan said. "Suffice it to say that old Dev here is a criminal who's finally been stopped in his tracks." He jerked his chin at the window. "Get me those tiebacks."

While Aidan bound Devonlea's hands and feet, Stoddard assisted Laurel in helping Beatrice into a chair. Stoddard knelt before her and took her hands between his own. "Are you all right?"

Beatrice nodded, then managed a croaking reassurance.

"Goodness, my lady! Oh, has Lord Devonlea taken ill?" Rose, Beatrice's personal maid, scampered into the room and came to an abrupt halt. She gaped with no small amount of puzzlement at her bound master sprawled across the floor, and at the trail of potting soil strewn beneath him. "Eloise and I heard such frightful clunks from belowstairs that I came up straightaway to investigate. What on earth has happened, ma'am? Shall I send for a doctor? A constable?"

"First things first," Laurel said with an air of authority. "Please bring Lady Devonlea a glass of water and a poultice. Oh, and perhaps one for Lord Devonlea as well, though he doesn't deserve it. And *then* alert the authorities."

"Right away, ma'am." Rose hurried off.

Deciding the time for answers had arrived, Aidan dragged a chair close to Beatrice's and sat, leaning forward with his elbows on his knees. He regarded both Beatrice and Stoddard, still kneeling at her side. "Would one of you care to enlighten me as to what you each knew, and when?"

"I still don't know anything," Stoddard protested. "I'm as confused as you are."

"Then what are you doing here?" Aidan demanded.

Stoddard had the unexpected humility to blush. "A gentleman doesn't like to say...."

"It's ... all right." Beatrice's voice grated. Coughing, she pressed her palm to her throat and whispered to Aidan, "This is all my fault. I should have stopped it. Instead I acted the coward."

"You encouraged Fitz to continue your father's project, didn't you?" Aidan spoke gently, but no less accusingly. "Even knowing it was fruitless and realizing how he might use it to hornswoggle others."

"No. George believes in his elixir. He never intended to swindle anyone."

"Did *you*?"

Standing behind Beatrice's chair, her hands lying protectively on Bea's shoulders, Laurel flashed him a cautioning look.

Tears formed in Beatrice's eyes. "You don't understand. I simply meant to provide him with a diversion. He's been so aimless, so lost since Father died. I thought it would . . . connect them somehow." She shook her head in a show of wretchedness. "George believes in the elixir wholeheartedly. It was *him*." She thrust a finger toward her unconscious husband. "Arthur devised the scheme to use the elixir to entice investments in the spa. I overheard him talking to Monsieur Rousseau about a fortnight ago."

"So then, you knew they never intended to build the spa," Aidan prompted.

"Didn't they?" Beatrice looked thoroughly confused.

"It's as much a fake as the elixir," Aidan confirmed. "Nothing but sham figures and a phantom investment firm."

"Good heavens, Arthur has been so very clever about the entire affair. Except for the elixir, everything else about the pavilion seemed so aboveboard." She reached out, clutching Aidan's sleeve. "I swear to you, I never imagined—"

He patted her knee. "I believe you."

"When I confronted him about what I'd overheard—" She broke off, darting a panic-stricken gaze down at Devonlea when he let out a groggy murmur. "He denied it all, of course. When I threatened to go to the authorities, he said he would kill me if I so much as breathed a word. I wanted to come to you with the truth, Aidan. I knew I should trust you, but he made me so afraid. . . ."

"There, now, it's all right." Laurel gave Bea's shoulders a squeeze. To Aidan she said, "That is quite enough for now."

He turned his attention to Stoddard. "And how the

blazes do you fit into it? Are you the reason Dev hasn't been sleeping at home lately?"

Stoddard opened his mouth to respond, but Beatrice said, "Arthur became impossible to live with. Julian knew nothing of his activities, but he has been a support to me throughout." Her eyes darkened as she regarded Aidan. "You of all people would not dare judge us for that."

"No," he conceded, "I would not."

Rose reentered the room. "Your water and compress, my lady." Holding a second compress, the maid looked uncertainly down at Devonlea.

"I'll relieve you of that," Laurel said.

Beatrice pushed to her feet. "Rose, help me upstairs. I've developed a crushing headache. Mrs. Sanderson, will you come, too? I . . . should like the chance to win back your regard."

"Of course, Lady Devonlea. Now that I have come to understand a thing or two about the difficulties you faced, I assure you, you have my utmost sympathies."

Retrieving his walking stick from the floor beside him, Stoddard, too, came to his feet, but he appeared indecisive. Aidan couldn't help feeling slightly sorry for him. The youth had landed one of England's most sophisticated and desirable women as his mistress. Quite an achievement for the second son of a marquess, not to mention one recently tossed out of university. But even a man of Lord Julian's scant experience must know their affair could not continue after today. Beatrice would insist on breaking it off now that someone else had learned their secret.

Laurel handed the compress to Aidan. Their fingers touched briefly, sparking warmth. "Thank you," she said very quietly.

"For what?"

"For being here when you were needed. When *I* needed you. For always doing what is right." Shrugging, she smiled and blinked away a suspicious trace of moisture.

He wanted to pull her into his arms and kiss her. He wanted to promise her all that he most feared. But those things—love, marriage, family—propelled his heart against the wall of his chest and rendered him mute.

How could he continue his life without her? But how could he go on if once he experienced the joy of a life with her, he then lost her?

Did he always do what was right? Would he now? He met her gaze, a gaze filled with such hopeful yearning he felt himself drowning in his own uncertainty.

"Laurel, I . . ." He drew a steadying breath. "We'll talk later."

Laurel had hoped for more. She had searched for some sign in Aidan's manner that might silence her awful dread that once she left Bath, she would never see him again.

But he had granted nothing except a vague promise to talk. Talk about what? About how high he held her in his esteem, but that he simply did not share her feelings? Or how pleased he was to have made her acquaintance and that he wished her the best in all her future endeavors?

Oh, God. How would she bear it? How would she bear the next several minutes or hours, or however long it would be before he reiterated his inability to share more than these past days, days filled with deception and danger . . . and excitement and discovery and love? Love most of all.

Her love, *her* heart, given without limits or conditions or regrets. Except that . . .

She fought back the encroaching tears. Lady Devonlea needed her. She and Rose were waiting in the doorway, watching her quizzically. Tearing herself away from Aidan, she started toward them.

Lord Devonlea groaned. His eyes fluttered. "Help . . . ah, God . . . what the . . ."

He struggled against the drapery cords. His head lolling from side to side, his gaze suddenly landed on his wife. "You! It was you . . . and—"

Whack! Julian Stoddard brought his walking stick down on the side of Lord Devonlea's head, sinking the man back into unconsciousness. The act drew a startled cry from Laurel.

Aidan seized the young man by his shoulders. "What the blazes did you do that for?"

"He was about to start threatening her again," Lord Julian blurted. He rapped the tip of his cane against the floor for emphasis.

"He's tied up," Aidan yelled. He gave the youth a shake. "He can do no harm. You don't hit an incapacitated man."

Lord Julian seemed to shrink several inches. "I'm sorry. I couldn't bear to hear the scoundrel malign poor, dear Beatrice again."

Aidan released him. "It's all right. Why don't you go on home before the authorities arrive? I see no need for you to remain."

Lord Julian tossed a disgusted glance down at Lord Devonlea and nodded. He made his way across the room, rapping his walking stick on the marble tiles every few steps. A strange sensation crawled up Laurel's spine. . . .

When he reached the doorway, he raised his free hand and stroked the backs of his knuckles across Lady Devonlea's cheek. "I'll look in on you later."

With a flair of her nostrils, she turned her face away from him. "That won't be necessary."

Lord Julian stared back at her. With the beginnings of a scowl, he moved around her and started down the hall, this time limping slightly without the use of the cane.

Several things happened then, all converging in Laurel's mind in a blur of perception. In the parlor, Aidan swore loudly. Laurel heard his footsteps, but she found she could not take her eyes off Lord Julian. Gripped by an awareness she could not name, she watched as he held his walking stick loosely in his fingers as one would a baton. Casually he tapped the handle against the wall as he headed toward the front door.

The knock sparked a memory and sent her unthinkingly after him. "Good heavens. Aidan, it was him. It was Julian we heard beneath the city."

Julian whirled around as she reached him and, gripping his walking stick in two hands, gave it a twist. The shaft came free from the handle; he tossed it away. As it clattered across the floor, he reached out and seized Laurel's wrist. Turning her, he pulled her back against him. The foot-long stiletto that had been secreted inside his cane flashed before her eyes. Julian swung the slender weapon against her throat.

Down the hall, Rose screamed, the sound abruptly stifled when Lady Devonlea slapped her. Rose stumbled backward against the wall and froze, her eyes huge with fear.

"Let Laurel go." A pistol extended in his hand, Aidan stood just inside the archway of the dining hall, half hidden by shadow. "There is nothing to be gained from another death, Stoddard. Not even yours."

Julian laughed and pressed the dirk tighter beneath Laurel's chin. The blood drained from her face and her knees turned wobbly as she realized that if Aidan fired, odds were that he would hit her and not the man holding her.

"Lady Devonlea, you and Rose go below. Now," Laurel said.

"Stay where you are," Julian countered. "No one goes anywhere until we get a thing or two settled."

"You can't kill all of us, Stoddard." Aidan stepped

forward into the light, stopping when Julian jerked the stiletto and forced a cry from Laurel.

"I can kill *her*," the young man said breezily. "And I don't think you'd much care for that, Barensforth."

"Julian, don't be ridiculous." Lady Devonlea came toward them.

Holding Laurel tight, Julian swung toward the viscountess, then just as quickly swung back toward Aidan. "Don't come any closer, my love. Someone might inadvertently get hurt."

To prove his point, he flicked the dirk against Laurel's skin. A warm drop of moisture trickled down her neck. Aidan saw it—Laurel caught the flash of terror in his eyes, mirroring her own rising panic. His gaze locked with hers, and in it she perceived a desperate plea for her to do nothing that would prompt a violent reaction from Julian.

All her life she had been strong for her sisters. She had come to Bath intending to be strong for Victoria. Now she needed to be strong for herself. She needed to gather her courage, her composure, and her faith—in Aidan. He had rescued her so many times before. He would not let harm come to her now. He would not let her die.

Holding her breath, she held herself utterly still in Julian Stoddard's death grip.

Aidan's features smoothed to a semblance of calm. "Perhaps I can help you, Stoddard. I believe I understand what happened. This plan of yours, my God, it's ingenious. I only wish I'd thought of it myself. Was Babcock in on it, or did he find you out and threaten to expose you?"

"Babcock was a fool." Despite his vehemence, Julian's arms relaxed a fraction around Laurel. "He became suspicious about Bryce-Rawlings Unlimited and began digging until he learned the truth."

"That the company is merely a facade for some intricate financial manipulations."

"Precisely."

Aidan lowered the gun but still managed to keep it trained on Julian. "So you waited until you had him alone at the Cross Bath, knocked him senseless with your walking stick, and dumped him into the pool to drown." He cocked his head as if considering how to play his hand at the card table. "How did you keep the attendants distracted long enough to do the deed?"

Laurel fought from shivering when Julian's soft chuckle grazed her nape. "I regained his trust by confiding that the money for the Summit Pavilion had been used to fund Rousseau's research, that it was ground-breaking work, but the Frenchman had become unreasonable, demanding higher and higher fees for his services. I convinced Babcock that the old king's map revealed an entrance to Rousseau's subterranean laboratory beneath the Cross Bath, and I proposed that he and I go there together and learn Rousseau's secrets for ourselves. Then we could decide whether we needed him any longer. The plan was for Babcock to go to the baths, conceal himself until after closing, and then let me in."

"At which time you murdered him." When Julian nodded, Aidan's fingers tightened almost imperceptibly around the pistol. Inwardly, Laurel braced herself for the possibility that he would risk taking the shot. Outwardly, she didn't move a muscle as Aidan grinned in admiration. "As I said, ingenious. But what now, Stoddard? It seems we have reached a stalemate."

"I know you to be a man of very little integrity, Barensforth."

Aidan pressed his free hand to his chest. "You do me wrong, boy."

"I meant it as a compliment. Tell me, can you be bought?"

Aidan's eyebrows went up, but his grip on the gun didn't loosen. "Depends. How much are we talking about?"

"A great deal."

"Then yes . . . I suppose I can."

Above Laurel's shoulder, the two men locked gazes. Aidan's turned steely, determined. His wrist came up a fraction of an inch and his finger twitched on the trigger. Beneath her chin, the stiletto nudged, shifted, prodded. Warm blood drizzled down her neck to pool in the hollow of her collarbone. The tension in the room arced, as taut and sharp as the blade.

A knock on the door drew a gasp from Laurel. Julian flinched, turning toward the sound. The door burst open and Lord Munster strode across the threshold.

"I know you t-told me to wait. . . ." His eyes popping wide, he stopped short just inside the doorway. "What the b-blazes?"

Aidan's gun exploded with a deafening blast.

Chapter 27

Powder burns singed Aidan's fingers. The gun's report stung like a thousand wasps against his eardrums. Through the acrid smoke clouding the hall, he stumbled, the harrowing sound of Laurel's scream dredging up his most primal need to assure himself of her safety.

As he reached her, that same instinct had him assessing the scene even as his hands closed around her shoulders and he drew her to his chest. Stoddard lay on his side on the floor, the shoulder of his coat already soaked with the blood leaking from the gunshot wound. His face gone pasty white, he panted for breath and stared unblinkingly at Aidan's shoe.

With a kick, Aidan dislodged the stiletto still clutched in the young man's hand. Stoddard let out a shout of pain. The weapon skidded across the floor and came to rest in the dining hall.

"Oh, thank God." Beatrice's shaking voice echoed down the hallway. "Is everyone quite all right?"

"Yes, Lady Devonlea," Laurel replied, her voice muffled by Aidan's shirtfront. "Except perhaps for Lord Julian, but I expect he shall live."

Beatrice drew the maid away from the wall. "I'm sorry I slapped you, Rose. I feared your cries would unnerve Lord Julian, and he would do something rash."

"Fitz," Aidan said, "see to your sister. And to Devonlea. He's in the parlor."

Then he buried his face in Laurel's hair and hugged her tight. "I'm sorry," he repeated more than once in a shredded whisper. "I didn't wish to do that, didn't want to take the shot, but I feared that if I didn't . . . Christ."

"I trusted you." Her voice came an octave higher than normal. Her trembling traveled inside him. "I held as still as I could so I wouldn't be in your way."

"Good God, I'm proud of you. So proud." Reaching into his coat pocket, he withdrew his handkerchief and pressed it to the nick in her flesh left by Stoddard's blade. "You could not have been braver."

Her light laughter wrapped itself around his heart and squeezed. "I was terrified. But I knew you wouldn't let him hurt me. I never doubted."

He had doubted. From one second to the next, he hadn't known whether Stoddard would take the lethal swipe and end Laurel's life.

If she had died, would he have turned his own pistol on himself? There had been a moment, as the blood had trickled down her throat, when he hadn't been sure. When he had been seized by the same immeasurable desperation that had sent his father over the edge of despair. In that moment, he had understood and even forgiven his father for what he had done.

But he hadn't known what *he* would do. He still didn't, and his soul trembled at the notion that he could love her that much.

"I s-say, old boy," Fitz called from the parlor, "poor Dev's awake and d-demanding to see you."

Unwilling to let Laurel out of his arms, much less out of his sight, he asked Rose to keep an eye on Stoddard and let out a yell should the youth move more than an inch in any direction. In the parlor, they found Devonlea unbound and sitting up in a chair. He held one of Rose's poultices to the side of his head. For once, his impeccable appearance had suffered from ill-treatment. His slicked-back hair fell in disheveled shanks over his brow and his clothing hung in rumpled folds.

"Sorry, Dev. But surely you understand how it looked." Aidan offered the man his hand, and after a slight hesitation, Devonlea shook it.

"Munster tells me the entire Summit Pavilion was a hoax." The viscount groaned and shifted the poultice. "I knew the elixir was a fake but–"

"It's more than a fake," Aidan interrupted. "It's laced with absinthe."

"It's t-true, Dev," Fitz concurred.

Devonlea's surprise was palpable, in Aidan's estimate too much so to be feigned. "I swear I didn't know that, either. I've never been inside Rousseau's laboratory. I'd believed that, with a little help from his miracle cure, the pavilion would make us all richer than our wildest dreams."

"Are you certain about that, Dev? You threatened your wife's life should she expose you," Aidan reminded him. "That sounds like the actions of a desperate man, one with a great deal at stake."

"I was furious with her. I'd discovered her affair with Stoddard." He flicked a glance at Beatrice. Beneath the viscount's simmering anger, Aidan thought he detected a plea for reconciliation. "I thought, how dare she accuse me when she is guilty of her own offenses?"

"You might have considered putting me first for a change," Beatrice retorted. "Before cards and investments and whatever else you do for entertainment. Can you truly blame me for finding companionship in another man's arms?"

"Then you had no notion of what Stoddard had done?" A hint of accusation accompanied Laurel's question.

"Good heavens, no." Beatrice appeared genuinely shaken by the very suggestion. "Like everyone else, I took him for a handsome, charming, but quite harmless boy."

"He had us all fooled," Aidan agreed. "But you will all have some explaining to do once the authorities arrive. I'll do what I can to help you."

"Think they'll t-toss us all in M-Marshalsea?" The query came from Fitz. Poor, hapless, gullible Fitz.

Aidan clapped his shoulder. "I don't think so, my friend, as long as you cooperate and pay back any money you might have made in the scheme." He shot a pointed glance at Devonlea. "And I do mean *all* the money, not to mention whatever fines the court levies against you. Of course, Rousseau is another story. Deliberately drugging people is a serious offense, and I don't doubt that he'll soon be all too familiar with the inside of a prison cell. Stoddard, however, may end up swinging, son of a marquess or no."

Laurel reached out and grazed Fitz's coat sleeve with her fingertips. "You helped save my life, Lord Munster."

His eyebrows surged upward in astonishment. "D-did I?"

"You surely did. I shudder to think what might have happened if not for your timely arrival." She stepped up to him and kissed his cheek. "I'll always be grateful, sir."

Fitz blushed several shades of crimson.

Aidan retrieved the drapery cords that had held Devonlea's wrists and ankles. "I can think of a good use for these." With Laurel's hand firm in his own, he went back out to the hall. "Rose," he said, "let us summon those constables now, shall we?"

Two mornings later, Laurel stood in the drawing room at Fenwick House and gazed out over the rain-slick city of Bath, its spires poking through the clouds that drifted low over the valley.

Following Julian Stoddard's arrest, she had left her Abbey Green lodging house and moved in here. Melinda had insisted and Aidan had concurred. In fact, he had balked at the idea of her staying alone, as if he dared not trust that the danger for her had passed.

When the local authorities had arrived at Lady Devonlea's home, she and Aidan had assumed the roles of outraged bystanders who had, through no fault of their own, become victims of Julian Stoddard's ill intentions. Phineas Micklebee had turned up with another man whom Laurel assumed to be with the Home Office as well, but as they conferred with the Bath officials, neither agent had given any indication that they knew Aidan Phillips other than by reputation. Although once, when no one had been looking, Mr. Micklebee had flashed Laurel a conspiratorial wink.

Everyone in the Queen Square town house had had to give an extensive account of all they had seen and heard that morning, including a very distraught Rose. With an admirable show of kindness, Lady Devonlea had stayed at the maid's side throughout, patting her shoulder and coaxing the poor woman through her testimony.

Julian Stoddard was taken first to Dr. Bailey's surgery to have his shoulder wound tended. Later that day he was incarcerated in the local jail to await his arraignment. Likewise, Claude Rousseau was taken into custody on multiple charges of fraud and reckless endangerment.

Regrettably, without Julian's cooperation it would take weeks and perhaps months to wade through the maze of financial transactions, recover the funds that had not been squandered, and reimburse the many investors of the Summit Pavilion. The Bath Corporation was assisting in that endeavor.

Outside, a carriage pulled away from the house and proceeded down the muddy drive. A footman and the housekeeper's assistant were on their way to town to make the weekly purchases and to post a letter for Laurel. In it she had set Victoria's fears of treason to rest, assuring her that her cousin had never intended to betray her. However misguided, George Fitzclarence had sought to establish a legacy for himself in place of the royal birthright that had been denied him.

Laurel wondered where Aidan had gone that morning, for he, too, had taken up temporary residence at Fenwick House. Melinda was dying. They all knew it now and acknowledged it openly, Aidan with a look of hardened pain in his eyes, Laurel with an intolerable pinching in her throat, and Melinda with a stoic smile and a dismissive wave of her hand.

"I've led a good life, better than most, and I've precious few regrets," she had said.

Her daughters had been sent for. Until they arrived, Laurel and Aidan were helping her make her final plans. At night, when Melinda lay sleeping, Laurel and Aidan found solace in each other's arms.

Unease fluttered in Laurel's stomach. Aidan had been up and out so early today, and he hadn't left a note. . . .

A sound in the doorway sent her spinning about, and her heart thrilled at the sight of him. He must have ridden up the drive and entered the house while she had been in Melinda's bedchamber. His hair still bore a gleam of moisture from the rain. He had removed his coat and as he entered the room, his fingers worked to undo the knot of his neckcloth.

Tugging the length of linen free and tossing it over the back of a nearby chair, he strode across the room, took Laurel in his arms, and kissed her soundly, possessively. The rainy chill clung to his skin, yet she melted against him, yielding herself entirely to the pleasure of his embrace, his strength, and however many moments like this were left to them.

They had not spoken of the future. Melinda's needs

took precedence over their own, of course, and Laurel had been content simply to be near him, to offer what comfort she could, and to share in the grief of losing a dear friend, as least as far as she was able.

His sorrow, she now understood, was a thing of unfathomable depth and breadth within him, a twisted skein of past and present, of perceived failings and self-punishment and hoped-for redemption. Last night, after making love, he had confided in her about his parents. In the dark, her arms around him, she had listened and cried silently and loved him more than she had ever believed possible.

And yet now, as though nothing were wrong, he smiled wolfishly, tipped her backward in his arms, and pressed his lips to her neck. "You're so warm. Ah, you feel wonderful."

"Where did you go this morning?"

A casual enough query, but she inwardly berated herself for asking . . . for questioning him at all. As if she had a right to know his business, or to demand more than he was willing to give.

"You don't have to answer that," she said.

He caught her chin and raised it until she met his gaze. "I had business in town. Business that concerns us both. But first I stopped at my town house and found this."

He fished into his trouser pocket. Raising her hand, he placed a small object in her palm. Her stomach flip-flopped at the sight of the gold and onyx signet ring that had slipped off the hand of her attacker that night at the Circus. The piece so repulsed her, she all but tossed it into the hearth.

He held up a second item. The button she had saved from her old life caught the light from outside as it swung back and forth on its gold chain. "You left this on my nightstand."

"Why have you brought me these?" She frowned

down at the signet ring. "They only remind me of danger and lies and everything I have lost. They taunt me with all I will never know."

"That may have been so, but I swear to you, no more." Scooping her into his arms, he brought her to the settee beside the hearth and settled her snugly in his lap. Gently he stroked her hair and cheeks as though she were still the frightened little girl of her past. "This button, this ring, they are my pledge to you, Laurel. Together we will discover their origin and what they mean to you and your sisters."

At his vow, her heart constricted. "You would make that promise to me?"

"That and many, many more, my Laurel." He shifted as he slipped a hand inside his waistcoat, this time extracting a velvet pouch. "This is what sent me to town today." He tugged open the drawstring and upended the pouch to reveal a second ring, a delicate gold band set with a teardrop ruby surrounded by tiny diamonds.

Laurel gasped as he eased out from under her and knelt on the floor at her feet.

"Well?" was all he said, but the hope brimming in his expression squeezed tears from her eyes.

She reached out, touched his dear face, and leaned closer to him. "Are you certain?" she whispered. She had no wish to ensnare him when he was vulnerable; would not allow him to make promises now that he might regret later. "All you said about not being able to offer me a future together because of your work—"

"Lies, every bit of it." He brought her hand to his lips, kissed it, and held it there. Then he said, "After my father's suicide, the Home Office became my shield, protecting me from ever feeling what my father felt for my mother. If I could never be close to anyone, then I could never know the despair of such a loss. But do you know what I've discovered?"

Not trusting her voice, she shook her head.

"A man can't protect himself from love. He can only feel it and trust it and draw courage from it, and stride daringly into the future—with you, Laurel, if you'll have me. If you'll take those strides with me. Will you marry me, my dearest love?"

She attempted to say she would, but her sobs reduced the words to a garbled, stammered utterance. She supposed he judged her answer by the joy on her face, for he grinned widely, kissed her heartily, and slipped the ring smoothly home.

Epilogue

Alone in the Knightsbridge Readers' Emporium, Ivy Sutherland tucked a recalcitrant strand of mahogany hair behind her ear and closed the ledger book she had been poring over these past many minutes. Tonight had been quiet, generating only a smattering of business, a rather unusual circumstance nowadays.

Hopping down from her stool behind the counter, she placed the CLOSED sign in the window, pulled the shade, and locked the door. She had manned the shop by herself tonight, since Holly, her twin, and Willow, the youngest, had donned their best new frocks and attended a play debuting in Covent Garden.

Ivy had gladly remained at home, for in her opinion plays were a great lot of stuff and nonsense. She had happily seen her sisters off, immeasurably relieved that their finances now stretched comfortably beyond the bare essentials.

Several factors had contributed to that happy circumstance. First, ever since sending Laurel on her fact-finding mission to Bath, Queen Victoria had seen to it that the Sutherlands had everything they needed, including weekly deliveries of the finest food to fill their cupboards. The queen had also let slip to several key individuals word of a charming little bookshop she'd once visited in Knightsbridge. Ever since, the bell above the door had tinkled nonstop, until Ivy had grown so weary of the sound she had finally torn the bell from the ceiling.

Then there was the most fortuitous change of all: Laurel's recent marriage to the dashing and quite wealthy Earl of Barensforth. Despite rumors to the contrary, Ivy's new brother-in-law had proved to be a kindhearted gentleman who insisted that his wife's sisters no longer needed to earn their own living; indeed, they were welcome to take up residence in any of his lavish homes.

But the Sutherland sisters had spent their lives tucked away on a country estate, and they had no intention of relinquishing their newfound independence now. They had developed a true fondness for their Readers' Emporium and took pride in its success. Even Laurel still enjoyed spending occasional afternoons sorting through books and helping customers with their selections. Her new society friends thought it eccentric, but rather charming.

At present, however, she and Aidan were away in France. Talk about Laurel hadn't stopped at her penchant for shopkeeping. Her ambiguous family background and supposed widowhood had fueled a wealth of speculation when she and Aidan married, and they had decided that taking an extended trip abroad would be just the thing to stifle the gossip.

"Will there be anything else tonight, miss?"

Mrs. Eddelson, the Sutherlands' new housekeeper, waddled downstairs from the living quarters above, puffs of exertion escaping her lips with each thump of her wide feet on the steps. As part of the compromise that allowed the girls to remain in their London home, Aidan had hired Mrs. Eddelson to look after them. The woman lived in the tiny rooms on the third floor of the house with *Mr.* Eddelson, who served as their driver and man-of-all-work, but who looked to Ivy like the sort of man who should be guarding the door of a gambling hell.

"I have locked up for the night," Ivy said. "You go on up to bed now, Mrs. Eddelson. When Mr. Eddelson arrives home with the girls, I'll let him know him you've retired."

Perched on her stool again, Ivy picked up the morning edition of the *Times*. She had not found a moment to read it that day. As she scanned the headlines, her eyes were immediately drawn to the lead story.

What was *this*? A priceless jewel stolen from Buckingham Palace? No leads as to who or why, or where the piece might be now ...

Ivy slapped the paper down in astonishment. Well, if anyone could recover the stolen property, it would be Laurel and Aidan. But they were not due home for weeks yet.

At a knock on the door, she started. It was far too early for Holly and Willow to be home. Who could possibly be seeking books at this time of night? Peeking round the edge of the window shade, she received a shock of surprise.

Quickly she drew the latchkey from her apron pocket and unlocked the door. A figure draped from head to toe in thick black wool hurried inside, drew back her hood, and grasped Ivy's hands in her own plump ones.

"Something dreadful has happened."

"I know," Ivy said. She pointed to the newspaper angled across the countertop. "I just read about it."

"My dear, there is more to the story than the papers— or anyone, for that matter—knows. Please, Ivy, I need your help. May I count on you?"

Ivy didn't hesitate. Smiling down into the queen's somber dark eyes, she said, "I am your friend and servant, Your Majesty, happily and most assuredly so."

In December 2010, the Sutherland
sisters once again become
Her Majesty's Secret Servants
in Allison Chase's

Outrageously Yours

Read on to learn their next mysterious
assignment. . . .

London, 1838

I vy Sutherland slapped the edition of the *Times* onto
the counter in front of her. Her shocked gaze darted
over the books lining the walls of her family's tiny shop.
Had she read correctly? She snatched up the paper
again, rereading the headline: PRICELESS JEWEL STOLEN
FROM BUCKINGHAM PALACE.

Her eyes skimmed over phrases such as "without a
trace," "no clues," and "queen distraught."

The rap of knuckles against the shop door made her
flinch. She had locked up not ten minutes ago, shortly
after her two sisters, who helped her run the Knightsbridge Readers' Emporium, left for the opening of a new
play across town. Ivy hesitated. Ever since her eldest
sister, Laurel, had returned from Bath last spring, there
had been changes in the Sutherlands' lives. Laurel's new
husband, the Earl of Barensforth, saw to it that his three

sisters-in-law enjoyed heretofore unattainable luxuries such as plays, new frocks, and more books than Ivy could ever hope to read.

There had been other changes, too, such as a pair of servants, the Eddelsons, who lived in the third floor garret. With his once-broken nose and tree trunk of a neck, Mr. Eddelson seemed, in Ivy's estimatation, to be more suited for prowling London's back alleys than for carrying in deliveries and driving the sisters about town in their shiny new phaeton.

Then, there was that morning not long ago when Ivy had spied Mrs. Eddelson sharpening the kitchen knives in their tiny rear garden. As Ivy had watched, the woman had cast a circumspect glance over her shoulder before grinning and sending the meat cleaver sailing end over end to sink some two inches into the trunk of the stunted birch growing in the corner.

It hadn't taken Ivy long to conclude that their brother-in-law's precautionary measures stemmed from more than mere prudence. Something had happened during Laurel's adventures in Bath to warrant stringent safety measures—such as never opening the door to strangers at night.

Another knock resounded, louder and more insistent than the first. Slipping off her stool, Ivy went to the window and peeked through the gap in the curtains. A coach and four of the finest quality stood at the curbside. No identifiable crest adorned its sleek panels. The plain livery of the three attending footmen gave no clue as to the individual they served.

No clue, that was, to anyone but the Sutherland sisters, who had seen this coach before. Recognition rushed through Ivy. With a gasp, she hurried to the door and turned the key.

A figure draped from head to toe in black wool stepped over the threshold. "Quickly, shut the door!"

Once Ivy had complied, a pair of softly plump hands

flipped back the cloak's hood and then reached for Ivy's own hands. "Something dreadful has happened."

"I know." Ivy pointed to the newspaper angled across the countertop. "I just read about it."

"Yes, well, there is more to the story than the papers, or anyone for that matter, knows. Please, Ivy, I need your help. Can I count on you?"

Ivy gazed down into the dark solemn eyes and sweet features of England's nineteen-year-old queen and smiled. "I am your servant, Your Majesty. Now please, dearest, come up to the parlor and tell me everything."

The hired barouche jostled laboriously along the weather-pitted highway north of Cambridge. Inside, the single passenger—dusty, hungry, and exhausted from the two-day journey from London—entertained grave doubts about the rash decision that had brought her here.

Lady Gwendolyn de Burgh had done a very, *very* bad thing, and now she didn't know how to set about making it right. It hadn't seemed so terrible when the idea to take the queen's stone had first occurred to her. It was really nothing but a rock, after all—not shiny and faceted and richly hued, but a jagged, granitelike hunk speckled with bits of silver. Other than the odd, tingling energy that emanated from its surface, there was hardly anything remarkable to be said for Her Majesty's stone.

Except that it had been a gift from that German gentleman, the one the queen strictly forbade her ladies-in-waiting from mentioning outside the private royal chambers. That man, Albert, believed the stone held special properties—electromagnetism, the queen had said—which was what had prompted Gwendolyn to steal—*borrow*—the stone in the first place.

Gwendolyn's gaze fell to the ornate box on her lap. Even through the carved wood, with its inlaid design of jade and ivory, she thought she perceived a faint vibration beneath her fingertips. Or did the sensation originate from her jangling nerves?

In the distance, beyond the flat, boggy fens streaming past the carriage window, a lingering splash of sunlight turned Cambridge University's highest towers to amber. As the vehicle rambled farther away from the city, a box hedge sprang up along the roadside, replaced all too soon by familiar high stone walls topped by lethal-looking spikes and a wrought-iron railing.

Gwendolyn was almost home.

With a rap on the carriage ceiling, she called out, "Stop here."

Here was the base of the curving drive that snaked through a heavy growth of oak and pine planted nearly a hundred years ago by the first Marquess of Harrow. That the iron gates stood open did not make the shadowed entrance of Harrowood any more welcoming. Clinging to the safety of the open road, Gwendolyn hesitated before ordering the coachman to turn in. Would the present marquess, her brother, welcome her back after all these months?

A chill of doubt crept across her shoulders as the last of the sunlight slipped away, plunging the road into sudden darkness. The box on her lap seemed to give off a cautionary tremor.

Above the trees, a fiery burst of light illuminated the house's sloping rooftops. Gwendolyn gasped. From Harrowood's central turret, an angry conflagration of sparks shot upward. The carriage jolted as the pair of grays whickered and tugged at their traces. In the stillness that followed, a crack like thunder echoed down the drive, rousing a flock of black birds from their nests; in a panicked flurry they scattered across the twilit sky.

"Ma'am?" The coachman's voice rose an octave and caught.

This was a mistake, Gwendolyn concluded, a foolish,

dreadful, ill-advised mistake. Now what? A new idea occurred to her, a better, safer plan.

"Drive on," she cried as another flash lit the night sky.

Simon de Burgh, Marquess of Harrow, cursed the cinders that showered back down into his laboratory through the turret's open skylight. With an exasperated sigh, he seized the woolen blanket from the table behind him and smothered the tiny flames dancing among his equipment. Then he moved through the room, stamping out each glowing ember to prevent the oak floor from catching fire.

Only when he was satisfied that flames no longer threatened his ancestral home did he pause to survey the damage to himself. His singed cuffs indicated the ruination of yet another shirt. His palm and fingertips stung as well. At least this time he smelled no burning hair, though his ears would undoubtedly ring for the next day or two.

Taking up the blanket again, he waved it up and down to clear the smoke from the circular room set high above Harrowood's sprawling wings. Damn and double damn. He had been so certain that *this* time his calculations had been correct, that the current flowing from his electrical generator was at the proper level. He believed he had taken all the necessary precautions, made all the needed adjustments to negative and positive charges. He had recalibrated the force of the steam passing through the conducting coils and positioned the electromagnets with meticulous care.

But flipping the lever and releasing the energy that had accumulated in the steam duct had brought only flames, sparks, and dashed expectations. Cursing again, he crossed the room to the brandy he kept on the bookcase beside the southern window. The wide stone still offered a convenient perch. He loosened his neckcloth, propped up a booted foot, sipped the burning liquid, and considered.

Perhaps it was time he admitted defeat. Perhaps, as people continually said behind his back and occasionally to his face, he *had* been tilting at windmills in this laboratory of his.

But as the pungent spirits spread warmth through his veins and eased his smarting fingertips, the old tenacity surged back. Simon was far from ready to surrender, and he couldn't deny a certain fondness for windmills, with their wide-open arms and their ability to harness one of nature's greatest powers and tame it for practical use.

That was all he wished, really: to tame a natural force and put it to good use. But perhaps he couldn't do it alone.

Alone. How he had come to hate that word and the way it had redefined his life, his very identity. How he detested the sidelong glances of his acquaintances, their gentle queries into his welfare, and, worst of all, the pitying whispers they thought he couldn't hear. How he dreaded waking to the deafening roar of those midnight silences that could not be filled because . . .

Because he was *alone*, and there was no longer anyone to talk to or reach for or hold.

With another generous draft he banished those and other pointless broodings. Life was what it was. His gaze drifted out the open window. From this vantage point, he could see clear across the open fenland to the cluster of lights twinkling in the city. Something closer caught his attention. Was that a coach speeding away down the road? Had someone passed his gates as the flames and sparks had shot up, or had they simply remembered that the Mad Marquess lived here, and urged their team to a gallop?

It didn't matter; it was no concern of his. No, Simon knew what he needed to attain his goal. But he also knew that what he needed would not come easily if indeed it came at all.

Ivy poured tea, added cream and the heaping teaspoons of sugar Queen Victoria favored, and passed the cup and saucer into her royal guest's hands. "Drink this, dear. It will help calm you."

Victoria obeyed with a small sip, then set the cup on her lap and shook her head. "You don't understand. I cannot be calm until the stone is recovered and back safe with me. Oh, I'll be a laughing stock, and Albert might never wish to speak to me again. . . ."

Wondering who this Albert was, Ivy held up a hand. "Please slow down and tell me why this stone is so special. You say it is not a priceless gem as reported in the newspapers?"

"Indeed it is not—at least not in the usual sense. But I dared not let the real truth be known. You see"— Victoria's bosom rose on a sigh—"it is infinitely more precious than a jewel. It was a gift from . . ."

"Yes?" Ivy gave Victoria's shoulder a reassuring pat. "You may speak freely. My sisters and I would die before we betrayed your confidence."

A fleeting smile of gratitude softened Victoria expression. "The gift came from Albert, my Saxe-Coburg cousin. He is a dabbler in the sciences, you see, and this stone . . . it is believed to have fallen from the sky. . . . A meteorite. And, oh, Ivy, it is extraordinary, indeed."

"How so?"

"There is a certain energy about it." The queen's voice dropped as if to prevent her words from being overheard. "A kind of warm field that at once pushes some objects away from it and draws others to it."

"It is magnetic," Ivy ventured.

"Oh, more than that. It is *electro*magnetic, and Albert believes it might even be a key to providing scientists with the means of generating . . . someday . . . useful and efficient electricity."

A ripple of excitement traveled Ivy's length. "To replace fire and steam in the powering of our industries, yes?"

"I suppose. . . . To be honest, I'm not quite certain what all this hocus-pocus will be used for." Victoria raised her cup for another sip.

Then her features crumpled in dismay. "What does it matter? Albert entrusted this stone to me as a symbol of our commitment to each other." In a whisper she said, "Oh, Ivy, he has asked me to *marry* him."

In a burst of elation, Ivy threw her arms around her younger friend, careful not to upset her tea. "That is wonderful news. My dearest, I am so happy for you. When will the joyous occasion take place?"

She didn't ask whether she would be invited, for she knew the answer to that. The Sutherland sisters had stopped being suitable companions for the then–Princess Victoria some seven years before, when she had become heir apparent to the throne. Soon after, they had lost touch with her, only to reestablish ties—secret ones—last spring when Victoria had appealed to them for help in a matter requiring the utmost discretion.

"I don't yet know," Victoria replied. "These things must be handled through the proper channels. But once we *are* married and Albert is here in England, he intends to put the stone in the hands of the right man, a scientist of singular brilliance. But now I have lost it and . . . Oh, Ivy! Albert will be so angry with me! And so will my dear Lord Melbourne."

"Your prime minister?"

"Indeed, yes." Placing her cup and saucer on the sofa table, Victoria leaped up from the settee and began pacing the small area of carpet in front of the fireplace. Ivy noted that her petite figure had grown plumper in the months since her coronation, her youthful features more careworn. Or was the latter due to her present predicament?

"I don't understand why Lord Melbourne should care one way or another about such a private matter," Ivy said.

Victoria came to an abrupt halt and faced her. "That is exactly the point."

When Ivy stared back blankly, the queen continued impatiently. "My dealings with Albert should never have *been* a private matter. I am a monarch, and for me there can be no affairs of the heart, not in the truest sense. Such matters are to be conducted through proper diplomatic procedures, but Ivy, Albert and I have been skirting those procedures on the sly. Nothing has been officially approved. In fact, I have led most of my courtiers to believe that I don't particularly care for Albert. Should anyone find out that I have already pledged my hand ... why, think of the scandal!"

Ivy could indeed imagine the tittle-tattle certain to fill England's drawing rooms should it become known that the queen had behaved in a manner deemed inappropriate. "But it isn't fair. Your uncles—"

"Were men. It is one thing for a king to carry on with his mistresses, but let a queen set her big toe beyond the dictates of proper decorum, and *oh*!" She made a noise and tossed her hands in the air to simulate an explosion. "Royal or no, I am foremost a woman in the eyes of my subjects, and an impropriety like this ..."

"I understand." Ivy pushed to her feet and went to stand before her queen. "What can I do?"

"Find the stone, Ivy. It was taken by one of my ladies-in-waiting, Lady Gwendolyn de Burgh."

"Are you certain?"

"This morning the stone was gone, and so was Lady Gwendolyn—quite without my permission. Why, she'd been asking so many questions, I should have realized her interest in the stone was more than cursory. But I trusted her as I trust all my ladies, or most of them. Never could I have imagined such treachery from within my own private chambers."

Ivy's heart fluttered. If only Laurel and Aidan were home. If anyone could recover the queen's stolen property, they could. Last spring, Victoria had sent Laurel to Bath disguised as a widow in order to spy on George Fitzclarence, a royal cousin whom Victoria had suspected of treason. Together, Laurel and Aidan had followed a dizzying maze of clues to solve a murder, stop a financial fraud, and put a very nasty individual behind bars where he belonged.

But Laurel and Aidan were away in France on some mysterious business neither seemed inclined to discuss.

"If only Laurel were due back soon. . . ."

"No, Ivy, it is you I need."

"But I'm not the adventurous one. Everything I know I've learned in books."

"Precisely. I need someone bookish, someone who would fit in with scholars and men of science. I am all but certain Lady Gwendolyn has headed to her home outside of Cambridge. Her brother disowned her some months back, and I believe she intends on giving him the stone as a peace offering. You see, he's something of an amateur scientist—if a rather mad one—and the stone would be of particular importance to him."

At mention of Cambridge, home of one of Europe's most prestigious institutions of higher learning, all of Ivy's senses came alive with interest. What she wouldn't give to be allowed to attend lectures in those celebrated halls. The word *scientist*, too, had captured her attention. But she hadn't at all liked Victoria's one quick reference to the man's disposition.

"Mad?"

After a brief hesitation, Victoria admitted, "Some

call him the Mad Marquess of Harrow, but I'm sure it's merely collegiate fraternity nonsense. He maintains close ties with the university. That is where you will find him, Ivy, and perhaps the stone as well."

"I see," Ivy said when, in fact, she did not. "Then I am to appeal to him for the return of the stone."

"Goodness, no!" Alarm pinched Victoria's features. "He may not be mad, but neither is he known for being a reasonable man. He disowned his sister, didn't he?"

"Then . . . ?"

"You must earn his trust. It so happens he is presently searching for an assistant for his experiments. If you could manage to win the position, you would gain access to his private laboratory, where you could then steal back what is rightfully mine."

The outrageous proposal sent a chuckle bubbling in Ivy's throat, one quickly coughed away when Her Majesty's expression failed to convey even the faintest trace of humor.

This, apparently, was no jest, but a true call to Her Majesty's service, one that left Ivy more than a little perplexed. "How on earth shall I, a woman, track down a man in an academic setting? I wouldn't gain admittance through the front gates, much less the lecture halls."

Victoria smacked her lips together. "I have a plan for that, though admittedly a shocking one. More shocking, even, than when I asked Laurel to pose as a widow last spring and work her charms on my inebriate, adulterous cousin."

More shocking than *that*? Ivy dreaded to ask, but ask she did. And the answer she received stunned her more than anything she had ever heard in all her twenty-two years on this earth.

ALLISON CHASE

DARK OBSESSION

A Novel of Blackheath Moor

They wed in haste—Nora Thorngoode, to save her
ruined reputation, and Grayson Lowell, to rescue his
estate from foreclosure for unpaid debts. Each
resents the necessity to exchange vows that will
bind them for all time, and yet from the first,
passion flames between them—quickly engulfing
them in a sensual obsession.

But soon the lover that Nora married becomes a
dark stranger to her, a man torn apart by guilt over
his brother's recent, mysterious death—and driven
half-mad by ghostly specters who demand that
Grayson expose the truth. Has Nora married a
murderer whose wicked deeds blacken everything
around them? Or, together, in the secret passageways
of Blackheath Grange and along Cornwall's remote
coastline, can Grayson and Nora discover what
really happened that terrible night—and in setting
free the troubled ghosts, free themselves as well?

**Available wherever books are sold or at
penguin.com**